Prologue

March, 1813

"UNGRATEFUL WHORE!"

Lady Grace Abernathy's cheek burned where the back of her father's hand struck her, but she fought to conceal her emotions.

Crying could come later, but not before Father. He fed on weakness and fear. Tears would only add fuel to his fire. She refused to encourage him. "A whore, Father?" Grace focused on her nerves to refrain from stuttering. "What do you mean?"

How on earth had he learned what had happened? Could someone have hidden in the library and watched while the Earl of Barrow ravished her?

"You are a harlot! Barrow told the whole of White's how you pushed yourself at him during Lord Everton's ball. How he tried to convince you any sort of dalliance would be an enormously bad idea, but you refused to take no for an answer. Do you want to know who was in White's that night, Grace? Do you?"

Her father, the Marquess of Chatham, rose to full temper. His bulbous head turned an unnatural shade of purple and appeared as though it might burst at any moment. Grace rather thought she might like to see it burst. His eyelids twitched over his wide eyes, and the thin bits of greyed hair covering his scalp flopped back and forth with each syllable.

"The Duke of Walsingham! Your betrothed, that's who. A good half the *ton* was at White's. As soon as Walsingham learned of the trollop you truly are, he came to my library and called off the betrothal. He ripped our agreement and tossed it in the fire. You are ruined, Grace. No one will condescend to have you now."

He dropped into the chair behind his aged desk and held his head in his hands.

Grace's jaw dropped when she learned of the extremity of Lord Barrow's revenge for Father breaking off their agreement. And of course, her father and his drink-addled mind had fallen right into Barrow's trap, and Grace took the brunt of it. Why should she have expected anything different?

"But Father, no, that is untrue." He must understand. "I never dallied with Lord Barrow. He forced himself on me."

His head rose and he stared upon her with apprehension. A pit of ire rose up in her over his dubious expression. Would the man never believe her, not even over this?

"I tried to stop him, but I was not strong enough." Her words rushed forth. "He wanted a settling of the score with you, for not honoring the arrangement for our marriage."

"Lies. *Lies*! You are a whore. You are no daughter of mine." He spat the words at her. "After all I have done for you to secure an eligible match. You were to be a duchess. I would be aligned through your marriage to the Duke of Walsingham. But now what? All is lost."

Of course, everything inevitably rested on status. Father had never concerned himself with her welfare, but only cared about the connections he had within society and the coin lining his coffers. How could he do better than marrying his daughter off to a duke? Grace wouldn't doubt if there were some sort of monetary agreement involved as well—something which would be more favorable than whatever Lord Barrow had offered, since Father had blatantly ignored the agreement with the Barrow—therefore garnering the earl's wrath—and leaving Grace to deal with the consequences.

Why could Father not, just once, love her? He slumped forward in his chair and wept. She waited, still as could be, to see what he would do next.

After several long moments, her father looked up again, unseeingly, at her. "There is still a possibility to resume the broken understanding with Barrow. I will work on that prospect again, or on making some other advantageous match if I cannot settle things to my liking." He rose and paced his library. "Barrow absconded—er, I mean left—for the continent, and I know not when he will return. But that is of little consequence."

"Father, you can't really wish align yourself with a man who would ravish your daughter, can you? And why *does* the earl leave England so often?" The man's frequent trips abroad, with no explanation, left her unsettled—even more now that she would be forced to marry him. Something seemed out of place, though she couldn't quite put her finger on it.

"I neither know nor care. His concerns are his own."

Grace ought to have known her father would not enquire into such matters. He preferred to know the title, connections, and property of any of her possible suitors. Anything else held little concern. For that matter, their ages and temperaments caused him no concern at all. Grace would marry as her father ordered her to marry, and that was the end of that. Her preferences, and frankly her needs, carried little moment with him.

A throb built in her temples as she waited to learn what else he had to say. Her jaw twitched with a desperate need to scream at the man, but somehow she held her tongue.

"You claim he ravished you, but what reasonable chit would not make such a claim under the circumstances? Barrow says you offered yourself to him." Several moments passed as Grace's father considered these ideas, mulling them over much as he savored his liquor. "I have no reason to doubt the earl's word. But in all honesty, it matters not who tells the truth and who lies. Your ruin is taking place before my eyes, Grace, and your ruin means my ruin!"

He stopped pacing and faced her. His eyes were cold, unfeeling. "By God, I will do everything in my power to see my reputation and status maintained. Go to your chamber. You will stay there unless I call for you."

"For how long, Father?" She glared at him through a haze of red. Of course he would banish her to her chamber again. He always locked her away.

"Until I decide you should come out, that is how long!" He sat behind his desk again and poured whiskey into a glass.

Grace fled through the doors of his library, blinded by her rage. Was she truly so unlovable her own father would take the side of a jilted suitor over her?

One

April, 1813

GRACE TREMBLED AS she knocked on the door to her father's study. Rationality had never been his strong suit, and the few servants remaining in his employ considered him anything but kind. Delaying this discussion, however, would only mean putting off the inevitable, so she braced herself for the task at hand as well as possible.

A muddled grunt from behind the door seemed to be her invitation to enter. In the absence of a footman, she pushed the dusty-covered, heavy doors open and proceeded into the library.

Her father stared the books of his estates with a sinister grimace on his face as he passed over the same figures time and again. He pushed the papers about, placing them just so against each other, in an apparent attempt to make the numbers line up properly. The stench of whiskey and an overused chamber pot permeated her senses.

"What is it, girl? Can you not see I am busy?" He barely spared her a passing glance.

The impending confrontation would not be a pleasant one.

"Father, there is something I must discuss with you."

He rearranged his papers once more before spilling his glass of whiskey on the mismanaged ledgers and notes.

Grace stood her ground, bent on avoiding assisting in the cleanup process. Father had created the problem, and he could very well fix it himself. She was far more concerned with how he might choose to handle her own situation. He mopped at the spilled whiskey with his shirtsleeve while she waited for him to acknowledge her.

"Yes, yes. Well. We are still waiting on Barrow to return so your betrothal can be announced. I am quite certain he will not wish to wait for the banns to be called. The earl can obtain a special license. Your marriage will take place in due time, Grace. Never fear."

Ha. Never fear.

Father took a swig from the bottle and then eyed her from across his battered desk. "Why have you left your bedchamber? I told you to stay put. If you are even thinking of asking to leave Chatham House for any reason, the answer is no. I dare not add to the gossip."

Father did not seem to realize, through his ever-present veil of drunkenness, that hiding until the gossip blew over would only add fuel to the gossipmongers' fire, not quench the flames. She wished there were someone she could talk to, but he had kept her in veritable isolation her entire life. She never knew exactly why. Grace could only assume he did not want her to see how the rest of society lived. How could she think something wrong when she knew nothing different?

His wobbly hand reached again for the whisky decanter. "Barrow will surely put things to rights upon his return from the continent."

Grace knew without a doubt that while the Earl of Barrow may *put things to rights* in the eyes of her father, her life would become anything *but* right. A life spent with the man who had so foully abused her was the last thing she wanted, but under the current circumstances, marrying the scoundrel might be the only option to salvage her reputation.

Not that it would be Grace's choice, even if she had myriad options at her disposal. Doubtless, Father would simply make his decision and force her to comply. She had once thought she would do anything to be away from Father. But a marriage to Barrow? She fought to conceal the shudder that coursed through her veins, chilling her to the core.

What about running away? Now there was a thought. Grace would have to hold on to the idea. She might need to make use of it after telling her news.

Which brought her back to her current purpose in speaking to him. "Father, there is something you should know."

He waved her off impatiently.

"Please. A—allow me to speak." Her shaking increased to the point of visibility, perhaps in anticipation of his reaction to her news, or also possibly due to fear of his retaliation. There was no way around telling him—he would discover the truth for himself in time, and his wrath might be deadly if it came to that, or at the very least violent.

How revolting, that she had been lowered to begging him for anything. But she must tell him, whatever the cost to her pride.

"Go on then. I do not have all day." Her father downed another large swig of his whiskey, somewhat missing his mouth in the effort. A stream of the liquor trailed down his chin and onto his already stained shirt.

His large hands grasped the glass. The image served as a reminder of the mark on her cheek. Better to just get it over with. "Father, I am with child," she blurted out.

The glass fell to the desk and Grace jumped. Her eyes followed it as it spilled its contents and dropped to the floor, shattering into a vista of miniscule shards that glinted in the dim candlelight.

Father stared out at nothing, his face growing redder by degrees. The twitching in his eye increased to the point she thought a vein might burst at any point. Good. He deserved to be angry. The man could not even be bothered to love his only child. But what would he force upon her now? She wished she were bolder and could dare to speak her mind with him.

His breath quickened to short rasps. He staggered to the window, never deigning to look at Grace. "Barrow is still away. Lord knows when he will return. Walsingham will not have you. After Barrow's announcement of your indiscretions at White's, no other man of title and means will have you either."

His frosty words fell heavy in the room and hurt Grace more than a slap to the face ever could. Those words proved what she already knew—her father's prestige and position were more important to him than she.

He paced through his library, stumbling at times, never glancing in her direction. "You will return to your chamber where you will remain until Barrow returns, and then you shall be his problem, not mine. If he does not return before the bastard is born, it will be given to some family that needs another set of hands. And you will wait for him to marry you." He stared out the grimy window, his head nodding at varied moments. "If he refuses to marry you, you will leave Chatham House and never return. Seek employment as a paid companion or a governess if you wish. Or as a whore, since you seem already inclined to that profession."

Grace's chin rose in vehement defiance.

"But you will never step foot across my door again, unless you come as the Countess of Barrow. You are a *disgrace*." Father stumbled back to his desk and picked up the decanter of whiskey. He rang for a servant to clean the mess he had caused, cursing when none arrived. For years, he had employed no more than his personal valet, a cook, and the occasional butler, yet he rarely remembered such pertinent details when drunk as a wheelbarrow, as in this particular moment.

Why, if he kept servants, he would have to pay them! Father preferred to spend his money on gambling or whores to keep him warm, or any number of other things on which a wastrel might spend his blunt.

Grace's nervous trembling subsided, replaced by anger. If he believed he could hide her away only to take her child from her, he was sorely mistaken. She could not allow such a vile circumstance to come to pass.

But if he managed to marry her off to Lord Barrow, her lot would become far worse than it already was. The earl had already shown her the sort of villainous treatment she could expect from him.

She left the library and returned to her room. Her father could not win this battle. She refused to let him take her child away from her, and she would be damned if she would marry an abominable lecher such as Barrow.

Grace had only one option.

LORD ALEXANDER HARDWICKE borrowed a curricle from his eldest brother Peter, the Duke of Somerton, for his jaunt across town. His good friend Derek Redgrave, the Earl of Sinclaire (a bloody handsome chap, even if Alex must risk his virility to make such an assessment) passed by in a phaeton as he left Mayfair on Piccadilly Circus.

"And just where are you off to in such a hurry on this fine spring day?"

Alex glanced about to be sure no one was within earshot. "To see Priscilla and Harry. Come with me. I'll explain. I need to speak with you, anyway."

Derek's eyes darkened with curiosity, then he changed the direction of his vehicle and followed behind.

After a good ride, including several unnecessary, and only slightly erratic, twists and turns to throw off anyone curious about Alex's destination, they pulled into a drive before the functional home where he housed the woman and her small son.

Their companion, Vivian, opened the door to his insistent knock. "My lords, how delightful to see you today. Come in." She stepped aside to allow their rather bulky bodies through the small doorframe.

"Awwiks!" Harry's delighted squeal assaulted them when they ducked beneath the entrance to the cozy parlor. "And Dewik, too."

The two-year-old boy dropped his wooden toy and waddled across to where they stood. When he arrived at their feet, he raised both arms to the sky and demanded, "Up!"

"Yes, sir. Up indeed." Alex lifted the giggling child high into the air and pretended to drop him, only to catch him again at the last moment. Of course, this elicited another peal of mirth.

"If you do not greet him properly, Harry, I fear he might drop you on your head." Priscilla sat on a window seat at the far wall, where she was at work sewing a garment that could be for none other than her son. Her brown curls fell into her eyes and she blew at them, only to have them fall immediately back into their previous position.

"Nooo, Awwiks not dwop me."

At the challenge, he took the bait and lifted Harry ever higher and caught him just before his face brushed the floor. The boy's laughter threatened to rob Alex of all his breath.

Priscilla looked up for just a moment before she busied herself in her work again. "And to what do we owe the pleasure of your company today? I didn't expect you before the weekend." Her face filled with inquisitiveness.

Alex placed the boy on the floor and gave him a wooden block to occupy his attention before he and Derek took seats at the neat writing table near where Pris worked. Everything here always seemed so dainty to him here, even with the toddler around to make messes.

He took a breath and looked Pris in the eye. "I have to leave you."

"By Jove, man. What will you have her do?" Derek pushed back from his seat, his dark eyes flashing with fury.

Alex lifted his hands. "Easy, easy. You know me better than that. This is not permanent. Far from it." He tugged at his cravat so he could breathe again. Blast the fussy things. "I am traveling to Somerton for a while. Lord Rotheby sent for me. He wants me to visit him, and I want to get away from London for a time. Perfect situation, if you ask me."

"Get away from London?" Derek asked, perplexed. "Why? Good God, there is nothing of interest to do in the country. And Rotheby's a fussy old goat."

"There is nothing of interest to do in town, either! Truth be told, it is more Mama that I want to get away from than London."

Priscilla raised an eyebrow in an unasked question.

"Ah…well, she's matchmaking again, you see. Peter believes she will start with me, even when he is the far worthier candidate."

"Ha!" Derek's burst of laughter filled the small room.

"You needn't be so jolly about it."

"But what could be better? You, Lord Alex Hardwicke, are running in fear from your mother. Why is that, I wonder? The only reasonable answer I can see is you fear she'll be successful in her bid."

Good Lord, why had he shared what he did about Mama? He would never hear the end of it from Derek. The dolt would probably go tell Sir Jonas and the rest of the crowd at White's that evening, passing it all on like the latest *on dit*.

"I am most certainly *not* afraid of my mother, or that she could be successful. She can't very well make an offer for me, can she?" She had better not get such an idea in her head. He shuddered and a pregnant pause filled the air, loud and unwieldy.

"How long will you be gone?" Trust Priscilla to get things back to the point at hand. She pulled her stitch tight and knotted it before she looked at Alex again, ever at work at something. Dear God, he wished he could change things for her, make things easier for her—something.

"I don't know. For that matter, I'm unaware why Rotheby wants to see me. I only know I need to get away and he's given me the perfect reason to do so without upsetting Mama." Deuce take it, why did he have to bring Mama back into this conversation when he had just got her out of it?

"You've been unhappy here for a long time, Alex. This is a wonderful idea." Priscilla smiled across at him with genuine warmth lighting her eyes. "Don't fret about me and Harry. We'll be just fine."

"But I do worry about you. I will continue to worry about you. I made you a promise, Pris—"

"You made a very foolish promise a very long time ago." She forcefully pushed her stitchery away and struggled to her feet, reaching for the cane resting next to the bay window. "You know what I think, Alex? I think it's high time you found a wife, settled down, and stopped ambling through your life. Perhaps you ought to stay in London, after all, and allow your mother to do what she will."

Derek earned a glare when he barely stifled a snicker. Priscilla ignored him. "Now why would marriage be so ghastly? You cannot go on like you are forever, you know."

"But if I were to marry a lady from society, what would I do with you and Harry? How could I continue to care for you?"

"I told you long ago we do not need you."

"That is bollocks, and you know it, Pris. What would you do for money? Harry will need to go to school someday. How would you pay for that? Christ, you cannot even walk without assistance, so what kind of work could you do?" He flinched at the sharp look she gave him, then rushed on. "I cannot sit by and allow you both to fall by the wayside. I will not."

She frowned at him. "Alex—"

Why did the blasted woman even think he would consider it? "No, I told you before and I am telling you again, I will take care of you. Mama must accept the fact that I will not bow to her every whim." Alex paced through the room, careful to step over Harry and his toys. "Derek, I need you to look after them while I am away."

"But—"

"But nothing. I swore to you I would care for you, and I intend to do just that. Derek will help." He hoped he was right.

"Of course I will. If you need anything before he returns, you need only send for me." He leveled a glare at Alex. "I will ensure you keep your promise to Pris and Harry. They need you."

"I realize that. And you know I'll come back to you as soon as I can." He strode over to where she stood near the window and placed a chaste kiss on her cheek. "I promise." He took the cane from her hands and guided her back to her seat.

He would not leave them alone for long.

GRACE WAITED UNTIL she was absolutely certain her father had passed out from his drink. She could not risk discovery. For once, she was glad he kept very few servants. It made her task this evening much easier.

She chose a small valise and packed her meager belongings into it. When all her clothes were inside and still she had more room, Grace chose a few books to take with her as well.

Reaching beneath her mattress, she retrieved a few bank notes. Not much, but it should cover coach fare, at the very least. After taking one more cursory glance around the chamber, the only thing left to pack was her battered doll. She placed it gingerly inside amongst the clothing and books. Her child might someday need a doll, and she might not be able to provide one, otherwise.

Before she closed the valise, she dashed off a brief note to her aunt and uncle.

> *Dear Sir Laurence and Lady Kensington,*
> *I realize this is terribly short notice, but I have a need to visit you. Please accept my apologies, but I have no time for further explanation now. I shall strive to explain myself upon arrival in Somerton.*
> *Your loving niece,*
> *Grace*

She stashed the note in her bag and climbed down the dark stairwell, careful to avoid the creaky steps and the missing planks, before she let herself out the oak front door. It thudded to a close behind her and she scurried down the path to the street with her satchel at her side.

Bustling along the dark streets, she prayed she was traveling in the right direction. Grace had spent far too many years cooped up inside her chamber at Chatham House. The time had come for change.

Finally, she spotted the posting inn where the coach was preparing to leave. She took a moment to deliver her note to the postmaster and prayed the mail coach would arrive before the stagecoach. The Kensingtons needed at least some warning of her looming arrival, however little it may be.

The driver signaled to her time had arrived for their departure. He assisted her aboard and she settled in for the three day journey.

Grace hoped her travel would not be in vain.

Two

GRACE STARED STEADILY out the window of the coach in a studied effort to avoid looking at any of the other passengers. In short order, she'd learned that making eye contact signaled an open invitation for conversation.

Mrs. Laymore, the grey-haired, self-proclaimed mistress of entertainment of the coach, did not take the hint. "And my Poopsie, when he fell from the tree—which I don't know how he got into the tree in the first place, since I thought dogs did not climb trees. Anyway, when he fell down from the tree, from way up high on that limb up higher even than the roof of the house, he broke both of his back legs, he did. Mr. Laymore had a doctor in town fashion a contraption to put on his hind end, so the bones could heal. But then we were forced to carry the poor pup around. It's certainly a good thing Poopsie is a poodle and not a larger dog, because I don't believe I could carry one much larger than him."

Mr. Turner interjected, "A dog that climbs trees? Are you quite certain your poodle is not a cat, Mrs. Laymore? I have never heard of such a thing." His attire appeared to be from a previous century, with everything down to the cod-piece in position, and his teeth had seemingly not been cleaned since the days when a cod-piece could be considered fashionable.

"No, he is as much a poodle as any poodle, Mr. Turner, albeit a rather odd, tree-climbing one."

Grace closed her eyes and pretended to sleep, but was jarred when Mr. Turner kicked her foot. Her eyes flashed open and she bit back a howl of pain.

"So sorry, Lady Grace," Mr. Turner said with a look of abject horror on his face. "My gout is acting up again, it is, and I needed to move my foot to a new position. I never meant to kick you, ma'am. I promise it won't happen again."

His gout would be the death of Grace, if the man refused to stop talking about it. She had heard about gout ad nauseum today and learned more about it than she ever cared to know in her lifetime in the bargain. She was tired of discussing the various accidents of Mrs. Laymore's precious Poopsie and the gout plaguing Mr. Turner. She just wanted to arrive in Somerton. That ought not to be too much to ask, after two full days stuffed into a coach with these insufferable strangers and another day to follow.

Grace shook her head. When had she become so intolerant? Obviously her concerns weighed so heavily on her mind that listening to the concerns of utter strangers was no longer as simple as it used to be—or even as simple as it *should* be, for that matter.

Being hungry didn't help matters, either.

She had spent almost all the money she had procured before leaving London on the coach fare and on rooms at the posting inns where they stopped along the way. Food was a luxury she could scarcely afford, so she ate only a small bowl of thin soup each day of the journey, casting envious glances at the crusty breads and mutton pies her companions ate with robust vigor.

Grace fell asleep after staring through the dusty window, even though she had tried desperately to stay awake.

It was the same nightmare she had experienced for weeks now. His eyes, cold and black, stared into her tear-filled ones through his untidy mop of blackish-greyish hair. His rough hands tore at her clothes and body. She shuddered at the grim set of his jaw as he forced himself on her, above her, into her.

Grace jolted awake in a cold sweat as the coach launched itself into a colossal rut in the road. She glanced about to see if any of the other passengers were aware of her nightmare, but none of them were paying her any attention. She turned her focus to slowing her breath and calming her pulse, even through the hollow rumble from her stomach. Perhaps the Kensingtons would provide her with a meager tea upon her arrival. She didn't want to raise her hopes, though.

She had neither seen nor heard from them since shortly after her mother's death, so she had no reason to expect they would take her in. At best, she could hope they might allow her to stay for an evening, perhaps through the end of the week if they were feeling terribly generous. But once they learned of her true reason for the visit (if it could even be termed as such), Grace held every expectation they would turn her out. She ought not to expect the same amenities she was accustomed to receiving in her father's home, however marginal they may have been.

She returned her gaze to the scene passing by outside the carriage window. After an interminable day of travel, houses and small shops started popping up along the roadway amongst the trees and wildflowers. What a relief. They must be approaching the posting inn where they would stop for the evening.

Within a few minutes, the coach pulled in front of the run-down building. The driver climbed down and handed them out. Grace rushed inside, hoping to get away from her irksome traveling companions and to the privacy of her own room. She needed a meal, a bath, and a good night's sleep—preferably in that order.

WHEN GRACE BOARDED the coach the next morning, she couldn't decide whether to be pleased or upset. A young woman with two toddlers and an infant sat in the coach, but there was no sign of either Mrs. Laymore or Mr. Turner. Thank goodness.

At least the day would be a short one. They should arrive in Somerton by about midday. Thankfully, no other passengers boarded, and Grace breathed a sigh of relief.

The coach departed with a jolt. What would life would be like for her in Somerton, should she be allowed to stay? Grace had very little memory of Sir Laurence and his wife, and the bits she did remember were spotty, at best.

After her mother had died, her father had stopped allowing the Kensingtons to visit. Letters from Somerton had slowed to a trickle, and then came to a complete stop. They could be as horrid and heinous as Father, for all she knew. Oh, *why* had she thought this would be such a grand idea again? Her misgivings threatened to take over. Perhaps she could convince the driver to stop before Somerton, and she could get off there. Then she wouldn't have to deal with such a dreary outlook. Of course, then she would never know the truth, too.

An argument between the children interrupted her thoughts.

"It is my dolly!" cried the female child. The little girl could be no more than three.

"No it's not. Mama, I had it first." An older boy pulled the doll from his younger sister's grasp and she wailed in distress.

"Christopher, you promised to let Annabel play with the doll today, did you not?" The young woman gently pried her son's fingers free of the toy and returned it to Annabel. The girl stopped weeping almost instantaneously and placed a thumb in her mouth while she held the doll.

"I do apologize, ma'am. Travel is difficult on children." The woman's face pinched when the infant began to cry. "Oh, lud. I hoped she'd sleep through this. I'm very sorry."

The older children seemed to take the baby's cries as an invitation to resume their argument. Christopher pulled the doll away from

Annabel. She screamed out loud before she bit the boy's arm. He retaliated by sitting on her.

The young mother seemed overwhelmed, sitting and watching it all happen with wide, fraught eyes. She made no move to intervene, so Grace took matters into her own hands.

She plucked young Annabel up from beneath her brother and sat her on the bench alongside herself. Grace pulled the young girl close and held on to her, soothing away the tears. "Christopher, sit next to your mother. You can keep that one." She dug through her valise and found her old, beat-up doll. It was one of the few things her mother had given her that Father had not confiscated to sell. Grace handed the doll to Annabel. "Here you go sweetheart. You can play with this."

Annabel's eyes twinkled, and she took the doll from Grace and held it in a close embrace.

Their mother stared at Grace from across the coach, her expression that of weary gratitude.

Grace gestured to the infant still crying in the woman's arms. "Do you need help with her, too? I could hold her for a stretch." The woman's jaw dropped open in dismay. She must never receive any help with her children. It must be overwhelming at times.

The woman did not respond, but held the baby out to Grace. She placed the infant over her shoulders and rocked back and forth, cooing and whispering until the child slept once again.

"Thank you, ma'am." A single tear slid down the mother's haggard face. "You are most kind."

Grace smiled at her. She didn't want to let the baby go. There was something very comforting about the feel of a baby sleeping in her arms.

The two older children each played with their respective dolls and refrained from further arguments, the mother slept, and Grace fervently prayed she would someday be able to hold her own baby like she held this stranger's baby.

When they neared Somerton, the woman awoke as the baby once again cried. "I believe she has a wet nappy, ma'am," the young mother said. Grace passed the child back to her mother's waiting arms, reluctant to let go. "Annabel, give the lady her doll back."

Annabel's eyes filled with tears as she lifted the toy up. Grace pushed the doll back into her grubby hands. "No, you may keep her, Annabel. I have no need of this doll anymore, but I can see you do." It hurt Grace to let go of this piece of her mother, but not as much as seeing the little girl cry. She would somehow find a way to provide her own child with a doll, but this one must go with Annabel.

"Thank you again, ma'am. You've been most generous with us." The mother worked to situate her children and all of their belongings, and Grace stared out the windows again.

As the coach pulled into town, the driver stopped in front of the Brookhurst Inn. Grace glanced about the street as the coach door opened and the driver set down the steps.

A tall, well-clad man with rich, auburn hair a bit longer than would be considered stylish stepped out of the inn, heading toward the stables. His breeches hugged his thighs so closely she could almost feel the power they possessed. The man's greatcoat, as snug as possible over him, displayed a broad expanse of muscular back and arms. Oh goodness. Now that was a man who cut quite the dashing figure. Grace flushed at the tingling sensation forming in her bosom, a most inappropriate and even *wanton* reaction, to the merest sight of a stranger. She had not even seen his face!

"Thank you again for the luncheon, Mrs. Derringer," he called out. "It was excellent fare, as usual." He nodded toward the unseen woman and continued on his way.

The stranger's gaze caught Grace's eyes as he walked past the coach. His eyes were clear—kind. There was something, she could not be sure what, but something *light* about him, light and good and true. Her gaze passed to his straight, Grecian nose and angular jaw line. He smiled, a smooth, gentle smile, with just a touch of wickedness—enough to let her know he was no angel. Still, most of the men she had encountered through her father's acquaintance were quite unkind. The compassion, even sweetness, she sensed in this stranger intrigued her.

He was a large man, certainly capable of overpowering her should he desire to do so. Yet without ever speaking a word to him, Grace felt safe. She somehow knew he would never hurt her. He would never be like the Earl of Barrow. She imagined this stranger to be the Greek god Apollo—handsome and light—before the absurdity of such a thought struck her.

He broke eye contact before it became improper, but he looked at her over his shoulder before turning the corner and moving out of her line of sight.

When he disappeared, her thoughts returned to the immediate. It was childish of her to let her mind wander in such ways, especially in regards to a man she had never met. For all she knew, he could be just like her father and all the men he had, at various points, desired to marry her off to.

No respectable gentleman would have her now. Not only was she damaged through Barrow's actions, but she would soon give birth to his bastard child. She would be lucky indeed if she managed to find suitable employment after her confinement. Her prospects for employment would depend on just precisely how far the arms of the gossip mill reached. Returning to London would be out of the question. Grace would have to travel to find an employer. She must never forget her present circumstances would forever determine her lot in life, fair or otherwise. But she couldn't fret over that now.

The coach driver was waiting to assist her as she climbed down from the coach. She was surprised to find another carriage and driver waiting for her, apparently sent by her aunt and uncle.

"Lady Grace?" The new driver bowed. He was an older man, with streaks of grey mixed in with his neatly trimmed chestnut brown hair and a slight stoop in his posture.

"Sir Laurence sent me to fetch you to New Hill Cottage, ma'am, as soon as he received your letter. It's a good thing, it is, that the post travels so fast these days or we would never have known you were coming, ma'am. No, we most certainly would not! I'm Barnes. If you would please show me which bags are yours, I'll help you into the carriage before I collect them, and then we'll be off to the cottage in a jiffy. I imagine you're right weary of all your travels by now and would like a spot of tea. We'll have you home in no time."

Her uncle had sent a carriage for her? Why would her relatives take such pains to assist her? She would be a burden upon them, so why should they care for her comforts?

While she had only meager belongings, making the trek on foot would have been rather difficult. She didn't know if any hired hacks were available for public use in Somerton. Even if she found a hack, paying for one to cart her and her bag was out of the question since she'd spent every last farthing she owned on her journey, lodging, and sustenance during the travel.

Thank goodness they were willing to help.

She pointed out her valise to Barnes, and he assisted her into the carriage before loading her bag on the back. Within a few minutes, they were, remarkably, on their way to New Hill.

ALEX PAID HIS tab at the Brookhurst Inn and headed out the doorway. Mrs. Derringer, the amply-curved cook and housekeeper who had been employed at the Inn for as long as his memory served, smiled and waved at him on his way out.

"Don't you be a stranger around these parts while you're visiting, Lord Alexander. You come back to see us, if you please."

Unable to resist a harmless flirtation with the woman, he flashed what he hoped to be a devilish smile. "Thank you again for the luncheon, Mrs. Derringer. It was excellent fare, as usual."

She tittered like a schoolgirl as he nodded and headed out the door. When he ambled toward the stables to fetch his horse, a coach being unloaded of its baggage and passengers caught his eye. This was an entirely ordinary and unremarkable occurrence, to be sure, yet for some reason, he couldn't look away.

Initially, he only glanced at the passengers, but then he caught sight of the most intriguing pair of icy blue eyes he had ever seen on a woman. They were crystal clear, with just the smallest hint of a silvery tone to accompany the blue.

More than their color though, the eyes captured his interest because of what he sensed beneath the surface. These two eyes spoke of something Alex could not quite determine. Sadness perhaps, or fear. He wondered what would cause such intense emotions.

She was young, likely not yet one-and-twenty, with midnight black hair pulled into a severe knot at the nape of her neck. Her traveling gown was a soft shade of blue more akin to a summer sky on a clear morning rather than to the shade of her eyes. And her skin—it was sheer perfection, all soft and pale and blushing at the same time, or at least he imagined it to be soft. How could the skin of a heart-shaped face so luminous, so radiant, be anything but smooth as silk or satin?

Dash it all, he was staring. He broke his gaze away from her and moved on toward the stables, where another carriage was situated alongside the Inn. The driver climbed down and called into the coach, "Lady Grace?"

Could Lady Grace be the young lady whose eyes had so fascinated him? Blast, he had no business even thinking along those lines. His entire purpose in coming to Somerton was to avoid Mama's matchmaking. Well, that and his summons from Lord Rotheby, of course. But really, if he were being honest with himself, it was to avoid being caught in the parson's mousetrap. If anyone in the world were capable of trapping him that way, he was sure it was his mother. The woman was bloody determined.

His horse had been fed, groomed, and saddled, and was ready for the last few miles of their journey. Alex had sent his carriage, along with his valet, ahead of him to Roundstone so he could enjoy the last portion of his trip alone. Any more time trapped inside the damned interior of that carriage, and he would lose his mind.

Besides, he loved a good ride in the outdoors, and he missed Somerton—the open air, the nature all around him, the people. He could breathe here. In truth, that was why he had chosen to eat his luncheon at the inn instead of traveling on to Roundstone Park. He wanted to catch up on all the things he missed from his childhood.

Fiend seize it, those eyes were back in his mind. He had to forget that woman. Alex held every intention of enjoying his stay with Rotheby—a man who had become something of a father figure to him in recent years, since the heartache of his own father's death. Doing that meant not wasting his time thinking of some chit suffering from a fit of the blue devils.

Sampson set off at a good clip, and Alex looked around at the familiar surroundings. The horse seemed to enjoy the open roadways, and frankly Alex couldn't blame him. He loved to look about and see more signs of nature than of a bustling city. The weather was a touch cool, but the sun was out and the roads were dry. All in all, it was a beautiful day.

Alex took his time on this final leg of the journey. There was no great hurry. Gilbert Thornton, the Earl of Rotheby, would not expect him until at least tea time. Alex and his horse wandered about Somerton and reveled in the freedom of open road and open sky. The late spring crops were maturing and flowers—crocus, daffodils, and foxgloves—were budding along the lane. The quiet atmosphere spoke to his soul.

He made the final turn into the lane where Roundstone Park stood. The manor house boasted an elegant but never fussy park and giant shade trees that created an arch overhead. The twitters of birds and familiar yaps of Rotheby's border collies created a pleasing welcome.

At the end of the drive, Roundstone came fully into view ahead of him. Ivy and vines climbed up the tall, stone sides of The Park. Large windows allowed sunlight into every room, with their drapes pulled back to soak it all in. Cobbled walkways ran between stone fences and a trickling creek, and bushes and flower beds lined more walkways, twisting and turning like a labyrinth through the garden, with the occasional bird feeder, statue, or water fountain. A creek trickled behind the manor house and whispered its way to join the Cary River before making the final run to the sea.

Alex inhaled deeply and enjoyed the newness of life in the air. The scents of spring were heady, even amongst the old structures they surrounded—Roundstone had been built more than two centuries before.

The head groom met Alex at the entry to the stables. "Good afternoon, my lord. I trust you enjoyed your ride today." He reached up to take the reins from Alex as he dismounted.

"Yes, thank you. Is Lord Rotheby at home this afternoon?" Alex took long strides across the lawn, not expecting a response. If the groom gave one, he didn't hear it. He wanted to see the old man and learn why his company had been requested—nay, commanded.

More than anything, Alex eagerly anticipated catching up with the earl. The two had always had a unique bond. The time they spent together was special to them both.

Jasper, Roundstone's butler, met him at the front door. The man had filled the post for the whole of Alex's life, and if appearances proved correct, that post would not be changing hands any time in the foreseeable future, despite the butler's curmudgeonly demeanor. He looked set to live the next century or so.

"Lord Alexander, his lordship is awaiting your arrival in the yellow drawing room," Jasper said. "I have prepared a suite for you and your valet has seen your belongings safely delivered there. Would you like to visit your suite first, or shall you attend to his lordship immediately?" During the course of this speech, Jasper had deftly escorted Alex through the door, removed his coat, and sent it off with a maid to be placed upstairs in the appropriate suite. Somehow, the butler did all of this without ever saying a word to the staff or even giving a signal. Roundstone Park always ran smoothly under the old goat's tutelage.

"Thank you, but I believe I will go in to see Lord Rotheby, if that's acceptable. I freshened up at the Brookhurst Inn just a short while ago." His eagerness must be evident to the servant, but sometimes such things could not be helped. And really, who gave a damn?

Jasper would likely be aware of Alex's eager demeanor even if the man were blind. He had a knack for picking up on moods—a skill Alex sometimes found exasperating, but more often recognized how such a quality in a butler could be useful. He might enjoy having a butler with such skills himself. Someday, that is. Someday in the rather distant future, when he had a home of his own which would need a butler.

"Very well, my lord. I believe you remember the way?" Jasper gave Alex a pointed look with a raised brow, perhaps remembering the way the Hardwicke siblings had run herd through Roundstone as children.

Alex nodded then turned in the direction of the parlor. A footman opened the door and announced him before leaving the two men alone.

A fire burned in the hearth, and a comfortable, brocade wing chair sat close to the warmth it radiated. "Come on in, boy, and be sure they close that door behind you. You are letting in a draft."

Alex closed the door himself and moved closer to the voice calling out to him. The earl was bundled tightly beneath two blankets. His skin held a greyish pallor, and a sickly smell hung on the air. Not a good sign.

"Have a seat, have a seat. Pull another of those chairs over here where I can see you."

Alex did as requested—even though he was more than amply warm, and the proximity to the fire might soon cause him to be over-warm—keeping a curious eye on Lord Rotheby. Had he come down with influenza? He hoped not.

The earl gave Alex a thorough once-over. "Goodness, are you taller than you were at your father's funeral? I would not have thought that possible, but my eyes tell me it is."

Alex gave a wide smile. The earl wanted to discuss his height, of all things under the moon? "My lord, I don't believe I have grown at all since I turned about twenty, but my valet could be more certain. He would have had to adjust my clothes. Shall we ring for him and ask?" He loved to tease the older man.

"*Lord* Rotheby? Hmph. You are still a cheeky lad, aren't you? What is this 'Lord Rotheby' business? I told you years ago. You are a man now, as am I. Call me Gil." The agitation in his words did not quite make it through to his voice or his face.

Try as he might, Gil would never pull off the part of the crotchety old man—at least where Alex and his siblings were concerned. Others might not agree with that assessment, but the earl had long ago developed an affinity for the Hardwicke family.

He lacked the acidity required to be considered cantankerous in his dealings with them—though rumor had it that his grandson and heir might have felt a bit of it from time to time.

Still, Gil could never be truly cross with Alex, though he had tried to be on a number of occasions. "All right, Gil it is. Although, my father taught me to always *respect* my elders." He ducked his head as Gil launched a crumpled piece of parchment at him. They both laughed. "It is excellent to be here again. It's been too long. I've been in need of a break from Town for a while, and your invitation arrived with perfect timing."

The earl raised an eyebrow at Alex in an unasked question.

"Mama is scheming. We'll leave it at that for now."

Gil chuckled, but he didn't push for further explanation. Surely, he remembered the dowager duchess's plots and plans as well as anyone.

"So why did you ask me to visit you?" It didn't really matter why Gil had asked. Alex had wanted to come—actually, he had been adamant about the visit. It would just help him to rest easier if he knew this was just a visit and nothing more.

"Does an old man have to have a reason to ask a friend to visit? Just stay for a while, and relax. We don't see each other often enough."

There was something in Rotheby's eyes—something Gil wasn't telling him.

Hmm. We shall have to see about that, my friend. But now was probably not the best moment to push for answers. He had, after all, just arrived. There would be plenty of time for such things.

No they certainly did not see each other often enough.

Three

BARNES DROVE GRACE in the Kensington carriage to the front door of New Hill Cottage.

Cottage was probably not the best term for the structure, as it could easily host a sizeable house party for society, should the Kensingtons wish to do so. The structure had two floors and appeared quite spacious, with a thatched roof, a delicious cream color with chocolate brown accents, multiple chimneys, and an exquisite combination of first stone against wood, and then against stone again.

Grace instantly fell in love with the thatched windows peeking out over flower gardens that were wild and unorganized enough to border on being unkempt. Daisies, thistle, and poppies fought with each other for control of the landscape, alongside dots of stones, fountains and a delicately carved bird feeder.

A footman bustled down the stairs to hand her out of the carriage. After she had safely descended, the butler who had followed the footman bowed deeply to her. "Good afternoon, Lady Grace. I trust Barnes did not keep you waiting overlong. Mason is my name. Your belongings will be taken to your rooms immediately. If you're in need of anything, I ask that you inform me of it right away, ma'am." Mason nodded smartly to her in lieu of another bow.

The deference of these servants at New Hill Cottage left her flustered. She had expected treatment as an unwelcome, uninvited guest. True, she *was* the daughter of a marquess and therefore a lady, but Grace had gone a long time without many servants about—and even longer since the ones who remained showed her any deference. Perhaps, of course, her aunt and uncle demanded such conduct from all of their servants. How very odd—or at least very different from what she had become accustomed to in her father's home.

"Thank you. I am certain everything will be quite unexceptionable."

The butler led the way in to the cottage. "If you'll follow me, ma'am. Sir Laurence and Lady Kensington anxiously await your arrival, my lady, but wish for all of your comforts be seen to before you join them for tea. Please allow me to introduce our housekeeper, Mrs. Finchley. She will show you the way to your chamber." He nodded toward an older woman, dressed in a plain black gown and white apron.

Her grey hair was knotted in a neat bun behind her head, and a mobcap that matched her dress perfectly rested above her chignon. Mrs. Finchley looked upon Grace with a welcoming smile and a curtsy.

She followed the housekeeper up a flight of stairs and along a hallway, and instantly felt comfortable. Handmade quilts and embroidered pillows draped plush sofas and chairs. These adornments were obviously used on a regular basis and not simply for display, showing pulls in the lightly faded fabric and the occasional darned hole—all of which gave them character. Candles were scattered on desks and tables in positions where they could easily provide light for letter writing, needlework, or reading.

Paintings lined the walls, outlined in gilded frames. Grace stopped before one, wondering what artist had created them, but then scurried along to keep up with Mrs. Finchley before she lost sight of the housekeeper. The paintings were of landscapes and the like. She thought she might have passed some of the scenes depicted in the artwork on her journey. Perhaps the artist was someone nearby.

"I understand your father did not send a lady's maid with you, ma'am," Mrs. Finchley said as they made their way through the halls. "We have arranged for my niece, Tess, to fill that role for you, at least on a temporary basis."

Grace's jaw dropped. She never had a lady's maid before, and had not even had a governess or a nursemaid in many years. Why, she had expected to be treated more as a servant herself than as someone to be served. If, that is, she were allowed to stay at all.

"Tess has not served in such a capacity before," Mrs. Finchley rushed on, as though Grace's shock were that they had already designated who would fill the role, "but she is a fast learner. If she is not adequate for your needs, you just let me know and I'll arrange to find someone more suitable for you immediately. Will this do?" The housekeeper came to a stop before a sweetly decorated bedchamber, complete with a silver mirror and brush set laid out on the vanity. The walls were a creamy white, with rich rose and sage green accents. Hand-stitched quilts in the same vibrant colors blanketed the bed, along with more pillows than she could imagine how she would ever use.

A young woman with honey-brown hair and a shy smile stood in the corner. She minced out of the way as a footman carried in Grace's small trunk and placed it beneath the window.

Grace took a tentative look around her new bedchamber and breathed a sigh of relief. "Yes, this will more than suit. Thank you." Grace might actually be able to rest in a room like this. Any form of relaxation, these days, had become a precious commodity.

"Of course ma'am. I shall leave you and Tess to it, then." The housekeeper started to back out of the room but stilled at the doorway. "Shall I come by when tea is ready, to show you to the parlor?"

Tea in the parlor? Her aunt and uncle wished her to enjoy tea with them. Maybe she would not be immediately turned out, after all. "That would be lovely."

"I assume you would like to be shown the rest of the cottage as well," the housekeeper said with a wink. "I'll be glad to give you a tour anytime you desire. Just have Tess inform me when you need anything."

Mrs. Finchley started to leave again, but Grace's call stopped her. "Oh, and Mrs. Finchley? Might I ask for a bath to be drawn?"

After three days of travel, the only thing more appealing to Grace than food was a bath. A rather startling discovery, that. The inn where she had stayed the previous night had not provided her with a bath (well, to be fair, she didn't have enough money left in her reticule to pay for a bath), and she couldn't imagine it would be too great an imposition on the staff—at least she hoped it wouldn't.

The housekeeper looked scandalized at Grace's hesitation. "It has already been ordered, ma'am. The maids will bring it in shortly."

Grace turned to Tess as Mrs. Finchley took her leave of them. The girl was shy, but efficient. She had already begun to unpack Grace's clothes.

Tess glanced up at her with a blush coloring her cheeks. "Shall I place your clothes in the bureau, my lady?" Before waiting for an answer, the girl started to do just that.

"Yes. Thank you," Grace replied. "Will you also set out a clean gown for after my bath? The lilac cotton would be perfect." She pulled the pins from her hair and shook away the tension. With a sigh, she sat on the edge of the bed and assisted her lady's maid with sorting through her possessions.

The girl's blush only deepened. "Ma'am, do you not wish for me to do this for you?"

Oh, dear. Grace had always done such tasks on her own. Having a servant assist her would require an adjustment period for both women, it seemed. "Of course, you may help me. I have never had a lady's maid."

Tess's eyes widened.

"We shall learn our new roles together. Does that sound all right?"

36

"Yes ma'am. That sounds perfect." Tess visibly relaxed, and the two worked together until the job was complete. By that time, a few other maids had pulled in a tub and filled it with steaming water.

Grace sank into it with a sigh. She allowed the heat to soothe the tension from her body, at least for the moment. She could always worry later. Nothing, after all, had changed.

And yet everything had changed, altogether.

"COME WITH ME, Alex. I plan to have a look about the property while it's still early, and I desire your company."

Lord Rotheby looked much better after a spot of tea and a bit of rest, so Alex was not as worried as he had been upon first seeing him that afternoon. Likely the older man had come down with a chill or some other brief illness. He'd be all right. Alex was certain. Nothing could keep the man down for long.

The groom prepared a couple of Gil's horses for their use. Sampson had earned a rest after the journey from London to Somerton, so Alex rose one of the earl's geldings for the day. They set out at a leisurely pace, taking in the glory of nature around them.

Alex marveled at the familiar landscape around the manor house. The Hardwicke family had spent the majority of their time in their father's principal seat, Somerton Court, while Alex and his siblings grew up. But their parents had moved the entire family to Hardwicke House in London eight years before so the siblings could participate in the marriage mart. Even with all the years Alex had spent in Town, he had always held an affinity for the country. The quiet spoke to him, soothed him, gave him something to think and dream about other than cards and balls and women.

Rotheby used to invite the erstwhile duke and his family to Roundstone Park for regular visits—he had looked at the late duke as the son he wished his had been—and it was not uncommon for the Hardwicke brothers to wrestle their way through the gardens or to leap, fully clothed, into the creek that wound through the property.

Gil seemed happy to have Alex with him again, today. His face came alive and his eyes were alert when he spoke. He took Alex through the entirety of the Roundstone property. "That oak over there? I seem to recall a day when you thought yourself man enough to jump from it into the creek just like Peter and Richard. You were a scrapper. But once you got on the branch, the height was more than you bargained for."

"Ah yes, was that the time you climbed up after me, to rescue me from the impending and everlasting shame of not completing the jump?" Alex chuckled at the memory.

"The very one. I took you by the hand and leapt. You fell down with me, but at least your brothers left you alone after that."

"For the day, but no more."

"Ah, well. At least for the day." Gil coughed again. "More importantly, you proved to yourself you could do it."

A far more important task, in the grand scheme of life. Jumping from the tree was only one of many things Alex proved to himself he could do, with the earl's prodding and assistance. No wonder their bond continued to this day.

They rode a little further in silence. Up ahead, a fence with two mangled posts loomed. "Goodness, why have you never fixed those, Gil? They were ruined years ago."

The older man strained his eyes in the direction Alex was pointing. "Oh yes. Well. They are still in the same shape as your mother left them. I haven't touched them so she'll remember every time she sees them."

Alex choked on his surprise. "My mother?" How could Mama be involved in something like that?

"Don't forget, you're the one who earlier pointed out her scheming. Don't you recall how those fence posts were undone? Surely you do."

He searched his memory, but nothing came to mind.

"You and your brothers wanted to race through the fields, chasing my dogs. Your sister, Sophia, thought she ought to be included. But she was a *girl*, and you boys felt she was too young and too female. So you left without her."

"I apologize, but I'm having difficulty making any connection to Mama with all of this."

"Slow down a minute. I'll get there. You are so impatient." Rotheby huffed out a sigh. "Some things never change."

Alex chuckled and bit his lip so he wouldn't rush the old man again.

"So Sophie ran to your mother and cried that you boys were leaving her out. She wanted to play with the older children, not be stuck at home with the baby—yet another boy, of course. Poor Sophie never stood a chance against you scoundrels-in-training, all cock-sure that girls had no place playing with boys. But I digress. Your mother thought she was right, Sophie *should* be allowed to chase after the three of you. The woman found a spade out in the garden shed—*my* garden shed, and *my* spade—and gave it to Sophia. Your sister went out and dug under those two posts to loosen them. Once she had them free, she pulled them to the side so she could climb through them and chase you."

"Mama did not. She would never encourage any of us to destroy your property." At least, he could not imagine it if she had.

"Is that so?" Gil frowned over at him. "Sophie ran after you boys, and your mother tried to fix my fence. All she managed to do was break loose more of the wood, though. When your father and I came upon her, she had Neil strapped to her back in some sort of sling she had created, my spade in her hand, and dirt everywhere—most especially all over her and that poor infant. I can promise you, it was a sight I shall never forget."

Alex laughed. "I doubt I'll ever forget it either, now that you have painted it so clearly in my mind. Mama is trouble, there's no doubt about that."

"No, no doubt at all. She's quite the minx, irrespective of her age."

Gil took time during their ride to point out various features of the estate and discuss their care. He told Alex which of his gardeners cared for which aspects of the park, how often he visited his tenants, the best time of year to travel into Bath to order supplies, and which merchants were honorable to deal with and which were just out to rake one over the coals.

Alex's suspicions about the earl's health were roused again by these details about the running of Roundstone. Why was he telling Alex? Why hadn't he summoned Quinton, his grandson and heir, to inform of such matters? But perhaps now wasn't the best time to press his friend on these matters. For now, he just wanted to enjoy their time together.

Near the end of their evening ride, Gil's eyes were bloodshot and droopy, and he slumped forward in his saddle instead of riding proud and erect as he had been previously.

"Should we head in for the evening?" Alex asked. "We can resume our jaunt through your grounds in the morning." The cold plaguing his friend must be getting the better of him tonight.

"What? Are you accusing me of being *old*? Rascal. You've always been a rascal." The glint in the earl's eyes showed some signs of revival, the weariness still won out. "Yes, fine. We'll call it a night."

Such a concession mustn't be easy for Gil. The earl had always been able to keep up with every man in any situation. He held it as a point of pride. Blast, he might be in worse condition than Alex had initially feared.

But Alex tried to force the fears aside. It could solve nothing. Nevertheless, it grasped him like a spider holding its prey.

They turned toward Roundstone Park with the last dregs of sunlight warming their backs. "What do you have planned for the rest of our visit?" Alex asked. "I'll be here with you for at least a few weeks. Would you like to go for a hunt?"

Maybe he could discover a bit more about the purpose of the Rotheby's request, even if he had to sort out the clues himself. The longer he was with Gil, the longer he was away from Priscilla and Harry—and unable to do anything for them but hope Derek looked in on them as often as possible.

"Oh, just a bit of this and that. I have some friends who live in Somerton, over at New Hill Cottage. The Kensingtons. I invited them over for tea tomorrow. I always enjoy spending time with them, but I don't want to put you out. I'm sure spending time with a bunch of older folks will quickly bore you."

"Oh no. I could only be, er, enlightened by—"

"Do not lie to me. I know you." The earl's eyes narrowed, as though he could see through Alex's head and into his very thoughts, but he chuckled. "I'm certain there will be some entertainments around town to keep you busy. We'll ask the Kensingtons tomorrow. They keep up with those things better than I do these days."

Alex wanted to say he would be better entertained by spending his time with Gil—because *perhaps* he would—but he heeded Rotheby's advice and kept quiet. Lying to the man would serve no purpose, and his friend deserved better. "All right," he conceded, "we'll see what they have to say. I promise to try not to become too terribly bored while talking with three decrepit invalids." He chuckled at Gil's glare as they dismounted. "I'll at least endeavor to hide my boredom, and not snore should I fall asleep."

The headed back inside Roundstone Park, side-by-side. It had been a good day. But the day left the nagging question of Gil's health working in his mind.

Four

Mrs. Finchley led Grace down the stairwell and turned into a broad hall. Off to the right, a large doorway opened into a spacious drawing room decorated in soft primrose with accents of a deep green. The late afternoon sun poured in through a wall consisting almost entirely of thatched windows, with the patterns creating a latticework shadow across the room. Handmade quilts and embroidered pillows draped the furnishings, the same as in the rest of the house. A fire burned quietly in the hearth, snaps and pops of sparking wood only occasionally disrupting the general silence.

"Sir Laurence and Lady Kensington, your niece, Lady Grace Abernathy." Mrs. Finchley executed a curtsy left the room upon a wave from her employer.

Grace tried not to let her nerves show as she perused her relatives—relatives she had not seen since she was a very young girl, and whom she remembered little, if any. Relatives who might set her out, should she not come up to scratch. As if she knew what they would consider up to scratch anyway. This was all terribly daunting.

Sir Laurence had obviously been quite handsome in his day and still maintained much of his youthful glow. He had filled out a touch about the middle, but his face held an easy smile and warm brown eyes to match the brown hair mixed with grey.

Lady Kensington could still pass as one of the most beautiful ladies of the ton. Her fair skin and black hair matched Grace's, though hers had begun to turn silver just at the temples. She stood with an elegance that spoke to her position, though her attire was certainly more comfortable than fashionable. Still, there could be no doubt this was a woman born to privilege.

Grace paused, unsure what she ought to do next. Her circumstances to this point had proven far from what she expected. Should she curtsy to her aunt and uncle? Walk across the room and take their hands? Hug them? Burst forth with her thanks at their allowing her to stay, even if only for one night? Her mind raced.

They didn't even know *why* she was there to begin with, so she should likely start with the reason for her visit. But how? Oh, goodness. She truly ought to have thought this all through a bit more before she just up and left her father's house. But she could *not* have stayed there any longer. Not one more moment.

She would simply have to become more decisive. Starting immediately.

All of her planning proved pointless, however. Grace's aunt remained seated and silent for several moments. But then she stood and virtually flew across the room to pull Grace into a tight embrace, complete with tears and sniffles.

"Oh, Gracie! Sweetheart. We are so, so glad you are here. Your Uncle Laurence and I have missed you terribly. Oh goodness, you were only a little girl the last time we saw you."

Lady Kensington finally released her and unabashedly wiped away the wetness she left behind on Grace's cheeks. The older woman grabbed her by the hand and pulled her across the room to sit on a sofa. Grace had no choice but to follow, dignity be damned.

"I've no idea what circumstances have changed so you can be here for a visit with us, but we are thrilled. Thrilled! Lud, Laurence, she looks just like Margaret."

Grace's head lifted at the mention of her mother. She barely remembered the woman, but a few pleasant memories remained—singing, playing games, being rocked and tucked into bed.

"Margaret had those same eyes," Lady Kensington continued softly. "I always envied your mother her eyes, dear. Mine are just a horrid, dull brown. It was truly unfair for one sister to have the most perfect shade of eyes in the world, and the other to receive eyes so dull. Oh well, I promise to enjoy yours." Lady Kensington patted her on the cheek and brushed at her hair until a few wisps came loose from their knot. "So beautiful…"

The effusive welcome threatened to turn farcical. If Grace's aunt did not allow her a moment to regain her bearings, she could surely not be held accountable for her actions. Could she? Oh dear. The entire situation was becoming inexplicably ludicrous.

"Dorothea, would you give Gracie a moment to breathe? I wager you have not taken a breath yourself in a good five minutes." Sir Laurence took a seat on the other side of Grace and pulled her in for a brief hug.

"She is not always like this, you know Grace. It is just she has been so excited since we got your letter informing us of your visit. Your Aunt Dorothea will become a normal woman after a day or two, once the newness of having you here wears off. Then she will merely talk your ear off during most hours of the day, all the while making you dizzy with moving about nonstop. You will become accustomed to it. I certainly have. Of course, I've had a good number of years to learn to love your aunt's quirks." He chuckled and touched her gently on the back of her hand.

Mrs. Finchley entered again, carrying the tea service. She placed it on the table before them and left once again, just as unobtrusively as she had come.

"Dorothea, can you manage to pour, or are you too flustered?" Sir Laurence gave his wife a wicked grin, proving the facetious spirit in which he delivered his query.

Lady Kensington frowned at him but served the tea anyway.

"Grace, have you settled in?" Sir Laurence asked. "I hope the chamber is to your liking. We have some larger suites, but we thought you might appreciate the coziness of the one we chose. It is bright and cheerful in the mornings."

Cheerful in the mornings would be very much appreciated, indeed. Grace hadn't felt cheerful in far too long. But that must mean they were prepared for her to stay for more than only one night. Would that change if they learned the truth?

"Yes, my lord, the room is lovely. It will be more than adequate."

She accepted the cup of tea and plate of sandwiches, scones, and cakes, trying desperately to be dignified in all of her speech and responses. Perhaps she could make herself acceptable to them yet.

Her aunt and uncle would surely not be pleased with her if she spoke out of turn or said something inappropriate. Grace focused her attentions on her manners, trying to eat slowly and neatly. Having eaten little for the last few days though, she was ravenous. Soon, she was shoveling food into her mouth in a most unbecoming manner, decorum tossed aside in favor of satisfying the beast inside her stomach that threatened to eat her alive if she did not provide it with ample sustenance in short order.

"Go on, go on, my dear," her uncle said. "Eat up. You must be famished. And just to be clear, there will be none of that 'Sir Laurence' or 'Lady Kensington' business. You should call me Uncle Laurence or just Uncle. The same will go for your aunt. She is either Aunt Dorothea or simply Aunt. We are not so terribly formal around here."

She glanced up sheepishly from the task of filling her stomach as her aunt nodded in vigorous agreement with her husband. This would mean even more adjustment.

At her father's house, she rarely even called him Father. He expected her to call him 'my lord' more often than not—and always in front of servants or guests.

Aunt Dorothea refilled Grace's teacup before giving her another helping of scones. "I do not imagine you had much to eat on your journey, did you dear? You seem fair gutfounded. That is quite all right. Have as much as you like now, and there will be plenty more at supper. I'll be sure Cook prepares a feast. We'll not have you go hungry. No ma'am, not in my house, you will not be hungry. The abomination of the thought!"

Aunt Dorothea seemed to have calmed, now showing immense interest in seeing to each of Grace's comforts. What a truly odd sensation, being looked after. Not uncomfortable. Quite the opposite, actually. But very, very different. She mustn't become too accustomed to such treatment. It would only make it more difficult when she must eventually take her leave of their generosity.

Uncle Laurence settled into a nearby armchair and tucked into his scone. "Do you think Tess will work out for you as a lady's maid? She has never served in any position, really, but she grew up in our home. She has been with us since she was just a wee tot, still in leading strings. I would like to find her a position here at New Hill Cottage, where she can stay with her aunt."

Grace's eyes widened again. They cared enough to provide her with a personal servant for not only the duration of her stay, but possibly as a permanent position? Oh dear. She had not expected this—not any of this. It was all quite more than she had been prepared to accept. Everything had started to look up for her, literally out of nowhere.

Yet she could virtually see a mountain of debts she would soon owe to her aunt and uncle piling up before her, with no real way to return the favor of their kindness. She'd have to find a way to make herself useful, if she were to stay for very long. They could not simply give and give and give her more, without her doing *something* for them in return. But what?

She'd figure that out soon enough, she supposed. "Yes, Uncle. I am certain Tess will be wonderful for the position. I have never had a lady's maid before, so she and I can learn how things should be done together."

"You have *what*?" Aunt Dorothea dropped her napkin to her lap. "Never had a lady's maid? Laurence, did you hear that? Goodness child, your father is a marquess! Could he not part with enough of his precious coin to hire someone to care for your needs?"

"No, ma'am. Father did not employ very many servants. He thought his money better spent elsewhere."

She flushed at the memory of just exactly how her father found better use for his funds. Grace did not feel it pertinent to share the precise manner in which he spent his money. He may not be a kind man, but he was still her father. Not knowing her Aunt and Uncle Kensington very well, she had no idea how they would handle such information.

They could very well be some of the biggest gossips in society. If so, word could spread all over London that her father was a drunkard who loved to gamble and whore. Granted, word could already be all over London about that—and it would be true—but it was not Grace's doing.

She needed to keep her location secret. No one could discover her, unless absolutely necessary.

Of course, letting such information about Father slip might allow Grace a means to gauge the Kensingtons' possible reaction to the fact that she had run away from him. Goodness, how could they have allowed her to stay in their home for even this long without demanding an explanation for her arrival?

Uncle Laurence set about calming his wife again, patting the back of her hand and muttering something about "things will be different for Grace while she is with us."

Grace returned her focus to the food before her. After a third helping of sandwiches and the like, she finally started to feel some relief in her stomach. She slowed her eating and returned her attention to the conversation of her relatives.

When they reached a lull, Grace took the opportunity to satisfy her burning curiosity. "Might I enquire what artist painted all of the pieces here? They seem to be of the local area. Is it someone who lives nearby?"

Aunt Dorothea brimmed with pride. She glanced over to Uncle Laurence, then spewed forth when he did not respond within about three seconds, "Why, your uncle is the artist!"

Grace covered her surprise by taking a sip of tea. Uncle Laurence good-naturedly allowed his wife to gush about him until she had spent the full frisson of her emotions and moved on to the next subject.

"Laurence is a wonderful painter," Aunt Dorothea continued, "though I have never yet convinced him to do my portrait." She feigned a pout in his direction.

"I will not have you filling the girl's head with fabrications. I can paint a landscape with the best of them, but I am no portrait artist." He glanced at Grace, and told her as though he were confessing to a cardinal sin, "I cannot quite seem to get the details in a face right—the lines and angles are all wrong. Portraits are some artists' specialties, but not mine. I shall stick to my landscapes, even if she badgers me to my grave about doing her portrait."

Grace didn't manage to suppress a grin at the huff her aunt expelled.

It seemed staying with the Kensingtons would turn out to be all right after all. They were genuinely kind and considerate, and appeared to enjoy teasing each other. For once in her life, Grace might live in pleasant surroundings—at least for a time.

Though, one could never tell when one might be turned out. If only she had known them better through the rest of her life, she might know better how to interpret their moods.

Once more, Grace gathered her courage and prepared herself to be disappointed, even though it had become apparent they would deny her nothing within their power. Still, asking for things she wanted went against her nature. It was rather uncomfortable to break free from the mold into which her father had her so firmly planted. Nevertheless, she barreled through. "Uncle Laurence, might I join you sometime on a painting excursion? I brought a few oils and brushes with me. I would love to see more of the area."

He beamed at her. "Of course you can, Grace. We'll head out early next week if you can wait so long. I've wanted to go over to the Cary River and paint for a while, if that sounds like a good destination to you."

She nodded. All it had taken was for her to ask for what she wanted in order for it to be granted. Life here would certainly be rather different from life with Father.

Maybe, just maybe, she would not be forced to leave them, at least for a time. Perhaps they would allow her to stay at least long enough to form a new plan.

Uncle Laurence patted the back of her hand. "Your mother told us you were becoming a little artist when you were only three or four years old. It seems your father did not break you of that, at least." He winked at her over his cup.

Could they know? Did the Kensingtons realize what her father had been like all that time? What her life had been like? It seemed unreal she could be granted such a reprieve as to stay with people who cared for her, who wouldn't keep her locked in her chamber, and who would allow her to get out in nature and experience some of the joys of life.

"Oh, wonderful!" Aunt Dorothea said. "I'll come with you, and we can make a picnic of it. Gracie…oh dear, I hope you don't mind that I call you Gracie, being a grown woman and all now." She frowned and brushed a stray hair back into place. "It is what we called you when you were just a little girl you know, and old habits are difficult to curb my dear. I am not much for painting, myself, or drawing for that matter. But I'll bring a touch of embroidery with me and it will keep me busy while the two of you deal with your canvases. I'll just keep to myself and won't be a bother to anyone."

Aunt Dorothea prattled on, and Grace and Uncle Laurence allowed her to do so. Grace no longer knew what her aunt was talking about—it didn't really matter. The non-stop chatter comforted her. Finally, she could breathe again.

She spent some more time swimming about in her thoughts while her aunt talked. Perhaps she could stay with the Kensingtons—if Father never found her, of course. And if they would forgive her for coming to them in such a condition, and if they dared to risk the ostracism of what it would mean, and—

"—and we shall travel to Roundstone Park tomorrow afternoon to visit and take tea with Lord Rotheby, Grace."

Grace jolted into the present. She ought to have been paying closer attention. Lord Rotheby? Oh, dear.

"I hope you will not mind paying a social call so soon after you've arrived," her aunt rushed on, "but we accepted his invitation before we knew you would come to stay with us, sweetheart. The earl really is a dear old man, and will not mind in the least if we bring you along."

A visit for tea with an earl? Oh no. Father might find out, if word traveled to Town. Surely, as a peer, Lord Rotheby must know her father. She had to think quickly.

"I'm terribly sorry, Aunt, but I don't think Father would approve of my visiting with anyone in town while I'm here." She searched her mind for a good reason he might have for such a disapproval. Drat! "He...er, well, he wishes to keep me away from all society until I can be properly introduced."

Please let them not have heard she had a come-out last Season, however paltry the affair turned out to be, with only attending a single ball before the Duke of Walsingham and her father came to their agreement.

Aunt Dorothea looked horrified. "Oh, lud! Your father can—"

"Dorothea," Uncle Laurence cut in. "Watch yourself. Chatham is still Grace's father, despite how you and I may feel about the man." Uncle Laurence turned to Grace and held her gaze. "Grace, your father obviously sent you to stay with us, and therefore he chose to trust your aunt and me with your care. As such, some decisions we make for your well-being may not line up precisely with what his decisions might have been under the same circumstances. Are you all right with that?" He paused and allowed her time to react.

She merely nodded in assent. If word somehow did travel to London, hopefully she would have enough time to escape again. Father would not force her to marry Barrow.

But, oh, how she wished her aunt had said whatever she had planned to say before Uncle Laurence had interrupted her. Surely it would have been wicked. Grace desperately wanted to be wicked, just for a moment. But if *she* could not be, perhaps she could just listen in while her aunt was.

"Excellent. Your aunt and I do *not* agree that hiding you from society is in your best interest. We feel it would be propitious for you to interact with other people of high caliber. Still, we won't force you to come if you don't find the idea pleasing. Is that agreeable to you? Would you like to join us?"

Again, Grace nodded. How could she refuse, when they were allowing her a place to stay? And on top of it all, the Kensingtons had required no explanation as to why she'd come, at least as of yet. Of course, the likelihood Father would find out was rather slim, but she still sat in awe of her decision.

Even more than awe, she felt something more—was it courage? She marveled at her own boldness. For the first time, Grace had taken just the tiniest bit of control over her own life.

She felt wonderful.

Five

ALEX FELT QUITE the grouch the following day. He wracked his brain to determine the cause of his foul mood, and found only one possible cause—a significant scarcity of sleep, due to incessant dreams.

They were not *un*pleasant dreams, exactly. They were filled with a pair of soft blue eyes.

The situations in the dreams had changed, but the eyes remained the same. They stared at him, piercing him through, eating at his psyche. He couldn't ignore them, even if he tried—but he couldn't quite bring himself to try, either. He was far too fascinated, even enamored, by them.

In some of the dreams, they implored him for help. What help did she need? He didn't know, but her eyes were almost begging him. Even still, these eyes told him more than she ever would—of that, he was oddly certain.

If only he knew what help she needed. Had she been left destitute? Did her husband die? Maybe she was running from someone—or possibly *to* someone.

Then again, it had only been a dream. Even if he knew what help she needed, how on earth would he ever find her? He didn't know her name or her destination. He knew nothing about her.

Nothing, that is, except the eyes that haunted his dreams in a silent plea for something unknown.

"IT'S QUITE A nice day out, ladies. Shall we take the chaise to Roundstone Park? I think it would be pleasant to enjoy some air on the trip." Uncle Laurence was bursting at the seams in his eagerness to be on the way.

Grace, however, felt uneasy. She chided herself for her nerves. Obviously the Kensingtons were good friends with the earl, and therefore they trusted him and expected she would, as well. But the nerves remained.

Of course, she was still so early in her pregnancy it was impossible for anyone to tell. She ought not to fret about the possibility of discovery. If only she had already informed her aunt and uncle of her situation—but they had not given her an opportunity. Or perhaps it was that she had not taken the opportunity when it had been presented. Either way, she wished they knew. Maybe then, they would allow her to stay behind.

But the pregnancy was certainly the least of her worries, the most of which being word somehow traveling to Town about her location. If Father knew where to find her...

Aunt Dorothea brightened. "Oh yes, Laurence, let us enjoy the sunshine. We always have so much rain, we might as well take advantage of the sun while we can. Grace, do be sure to wear your poke bonnet so you can protect your complexion. It would just not do for you to be covered in freckles. You have such a lovely complexion." She fluttered about the drawing room to put away her embroidery and collect her own bonnet.

In the brief day that Grace had been with her aunt and uncle, she was continually amazed at her aunt—the woman was always in motion, always talking. She never seemed to take a breath. Yet the incessant action wasn't bothersome—far from it. While she could have easily become flustered from all of the commotion, it calmed her instead.

Traveling by chaise, Grace saw the surrounding area for the first time. It was a much different view than she had while stuck behind the dusty windows of the coach. Wildflowers littered the fields: violets, hyacinths, foxgloves, and daffodils dotted the road and created a landscape of blues, pinks, purples, and yellows that Grace's fingers itched to paint.

The trip to Roundstone Park was brief. "The earl," Uncle Laurence informed Grace, "is our closest neighbor at the cottage. We have become quite good friends in recent years. I daresay we visit him or he visits us at least every week, if not rather more frequently."

Barnes drove the chaise over a bridge that brooked a creek and took them to the front drive. The manor house stood proudly at the end of a lane of trees, which created an archway of branches overhead. Sunshine twinkled through the leaves which danced like dervishes as they moved.

A grand rose garden behind the house caught Grace's eye and enchanted her with the variety of colors—even more colors than lined the roadway. She pulled her gaze back to Roundstone and was awed by its size. While London boasted any number of great residences, she had not expected to find one to compare with them so far from Town.

Grace feared her ignorance due to isolation would soon rear its head and reveal itself to the entire world. What great blunder would she make first? Then her gaucherie would pronounce itself to all and sundry, and she would have to hang her head in shame.

The home she lived in with her father since Mother passed away was anything but grand. Father had also sold all of his other estates which were not entailed to his heir, in order to further fund his habits. Grace was very much used to modest living and had rarely ventured outside her home (due, as usual, to Father's edict, in addition to her own fears of being discovered for the uncultured, ungainly, uncivilized chit she so obviously was).

The splendor before her at Roundstone Park caught her unawares, with the ivy climbing the edifice of the house and huge picture windows looking out. They seemed almost to soak in the warmth of the sun. And oh, how many rooms there must be! Even with its drab grey stone exterior, it seemed so much cheerier, so much brighter, than Chatham House had always seemed.

As they drew closer still, even more flowers came into view in the various parks, with neat, cobbled walkways spread about. Benches, fountains, and marble statues dotted the way, surrounded by bursts of color in every hue of the spectrum. Grace tried to memorize every detail, every line, every shape and texture and sound so she could someday recreate it with her oils.

She could become quite settled with this new life, if she allowed herself. If *fate* allowed her.

As they came to a stop before Roundstone, a footman came from the house to assist the ladies down. Uncle Laurence led them inside.

"Sir Laurence and Lady Kensington. Ma'am." The stodgy butler inclined his head in their direction. "Lord Rotheby is expecting your arrival, though he did not mention a third guest. How shall I announce your arrival?"

"Inform the earl that the Kensingtons have arrived, complete with their niece, Lady Grace Abernathy."

The butler indicated the guests should follow as he led them to a downstairs drawing room. Grace tried not to gawk at the opulent furnishings. Brocades and silk satins upholstered every chair and sofa in periwinkle and puce, and wooden tables and bookshelves gleamed with rich oak finishes—so shiny they looked to be covered in glass.

The butler cleared his throat. "My lords, Sir Laurence and Lady Kensington and Lady Grace Abernathy." He waited until signaled by the old earl, then continued. "Shall I bring in the tea now, my lord?"

Again, the elderly man nodded in assent. He was bundled beneath multiple blankets, though Grace thought the room to be plenty warm. Another, younger man stood near the windows—a tall man with auburn hair. Oh, no. What if he were the same man from the inn?

But she oughtn't to worry. Even if he were that man, he surely wouldn't recognize her. And if he did, what of it? He knew nothing. She tried to relax herself and slow her pulse. Nothing opportune could come of becoming a bundle of nerves.

"Come in, come in." Lord Rotheby waved them inside the room and rose to unsteady feet. "Please, make yourselves comfortable." He motioned to a sofa and an armchair, and the ladies drew near to him.

"Gil, I hope it is all right that we brought another guest with us," Uncle Laurence said. "Lady Grace is our niece. She will be with us for an extended stay and just arrived yesterday, but I was sure you would not mind if we brought her along."

The earl's smile seemed adequate confirmation. It reached his eyes, at least, even if it didn't quite stretch his lips as it might have once done.

"Lady Grace, may I welcome you to Roundstone Park?" Lord Rotheby asked before being seized by a round of coughing. He settled himself as soon as possible. "I am glad you will be joining us today. My good friend, Lord Alexander Hardwicke, has joined me for a likewise extended stay. I'm sure he'll be glad to have a younger person to converse with this afternoon."

Lord Alexander turned from the window and gave a polite smile to them all. She froze when his gaze landed on her for a moment. He was the man from the inn. She flushed at the open stare he gave her. Her cheeks heated, at which point his stare became even more intense. His gaze changed in a moment from an inquisitive glance to a thorough inspection of her.

Grace timidly returned his inspection. Lord Alexander was quite handsome. His hair bordered on being too long for the current style, and his eyes shone an intense green—darker than the forest, almost like midnight, with golden flecks bouncing about the edges, giving them a hint of the lightness she sensed the previous day. He was fair of skin and had a long, straight nose, narrow as was the rest of him.

His cravat was ever-so-slightly loose at his neck, as though he had tugged at it in impatience, though the rest of his attire was utter aristocratic perfection—the long, black coat over an ornate waistcoat, all snug against his strong chest, and buff knee breeches enhancing rather large thighs, tucked into immaculate, well-shined Hessian boots.

Grace couldn't help but be impressed with the sheer beauty of him. Drat, she had no business thinking in such a manner. She tried to banish all such thoughts from her mind. After all, she must remember she would soon bear a bastard child. No man of Lord Alexander Hardwicke's standing would want anything to do with her.

Not only that, but she was not yet of age. She could not marry without Father's consent. Obtaining his consent would be next to impossible, as well as dangerous, now that she'd run from him. If he learned where she was—oh, she dreaded to think what he was capable of.

How she wished things were different!

Grace couldn't tolerate the idea of raising her child alone. Would it not be better for the child to have two parents, and to not go through life with the label of bastard? Of course it would. But how could she provide her child with a father? No man would have her now. Well, none she would have.

Lord Rotheby continued, "Laurence, my lady, I am sure you both remember Alex. Although I would wager he was hardly more than a boy the last time you saw him. He is still as much of a rascal as ever, I can assure you." He chuckled, despite the fact that it caused him to cough again. "I am so sorry. My health is not quite the thing today."

The butler returned with the tea and poured a cup to ease Lord Rotheby's cough before excusing himself.

Alex smiled and greeted the Kensingtons warmly. "My lord, my lady, it is certainly a pleasure to see you again. Gil tells me you keep him company while he wastes away here in the country." He passed a facetious grin in the earl's direction, and Grace tried to cover a laugh by taking a sip from her cup. "It is good to know he has some friends nearby who can put up with him in his old age."

Then he turned his gaze on her, and her cheeks heated again. "And Lady Grace, it is a privilege to make your acquaintance."

Lord Alexander took a seat in an armchair next to Lord Rotheby and across from Grace, and she tried not to stare at him. She sat on the couch, nodding and making her "Mm's" and "Ah's" in the appropriate places, but paying more attention to her own thoughts and the man she had encountered the previous afternoon than she did to the discussion. She peeked at him over her teacup a few times, hoping not to be caught in such a bold act.

Why had he twice stared at her so forthrightly? She hoped she could to find the reason in his eyes or his deportment. He was not being intentionally churlish in his assessment of her, but he more than put her nerves on edge.

Why was his curiosity about her so strong? Could he be aware of her identity? Maybe he had followed her—possibly at Father's command. Or perhaps he had been one of the men at White's the night Barrow had told his tale of her so-called *indiscretions* with him.

She hoped not. Grace had hoped Somerton could provide her with some privacy, with a place to hide. The last thing she needed was for someone other than her aunt and uncle to know why she was there. If they were to spend much time in his presence, and he *knew*—she did not think she could hide her shame. On top of it all, her aunt and uncle did not yet know the true reasons for her visit.

Oh gracious heavens. What would she do if he informed them before she could? They would turn her out in an instant.

After yet another long gaze at Lord Alexander over her teacup, Grace caught sight of Aunt Dorothea's knowing stare focused her. Drat it all. She looked away quickly. She had no idea if her aunt was the matchmaking sort, but since Grace was not matchmaking material, she saw no reason to encourage such behavior one way or the other.

One thing was certain—Grace needed to spend as much time *away* from Lord Alexander as possible, which did not seem a terribly easy prospect at this juncture. She would likely be thrust into his path at many turns, since the earl and the Kensingtons were dear friends. The last thing she needed was Aunt Dorothea trying to increase the amount of time she would be required to be in the blasted man's presence.

Grace tried to return her focus to the conversation at hand, while attempting to avoid the gazes of both her Aunt *and* Lord Alexander. Neither of which turned out to be easy. Lord Alexander brazenly watched her, and Aunt Dorothea cheerily eyed them both.

This could turn out to be a very long tea, indeed.

WHEN ALEX TURNED to greet Gil's guests, he pasted a smile on his face. He remembered the Kensingtons from his years growing up in Somerton, though not well, and he mentally braced himself to play the gallant gentleman for their young niece.

He expected Lady Grace to be a young chit, not yet out in society. After all, if she was already out in society and still unmarried, why wouldn't she stay in Town for the season? What young girl would choose to remain in the country when she could enjoy the grandeur of London in spring? Instead, he was shocked to find the very young woman whose eyes had haunted his dreams last night.

Alex studied her eyes, searching to see what was real and what had been only a dream. A hint of sadness rested in their depths, and also the shadow of fear. He stared far longer than was polite, but couldn't seem to turn away from the cold, blue eyes that had frozen holes into his mind, nor from the face of their owner.

She had porcelain skin and hair as black as midnight. Like yesterday, it was pulled into a tight chignon at the back of her head, with not a single strand out of place. A pale, rose bonnet sat atop her lap and matched the cambric of her simple dress—one with none of the lace and bobs his sisters seemed so inclined to adorn their own with. An unpretentious ribbon tied her hair in place.

She needed no adornments. Lady Grace was as close to perfection as Alex imagined he'd ever see in his lifetime. An unwanted vision passed through her mind—this revelation of a lady with her hair flowing free around her shoulders in some sheer, gauzy confection. The image turned his thoughts in a much different direction, and he forced himself to think of something else—anything else—lest he embarrass himself before Gil's guests.

He greeted them with a lighthearted joke to ease his way into the conversation. Then he settled in an armchair next to Rotheby as they smiled and nodded in his direction. His friend's coughing was certainly a concern, but focusing on anything at all soon proved virtually impossible.

Anything, that is, other than Lady Grace Abernathy.

The young woman had the English rose complexion currently in favor, but her dark hair gave it an entirely different effect than was *de rigueur*. She was hardly what most of the *beau monde* would fawn over at all. For that matter, she wasn't even cheerful. He had no idea why she ought to consume his thoughts in such a way. Alex had never heard her utter a word. Christ, she could be mute or dumb, for all he knew.

On top of it all, he had come to Somerton to get away from Mama's matchmaking schemes and determine how he was to spend his time to for the remainder of his life. Matters had not yet been settled for Priscilla and Harry. He had no business thinking of Lady Grace; he needed to determine his own course before he could worry about becoming responsible for anyone else.

But focus on her he did. Blast it, why was he thinking about how she'd look in something sheer? He didn't even *like* the girl, for God's sake.

As the small party talked, he occasionally caught a glimpse of Lady Grace looking slyly over her teacup to watch him. He'd be damned if she didn't remember him from the inn as well, though she gave no outward indication to anyone else. Why was she so curious about him that she would sneak covert peeks at him?

Lady Grace never interjected anything into the conversation other than a hum of assent or the like, yet Alex couldn't seem to remove his eyes from her, catching a knowing glimmer here and a bashful retreat there. For some unknown reason, he yearned to discover what was going on inside her head and why she felt compelled to keep it all to herself. It was almost like an illness.

He looked away from her for a moment, just in time to catch Lady Kensington eyeing the two of them equally with a mischievous glint in her eye.

Damnation, could he not escape meddling women even in Somerton? He might as well have brought his mother with him. Better the devil he knew very well, than one he knew not at all.

At precisely that moment, Lady Kensington chimed in. "Goodness me, Laurence, we have been boring these youngsters to tears. Have you noticed that neither of them has spoken a word other than to mumble something incoherent in a good long while? How awful we've been! A group of old friends rambling on and on about the crops and hunting and such, while these young people would obviously prefer to discuss more fashionable things, I am sure."

"Oh, no ma'am, I am delighted to discuss—"

"Aunt Dorothea, I assure you I am not bored by—"

But Lady Kensington interrupted them both.

"Lord Alexander, I believe our Gracie was admiring the earl's rose garden when we arrived. Would you be so kind as to escort her for a walk through them?"

The younger woman's eyes widened in protest, but her aunt pushed on.

"I do not believe Lord Rotheby would miss your company for a short bit, and the air would do you both good, I am certain."

Well. Alex supposed that settled that. There could be no harm in walking with Lady Grace through the gardens…could there? Perhaps she would prove more talkative than she had during tea, but if not he would still manage.

"Of course, ma'am. I would be honored." He held out his arm to assist the younger woman from her seat. "May I?"

Lady Grace placed a tentative hand on his arm and rose awkwardly from the sofa, using her free hand to straighten her gown, pat at her impeccably coiffed hair, and resituate the bonnet atop her head. She glanced to her uncle, seemingly looking for a reprieve from the horror of spending a few minutes alone with a strange gentleman, to Alex's view.

Was he really so dreadful? Maybe he hadn't scrubbed his teeth well enough this morning. He couldn't understand Lady Grace's hesitation. Still, after a moment, she walked beside him outside into the rose gardens of Roundstone Park.

This ought to prove interesting.

Six

GRACE COULDN'T BELIEVE her aunt had the audacity to thrust her into company with Lord Alexander completely alone. Not even a chaperone! What on earth was she supposed to say to this man?

Hello, Lord Alexander. Despite my aunt's machinations, you should endeavor to stay clear of me. I am damaged goods and unfit company for a gentleman. For the sake of your reputation, kindly avoid me. Such a line of conversation could only be awkward, and anything less would be a far cry short of the truth.

With her aunt, uncle, and Lord Rotheby for company, she had not been forced to take part in the conversation. But alone with a gentleman? She could hardly avoid having to converse.

Living with her father, Grace had long since learned it was usually best to keep her thoughts to herself. Father only occasionally struck her, but his words and actions left scars on her heart far more permanent than any bruise. Due to his edicts, she had had little interaction with those of Quality, living as a virtual hermit. Grace typically spent her days alone, working with her paints, reading, or mending her clothes. The less notice she attracted—and particularly that of her Father—the better.

And now, she'd be lucky, indeed if she managed not to trip over her words while attempting to speak to this man. A man far too handsome for her comfort.

He was dangerous.

If her uncertainty with regard to her aunt and uncle were not enough, now she was expected to be good company for a handsome, eligible gentleman to whom she felt an atrocious and exceedingly irksome attraction. Grace tried to school her features so he wouldn't see her panic.

Lord Alexander led her through French doors onto a veranda, which then led out to the main path through the gardens.

Blast, why could she not stay in the drawing room with her aunt and uncle? There, she would not be nearly so tempted to let her mind drift and think of all the what-ifs of her life. What if she had not been ruined? What if she were not with child? What if she had stayed in London and her father would allow her to marry a gentleman other than Barrow?

Still, it would not behoove Grace to allow her mind to wander to those places, but this jaunt through the gardens with Lord Alexander made it difficult not to play such games. He was entirely too…too…too *something*. She shook her head as if to clear it. His proximity was leaving her muddle-headed.

Gauche girl that she was, she took his arm and almost tripped from the shock of contact. Goodness, his skin was hot. The heat pulled her closer when she ought to have pulled away. It radiated across her entire side, mustering an onslaught of unwanted reactions in her body. She tried to remember to breathe, but her lungs and nostrils were quite non-compliant all of a sudden.

Much to her relief, he initiated their conversation. Drawing a full breath was difficult enough on its own at the moment, without the added discomfort of finding something agreeable to discuss. "We are experiencing excellent weather of late in Somerton, Lady Grace, wouldn't you agree?"

The heady scent of the roses in full spring bloom wafted over them as they strolled in the early evening sun.

"Yes, my lord, quite." Where could she turn the conversation next? They couldn't very well discuss the weather for more than a minute or so. Something else would have to be said, but Grace was at a loss for anything congenial.

What did polite company speak of? Her father had kept her far too sheltered to be prepared for such an encounter. Of course, he had never intended for her to have relations of any sort with eligible gentlemen, other than her betrothed. She was to go straight from where he kept her under lock and key to her new husband's home, where she would discuss only those subjects her husband wished to discuss. Or, perhaps, nothing at all, should he desire her silence.

She'd be lucky, indeed, if Lord Alexander wasn't soon expressing frustration over her lack of conversational skill, but he seemed more amused, if anything. A devilish gleam passed over his eyes. "Have you enjoyed yourself with Sir Laurence and Lady Kensington? They live at New Hill Cottage, if memory serves."

Well, at least he asked her another question. For the moment, she could simply answer him and not scrounge around in her feeble mind for something appropriate. But how much should she tell him? She'd do best to keep personal details to a minimum, in the event word ever traveled back to London. The last thing she needed was for Father to hear of her location. She'd defied him and run from him, and he'd likely come after her and force her to return with him, whether the Kensingtons condoned her behavior or not. However much she wished to be free of his grasp, she must never forget how much control he could still exert over her life, should he find her.

Grace also didn't want to allow anything to slip to him as to the true purpose of her visit.

She proceeded with caution. "Yes, my aunt and uncle live at New Hill. They have been quite amenable to all of my needs, my lord, thank you for asking. Our visit so far has been quite…pleasant." She looked up at him with what she dreaded to be an uncouth, foolish half-smile. Should she say anything else? And good gracious, how much more stuffy and stilted could her conversation be?

Her internal debate proved rather foolhardy, as Grace stumbled over her own feet. Before she could fall, Lord Alexander caught her and set her to rights. He steadied her in his arms and leaned her gently against his sturdy frame for a moment, until she could stand on her own.

His strong arms braced her, and she took in a long breath. Probably not the brightest move, since his scent poured over her—warmth and cleanliness, and the barest hint of the woods.

She rested in the cocoon of his arms for longer than she ought to have done, but he felt too good to leave. The length of their bodies melded together perfectly—so perfectly it seemed entirely natural to stay in this position. How could she be so comfortable, feel so safe, being held by this man she barely knew?

"Easy, Lady Grace. Are you all right? Perhaps we should rest for a moment."

His concern seemed genuine. Grace wanted to alleviate his worries. It wouldn't do to have him thinking of her any more than absolutely necessary, for any reason.

She separated herself from his grasp and straightened her gown. "Oh, how terribly clumsy of me. I am very sorry, my lord. I assure you, I am quite well. There is no need to rest."

She flushed again. Blast, her cheeks must surely match the color of her gown by now. The heat was rising to her head, and it only intensified when she remembered how long she had allowed herself to stay in his arms. She was behaving in a most dreadfully improper manner.

Lord Alexander raised an eyebrow dubiously, so Grace started walking to prove her point. "The earl's roses are rather lovely, are they not?"

He walked alongside her—this time grasping her arm, where before she had held onto his. Good Lord, even his *hand* was strong. She shivered slightly and looked away from him.

"There are so many colors, and the roses are all abloom. I would love to paint them sometime." Drat. Why had she mentioned painting? She had wanted to avoid telling him much about herself, and to simply fill in the conversation where appropriate. Apparently, she was destined to fail miserably at her seemingly simple goal.

"You paint, ma'am? I've never had talent for it myself, but my youngest sister, Charlotte, is quite the artist." He stopped to pluck a single pink dog rose from its stem. It was almost the exact shade of her gown. He tucked the flower into her hair, just above her ear. "There, that looks just about perfect now."

His gentle touch left her flustered. Every nerve ending in her body was thrumming and felt alive. Grace began to walk again, at a swifter pace this time, lest he discover just how easily he had discomposed her.

What to talk about? She needed to find something. Perhaps she ought to ask him about his family, since he'd mentioned a sister. Or maybe she should ask him about the talents he did possess, if not painting. There were any number of directions she could turn the conversation, but all she could think about was getting away from him—as fast as possible.

However, he stayed close behind her. He took hold of her wrist and pulled her to a stop. His proximity clouded her judgment—that warm, woodsy, masculine strength he exuded made it impossible for her to form a coherent thought, and she feared she might do something wrong.

"I apologize," he said. "It was highly improper of me to take such liberties. Please forgive me." His eyes were filled with sincerity.

Of course there was nothing to forgive. All he had done was help her to regain her feet and place a flower in her hair, nothing more. She had overreacted. "Please, don't apologize, Lord Alexander. You've done nothing wrong. I—I am the one who ought to apologize. I don't know what is wrong with me." He could never understand her reactions, even if he knew the whole of the truth. And letting him know *that* was an utter impossibility.

After all the recent events of her life, Grace couldn't possibly deserve such attentions from a gentleman. But how could she tell him such a thing? He couldn't know the turmoil going on inside her, and she couldn't very well let any of it out in front of him.

After a few moments, a wry grin emerged on his lips. "Lady Grace, you recognize me from the Brookhurst Inn yesterday, don't you?"

He did recognize her. She nodded and smiled, but ducked her head.

"When I saw you on the coach, I felt time stood still. Your eyes—they are quite haunting."

She turned her gaze to the orangery nearby, scanning desperately for something to look at—anything but him—but remained where she stood. Allowing him to see her fear wouldn't do, but she refused to run. Her escape from Father had been more than enough running in her life. She would not grant this man so much power over her.

Grace was no coward.

Her reaction to this gentleman was confounding—he'd done nothing to cause her fear, so why was she so afraid of him? Was it because he'd admitted to an attraction to her, even if he did it in a circuitous manner? It would be altogether better for them both if they had a strong distaste for each other, but the opposite seemed to be occurring.

Still, whatever the reason for her fear, it stood there before her like a great, hulking oak—solid and immovable. Somehow, she needed to force it aside. What else could she do?

ALEX HAD NO idea why Lady Grace had turned from him just then, but he pressed on. "They are so beautiful, so clear, your eyes—but they seem so sad. I dreamed of your eyes last night."

Devil take it. What on God's good earth had possessed him to tell her he'd dreamed about her? But now his cards were all laid out before her. He couldn't take the sentiment back, even if he wanted to—which, surprisingly, he didn't. He might as well keep going. He placed a hand on her shoulder, gentle but firm, and allowed it to rest there for a few moments. Her breath quickened, and she looked timidly over her shoulder at him.

She seemed so lost and fragile, yet somehow still in rigid control of herself. He needed to break a small piece of her control, just for a moment. He wanted to help her—but how? So he did the only thing in his head.

He couldn't stop himself. Alex had no right to touch her, and as a gentleman, he absolutely should do nothing to compromise her. But how could he resist a kiss? He turned her so she was only a whisper away, then he stared down into the frosty depths of her eyes. Her fear had returned. He almost decided to stop.

Almost.

But he had to know. He needed just a taste, just a touch, and then he could walk away. His fingertips brushed against her cheeks and nose. She shivered but didn't pull away. When Alex traced along the lines of her mouth with the pad of his thumb, her eyes locked with his.

He waited until he could wait no longer for the fear to leave her eyes, and finally received his reward. They softened before him and turned azure with curiosity.

Softly, gently, he pressed his lips to hers and tried to coax her to open. She didn't yield, at first—but she didn't run screaming from him, either.

Her restraint made him burn for more. He wanted her to feel the same desire he felt. Alex pulled her against him and deepened the kiss, his tongue pressing between her lips while his arms kept the heat of her body pressed against him.

She softened finally and took a tiny, tentative step toward him.

Thank God. He moved his hands to the back of her head, tilting her for deeper access to the warmth of her mouth. She let out a low moan against his lips. Her tongue stroked ever-so-shyly against his as he stabbed, twisted, and tangled. His intention had never been to take the kiss so far, he was damned if he could determine how to stop how. Her soft sounds and eager, unskilled efforts were enough to drive him to the brink of madness.

Alex was ready to dive over that cliff. Damn, he had to stop this—he had to move away from her. With sincere regret and a significant amount more control than he thought himself capable of, Alex broke off the kiss and stepped back. Lady Grace's rumpled hair and pink, swollen lips seemed to beg him for more. He placed a few paces between them so he would not be tempted to grab her and finish what he had started.

Her eyes were like blue fire ringed with smoke. Alex had never wanted anything more. He couldn't quite muster the mortification he knew he ought to feel, though. It had felt so very right, even though he ought never to have allowed it to happen.

By degrees, the fire fled from her eyes and they filled again with the sorrow and fear that seemed ever present.

He'd caused the fear, this time. This time, he was the bastard. He'd meant to keep the kiss soft and sweet, but instead he'd pawed at her. His passions got the better of him.

His behavior was beyond reproach—what a lecherous cad he was, and certainly no gentleman. After several moments of silence, she turned and walked away from him.

"Lady Grace." He started after her, and with his long legs soon caught up to her. Again, he placed a hand on her shoulder to stop her progress.

She froze in place, neither looking at him nor saying a word.

"It seems I must apologize again. I should never have allowed myself to take such liberties. Please, may we pretend it never happened?" He waited for what seemed an eternity before she responded in any way.

Finally, she nodded. Her silence condemned him for the lecher he was.

Alex exhaled audibly and closed his eyes for a moment. "Shall we continue our walk through the gardens? Lord Rotheby's arbors are relaxing this time of year."

Good God, she had to say something—anything. Her silence was slowly but surely destroying him.

Lady Grace hesitated. "Yes, the arbors would be fine." She still didn't face him, but at least she walked alongside him, even if she watched her feet as she moved. Her struggle to maintain that thin veneer of control was betrayed by the firm set of her jaw and the slight tremble of her lower lip.

He needed to lighten the mood. He couldn't stand to see her anguish, especially since he was the cause of her current distress. "I mentioned my sister, Charlotte, earlier, didn't I?"

Lady Grace gave a slight nod of her head, but remained mute as a church mouse.

"I don't believe I mentioned I am only one of six. Our father passed away a few years ago. Mama's made it her personal mission to see each of us happily married off. The sooner the better, I'm afraid. She is not overly concerned with the advantageousness of the matches. Mama's ideas…well, they are quite unconventional, at least as far as the beau monde is concerned." Alex chortled. Mama could accomplish anything she set her mind to, which was somewhat frightening. "That is part of my reason for being in Somerton this summer. I'm not prepared to face Mama's incessant interference. She can be quite the bear."

For the first time in their brief acquaintance, Lady Grace laughed out loud in his presence.

"Oh, she is not truly a bear," Alex rushed on. "She is just determined. Possibly to the point of obstinacy, but she means well. Please don't think poorly of her because her son is terrified of her."

Lady Grace laughed louder this time, more gaily. For the first time since they met, she seemed carefree. She visibly relaxed her jaw and looked at him with eyes full of mischief. "My lord, I'm certain I couldn't think poorly of a woman who had borne six children. Simply putting up with all of you was likely enough to create more than just a touch of stubbornness. Why, I'd imagine most women in her circumstances would be on the verge of madness from you alone."

"Touché, my lady, touché."

Finally, she'd said more than a single sentence of response. Thank goodness. Maybe she would not be such poor company after all.

Lady Grace stopped and looked out at a section of the gardens filled with poppy, pimpernel, and clover, all dancing in the soft breeze. "You don't truly fear your mother, do you? I have a difficult time imagining a mother who should be feared. There are plenty of other things in this world to be afraid of." She bent to smell a bright red poppy.

Every bone in his body itched to learn what she feared, but he wanted to keep her talking. She might very well turn reticent again if he were so impertinent as to ask. That could wait for another day. "Fear Mama? No, of course not. She's a wonderful lady and loves her children as no one has ever loved before. All six of us."

Her smile was as bright as the sun when she stood to rejoin him, brightening her face and softening her eyes. He wished he would never see her in any other manner again, than at that moment—smiling in the evening, summer sun with a flower tucked behind her ear, without a care to weigh her down.

"Tell me about your siblings," she said. Then she blushed again. He'd never seen anything more lovely. "That is, will you? Please."

So very charming, this Lady Grace, even with her social ineptitude. He wanted to kiss the chagrin out of her expression.

"My siblings? Peter's the eldest. After our father passed away several years ago, he became the Duke of Somerton. None of us could be better suited for the task. He takes his responsibilities quite seriously, so some people think him a little overbearing. But underneath, he's just Peter. He's a widower now, with two little ones running amok, helping to make him crazy."

She placed her hand gently on his arm again, and he led her through the garden again. "There is a wilderness walk up ahead," he said. "Would you like to explore that? It's rather beautiful all year long."

Lady Grace inclined her head, so he headed in that direction.

"Where was I? Oh yes—Richard. He's the one all the unmarried young misses of the ton fawn over at the balls. A handsome devil, if ever there was one. Tall and broad, and perfect, all the ladies tell me." Alex chuckled. "He's been in the military for several years now. A major. Mama wishes he would sell his commission and come home, but the military life seems to suit him. He is different now. Changed. Serious. Well, he always was serious, so I can't blame the change entirely on the wars."

"It must be quite difficult on you all to have him so far away. It sounds as though you're very close to your family."

"Yes, we're a close lot. Almost a clan, if you will. We even share the same hair color."

She laughed again, a lilting sound.

He could become accustomed to hearing it with no complaints. "Sophie is the eldest of the girls—she comes just after me. She's always wanted to do things her own way, not the expected way. I suppose she manages due to her position in society. But she's already bucked tradition a bit too much for Mama's tastes, by remaining a singleton far after she ought to have selected a husband and started filling a nursery."

"And she is allowed to do so?" Lady Grace's eyes held curiosity more than shock.

Alex nodded. "Peter won't force her to marry. He won't insist on any of us marrying if it isn't what we want—not after...well, never mind that. Besides, she reached her majority long ago. Sophie can do as she pleases, no matter how stricken in years she might become."

"Oh…"

When he looked down upon her, her lips formed an O shape. His family must be very different from hers, to have such an effect upon her.

"Neil came next, much to Mama's chagrin. He is rather enjoying himself, I imagine, doing all the illicit things a young man about Town will do. None of which are appropriate for tender ears, so I shall leave it at that for him."

"Is he a…a rogue?" Her free hand rushed to her lips, those delicious, delectable lips, almost to take the word and replace it where it had come from.

Alex chuckled. "I doubt he has fallen *too* far into depravity, ma'am. Peter will rein him in, if he needs to. But for now, he is being allowed to sow his wild oats."

"I see. So your mother—she does not take a hand in such discipline?"

Her curiosity about his family seemed odd. The Hardwickes were not all *that* unusual, as far as aristocratic families went. The girls may have slightly irregular views on the world, but overall, they were rather…normal. Almost boring, even, at least in the eyes of the *ton*. What must Lady Grace's family be like, for her to seem so thunderstruck by them?

How very intriguing.

He shook his head. "Once Father died, Peter became the head of the family. Mama sees to certain aspects, of course, but Peter ultimately makes any family decisions."

"Oh. Of course."

Of course? How he wished to understand the workings of her mind. "And the last member of the Hardwicke clan is young Charlotte. She's still in the schoolroom, not yet out in society, but I daresay she will turn heads when she makes her debut. Char is…well, she's hard to pin down to any one thing. She is exuberant and gay and will utterly charm your stockings off, but at the same time, she is very…I don't know how to put it other than to say she's special and not disinclined to scandal. As I've already mentioned, she's an artist, like you. She paints in watercolors."

"Oh, I daresay I might like her."

He cocked a brow in her direction. "You might? Are you inclined to scandal?" Her cheeks turned a delicious shade of pink again.

"Well, no. I'm not. I mean, I don't wish to be." Her eyebrows scrunched together.

What a very odd sentiment. She does not *wish* to be inclined to scandal. Lady Grace grew more intriguing by the moment.

"I mean that Lady Charlotte sounds very interesting to me because she has something she is passionate about."

He could almost see the thoughts racing in her eyes.

"I should think I would quite like her." Lady Grace nodded after a moment, a very forceful, made-up-her-mind sort of nod.

"I think you would as well," Alex murmured. "Perhaps someday you will meet her and become friends."

They walked in silence for a stretch along the wilderness walk, amongst the trees and a pond, and an abundance of flowers. It was not uncomfortable, rather companionable. But the end of the walk drew close.

"I am afraid we'll be forced to turn back now, Lady Grace."

She slowed and glanced ahead of them. "My lord, what is that, up by the hill?" She stretched onto her tiptoes and pointed off to the horizon.

"Oh, that's my brother's estate, Somerton Court. You can almost see the main house from here, though it is still a good way off."

Her eyes squinted in concentration. "The duke? Peter?"

"Yes, Peter. His property borders Lord Rotheby's property. We all spent a good deal of time tromping through his fields as children, and otherwise getting into things we ought not to have done."

They looked for a few more minutes, and then she sighed. Turning to head back with him, she took a single wistful glance over her shoulder.

"Well, we spent the entire walk out discussing my family. Will you tell me about yours?" Apprehension flickered through her eyes. He rushed on. "Do you have any siblings?"

Her hand tensed on his elbow and the carefree look was instantly gone. "No, I have no siblings."

He waited, but she said no more. "What about your mother? It doesn't sound as though you are afraid of her?" Alex winked so she'd know he was teasing her. He hoped to keep her talking. Her gentleness beckoned to him and drew him closer—which he rather enjoyed, almost despite himself.

Lady Grace's smile fell completely away from her face and her eyes returned to their cold stare. "My mother passed away many years ago." Then she fell mute again. They walked in silence for several more minutes.

The quiet would kill him if it went on much longer. "I am very sorry, my lady. I did not realize. It seems I'll spend the whole of the evening apologizing to you at this rate. Forgive me." He searched for another topic, something to return the lightness to her visage.

Before he could speak, Lady Grace blurted out, "I believe I should return to my aunt and uncle. They will miss me. You must excuse me, my lord." She abruptly removed her hand from his arm and set out toward the main house at a brisk pace.

Alex cursed beneath his breath and jogged behind her. "Lady Grace, please at least allow me to return you to your relatives. I don't wish for them to believe I have been such a cad as to have abandoned you here on the wilderness walk." Never mind the fact he had done far worse.

He placed a firm hand on her elbow, which slowed her pace to a more decorous walk. She continued on her way, never once deigning to look at him again. He admired her quiet reserve, almost despite himself. Alex deposited her with Sir Laurence, Lady Kensington, and Gil before taking his leave.

He needed to ride and cool off. He bloody well needed to stop thinking about this woman, a woman whom he had told virtually everything about his life, but who could not be bothered to tell him one whit about her own. A woman who set his blood to boiling in more ways than one. A woman who confounded him at every turn.

A woman he might never stop thinking about.

Seven

GRACE HAD BEEN with the Kensingtons for the better part of a fortnight and was much happier now than we she arrived, even though she still hadn't told them the reason for her rather abrupt arrival. She had started to confide in them more about her life, often while working on needlework with Aunt Dorothea or digging in the gardens with Uncle Laurence.

Mr. Finchley, the gardener, had gone into fits the first time he caught the two digging together, but Uncle Laurence had calmly explained to him that he would have to accept their interference in his job. Since then, Mr. Finchley watched from a distance with a frown, but kept his opinions to himself.

Grace still listened more than she talked, and thought more than she listened, but her laughter had somehow become a frequent occurrence at New Hill Cottage. More and more often, she even caught herself smiling—something she had done only infrequently for years.

Sometimes at night, she still woke with nightmares. They served as a reminder her of her reason for being there. Not that she could forget if she tried.

Nearly two months had passed since Grace last saw her courses, and now she was experiencing several of the other joys of being with child—if one could call them that. Occasionally she would lose her breakfast, and the smell of fish turned her stomach in an instant. Afternoon walks with Uncle Laurence quickly tired her. She frequently retired to her bedchamber for a nap, sometimes even missing afternoon tea due to her growing fatigue.

Only two days previously, she had fallen asleep while working on some needlework with Aunt Dorothea. She didn't wake until she pricked herself with a needle.

Fortunately, there were still no visible signs of her condition. Here, Grace was able to live a somewhat normal life with the Kensingtons. She rejoiced in their kindness, but she must tell them of her condition, and soon. They had to be growing suspicious of something being out of the ordinary, simply due to how easily she tired.

Sir Laurence and Lady Kensington had accepted Grace as though she were their own daughter. They had never had their own children, and seemed thrilled to pretend—at least for the time being—that she belonged with them.

Grace was all too happy to go ahead and pretend alongside them. Of course, she could only stay with them for a time, so tried to brace herself against the heartache of impending separation by not growing too close. It would only hurt worse when she was forced to leave.

She had so much more freedom in Somerton than she had ever experienced with her father. While she was with the Kensingtons, she could forget for a time that she would be forced into a marriage with whichever gentleman her father could convince to marry her— assuming he ever located her. She let herself imagine she could stay with the Kensingtons forever, that they could be a happy family without the threat of her father's retribution.

She still shivered at the thought of a life with Lord Barrow. It was best to hope she would never have to return to London.

Her daydreams were filled with images of raising her child with her aunt and uncle at her side, allowing the tot to run wild through the gardens at New Hill. Some days, she dreamed of a man alongside her—a tall man with auburn hair, laughing and playing with her child.

But dreams were not reality. They could never be.

Even so, today would be favorable. Grace was going to paint the English countryside on the banks of the Cary River. She would put the tempest of her feelings onto canvas in swirls and streaks of color and texture in a way only she could do. Grace would never be considered the finest artist in England, but she did have a knack with her brushes.

She had a spring in her step when she joined her aunt and uncle for breakfast. The sky was overcast, but the wind was calm. It should be a perfect day for their picnic by the river.

She and Uncle Laurence planned to take their paints, canvases, and easels. Aunt Dorothea, in the process of embroidering a pillow to put in the morning parlor, planned to work on a spot of needlework. She said she could think of no better place to work on it than in the out of doors, as long as the weather cooperated.

"Good morning, Gracie," Uncle Laurence said. "You seem chipper today." He looked up from his papers when she joined them at the breakfast table.

Grace grinned across at him. "Good morning, Uncle. Is anything interesting in your papers today?"

It took several days for the papers to reach them in Somerton, so by now the news he was reading was close to a week old. The lack of timeliness never stopped him from poring through them each morning.

He flicked the paper and looked over it at her. "Why, I would say so. It seems the Duke of Walsingham is engaged to a Miss Barbara Flynn. Young Miss Flynn was not pleased at the prospect of becoming his duchess, it would appear, as she took a dive from a second floor balcony at the engagement party given by her father. She suffered an injury to her arm in the fall, but her father assures all she will be quite fit to say her vows in a fortnight's time."

Grace's heart plummeted to the floor. The poor girl! "My pity goes out to Miss Flynn, then. I am thankful I didn't have to make such a choice." Of course, she had been forced to make other choices. She turned back to her breakfast and tried not to think about how much the path of her life had changed of late.

Uncle Laurence leaned across the table and whispered to her, "I suppose there are some small favors granted to us in life." He patted her on the top of her hand and resumed reading his papers.

She hated herself for not revealing her ruin to them before now. The Kensingtons had been more than kind to her, with not a single question asked about anything. They had simply accepted her. Grace took another bite and steeled herself to divulge her secret.

No time like the present.

"Uncle, Aunt. There is…there's something I must tell you. Well, several somethings, actually."

Uncle Laurence set his newspaper down on the table and gave her his undivided attention while Aunt Dorothea reached across the table to grasp her hand. "Go on, dear," her aunt said. "You can tell us anything, you know."

Grace took a breath and rushed out with it before she could think better of it. "I have run away from Father." Their disgust and anger were sure to come at any moment. She squeezed her eyes closed so she wouldn't have to see their reaction.

"Yes," said Uncle Laurence. "Your aunt and I had surmised as much, Gracie. Why, your father cut off all contact with us years ago. He certainly couldn't know you were here with us now. I don't imagine he would have allowed you to visit it. What we have not discovered for ourselves is why you felt the need to do something so rash."

They would hear her out? Shock set in that they weren't turning her from their door immediately. She had difficulty finding her words. "I…he—the earl, that is" Goodness, where should she start?

"It is all right, sweetheart," her aunt said. "Take your time. Your uncle always tells me it is best to begin at the beginning. I do often have difficulty finding where the beginning might be, myself, but I am certain he's right."

"The beginning?" Grace took a sip from her cup of morning chocolate to stall for a bit more time. Where had it all started? "Well, you see—I've been ravished."

"Gracious heavens. Laurence, you must find the scoundrel and challenge him at once. Who did this to you, Gracie? We shall not stand for it, by gad. He will come to justice!" Aunt Dorothea rose from her seat and paced through the room. "I tell you, Laurence, I knew something horrible had happened to our Gracie, and that man—her *father*—he's done nothing about it, has he? Of course he hasn't. The vile, despicable—" Tears sprung to her aunt's eyes.

"Dorothea, let the girl continue her story." Uncle Laurence looked to Grace with understanding eyes. "She has not yet finished. Have you Gracie?"

She stared down at her hands folded on her lap. "No, Uncle. I—well…"

"Who was he, Gracie? Tell us the blackguard's name and your uncle will challenge the deuced coward like your father should have done."

A look from Uncle Laurence silenced her aunt again. "Dueling, my dear, is illegal, as you well know. His name is not important at this precise moment. Go on, sweetheart. Your aunt will not interrupt you again."

If only she would. Those interruptions allowed her to put off the telling, even if only for a moment or two. "I'm…with child." A single tear fell down her cheek, followed by a virtual flood. Her aunt was at her side in an instant, pulling her close.

"And is that why you left, Grace?" Uncle Laurence moved closer to where she sat.

She nodded, unable to form words as she succumbed to a bout of hiccups. Once they slowed, she tried to continue. "Father…he—w—when I told him, hic—he was so angry. He wants me to marry the man—"

"Oh no, you most certainly will not marry that man! I will never hear of it. The nerve of your father!"

Uncle Laurence placed a calming hand on his wife's shoulder to quiet her. "Go on, Grace."

"And if…if he will not have me, then I am to—to—to give the child away to a family in need of more hands and marry whoever else he can arrange for."

Aunt Dorothea burst from her position to pace through the breakfast room. "What? I am appalled. Appalled!"

"So I came here to you," Grace continued. She had to get through it all or she'd never finish. "I didn't know where else to go. I'll leave if you want me to. You have been more than kind to allow me to stay as long as you have. I don't want to be a burden on you—"

"A burden? A burden! Laurence, the child thinks she is a burden on us. Goodness, Gracie, if you try to leave, I'll be furious with you. Why, wherever would you go? You cannot do this alone, dear. I'll not hear of it."

Uncle Laurence nodded. "Your aunt is right. You must stay with us. Why, how would a woman in your situation get by? No, your leaving is out of the question."

"But what if Father finds out where I am?" He would be irate if he knew they had willfully defied him. Murderous, even.

"Let me worry about that. I can handle your father." Uncle Laurence's eyes held a grim expression quite unlike his usual calm demeanor.

"And the baby?" How would they explain her situation to their neighbors? Oh, no, she couldn't stay through her confinement. It would bring her shame upon them.

"The baby? Why, Gracie, your baby must stay where you stay. I'll quite enjoy having a little one about, I daresay." Aunt Dorothea puttered around the room, picking up objects from one position and moving them to another, in a random fashion. "Laurence, the next time we travel to Bath, I must purchase some yarn. I'll need to begin knitting for the little one. Lud, do you think your child will have your eyes? I do hope so. Such pretty eyes. So unlike my boring, brown eyes. I always envied your mother those eyes, have I told you that?

Why, I declare, they are the most fascinating shade. I could never tire of looking at them—and if I can stare at them in the face of a babe, oh, I'll simply be in heaven…"

Her chatter droned on, but Grace could no longer concentrate on it. Her thoughts lay in only one direction. She could stay. And she could keep her child.

Everything would be all right. She finished her breakfast and prepared for the day ahead—a day of painting at the river with her aunt and uncle.

GIL'S COUGHING FIT wracked his body as he and Alex rode. They were headed through the countryside to inspect the land by the creek and the Cary River. Rotheby's land only covered the area surrounding the creek, but he kept emphasizing to Alex the importance of making certain things ran in a smooth manner all along the river.

His continued illness left Alex more than unsettled. It had gone on through the entire course of his visit, without even the slightest hint of improvement. Gil had coughing spells, tired easily, always complained of the cold, and had a sickly pallor to his skin. There was an easy answer as to why the illness lingered, but Alex didn't want to accept it.

Gil was dying.

Now the reason for his invitation was clear. The earl must want a friend with him during this time. He'd never said as much, but why else would he have summoned Alex to his side? And why Alex, when it would make more sense to send for his grandson. Quinton was Gil's heir, after all. Though, admittedly, their relationship had been rather shaky. Maybe Quinton wasn't the best to have around at such a time, after all.

Alex admired the earl. He would even go so far as to say he loved the man. Because of that love, he intended to do all he could to make certain Rotheby was content during their time together, however long it may be.

So, when Gil wanted to go for a ride, they rode. If Gil wanted to visit a friend or a tenant, they visited. When Gil wanted to tell stories of Alex's childhood, or even of his own childhood, Alex listened with his utmost attention. Hence the reason for their current ride, even if Alex couldn't understand why the earl was teaching Alex all of these things and not his heir.

Once Gil's coughs subsided, Alex turned in his saddle to face him. "Are you doing all right, Gil? We can head back to Roundstone any time you're ready."

He didn't want to seem overly protective—but it was a tricky business, in a time like this. He'd witnessed his father's sudden death from apoplexy a few years back. Alex didn't want his time with Gil to be shortened any more than necessary.

The earl glared at him from beneath the brim of his hat. "I most certainly am not ready yet, whippersnapper. Mind yourself."

As usual, the older man was all bark with no bite. Alex laughed.

They rode down the bank of the river in silence for a distance, enjoying the warmth of the air despite the lack of sunshine. A group of picnickers were up ahead of them on the embankment. As they drew closer to the party, Alex could make them out finally: Sir Laurence, with his wife and Lady Grace.

Alex hadn't seen any of them since the day at Roundstone when he had kissed Lady Grace in the gardens and made a complete arse of himself. Not only had he not seen them, but he was glad for that fact.

Well, at least glad he hadn't seen Lady Grace. In less than an hour's time that day, he'd been forced to apologize to the woman three full times. He had no desire to reprise such a performance.

Although Alex hadn't seen her in person in close to a fortnight, he continued to see her in his dreams. But where initially her eyes haunted him with their bleak emptiness, they now woke him with their fire. There had been heat in her blue ice when he kissed her. She couldn't deny it, and he wouldn't dream of it. He couldn't blot the memory from his mind—but he couldn't act on it, either. He should be trying to guard her virtue, not destroy it.

Nonetheless, he had told himself all along he had no intention of becoming entangled with a female. Any more contact with Lady Grace beyond simple, polite conversation would most certainly qualify as an entanglement. There were already more than enough entanglements waiting for his return in London.

It would be best for them both if they avoided each other in the future. Judging by all indications from her, Lady Grace would be more than amicable with that solution. Why, she hardly said a word to him on their previous encounter. He had gone on and on about his brothers and sisters—his whole life—and she barely strung together more than five words at a time.

She could have no objection to him staying clear of her company.

Today though, it appeared he must make an exception to this new rule of avoidance. He and Gil had come within calling distance, and Sir Laurence lifted a hand in greeting.

"Gil! And Lord Alexander, as well. What a pleasant surprise. We were just sitting down to luncheon." With a smile, he glanced through the basket Lady Kensington and Lady Grace were busy unpacking. "As usual, Mrs. Finchley has packed far more food than an army could down after going hungry for a week. Would you care to join us?"

Sir Laurence walked to the two horses and held out a hand to aid Gil in dismounting, not waiting for a response. Apparently, a 'yes' was assumed. He led the earl to the blanket spread beneath an oak tree and assisted him in gaining a seat while Alex saw to the horses. He tried not to curse out loud about his rotten luck.

He put on a cheerful face before joining the others beneath the heavy cover of branches, hoping to hide his brooding. "Ladies, Sir Laurence." Alex nodded to each in turn. "It's kind of you to share your meal with us. We've been riding for a good spell now and I, for one, am famished."

He sat next to Gil—and as far away from Lady Grace as he could manage without seeming altogether a cad, yet again.

The group ate and talked and laughed. Everyone took part in the conversation this time, including Lady Grace. She seemed much more vibrant than she had on their first meeting (other than those few rare moments when she had let down her guard) and not nearly as shy.

She looked stunning, sitting on the quilted blanket beneath a cloudy sky. Her smile reached all the way up to her eyes—to the point they sparkled like diamonds.

But she did her best to ignore his presence.

She spoke with Lord Rotheby, telling him of the painting she and her uncle planned to perform after their meal. She enquired after his health. She even asked his permission to someday visit and paint in his flower gardens, if he was so inclined to allow her intrusion. She talked and teased with her aunt and uncle. But she never spared Alex a glance, nor included him in her conversation.

Still, he could not keep his eyes from her. Even before, with the sadness blanketed over her features, Lady Grace was an absolute vision. With it removed, she honestly stole his breath.

He tried to focus on the conversation, but had little success. Alex even attempted to become cross or upset about her obvious exclusion of him from her part of the conversation, but couldn't muster the emotions. He refused to feign them. He'd keep his dignity, even if it killed him.

All he could think about was her heat when he pulled her close, the light scent of something floral and sweet on her skin, and the passion in her eyes just after he kissed her.

"Lord Alexander?" Lady Kensington frowned over at him for a moment. "Lord Alexander?"

He snapped to the present with a jolt. "I am so sorry, ma'am. I was woolgathering. You were saying?" Blast, if he hadn't been living in his own world for a great good while.

She patted his arm and gave him an indulgent smile. "I understand, sir. Our Gracie is certainly something to look at, is she not?"

Sir Laurence cleared his throat in an obvious warning to his wife. She sent a glare in his direction as she continued her new conversation with Alex.

"I was merely wondering if you had finished or if you wanted another sandwich. We certainly have more than enough, but you've hardly touched yours and everyone else has finished. Aren't they to your liking? Anyway, feel free to help yourself to more if you wish."

She cleared their luncheon away as she continued to speak, leaving a plate of cucumber sandwiches out where he could reach them. "I believe Laurence and Gracie are set to work with their paints for a bit now, and it seems your Lord Rotheby is prepared to take a bit of a nap. I think it is best if he just stays here to do so, rather than attempt to ride all the way back to Roundstone. How lucky we are, I planned ahead and brought a few extra blankets and such with me. I've been working on my quilting and embroidery, you know, and one can just never tell how much one will finish in a day!"

As Lady Kensington rambled, her niece stood and assembled easels and painting supplies for herself and her uncle, placing oils by her own canvas and watercolors by Sir Laurence's.

The baronet helped Gil settle in a secluded spot under a nearby willow tree. Lady Kensington was right about Gil being too tired to make the return before succumbing to sleep. He stumbled as he walked with Sir Laurence. Alex supposed that meant he would have to spend even more time in the presence of the minx while she ignored him.

Deuced infuriating, that.

He ate and Lady Kensington droned on and on, about subjects he had neither the desire nor the intention of following. Alex nodded and occasionally raised an eyebrow, which seemed enough to keep the lady generally appeased. He didn't think she really cared if he paid attention—it seemed to be more an issue of her own comfort. He doubted she was capable of sitting in silence for longer than a few seconds without sleeping, and he wondered if she was even capable of it at that point. She may be one who talked in her sleep.

While they sat, Lady Kensington worked on her embroidery and kept up a constant stream of chatter. He gazed at the river passing them by, but his thoughts kept returning to the two people who had been so consistently on his mind since his arrival in Somerton—Gil and Lady Grace.

After a while, he realized the garrulous buzzing of Lady Kensington's incessant speech had—miraculously—ceased. A quick glance in her direction revealed that she, too, was asleep. Now he couldn't even pretend to carry on a conversation with her, but must find some other way of passing the time until Gil had rested enough to carry on with their jaunt. So, he watched the two painters at their craft.

Sir Laurence was clearly a studied landscape artist. His piece looked almost identical to the scene before them, down to the smallest details like the rocks on the opposite side of the river bank. From an artistic standpoint, his work was perfect, while not necessarily inspiring. The painting was beautiful, but it lacked a certain finesse to take the piece from very good to great.

Lady Grace, however, was a true artist in Alex's mind. Her painting was night-and-day different from that of her uncle. She brushed her oils in broad, sweeping strokes and bold flashes of color. While it was clear she had painted the same scene as her uncle, her piece something contained more. There was a mood in the painting. It conveyed emotion. The sky was not merely overcast, but dark and ominous, as it threatened to chase the bold colors from the scene.

He was, in a word, flabbergasted by what he saw coming to life on her canvas.

Her brushes swooshed and swayed across the surface, with every flick of her wrist creating some new facet to convert the overall impression. As she worked, Lady Grace's eyes gleamed. A series of emotions ran across her face and bled through the brushes into her painting. Alex was in awe.

After what could have been minutes or hours, she stopped. She took two steps back and looked deeply at her piece for a moment, then turned around to face him. Lady Grace beamed at him and allowed him to share in her moment of glory.

The expression on her face at that moment, he never could have predicted—she looked regal, imminently satisfied, and fully at peace. All of the emotions that had been working through her were somehow transferred to the canvas and left behind, at least for that moment.

If he had not seen it himself, Alex would never have believed such an intense work could have come from inside this tiny, perpetually fearful woman. Well, if not for the fact she still took deep breaths from her exertions, had splatters of paint covering her from head to foot, and had her hair flowing freely after having escaped from her pins.

She was breathtaking. Perfection.

"Good heavens, Gracie, you are a sight!" Lady Kensington said, coming up behind Alex. Her shout of dismay woke Gil as well, and he started to put himself to rights while Lady Kensington fussed over her niece.

Rotheby walked over to Alex and silently observed the scene while Sir Laurence continued as he was, ignoring the tumult his wife created with her dither. The baronet must experience such things on a regular basis to display no outward reaction to her.

Alex allowed himself a brief chuckle. Their marriage must have been quite interesting, all these years. Sir Laurence obviously knew how to handle his wife flawlessly.

"Shall we gather our horses and head back to Roundstone, old chap?" Gil asked. "I think I am ready to call this one a day." He looked slightly refreshed after his nap, but Alex was not convinced he was recovered—certainly not fully.

"I am ready any time you are. I'll ready the horses while you give Lady Kensington our thanks."

Alex didn't want to think he was avoiding Lady Grace by readying their mounts—nor by taking his time about it. So far, he had made it through this encounter with her without being forced into offering his apologies for a single action. He'd like to keep it that way, if possible.

Once he had untied the horses, he led them to the group and waited for a lull in the conversation. "We are much obliged to you for sharing your luncheon with us, Lady Kensington."

She smiled graciously toward him before her expression turned a touch more devious. Oh, blast. What was she planning now? The woman had far too mischievous a gleam in her eye for his comfort— it made him think of the same look coming from Mama.

"Lord Alexander, join us for a meal any time you're in need of one, or even when you're not in need of one. Please, bring Lord Rotheby to visit at New Hill Cottage sometime."

Lady Grace chortled under her breath, but Alex caught it out of the corner of his eye.

"You both have a standing invitation," Lady Kensington. "Just drop in when you're in the area." The older woman could not have wiped the glee from her eyes if she tried. Just what he needed. Because, of course, the *area* was Somerton in general.

He didn't care to take her up on the offer at any time in the near future. But Gil would enjoy such a visit, and Alex wanted to make his friend happy. "I am sure we'll hold you to your offer sometime soon, won't we?"

The earl nodded vigorously.

Alex nodded to the group. "Well, we must be on our way. Sir Laurence, Lady Kensington." He took a long look at the woman who so fascinated him before he continued. "Lady Grace. It has been a pleasure, as always. I think Lord Rotheby has had enough for one day, haven't you, old man?"

"Bah! Whippersnappers. You think you know everything." Gil frowned, but it didn't reach his eyes. They walked away and gained their mounts. "Besides, I have already had a nap today. You, however, haven't. I'd wager I'm more up for a ride than you at this point."

It was good to see some of the old fire in his friend. "Are you up for a race, then? Now that our horses have had a graze and rest, they're raring to be let loose."

Gil's eyes twinkled at the prospect.

"I'll even let you have a head start," Alex said. "Sampson will beat Peregrine easily. Go on, then!" He waited a few moments before spurring Sampson into a gallop.

Racing through the countryside, Alex felt alive. He had spent the day being ignored by a woman he intended to avoid, but yet the very woman who consumed him. Then he had agreed to stop in on her relatives at some point in the near future. Lord only knew why he would have done such a thing. But the fact remained, it was done. Bloody hell, what had he been thinking?

He'd have to honor that commitment, for Gil's sake if for nothing else. Deuce take it all, now he'd have to spend even more time with the chit. And if today was any indication, she would continue to do everything in her power to pretend he didn't exist.

That irritated him to no end.

Sampson quickly caught Peregrine from behind. Alex dug in with his heels, encouraging his horse to run harder. "Watch out, old man! We're coming for you."

Sampson was within a head's distance of catching the other horse as they pulled into Roundstone Park's arched lane. By the halfway point through the trees, Sampson was almost dead even with Gil's mount. Alex pulled back, allowing Gil to take the win just as they pulled into the stables—doing his best to hide his actions. "Good race, old man. You beat me there at the end."

Gil's eyes narrowed. They dismounted and handed their reins to the waiting groom. "Yes, well. We'll have to try this again sometime soon. With no head starts next time! I like my wins to be fair." They walked side-by-side back to the manor house, a comfortable companionship between them.

How many more days like this would he have with his friend?

Eight

AUNT DOROTHEA HAD an invitation in her hands when she turned to her husband. "Laurence, Sir Augustus Wellesley has invited us all over for an evening of entertainments Tuesday next at Brightstone. Shall we accept? I think it would be lovely."

Aunt Dorothea pointedly avoided Grace's eyes.

Uncle Laurence never looked up from his papers and tea. "Sir Augustus? That should be fine dear. Do write out an acceptance and send it along."

An evening of entertainments? Certainly such things went on in the country almost as often as in Town, but shouldn't she avoid such an affair? It seemed the perfect way for word to travel to Father, and then he would know where she had run. Dare she take such a risk?

It was one thing to visit with Lord Rotheby and Lord Alexander and then picnic with them on the river. An entertainment was something else entirely. The risk seemed much too high. Besides, if someone there had heard of her situation, only shame and scorn could come to the Kensingtons for allowing her to stay with them. She couldn't allow such a thing to come to pass, even if they were willing.

"Aunt Dorothea," Grace said, hesitant to broach the subject, "would it not be more prudent for me to remain at New Hill…considering the circumstances? Perhaps you should accept the invitation for yourself and Uncle Laurence, but not for me."

Please let her aunt agree with her suggestion. Staying behind was clearly the only solution. She could avoid anyone who might know Father—and she could also avoid chancing another encounter with Lord Alexander. The man was far too handsome, not to mention virile, for Grace's comfort.

Truth be told, the opportunity to run into Lord Alexander was a far greater deterrent than her Father's discovery at the moment. She seemed to lose all control over her emotions, and also her body, in his presence. Not a good combination.

Not at all.

"Why, I'll hear of no such thing, Gracie. Of course, you must accompany us. Sir Augustus would be offended if we did not bring you along. Your Uncle Laurence told me just this morning about how he ran into the baronet on a ride through town, and they discussed your visit. You simply must join us. It would be most unpardonably rude to stay home."

Splendid. She bit the inside of her lower lip and frowned. There could be no point in further argument. Grace resigned herself to attending the event.

Would Lord Alexander be there?

ALEX DRESSED BEFORE a cheval mirror and tied his own blasted cravat. It took him far less time to accomplish the task on his own for some reason than with the assistance of his valet. He would have to speak to Thomas about that, after the man recovered from the chill he had taken. Granted, Alex couldn't attain the same level of perfection when tying the neck cloth himself, but that should be no excuse. He was liable to become an addle-pate during the time it took his valet to tie the deuced thing.

He'd flatly refused Gil's offer of his valet's services. Alex wanted to get this evening over with, and waiting around for servants to complete such simple tasks would only delay the inevitable. He had somehow convinced himself the end of the evening would arrive sooner if he and Gil got started with it sooner. Surely there was some logic in the thought—somewhere.

Once dressed, he made his way to the front salon of Roundstone Park.

Even with the services of a valet to tie *his* cravat, Gil had finished dressing before him. Alex definitely needed to have a firm word with Thomas. Good Lord—was he becoming a dandy? Impossible. Best to ignore such frightful thoughts. Dandies had no concern for speed and efficiency, but only with frippery and finery.

"Shall we be off, then?" Gil asked. He straightened himself out of the armchair where he was waiting and gingerly adjusted his evening coat.

"If you are certain you are up to an evening out, Gil."

The older man nodded brusquely.

"Well, if you tire before the night is through, we'll leave at once. Just say the word."

Alex wanted Rotheby to visit with his friends. He did. But wouldn't it be easier on his health for those friends to pay a visit to Roundstone Park? Surely they must see what he recognized about the earl's health. Alex could not be the only one aware of Gil's decline. Later, Alex would have to broach the subject with him—perhaps after they retired for the evening. Except that would mean discussing Gil's health, which as to that point, the man had staunchly avoided any such discussion about.

They left in Gil's carriage and traveled the short distance to Brightstone. Lanterns lined the walkways of the drive and carriages abounded as the various guests made their entrance.

The atmosphere was more relaxed than a typical *ton* ball. Good thing. Alex wasn't prepared for that sort of display. These revelers greeted each other as old friends—shaking hands, slapping each other on the back, and the like. They wore what he assumed to be their best evening wear, yet the attire worn by most of the guests would not be in quite the first stare of fashion according to Town standards. It was all far more comfortable in his estimation, and less cliquish.

Sir Augustus Wellesley, an elderly and portly gentleman with as much hair growing from his chin as from the top of his head, greeted them with a jovial smile at the front of his home. While Brightstone was not as grand in scale as Roundstone Park, it was certainly spacious and comfortable, with ample food and drink, and, of course, excellent conversation.

Alex was charmed the moment he stepped within.

He and Gil made moved inside, with the earl hailing his neighbors as they passed. Peers mingled with country gentlemen, and even with a few members of the merchant class.

The idea that they could all spend an evening together would be shunned by many of his contemporaries, but why shouldn't they all socialize together? They lived close by and did business together. There was no reason they should operate in entirely separate circles.

Alex enjoyed country life more and more the longer he stayed. Of course, he missed his family and a few friends in London as well, particularly Sir Jonas Buchannan, a jolly good fellow, and Derek Redgrave, the fiendishly handsome rascal. And, of course, Priscilla and little Harry. But he was content with the lifestyle of the country.

He had not told Gil, or anyone for that matter, but he had begun making enquiries about properties he could purchase nearby. None yet quite suited his needs, but he would not give up until he found the perfect estate to raise a family.

Because, rather frequently, he was entertaining thoughts about working the land. The life of a country gentleman held a good deal of appeal for him. Frankly, the idea had taken him by surprise, but it seemed to be the answer to all of his problems. He had come to Somerton to discover how he wanted to spend the rest of his life, and there it lay, right before him.

Alex would still be able to travel to Town when the desire struck, but he'd prefer to stay away from the hustle and bustle of the city, in general.

He wanted to find a wife, start a family, actually have a *home* of his own, and not continuously hang on his brother's sleeve. He wanted to be useful, to serve a purpose. To find life meant more than just wasting time at the gaming hells and gentlemen's clubs and balls, all the while watching hordes of money float away.

If he found some place to suit nearby, he could be close to Gil. Not to mention he would be close to Peter's principle seat. The possibility remained that Peter would someday take a new duchess and retire to the country—however unlikely such a possibility seemed. He wanted to be near his family. How better to arrange it than by purchasing an estate near his brother's?

On top of all that, if he settled in the country, he could bring Priscilla and Harry out here—away from the prying eyes in the city. They could be comfortable here. He could set them up with a small home, something that they could be comfortable. Somewhere that they could be close by. He hated not having them near.

He was startled from his thoughts when Lady Grace entered the ballroom with her aunt and uncle. There was no reason he should not have expected to see them at the evening's soiree. The Kensingtons were some of the more prominent residents of Somerton. Yet he was thoroughly unnerved by the sight of the woman he was trying his damnedest to avoid.

She looked very pretty this evening in a primrose silk with golden netting and a modest neckline that gave a hint of the bosom hidden beneath. Her black coiffure, for once, fell in loose curls about her face, beckoning him to twine one about his finger, even from a distance.

Alex hardened at the sight. Fiend seize it. He needed to think of something else—anything else. He shifted to remove her from his line of vision.

Miss Wellesley, the eldest daughter of the baronet whom he had just met, slid into place where Lady Grace had been in his vision. "My lords, we'll enjoy a game of charades in the drawing room, if you'd care to join us. And Papa has also mentioned there will be card games in the salon, if you would prefer that form of entertainment instead." She smiled prettily at them both and executed a perfect curtsy.

"Cards!" Gil said with an eager grin. "I daresay Sir Augustus will try to beat me again at whist, though he will fail. Miss Wellesley, Alex, please excuse me." The earl headed off toward the salon.

After watching him go, Alex turned back to Miss Wellesley. "Charades would be lovely. Please, lead the way." He glanced over to where he last saw Lady Grace. She was gone, and he chided himself for being concerning himself with her activities. It didn't matter one whit if she was to dance, or play charades, or gamble her entire life away on a hand of cards. He must stop thinking about her. She had made it quite clear by the river she wanted nothing to do with him. Forgetting her was his only option, however difficult the task.

Alex forced his thoughts instead to the young lady leading him to the drawing room. Miss Wellesley was the daughter of a country gentleman. Perfectly acceptable lineage. The girl had a perfect English Rose complexion, complete with the fair hair that was all the crack in Town. And unlike Lady Grace, Miss Wellesley was nearly as tall as he was, with the top of her head falling just above his eye line.

Maybe he ought to pay more attention to her tonight. If there was dancing later, he'd ask for her hand in a set. After all, what better distraction was there than another pretty young lady?

Miss Wellesley led him into the drawing room. A quick glance around had his heart thudding to a stop in his chest. Lady Grace had already joined the party. She locked eyes with his for the briefest moment and then looked away.

"Why don't we split the room in half?" their hostess suggested. "Mr. Maxwell, you'll join the group closest to the fire there to make the teams even." Mumbling and movement took control of the room for a few moments while everyone resituated themselves.

Lady Grace was assigned to the team with Mr. Maxwell, a large, rather boorish looking man with a long nose that took over most of his face. Alex found it difficult to keep his eyes anywhere but on the two of them.

Miss Wellesley started the game off. She pulled a slip of paper from Mr. Someone-or-Other's hat and stood before the group. When she held up three fingers, shouts of "Three words!" filled his side of the drawing room. Blasted games.

A movement near Lady Grace caught his eye. Maxwell inched closer to her until his arm almost touched the edge of Lady Grace's gown. Bloody bastard. Alex quelled the growl forming low in his throat. It wouldn't do to lose all sense of decorum in front of an entire houseful of people.

Miss Wellesley rubbed one hand against her mid-section with the other hand cupped against her ear. Another chorus of shouts rose up about him. "Sounds like stomach!"

"Stomach? A poet with a name that sounds like stomach?"

"Belly, you fools. Sounds like belly." No one heard Alex's mumbling, or at the very least they ignored his impertinence.

He tried ignore them all while Miss Wellesley touched her nose and pointed like a madwoman to some young miss near the hearth. And again, Maxwell drew his attention when the tips of his fingers grazed the netting of Lady Grace's gown. Alex's breathing became labored and shallow.

"That is correct! Miss Corkley wins a point for our team with Percy Bysshe Shelley. Excellent, everyone. Now, who'll go first for the other team? Any volunteers?" Miss Wellesley looked across the room with eager anticipation.

Maxwell piped up with, "I nominate Lady Grace. I believe she'll do jolly well."

A cacophony of encouragement sounded throughout the room as Lady Grace tried to demur with, "Oh no, I could not…"

Maxwell took her arm in an altogether-too-familiar manner and practically lifted her to her feet. Alex seethed. If the man had any idea what was best for him, he would unhand her within the instant.

"Lady Grace, we insist," Maxwell said. "Please, do us the honor. I daresay no one will give clues as skillfully as you this evening." The louse led her to the front of the drawing room with one hand on her arm and his other odious appendage resting at the small of her back.

She cowed before the room. She might actually be shaking as she moved to stand before the hearth. It took every ounce of Alex's self control to refrain from ripping the bloody fool's head off. Maxwell removed his hands from her person at the exact moment Alex thought he would lose his hold over himself and remove the blackguard's hands from his arms.

Lady Grace cautiously pulled a strip from the beaver hat held out before her and read its contents. She spent several moments without moving whatsoever.

He ached for her. She must be in agony in front of this gathering. Her demeanor was always so quiet and reserved, she must despise having the attention being focused on her.

But then she moved. Lady Grace held up three fingers.

Maxwell called out louder than anyone else in the room, "Three words."

Alex fought the urge to wring the man's neck.

She walked about the front of the room, marking off paces and indicating something on either side falling from the ceiling to the floor with her hands.

"What is that?"

"I can't tell, can you? I'm uncertain what she is trying to show us."

Lady Grace chopped with her arms against the imaginary objects, and swooshed to the center of the room again.

"Why, they are curtains," said some unknown gentleman. "Is it a play, Lady Grace?"

She touched the tip of her nose and nodded at him with a broad smile brightening her face. Pride beamed from every pore of Alex's being.

Then she sat on the floor before the hearth, cupping her hands and raising them to her lips, pretending to drink. After the counterfeit liquid passed through her lips, she fell to the floor in a heap. A few moments later, she roused herself and pushed an imaginary dagger through her chest, falling again to the floor.

Her portrayal of the death scene in *Romeo and Juliet* was exquisite. He waited for someone from her team to call out the answer. No one could mistake her intentions.

"Death? Dying? What on earth was that?"

"I don't know for certain, but I believe she might have been acting out *She Stoops to Conquer*. Why else would she be on the floor?"

"That has four words, not three."

Lady Grace's visage looked strained. Alex stared, dumbfounded. How could no one have guessed correctly yet?

"Well, what about *Oedipus the King*? That has three words. Surely someone was stabbed in it."

Alex couldn't stand it any longer. "Oh good heavens, that was *Romeo and Juliet!*" He immediately regretted his outburst, especially upon the look of mortification on Lady Grace's face. But his patience had run clear to Rome and back in the last few moments. He needed to do something. He needed to pace. He needed to get Lady Grace away from all the stares or he would end up in Bedlam.

"Lord Alexander, you are quite right. Bravo." Maxwell passed a faux smile in his direction. "However, you're on the wrong team. I believe it only fair that is a point for us."

Lady Grace didn't look at Alex but returned to Maxwell's side. She kept her eyes on the ground through the rest of the game. He knew, because his eyes never left her.

Again, Maxwell moved closer than he should and his fingers dusted against her arm.

Almost of their own volition, Alex's fingers curled into fists at his side. Blast it all, was he jealous? It couldn't be jealousy. It had to be something more like protectiveness, like he would feel if a man was manhandling Sophie or Char like that.

Alex wanted her to be safe, that was all—and this Maxwell was surely trouble.

The game came to a close with Alex having virtually not even participated, other than his outburst earning a point for the other team. Maxwell called out to the group, "Dancing! Let us all dance. Miss Wellesley, is there a young lady present who might play the pianoforte for us?"

Miss Ellen SomeSuchThing, a girl far too green to be out yet, spoke up. "Oh, do allow me. Mama and Papa allowed me to come this evening, and I should very much like to participate in some way." She blushed and lowered her voice. "I play the pianoforte tolerably well, my governess tells me."

"Then dancing there shall be." Miss Wellesley led the party into the main ballroom and seated Miss Ellen behind the pianoforte.

Couples paired off and situated themselves into lines for country dances. Maxwell asked Lady Grace for her hand and led her to the floor.

Fuming, but with no real idea why he should be, Alex forced his features to remain placid and turned to Miss Wellesley. "Might I have the honor?" Only a moment passed before she nodded in agreement. Alex made certain they were only one position down the line from Maxwell and Lady Grace. He wanted to keep an eye on them—in particular, on him.

When Lady Grace looked at him, tension crackled in the air between them. She turned away from him with some measure of force as the music began. She and Maxwell commenced the steps, and Alex was a few beats behind already.

During one figure of the dance, he passed next to Lady Grace, only a breath apart from her. The scent of roses and woman wafted over him. He was intoxicated.

Alex tried to concentrate on Miss Wellesley, but it was useless. She was perfectly lovely, a good dancer. She made proper and polite conversation. But Alex only had eyes for Lady Grace.

Maxwell brushed against her and ruffled the silk and netting of her gown. Alex fumed, then forced his eyes away. Then, in completing another figure of the dance, Maxwell held onto Lady Grace's hand longer than was necessary (*far* longer, if one were to ask for Alex's opinion on the matter). Alex clenched his jaw and returned his gaze to his own partner.

"Why, have I done something to anger you, sir?" Miss Wellesley asked, staring up at him in confusion.

"What? No. You haven't." Christ, he needed to soften his glare or risk sending his partner a thoroughly unintended message. Nothing to be done about it, though, until Maxwell's body was writing under his hands for daring to move into the presence of perfection.

Good Lord, he was becoming a madman.

Alex tried to take a cleansing breath with no luck. He refocused his efforts on calming his thoughts. He was being ridiculous about all of this. He was grown man, for Christ's sake.

And then Maxwell moved in too close to Lady Grace, brushing his chest against her bosom. Alex's hands turned to fists at his sides.

Finally, the music came to an end and the set was over. Lady Grace would find another partner with whom to dance. Alex could breathe again. Half an hour of holding his breath had proved far too long.

Another gentleman, someone Alex recognized but couldn't be bothered with remembering his name, walked over and asked for her hand. He wasn't nearly as objectionable as Maxwell. Whoever her current partner was, he refrained from leering, so he stood a rung higher on the ladder in Alex's estimation of his character.

Several ladies stood about the edges of the floor, watching and waiting for partners, so propriety dictated that he must dance again—but Alex couldn't suffer propriety at the moment. He had danced the first deuced set. That would have to be enough for now.

He watched Lady Grace's every move through the entire dance.

Before the next set started, Maxwell returned to her side.

Alex couldn't stand for this. He marched across the ballroom, intent to ask for her hand before she could accept Maxwell, but he arrived just a hair too late. Maxwell led her to the dance floor, glancing over his shoulder at Alex with a look of triumph.

The set was a waltz. Bloody hell.

The air in the Wellesley ballroom suddenly turned stifling.

Maxwell pulled her too close to his body, leaned too near to her face, touched her in ways that caused Alex's eyes to pulse in his head.

And she recoiled from his advances, placing a respectable amount of distance between them.

Good girl.

It took every ounce of his will to stay put and not pluck the slimy lout from the dance floor, haul him outside, and engage him in a bout of fisticuffs or ten.

When the waltz finished, Alex pulled Lady Grace from Maxwell's arms and led her away. "My lord," she said in some alarm. "Unhand me this instant." She struggled against him, until he passed her a glass of lemonade upon their arrival in the refreshment room. She took it and sipped, eyeing him over the top of her glass.

Another waltz was forming. He had vowed to stay away from her, but he could no longer keep such a promise to himself. It was, in a word, impossible. "Lady Grace, might I have the honor of your hand for this set?" he asked.

She had better not refuse him. He might become murderous if he had to watch another set with Maxwell's hands on her and was uncertain how much longer, if any, he could control himself.

Her eyes widened. She looked around, seeming to search for an escape, but then she demurely nodded her head in acceptance. Alex led her to the dance floor and took her in his arms. Her scent drew him closer. He took one of her hands in his own and placed her other on his shoulder, their bodies touching lightly through superfine, silk, and netting as they swayed to the music.

Nothing was said between them for a long while. He was too furious over the manner in which Maxwell had manhandled her to trust his own voice. On the other hand, her silence—at least in his presence—came as no surprise. She rarely had a word to say to him.

But then she bowled him over.

"My lord, I didn't know if I should expect to see you tonight." She took her time, seeming to choose her words with care. "Lord Rotheby's health did not seem quite—well—at the river last week. Has he shown any improvement?"

"None, ma'am. I fear…" he said and then broke off. How much should he divulge? It was not his own health he was discussing, after all. But still, she almost never said anything to him, let alone asked him anything. "I fear for him. I do not believe he'll live much longer, though he hasn't said as much."

"Oh, dear. I am sorry to hear that. It's good he has you with him." She added no more, and they continued to waltz.

Each time he spun her about, the scent of roses caught on the wind and wafted to his nose.

What in bloody hell could they discuss now? He knew little of her interests, because she so often ignored his attempts at conversation.

They passed Maxwell on the floor, as he twirled Miss Wellesley in their direction. Anger blinded Alex again at the sight of the man. "My lady, you shouldn't associate with Mr. Maxwell anymore," he blurted out without thinking. Why on God's green earth did he choose that particular line of conversation? He was making an utter cake of himself.

"Pardon me?" she asked, calm veiling the anger flashing blue lightning in her eyes. "And why should you be concerned with who I choose to associate with, or not to associate with, as the case may be? My lord, I assure you, I don't need your involvement in any of my affairs."

He cringed. How tactless could he be? "I don't mean to offend. Please forgive me." Yet again, was forced to apologize to the minx. Though, he must admit, that might be quite the longest speech he had ever heard her utter. Interesting. "I simply—ma'am, he has behaved like a lecher toward you this evening." Once the words began, they flowed at a speed over which he had no control. "He continually brushes against you in most inappropriate ways, he holds you far too closely while you dance, and he leers at you when you are not looking. For your honor—"

She stiffened in his arms. "My honor, sir?" she interrupted. "What could you possibly have to teach me about honor? And how dare you call another gentleman a lecher in my presence? You, who had the audacity to—to—to *kiss* me!" Her words scarcely rose above a whisper and her eyes, those haunting eyes, told him she would rather be anywhere but in his arms at the moment. "I hardly think you of all people have any right to disparage another gentleman to *me*, my lord."

Devil take it, she was right on all counts. Alex had behaved in a most ungentlemanly manner in Gil's gardens, and he had behaved far worse than Maxwell this evening.

Yet he knew he *had* to protect her. If only he knew how.

Nine

THE MORNING AFTER the Wellesley soiree, Grace sat in the parlor of New Hill Cottage and worked on her embroidery with Aunt Dorothea who, for once, worked in silence. Grace was glad. The quiet provided her ample time to think about last night's events in peace, without interruption from her aunt.

Grace hadn't enjoyed the company of Mr. Maxwell—not at all, in fact. He was barbaric and churlish, and entirely too forward. She had no desire for any of the attentions he had continued to lavish on her, despite her negative response. Nor was she happy with him virtually forcing her to participate in charades.

But none of that gave Lord Alexander any right to interfere in her affairs.

The insufferable man would be better served avoiding her. Grace didn't know how much more clear she could make herself on the point, short of thumping him over the head with a parasol. But hadn't she already done so, at least in essence? She'd have to be more explicit with the man.

Lord Alexander was entirely too handsome and masculine, and in general too desirable for Grace's comfort. The air between them felt alive. She would much prefer that not to happen.

She shivered, remembering the feel of his arms about her while they had waltzed and the way his scent had hung so close she could taste it—taste *him*. He elicited responses in her she had no right to own, sensations she should avoid.

Grace was to live the life of a spinster. Maybe with her aunt and uncle, or perhaps alone. But she would forever be an outcast, a social pariah. She mustn't forget.

But in his arms, she felt like all was right with the world, instead of like the world was closing in on her. The feeling was entirely unfamiliar, but not necessarily unwelcome. Except that she shouldn't welcome it. She *couldn't* welcome it.

The butler cleared his throat and interrupted their work, breaking into her daydreams. "Pardon me, Lady Kensington. Lord Rotheby and Lord Alexander are below stairs. Shall I show them in?"

Lord Alexander? Oh, dear. Panic and delight warred for control of Grace's emotions.

"Oh, wonderful, Mason. Please bring them up." Aunt Dorothea set her quilting aside and straightened her afternoon gown about her legs. With a raised eyebrow and a wave of her hand, she indicated Grace should do the same.

Grace sighed in joint frustration and curiosity while she complied with the silent order. Moments later, the two gentlemen joined them in the parlor and inclined their heads in greeting.

"Thank you, Mason," Aunt Dorothea said. "Please order some tea for our guests. And let Sir Laurence know Lord Rotheby has arrived, if you have not already done so. He shall very much like to visit with the earl, I would wager."

The butler left with a quick nod.

"Gentlemen, do have a seat. It's so good of you to join us. I must say, Gracie, I'm quite glad of their company." Aunt Dorothea gave her a pointed look. "Would you not agree that the morning has been dreadfully quiet after the excitement of last evening?"

Lord Alexander helped the earl into a chair near the fire before seating himself opposite Grace. She most certainly would *not* agree, however she answered in the affirmative, as clearly expected. "Indeed, Aunt."

All eyes turned to her when she spoke, and heat raced up her neck and over her cheeks to match the heat in Lord Alexander's gaze. His expression—one of pure desire, plainly—was sheer and utter impropriety. The warmth spread from Grace's face through the rest of her body and all the way to her most intimate, private places. How could any man such as he feel desire for her? If he knew, he would run to the hills to escape the stigma permanently attached to her.

She turned away from him, facing the earl instead. He was safer to look upon. "Lord Rotheby, I trust you have rested well after such a late evening. I would hate for you to become ill."

"Oh yes, my dear. I am doing very well—" he broke off to cough, "—very well, indeed. You are such a dear to ask after me. Alex told me you enquired after my health last night while you danced, as well." He smiled then, and it reached all the way to his eyes. "I daresay I was quite pleased to hear you danced with Alex. He's spent far too much of his visit following after me and checking on my health. It's good for young people to spend time with other young people."

A mischievous look passed between Lord Rotheby and Grace's aunt. *They were conspiring!* How could Aunt Dorothea continue with such behavior, knowing how unfit and ineligible Grace would be for any respectable gentleman?

Mason returned with the tea service just as Uncle Laurence joined them. "Gil, you are looking well this morning," Grace's uncle said. "Playing cards must agree with you, then."

Lord Alexander stood to greet Uncle Laurence, who commandeered the armchair the younger man had left vacant. Grace's heart sank when she realized the only seating option left open was to join her on the loveseat. He sat next to her, and she did her best to disguise her discomfort.

Grace had given him enough of her opinion of his character at the Wellesley revelries last night. Delving further into such a line of conversation would be pointless, particularly when surrounded by company; nor did she intend to allow Lord Alexander the satisfaction he could glean from her discomfiture at his proximity.

She did everything in her power to avoid thoughts of his nearness. Grace soon found the task quite impossible. Lord Alexander's large frame caused his legs to brush against hers in a most inappropriate manner, and she was altogether too aware of his presence—his heat!—at her side. Before his arrival, she had smelled the fire burning in the hearth and the scent of baking bread wafting from the kitchens. Now she smelled only *him*.

He spoke with his hands. As his animation grew, his hands drew circles in the air next to her and pushed the earthy, masculine scent of him closer to her nostrils.

When he finished speaking, his hands dropped to his side, where one of them brushed against the muslin over her thigh.

Grace wanted more of his touch.

She wanted the feel of him against her as when they waltzed the night before—or, however brazen the thought may be, as when he had kissed her in the gardens. How wanton she'd become!

He turned the fullness of his gaze on her and asked, "Would you not agree, ma'am?"

She flushed again. Drat! How embarrassing, to be caught without a thought in her head. Or at the very least, without a thought she could share.

"I'm dreadfully sorry. I—I seem to have been woolgathering. Would I not agree with what?" She prayed the color in her cheeks would soon return to normal.

He gave her a gentle smile. "Wouldn't you agree the weather is quite lovely for a walk through the gardens? Your aunt suggested we might enjoy some air while she and Sir Laurence show Lord Rotheby a painting they recently acquired."

A walk. In the gardens.

Alone with Lord Alexander.

Again.

Aunt Dorothea feigned innocence when Grace glanced her way, the wretch. "Gracie, do be a dear. It would be quite rude if we should leave Lord Alexander alone, you know."

And, of course, one must never be rude to Lord Alexander. She wanted desperately to ask why the man in question could not simply join them all to stroll through the gallery and admire the painting, but her blasted manners won out. "Yes, Aunt." She turned to Lord Alexander and forced a pained smile. "Shall we stroll through the roses, or would you prefer to see the arbors?"

He never broke eye contact. "The arbors should provide protection from the sun. Why don't we go there?" His voice slid across her like satin.

She pulled a light pelisse about her shoulders and led the way outside. Anything would be better than spending more time alone with him. Anything. Yet once more, her aunt had thrust her into just that situation.

She fought her fury down and struggled to control her emotions.

She wished he'd take her hand. It tingled in anticipation of his touch that wouldn't come.

ALEX BATTLED THE lust building in his chest.

He was determined to act the gentleman with Lady Grace today and keep his thoughts where they belonged. She was a *lady*. She deserved his respect.

But then she flushed again, and the urge to pull her under the cover of the trees and perform unspeakable, utterly delicious acts overwhelmed him.

He was no green youth. He'd had his share of women and paid them handsomely for their services—or taken what was freely offered, what that opportunity had been presented. Why did this minx cause him to lose his tight rein of control? She was a pixie, hardly more than a girl, yet lust raged a furious course through his blood.

They walked in silence among the trees outside New Hill Cottage, through well-worn paths that wound in and out of daffodils and poppies. The silence came as no surprise. He found it comforting, even commonplace, for the two of them. With any other lady, he would force himself to make conversation. But with Lady Grace, he felt no need to meet society's demand.

There was something very different about her. Why couldn't he determine what that difference was? For now, he chose to allow that aspect of their relationship to simply be. He wouldn't force her to divulge her secrets.

Still, he wanted very much to know her secrets, her thoughts. He wanted to know what it was inside her that created the art he'd witnessed. She tried to portray herself as cold, unfeeling— passionless, even. But he knew better. It was all a grand charade.

Passion had poured out from her, as though her very soul had been spilled onto the canvas. He'd felt her passion kindle in his arms.

She needed someone to help her past her inhibitions. Lady Grace knew no shyness or modesty when she painted. He wanted to incite such passion in her. The realization struck him unawares, and he stopped mid-stride.

"My lord, are you quite all right?" She slowed and turned to face him.

He marveled at her dainty beauty, at the idea he could be attracted to a woman so staid—her neat, midnight bun at the nape of her neck, her tiny frame, her figure that spoke more of a girl than a woman, and those eyes that cried out to him for something he couldn't provide.

He resumed his pace and she walked alongside him. "I apologize. It must be my turn to gather wool." Alex winked down at her.

Silence returned. They strolled through the arbor until they reached a creek that trickled down a grassy hill through a meadow of bluebells.

He slowed his gait and matched him. "Before we return, shall we take a rest?" Alex asked. "The willow here will provide us with ample shade." He didn't want to overtire her, particularly since he knew all too well how late they'd all been out last night.

Dark circles had formed beneath her eyes, and her skin bore an unnatural, uncomplimentary shade of green. She sighed in apparent relief. "Yes, that would be lovely."

He removed his outer coat and laid it on the grass, then helped her to sit on it. She stared at the view before them, likely taking in the mélange of rock formations and palette of colors for a later painting, never once looking in his direction.

His focus remained fully on her. With each passing minute, her color faded and his alarm grew. "Are you unwell? Should we return to the cottage?"

She didn't respond but stumbled to her feet. "Oh!" she cried and rushed away from his sight. Alex followed behind her as quickly as he could. She stopped near a tree and retched, then fainted into his arms.

He lifted her and rushed toward New Hill, leaving his coat where it still lay on the grass near the creek. Good God. She needed a doctor. He had to hurry. There was no time to waste.

Halfway there, she stirred. Her eyes flickered open and she regained some color. "What...where...Lord Alexander?" Her befuddlement almost aroused him—almost. He was not entirely a rogue, thankfully.

He continued toward the cottage. "You're ill. I'll return you to your aunt and uncle in moments."

She collected herself a bit more and struggled in his arms. "Please don't trouble yourself, sir. I am capable of walking on my own." Her squirms increased. "Set me on the ground, my lord." Her pert voice was indignity personified.

"I'm sorry, but I can't do that. You are ill. I can have you home far sooner if I carry you than if you walk." He tightened his grasp, pulling her to his chest so she had no choice but to accept his assistance.

She huffed up at him with the most adorable frown on her face, but thankfully ceased her struggles and arguments. Within minutes, he reached the cottage and carried her through the door held open by the butler.

"Oh goodness, Gracie!" Lady Kensington's shocked cry reverberated through the front hallway of the cottage. "Laurence, she's ill. Oh, Lord Alexander, I'm very glad you were with her to carry her home. Come. Come with me. We'll settle her in bed where she can rest. You poor dear, going for a walk to take some air, and becoming sick like that."

Lady Kensington led him up the stairs and pushed open the door to Lady Grace's bedchamber. She pulled back the bedclothes and plumped the pillows so he could place her in comfort, although it seemed to him the woman took more time to accomplish the task than necessary. He continued to hold Lady Grace tight in his arms and waited.

A maid stepped into the room. "Oh, my lady. Have you taken ill again?"

Alex's head whipped around to stare down at the. "Again? Lady Grace has been ill before today?"

The maid blushed prettily, then rushed forward to assist Lady Kensington in preparing the bed for Lady Grace. Her efficiency sped the process along a good deal, but she didn't answer his question. Finally, they had the counterpane pulled down and pillows situated just so. Alex frowned up at them both as he laid her in the bed, careful of placement for her comfort.

"It is nothing, my lord." Lady Kensington patted his arm before adjusting pillows around Lady Grace's head and tucking the quilt tightly against her sides. "I fear the cod she ate at luncheon didn't agree with her. Never you mind."

"Shall I fetch a doctor? I can ride into town and bring one in short order." Blast it, he felt helpless with empty arms.

"No. No, that's not necessary, but you are such a dear for making the offer. Gracie will be fine after a good rest." Lady Kensington stopped her ministrations and faced him. "Lord Rotheby is tired, sir. I thank you for bringing him to visit, but he desires to rest in his own home. Please see to his comforts and allow me to see to Gracie's."

Clearly, Alex had been dismissed. He returned to the parlor and fetched Gil, determined not to fret over Lady Grace.

On the return trip to Roundstone, he couldn't banish the feel of her in his arms as he carried her from his mind. She was so fragile, yet strong.

What a fascinating combination.

Ten

"GRACIE, SWEETHEART, I think we should go into Bath tomorrow and have some new gowns made for you." Aunt Dorothea's attempt at tact fell heavy on the air. "With your condition...well, you'll be starting to fill out around the middle before much longer, and your clothes will not fit you properly anymore. We must have a seamstress work on some garments more appropriate for your situation."

It was already mid-morning, and Grace had been unable to head downstairs for breakfast. Her stomach upset had assailed her far more strongly than usual, and she remained stuck in her chamber.

She groaned aloud as another wave of nausea passed over her. "Aunt Dorothea, new gowns cost money that I can't afford. Why don't we let out the ones I already own?"

Could they be let out enough to sustain her through the pregnancy? She had her doubts, but that approach seemed a better alternative than going without or wearing too-small gowns. Maybe she could use similar fabrics and combine them, if they wouldn't expand far enough to cover her about the middle.

Her aunt scowled over at her. "Oh, poppycock! Do you really think your uncle and I expect you to pay for such things yourself? Goodness, Gracie. If not for the fact your father would have spent it all on his gambling and lightskirts, we would have sent money all along for your education and expenses. Why, if I had known you had no lady's maid, I would have hired one and paid her discreetly so he couldn't steal that money as well. We will buy you some appropriate attire while you stay with us. Why, I never."

Aunt Dorothea puttered around the room, straightening things in no need of straightening, likely just to have something to do. "We'll travel into Bath tomorrow, and that, my dear, is that. Tess, sweetheart, you will need to pack a small trunk for your mistress."

The young maid stepped out from the shadows of the corner. "Yes, my lady. I'll take care of it, ma'am."

"We'll be gone for a week. Please pack her trunk this evening. And one for yourself, if you please. We'll require your services, I would imagine. One cannot sit in a hotel room and not be seen while in Bath, you know."

Aunt Dorothea turned to Grace on the bed. "Dear, I do hope you feel more the thing tomorrow. It will take us nearly the full day to travel. I should hate for you to be ill in the carriage. Nothing is more miserable, I can assure you." She patted the back of Grace's hand and smoothed the hair over her brow before she left the room.

Grace sighed to herself. There could be no avoiding it, once her aunt's mind was set on something. Brooding would accomplish nothing.

"Well, Tess, shall we start packing?" She descended from bed to select some gowns for the journey.

What would her aunt toss into her path next? Surely she would have to give up the foolish idea of finding a match for Grace soon. It wouldn't be much longer before her condition started to reveal itself, and then no gentleman would consider her, nonetheless.

GIL LOOKED UNCOMFORTABLE as he prepared to speak to Alex across the table while they ate luncheon. His face contorted a few times, and he twice attempted to speak only to stop himself short before anything more than an "ah" or "mph" came out. He shook his head each time he stopped.

"Spit it out, old man." Alex softened the rebuke with a fiendish grin. "We'll be here all night if you keep it up at this pace."

The earl took another bite before he tried again. "I need to take a trip, and I want you to come with me." He rushed on when Alex tried to interrupt with an argument. "Not a long trip. Just to Bath, for a few days. I want to take the waters there, and see if I can clear up this cough of mine. I have some business to attend to."

Alex's jaw dropped. Traveling, with the state of Gil's health, was a ghastly idea. Preposterous, even. And did the waters really do anyone any good? He had more than a few doubts about that. So why go through with the trip? It could only serve to complicate matters which needed no aid in complication. Gil would do much better to stay at home where his friends and doctors could see after him.

But Gil pressed on. "I'm going, Alex. With or without you. You can't stop me. I would appreciate it if you choose to join me, but you will not change my mind. I leave for Bath in the morning."

With that, Gil pushed away from the table and stalked from the room. Alex wouldn't be able to stand it if he allowed Gil to go to Bath alone and something happened to him. He supposed he only had one choice.

He was going to Bath.

GRACE HAD FELT fine when they departed from Somerton, but soon the nausea started again. She got by as long as her eyes remained closed.

Somehow, seeing everything in the carriage bounce and dance about caused her stomach to lurch. Keeping her eyes closed turned out to be a good trick in more than just that manner, as her aunt and uncle took it as a sign she was in no mood for conversation, and they left her to her own thoughts.

As the carriage rocked back and forth toward Bath, she let her mind drift to the painting excursion along the Cary River. She'd merely hoped to enjoy the day with her aunt and uncle and get in a spot of painting. The experience always relaxed her, as she put her vision onto the canvas. But this time had been different.

Painting the scene on the river became a cathartic experience. Grace had so many pent up emotions—hurt, anger, and sadness directed toward her father—and a good deal pointed at Lord Barrow as well. All of it had rushed out of her and made its way into the painting.

She had captured the vitality of the running water and the soul of the flowers that grew across the bank. But she also rendered the clouds as dark and menacing—they threatened to destroy all the vitality stretching along the river bed. None of it had been a conscious decision on her part. She had simply started to paint, and then lost herself in the moment. Her brushes had taken on a life of their own and willed her hands to guide them in a certain manner. They had reveled in victory when she acquiesced.

What an experience it had become, to give in to the moment. She felt so alive and energized when she finished with the painting—and so much of the hurt she kept locked inside was left in the clouds of the artwork.

When they arrived home at the cottage, she had selected a spot on the wall in her chamber where she would hang the painting once it was framed. She wanted to see it every day and remember.

Grace relived the moment she completed her painting—the full breath, the sense of accomplishment, and then turning to discover Lord Alexander staring at her.

She had no idea he had been watching her as she worked. He might have been there for only a moment or for hours, and she would have been none the wiser. But there he stood, with a look of utter surprise and awe.

Neither had said a word. In fact, she had said nothing to him the entire day. She didn't intend to be rude, but what should she say to him? Their previous encounter had ended with that kiss—that glorious, sinful kiss. What did a lady talk about with a gentleman after such an experience? She hoped he would initiate future conversation, so she wouldn't have to decide—if they ever had another conversation.

Even though she knew it was wrong of her, and for his own sake she should end their connection, Grace was desperate to see him, to hear his voice—to touch him again. She had spent many a night thinking of him before she fell to sleep and later chastised herself for wishing for the impossible. Sometimes, his woodsy scent assaulted her nostrils and she woke, only to realize the open windows had pulled the scent in from outside.

Aunt Dorothea had not helped matters any, with her countless unsubtle hints toward the man. The last thing Grace needed was for Lord Alexander to desire an attachment with her. It was the last thing he needed, too.

She could never marry him. Since she still hadn't attained her majority, such a decision would fall to Father. And asking for his permission was simply out of the question.

For a brief moment, she entertained the notion of letting Lord Alexander know the truth of her situation. It *could* convince him to avoid her. However, her luck often ran the other direction, and he might instead increase his attentions. That wouldn't do.

But how could she conceal the spread of her belly? Maybe he would no longer be in Somerton when it started to happen, so the point would become moot.

If her luck turned, he would be called back to Town on urgent family business or something of the sort. Anything, as long as he left so she wouldn't have to face him and the unwelcome feelings she experienced in his presence.

The nerve of her aunt, giving him an open invitation to New Hill! But what could Grace do about it? She relied on the Kensingtons' charity at this point, and saw no end to the situation for a good deal of time to come. They had every right to invite whomever they desired to visit at their home, and she had none to deny them. All the same, she wished her aunt would stop interfering in a relationship Grace wished would disappear.

But instead of disappearing, he had accepted the offer and shown up on their door—and the visit had ended in the most dreadfully embarrassing manner she could imagine.

It was not that she disliked Lord Alexander—far from it, actually. Grace was far too attracted to the man for her own good. From his behavior, he seemed fascinated with her as well, which could not serve either of them.

He deserved better than the risk of heartache from becoming too close to her. Nor did he deserve to be leg-shackled to a woman already ruined by another, no matter how it had come about. Lord Alexander deserved an untarnished woman, or at the very least one not bearing another man's child. Grace wished she could find some way to avoid him, but her control over matters slipped further and further from her grasp each day.

After a long day in the carriage with her eyes closed, she finally dared to open them. Thankfully, the nausea had passed.

They drew close to the city. More homes and shops lined the streets now than early in their journey. Thank goodness. She had a desperate need to stand and stretch her legs, and soon.

Traveling in her uncle's carriage was far more pleasant than the journey from London to Somerton on the stagecoach, however. Here, she was not constantly jostled about by the other travelers, and there had been no discussions of gout or poodles.

Uncle Laurence had arranged for them to stay at the Crescent Court Hotel on the Parade. As they arrived in town, people were out and about on the streets, shopping and taking the air. Barnes pulled their carriage up to the hotel and helped them to climb down to the street.

Uncle Laurence headed to the lobby to check in to their rooms as various porters and other workers unloaded their trunks and carried them inside. Grace and Aunt Dorothea followed along at their leisure, after a gander around town. While Bath was not new to her aunt, Grace had never been there before, so she took a moment to study ancient Romanesque structures, so like the ones she'd studied while she had been holed away in her chamber at Chatham House.

When they entered the hotel, Uncle Laurence met them in the lobby. "We have two adjoining rooms with a shared parlor area. Come along. They've already moved our belongings in for us." He led the way through wide, ornately decorated hallways and opened the door to their suites. "Do you think this will do, my dears?"

The room was pristine, with not even the tiniest item out of place. A large chandelier hung from the center of the ceiling, and candlelight danced over the floor and walls. Brocade drapes lined the windows, and the most opulent of silks upholstered the furnishings. While not gaudy, the room was certainly much grander than anything Grace had experienced with her father, and more ostentatious by far than anything she'd encountered in Somerton.

The grandeur of it all overwhelmed her.

Aunt Dorothea swiftly adjusted to their surroundings. "Yes, this room will be perfect. I believe we'll be quite comfortable here, wouldn't you agree, Gracie? Of course, you do. How could you not enjoy such finery?"

She puttered around as usual, unpacking things and finding them homes for the course of their weeklong stay in Bath, apparently unable to wait for a servant to do the job. "Shall we order tea sent up? I think it would be a lovely idea. And Gracie, you must get plenty of rest this evening. We'll stay in tonight, but tomorrow morning we must be seen at the Pump Room, you know."

Actually, Grace knew nothing of the sort, but she nodded for her aunt's benefit.

Why must they engage in social events here? Couldn't they simply do their shopping and return to Somerton? Many of Bath's residents must also be part of the London social circles. Word could too easily reach Father. He'd find her in no time.

Oh, why could they not have stayed in Somerton?

Aunt Dorothea winked at her. "I cannot have you becoming too tired or sickly in the morning, dear. Laurence, you'll of course join us at the Pump Rooms. After performing our social duty in the morning, we'll return here for luncheon, and then Gracie, you and I will begin our shopping. Oh, Laurence! You will allow us to use the carriage, won't you? I should hate to find ourselves caught out in the rain, and if we make a number of purchases, we'll need a way to return them to the hotel. You are such a dear man, you know." She patted the back of her husband's hand with affection. As usual, she plodded along with her solitary conversation without waiting for an answer to any of her myriad questions.

Grace sighed. After the journey to Bath, she desired nothing less than to be seen anywhere in the morning or to shop in the afternoon. But what could be done about it?

The shopping excursion was Aunt Dorothea's entire purpose for making the trip. Grace resigned herself to humor her aunt and prayed no one would recognize her or know of her father.

Eleven

"NOT SO TIGHT, Thomas. Breathing is desirable, if you don't mind." This was definitely not his idea of a good time—promenading through the Pump Rooms—but Gil wanted to take the waters, and it was what one did while in Bath. *Insufferable social customs.* "Would you hurry? I thought we discussed this."

The valet scowled up and him and gave another hard tug on the neck cloth, but didn't respond.

Alex groaned. His valet held far more concern for his appearance than he did. He just wanted to get this morning over with.

The previous day's journey had proven difficult for Gil. His coughing fits grew more pronounced, and more frequent to Alex's estimation, the longer they were in that blasted carriage. He would prefer to stay in their hotel that day, in order to allow the earl enough time to recover from the trip. Gil, however, seemed disinclined to listen to the *young whippersnapper's* ideas on the matter.

Taking the waters was never Gil's true intention in traveling to Bath. The actual purpose of the visit surely had more to do with his business than the Roman Baths. Alex had his own ideas on what that particular business might entail, but he wouldn't force his friend to disclose anything until he was ready. Lord Rotheby would be meeting with his man-of-business to discuss details of the entailments on his properties. What else could it be? It wouldn't surprise Alex one whit if the man was trying to keep as much as possible from his grandson.

Lord Quinton had always been a wild one, if memory served—though since his marriage, he seemed to have settled somewhat.

He should be in Somerton, resting at Roundstone Park, but instead he was traipsing all over Somerset, seeing to affairs that would no longer affect him after he passed.

Thomas finished his torture and excused himself just as the viscount arrived in Alex's chamber.

"Ah, good, I see you're dressed. Are you ready? I'd like to start our day." Gil slumped in his stance as he groped for his cane—yet another sign that he should stay at the hotel and rest instead of meeting some blasted social ritual. One couldn't tell from his tone that anything was amiss, however. He seemed as chipper and falsely gruff as ever.

Alex offered an arm for his friend to lean on. "I'm as ready to deal with this infernal business as I'll ever be, but I will have you know I'm not at all happy with it. But you already know my feelings on the matter." He let out an audible sigh at the look of grim resolve on the earl's face. "I've already ordered a carriage brought around. They should be downstairs preparing for our departure."

The walk to the Pump Rooms was not far, but Alex wouldn't risk overtiring Lord Rotheby so early in the day. If he must suffer through this ordeal, he would at least do everything in his power to take good care of the older man in the process.

Not that the earl made the task easy. He grumbled beneath his breath something along the lines of he could damned well walk, but what alternative did Alex have? He would concede to the older man on certain points, but on this one he refused to budge.

They traveled in silence. By the time they arrived, a number of fashionable people were already milling about the room in groups of twos and threes. Some stood near the Grecian columns and carried on in-depth conversations. Those who were sickly made their way to the end of the room to drink from the waters. Alex and Gil had scarcely arrived before various desirables made their way over to greet them.

The Countess of Trent swooped in on them like a huntress after her prey, with her greying yellowed locks in a loose knot behind her head. The woman's sharp nose led her forward, with the rest of her following close behind. "Lord Rotheby! How pleasant to see you in Bath again, sir. I see you've brought your friend Lord Alexander with you. *Quelle surprise.*"

She placed one arm through each of theirs and walked around the room, effectively trapping them in her grasp.

"You know, my lord, you really ought to grace us with your presence more often. Bath is not such a far jaunt from Somerton. It's quite unfair of you to hole yourself up in that manor house of yours. Why, Lady Kensington just told me how you visit their cottage all the time, and I thought to myself the Kensingtons were not sharing you very well with the rest of us. Of course, she failed to mention that you were also in Bath today, the wretch. I'll have to give her a piece of my mind for not sharing the most delightful news!"

The Kensingtons were in Bath? Alex stopped in his tracks momentarily, but Lady Trent soon pulled him along again. If the Kensingtons were here, then Lady Grace would be as well.

He searched the crowded room to catch a glimpse of her before berating himself. He was supposed to be avoiding her, not seeking her out. Blast, it wasn't any sort of an impossible goal. But how could he avoid thinking about the woman whose eyes had become his constant companion at night, who set his loins aflame with a simple glance?

Lady Trent then turned her attentions from Rotheby to him. "And you, Lord Alexander. Where have you and your family been hiding all this time? I declare, we have seen neither hide nor hair of any of the Hardwickes in an age. His Grace, your brother—he must be out of mourning now, isn't he? You know my youngest daughter, Lady Cecelia, would be just perfect for him. I'm certain she could help him to forget all about his first duchess."

The woman's audacity spawned a glare in him, which he neglected to quell.

"Oh goodness me, there are the Marquess and Marchioness of Coulter. I must speak with them. Please do excuse me, gentlemen. Lady Trent swooped away from them as fast as she had come, and Alex could not be more pleased to see her go.

He eased over to Gil's side to provide him assistance in walking without being too obvious. "Relax, Alex," the older man said. "She's moved on to her next targets. She'll not bother us again, but will simply gossip about us." He smiled weakly. "She's still convinced she will marry me. Ever since Trent passed away five years ago, she's been hounding me. All the woman cares about is money and status." He let out a heaving sigh and shook his head. "I think there are much more important things in this lifetime to focus my attentions on. Now, what did she say about the Kensingtons? Have you spotted your young lady yet?" The twinkle was back in the earl's eyes. "I think I'll go and take some of the waters while you search for better company." Gil straightened and detached himself.

"She is most certainly not *my* young lady," Alex called after his friend. The exasperation in his tone rang out in the grand hall. How would he ever convince himself to stay away from her if no one in his blasted life would cooperate?

"Well, if she is not your young lady yet, perhaps you should do something about it. Time is wasting, my friend. And you never know how much you'll have. If you do nothing, I'm quite sure another man will come along and snatch her out from under your nose. Perhaps a Mr. Maxwell?"

Rotheby walked away, leaving him alone in the center of the huge hall. He turned about, trying to spot anyone he recognized.

While he did find someone he knew, the particular someone he found was *not* anyone he wanted to converse with. Alex turned in the opposite direction, walking away from Lord Overstreet and hoping to find a diversion. The bastard had no sense of decorum, and Alex wanted nothing less than to be associated with the man.

In his haste to escape Overstreet's company, he walked straight into another, far more acceptable, acquaintance. "My apologies, Sir

Laurence! I didn't see you there. I must admit, my distractions got the better of me."

Sir Laurence glanced over Alex's shoulder and gave him a consolatory look before glancing across at Overstreet.

"Lord Rotheby just left me to take the waters," Alex continued. "I'm sure he would love to see you. We were unaware you had come to Bath."

Sir Laurence placed a hand on Alex's shoulder in a show of camaraderie and smiled. "Come, join us. We'll keep you company, and Overstreet will have no reason to interrupt. He and I have never been on the best of terms, to put it mildly." His conspiratorial tone made Alex like the man even more.

He led Alex to where his wife and niece were conversing quietly. "Look who I bumped into, my dears. Our neighbors have also come to Bath."

A brief flash of panic swept across Lady Grace's features, just as soon replaced by a bland expression she showed obvious difficulty in achieving. Apparently, she was no more in favor of their continued association than he.

"Ladies." Alex bowed his head to them.

"Oh, Lord Alexander. How fine it is to see you here. I assume you're not alone? Is Lord Rotheby with you?" Lady Kensington grasped his hand with clear euphoria before scanning the crowds for a glimpse of the earl. However much he may wish to avoid Lady Grace, he was unable to deny her aunt's exuberant display of affection for him.

"Yes, ma'am, he should return shortly. I'm sure you can speak with him as long as you like. Lady Trent was kind enough to inform us she already encountered your family this morning." He coughed beneath his breath.

"Oh, that beast of a woman! Such a dragon. Did she make a go at Lord Rotheby again? I would wager she did." Lady Kensington's face filled with color as she went into a rant about the countess. "She's been after Lord Rotheby since the day her husband died, if not before. I declare—oh! Why, Lord Rotheby, so good of you to join us."

"Lady Kensington, Lady Grace. Sir Laurence." Gil greeted them each in turn. He shook the baronet's hand. "How wonderful to see you all again, and quite surprising, I might add, to see you here in Bath. Are you here for some shopping?" He took a swig of the water in his hands. "I daresay there is little opportunity for that in Somerton, although we do have a few shops that will carry some decent goods on occasion. Lady Grace, you shall find much more variety and quality here. Myself, I came for the waters." He held up the glass, as though to prove his point. "I must say, I'm not very fond of their taste, but they are reputed to have excellent healing qualities."

Gil pulled a face as he took another sip from his glass. "I hope they shall help cure me of this interminable cough. After a few days of drinking from them, I suppose we shall see. If I live that long, that is. Tastes like it has been poisoned."

Alex wondered how many days the man considered a few.

At that moment, Lady Kensington looked across the room. Alex caught a gleam in her eyes the moment she started to speak. He'd be damned if she wasn't up to something again. The blasted woman schemed too much.

"Goodness gracious me, is that Captain and Mrs. Marshall across the way? I do believe it is. Laurence, Lord Rotheby, we simply must go and speak with them. It has been far too long. Hurry along, they are alone at the moment."

She hauled the two men with her. Lady Grace glared at her aunt as the older woman led Sir Laurence and Rotheby away. Then Lady Kensington feigned a sudden remembrance that Alex and her niece had been with them. "Oh dear, we are leaving these two without a thought! How horrid of us."

With a pleading look, she turned to Alex. "My lord, do be a dear and entertain our Gracie for us. We could take the two of you with us to speak with the Marshalls, but I do fear you would both become dreadfully bored in the company of so many older people."

She patted the back of his hand as if he were a good puppy, and turned on her way, leaving her niece seething beneath the surface, presumably because the chit was once again alone in his company. "What a sweet boy he is. He's quite good to us all, Lord Rotheby." Her voice trailed off as they disappeared through the crowded Pump Room.

Lady Grace tried to stifle a groan as she turned to face Alex, but he heard it leak through. They eyed each other warily. How would they ever manage to avoid each other at this rate?

She faced him with a look full of consternation. "I suppose it is my turn to apologize. It seems despite what our wishes may be, my aunt has other plans in mind. I'm very sorry."

What kind of response could Alex give to such a statement? Now he would to be stuck in a very public, very social setting, with a woman who wanted to be anywhere other than with him, for Lord only knew how long. He wanted to make the best of the situation, but honestly didn't have the first inkling how to go about it.

His mind drifted back to a few days before, when she had painted the scene at the river. He wished he could see her like that again, with all the joy and freedom she had experienced. But she only seemed to experience panic, fear, and discomfort while in his general vicinity— at least if she was aware of his presence.

"My lady, I truly believe you had nothing to do with that. There's no need to apologize." He glanced around the room for a few moments as he debated what else to say to her.

She remained silent—a trait he now expected in her but which rankled, nonetheless.

Her silence lasted just a touch too long. His aggravation finally got the better of him and he snapped, "Am I thoroughly disagreeable to you, ma'am? Am I so horrible you are unable to converse with me at all, or is something else wrong? I've apologized to you repeatedly for taking liberties in Lord Rotheby's garden, and for everything else under the sun. I don't know what else I can do to convince you to speak to me. You could at least make some effort at being civil. Lord knows I have made enough efforts for the both of us."

Her eyes grew wide, and then slowly filled with heat. "You…you…how dare you! May I remind you, sir, you are the one who took those very liberties you speak of with me." She stood with her hands haughtily on her hips and her icy eyes turned to deep, blue flames of anger. "I didn't ask you to do so, I didn't encourage you to do so, and I most certainly didn't want you to do so. That was entirely your choice. You've made it abundantly clear you only suffer my presence as a favor to Lord Rotheby and my aunt and uncle. Yet you continue to stare lasciviously at me, leaving me thoroughly baffled as to what, precisely, you want from me."

Her voice rose no more than a whisper as she built a head of steam. Now that she had started, Alex worried she might never stop her tirade. Yet this harangue of hers was intriguing. She suddenly had so very much to say.

He stood in the middle of the Pump Room with his mouth agape, unsure of how to proceed other than allow her to continue her verbal assault. So he did.

"I do not know how to act around you. I've tried to ignore you, as you seemed disinclined to my company, and I therefore assumed you would prefer that reaction. So how, pray tell, am I supposed to react? I've tried to stop you from making a gargantuan mistake, but you seem to have an aversion to accepting my assistance. I would very much like to help you by doing whatever it is you want, but I'm quite incapable of interpreting your thoughts. So, my lord, why don't you tell me what to do and save us both a good deal of trouble? It would alleviate the ache that is rapidly building in my head."

Lady Grace finally took a breath, and waited. By this point, most of the room openly stared at the two of them, some with their jaws hanging open, others seeming to note every word said so they could rush to the nearest gossip and fill them in on these newest, juicy on-dits. Her words, while hardly more than a whisper, seemed to echo in the spacious area.

Alex, too, heard every word she'd hissed at him. Yet he had listened to only a few. The passion she displayed entranced him. She was normally so cold and collected, never losing the veneer of control she kept such tight rein over.

Yet that had all gone by the wayside, and he could think of nothing but how beautiful she looked when angry. Her eyes had flashed and flared, and some strands of her hair had pulled free from the exacting knot and whipped about her face. He wanted to capture her passion, to hold onto it for a later moment when she resumed her cold demeanor.

Alex yearned to touch her.

Maddening. Most men would do anything to avoid infuriating a lady, but he was formulating ways he could do so again. He loved seeing her out of control, reckless and passionate. He wanted more. So much more.

Without a thought to the consequences of his actions or the audience that had gathered, he closed the distance between them and kissed her. Greedy this time, he took more than he gave. One hand fisted in the knot of hair at the nape of her neck and worked to free more of it than was already framing her face, while the other drew her closer to him so he could feel her length against him.

Their audience drew in a collective, scandalized breath, which appeared to register with Lady Grace. She struggled against him, but he would prefer to ignore them. However, she increased her struggles and pushed hard against his chest to separate them. Reluctantly, Alex relinquished his hold.

She took a calming breath, then another, and a third, all while glaring daggers of ice-blue fire into his eyes. Then she reached a hand up and slapped him across his cheek. "You forget yourself, sir," she spat out. Then she turned on her heels and fled, with the Kensingtons close behind.

Alex started to follow her as well, but Gil appeared as if from nowhere and placed a hand on his arm. "Let her go, Alex. This will all be sorted out. Just let her go for now."

So he did.

Twelve

MORTIFICATION WAS NOT nearly a strong enough word to describe Grace's current state.

She couldn't believe the way she'd behaved toward Lord Alexander in the Pump Room—losing control of her emotions. Such behavior was grotesquely inexcusable, compounded by the fact that a room full of people had listened to every word.

And then. Then! Oh, that dreadful man. How dare he kiss her *again*, and this time in public, before a gathered crowd? But what a kiss it was… Even still, how could she have allowed herself to enjoy the kiss, even if for just the briefest moment?

Word would spread throughout Bath about her behavior within the hour. How many peers had been present? Far too many for comfort. She'd be lucky, indeed, if word didn't reach her father in days. Lord help her if that happened. Why, Father could be in Bath before the week was out. Who knew what her fate would be if that happened. She would have to leave before he found her. He would *not* make her marry Lord Barrow, and he would *not* take her baby from her.

Grace was frustrated with herself, with Lord Alexander, with her aunt and uncle…with the whole world. She marched to their hotel, paying no attention to anything around her.

Maybe she should simply pack up her belongings and leave. She didn't know where she could go, but she didn't want her aunt and uncle to have to face the shame of her behavior any more than they already had at this point. Not only that, but she couldn't brook the thought of Father's retribution toward them should he discover they'd been harboring her all this time.

They had opened their home to her, treated her like a daughter— and she had repaid them by behaving like an untamed shrew toward a gentleman in public, and then allowing the man to kiss her before the whole of Bath. And then for her encore, she'd slapped him.

Her behavior was beyond reprehensible. Truly, how could she excuse it other than to say she'd lost her temper? As though she were not already enough of a social outcast, she had now secured the position for eternity.

As she strode through the hotel doors, Uncle Laurence caught up with her. Had he followed her the entire way from the Pump Rooms? She couldn't hide her embarrassment from him, however hard she tried—so she refused to even try.

He took her by the elbow without saying a word and led her toward their suite of rooms. Aunt Dorothea stopped at the front desk of the lobby before she followed behind them, and she closed the door once they were all safely inside. "Oh, my sweet dear, are you quite all right? Such an ordeal you and Lord Alexander went through, having a lover's spat like that in public!"

Lover's spat? What on earth was her aunt concocting now? Grace knew one thing—it wasn't good, whatever it was.

"But don't work yourself up over it, dear. I'm sure it will all be worked out in no time. He's an honorable gentleman, Gracie. He will do right by you." Aunt Dorothea tucked one of Grace's stray hairs behind her ear and patted her on the cheek. "I've ordered us all a bit of luncheon. They'll bring it in momentarily, and then we'll have a nice, calming meal. Then Grace, you and I will go shopping. After all, that is why we are in Bath. We must be sure to get you some decent clothing. So never you mind about all of what just happened. Everything will be quite all right in no time. Won't it, Laurence?"

"What love? Oh, yes. Everything will be fine. I'll make certain of it."

Panic squeezed Grace's chest, making it difficult to breathe. The set of her jaw soon caused her physical pain, so she made a conscious effort at unclenching it. What could they possibly mean? How could her uncle make certain everything would be fine?

Nothing could be fine.

Unless, of course, she left. Then their lives could go back to normal, and they could pretend they had never allowed such an ungrateful relative into their home to disgrace them.

"Aunt, Uncle, I...I think it would be best for you both if I were to leave you. I can go somewhere and seek employment. If Father hears of this...well, he will certainly not take the news kindly, I'm afraid, and I don't know what he will do. Surely the scandal will die out faster if I were no longer with you, so—"

Aunt Dorothea huffed. "Scandal? Oh, pish. A touch of scandal never hurt anyone, lovey. Now I'll hear no more of this nonsense of you leaving us. You will not leave us if I have to tie you to the bedpost. And don't believe for a moment I wouldn't do it."

Grace believed her, all right. The panic in her chest, that anxious, fluttering tightness, threatened to swallow her whole. She had to leave them. If only they would understand. But then, they'd never seen Father in one of his rages. They couldn't know.

"Now, why don't we have a lovely luncheon and then get on with our shopping this afternoon, hmm? Oh! I haven't told you yet, in all this excitement. We'll be going to the Assembly Room tonight, Gracie. There is an evening of dancing and entertainment planned, and we've been invited to attend. Of course, I accepted. Did you happen to bring an appropriate gown? If not, never fear. We'll see what Madam Yeats has ready-made to suit."

A dance? An evening of entertainments? Grace shook her head. If word wasn't already on the way to London after the morning's episode, surely being seen at such an event would ensure calamity.

A knock at the door signaled their luncheon had arrived, and Uncle Laurence allowed the servants to enter and deliver the food.

"Oh good, we'll be able to eat quickly and be on our way then. We'll begin at the linen drapers and choose our fabrics before we go to see Madam Yeats. Now, after we visit Madam Yeats, we'll also visit the haberdashers to obtain ribbons and the like. You'll certainly need a good deal of those, in order to match the new fabrics for your gowns. Oh, gracious, this afternoon will keep us quite busy. Be sure you eat up. You'll need plenty of energy."

Only after placing food in her mouth did Aunt Dorothea's endless train of plans cease for long enough to allow Grace to digest all that had happened. She forced the lump forming in her throat down, at the same time as she attempted to fight off the sudden wave of nausea that consumed her. Her aunt and uncle surely only wanted the best for her, but why, oh *why* could they not understand the necessity of staying away from society? Of course, they didn't seem to grasp even the simpler need for staying away from Lord Alexander, so why should she expect them to understand this more dire need?

It grew more difficult to be in the man's company, because as hard as she tried to dislike him, she enjoyed being around him. He created feelings in her she'd never experienced before—strange and wonderful feelings—that would make it so much more difficult for her if he ever discovered the truth.

She ate in silence and searched her mind for a way out of this convoluted mess—finding few solutions, if any. When Aunt Dorothea decided it was time to begin their shopping, she went along, even though all she wanted to do was crawl under her bed sheets and never come out.

ALEX PACED THE floor of the hotel sitting room he shared with Gil. He was furious with himself. Why had he allowed himself to get so caught up in the moment, watching the passion build in Lady Grace as she had berated him? He hadn't even paid attention to what she said to him, so he had no idea whether he deserved such a tongue lashing or not. All he could think was how lovely she looked when in pique, and how he wanted to see her that way more often.

So he kissed her. Again. And this time, with an audience.

He had sullied her reputation. She was ruined. If he didn't offer for her, and if she didn't accept, there would be no possible repair for her character.

He had spent the last hour and a half with Gil trying to discover a way he could help Lady Grace keep her reputation without marriage, since she seemed so disinclined to any attachment with him whatsoever, and since she knew nothing about Priscilla and Harry. But there was no alternative.

All of his good intentions were out with the wash. He'd tried to avoid her but failed. He'd tried to ignore his thoughts about her and failed. He'd intended to discover who he was as a man, what he wanted to do with his life, and how he could continue caring for his two responsibilities before he settled down to wife and family. He had only just begun to make progress in those areas, so he was well on his way to yet another failure.

Perhaps he should have stayed in London with his family and allowed Mama to do her worst. At least then he likely wouldn't have permanently and irreparably tarnished an innocent young lady's reputation.

He couldn't believe his own weakness when it came to Lady Grace. He never reacted this way with a woman or lost his ability to think clearly solely from being in a woman's presence. He accepted their affections when they were offered, but never forced his attentions on a woman—and he had always been too gentlemanly to kiss a gently-bred lady in full view of half a city before.

But this had not been just a kiss. It was hot and raw and needy. Lady Grace gave as much as she took this time, at least initially— before she realized their performance had an eager audience.

Perhaps marriage to her would not be so dreadful. They would certainly have a great deal of passion. There could be no doubt about that. A marriage to Lady Grace would never be boring.

"The fact remains I still haven't settled into a responsible and respectable life," he admonished himself, "and I have no property. Good lord, I've never even met her father. What if he doesn't approve?" Oh, God. Her father might not approve. But it was too late to worry about such things now. A wedding must be planned with all due haste.

Gil had, of course, heard his entire monologue. "I should think your first course of action would be to speak with Sir Laurence. He cannot grant you permission to marry his niece, but he might be able to aid your cause with her father. You should speak with him today, while she is shopping with Lady Kensington."

He broke his stride to consider Gil's advice. "Yes. Yes, I'll speak with Sir Laurence today. And then I must make the situation clear to her. She has to understand there is no alternative other than ruin." In other words, there was *no* alternative.

He would make her understand. She *must* become his wife.

"I suppose then I'll travel to London tomorrow to speak with her father. Gil, what if he finds me unworthy? What happens then? I don't believe she has come into her majority yet. She must do what her father wishes." A new thought struck him now. "He could already have an agreement with another man. She may already be betrothed!" Endless potential problems coursed through his mind. "Dare I consider Gretna Greene?"

A fit of coughs seized Gil, and Alex stopped pacing and rushed to the older man's side. Once the coughing subsided, Gil implored, "You'll worry yourself into creating problems that don't exist. Stop this claptrap at once." Gil took hold of his arm and pulled him down to sit in an armchair next to him. "You'll go this afternoon to speak with Sir Laurence. He'll arrange for you to speak with Lady Grace before the night is through. We'll pack tonight and be on our way to London in the morning."

"We? What is this *we*?" No way would he take the earl with him on such a journey in his state of health. "I must go to London, but the travel is too hard on you. You should stay here, take the waters, handle your business. I am certain the Kensingtons would be glad to return to Somerton with you when you are ready to go." The man was in no shape for the journey, and he didn't want his friend's health on his conscience, should it take a turn for the worse.

"I will not have you treat me like a child. I was a grown man when your father was still younger than you are now. I make my own decisions. I've decided to accompany you to Town."

Alex tried to interrupt, but Gil's hand stayed him.

"I'm not finished. This is one of the most important journeys you'll ever make in your life, and I want to take part in it. I can handle my business in London better than in Bath. We'll travel in the morning. You will not change my mind. I'm coming with you."

The set of Rotheby's jaw proved no amount of argument would dissuade him. Alex's heart dropped. With his current delicate health, Gil may never make it back to Somerton. But he would respect his friend's wishes. Nothing else could be done.

GRACE WAS EXHAUSTED—both emotionally and physically—yet Aunt Dorothea still insisted she attend the entertainment that evening at the Assembly Room.

She'd spent the day before in the carriage traveling to Bath with a constant case of nausea. Then this day. Oh, what a day it had been. It had started with the scene with Lord Alexander, followed by shopping that seemed to never end. Aunt Dorothea had found the fabrics at the first linen draper's unsatisfactory, so they visited three more before she found enough variety. Then they had gone to see Madam Yeats to order new dresses made. This, of course, required discussion about any number of patterns and designs, debates over which fabric should be used for which design, and endless chatter over all sorts of other details Grace would have preferred be made for her. After all of that, she had been *encouraged* to try on any number of gowns and select one for the entertainment that evening.

The first was too loose, the second too long, the next made her skin look sallow, the next too pale—the list of Aunt Dorothea's complaints went on far too long. Finally, after she tried on the tenth gown, they found one everyone could agree on.

Everyone, that is, except Grace.

The gown appeared too expensive for her tastes. She much preferred something very simple and plain. But she was overruled. She would wear a gown of silvery-blue gauze with lace accents. Madam Yeats and Aunt Dorothea, as well as a number of other patrons in the shops, were all in agreement. The silver made all the other gowns look like peasant frocks in comparison.

With all of their business completed at Madam Yeats's shop, they had headed to the haberdashery for ribbons and trimmings. As with the earlier visits to the linen drapers, Aunt Dorothea was not satisfied with the selection in the first haberdasher they visited, so they were forced to visit multiple shops. Grace simply must have the best ribbons to place in her hair and on her bonnets. Nothing short of the best finery would do for Aunt Dorothea. And of course, following the visits to the various haberdashery shops, Aunt Dorothea had declared they simply must also see a milliner. Grace's supply of bonnets would not suit. Following their previously set pattern, visiting one milliner was not sufficient for her aunt, so they made multiple stops.

Finally, after what she was certain must have been three days' worth of shopping all rolled into a single afternoon, they returned to the hotel for a spot of tea before they dressed for the evening.

Grace jumped as she entered their suite and saw Lord Alexander seated across from Uncle Laurence in the parlor. The two men immediately rose upon their entrance. Servants brought in countless boxes and bags full of the purchases she and her aunt had made throughout the day.

Lord Alexander glanced at her and smiled briefly before turning back to her uncle. "Thank you again, Laurence. You've been most kind and exceedingly helpful. I'll take my leave of you now." He inclined his head to the ladies before moving to the hallway.

Grace sent a questioning look to her uncle from across the room as she stepped aside so Lord Alexander could walk past her. He'd called her uncle by his given name. No one but a close friend ever called him by his given name. Close friends, or *family*. Oh, dear.

"Ladies, I do hope you have had luck with your shopping excursion." Lord Alexander bowed his head to them again and walked away.

Aunt Dorothea, as usual, became a flurry of words and motion. "Oh Laurence, we did have the most excellent luck today. I do believe we bought everything Gracie will need. And her gown for this evening! Oh, you will not believe your eyes when you see her in it. She is simply stunning. I didn't think she could be more beautiful than she already is, but I was quite wrong."

She seated herself on the sofa and unpacked bags and boxes, turning the parlor into a state of disarray. "And you've visited with Lord Alexander. How delightful. I do hope your meeting with him was productive."

There appeared to be some underlying hint to him, a secret code only those two could interpret. Grace was unaware of any business her uncle might have with Lord Alexander, but she sensed anything it could be would not meet her definition of *good*, especially since the man left and called her uncle 'Laurence.'

"Yes my dear, our meeting went very well. Everything's in order."

Aunt Dorothea sighed and sank back into the cushions.

"Do you intend to show me all of your purchases, my dear, or would these be better unpacked in Grace's chamber?"

Grace flushed furiously when she looked down. The items her aunt had unpacked were the inexpressibles they had purchased.

"Oh, lud. I don't know what I could have been thinking." Aunt Dorothea bundled the items again and handed them to Grace with an apology in her eyes. "Dear, you should go ahead and prepare yourself for this evening. There is no rest for the weary today. Off with you, now." Aunt Dorothea shooed Grace into her bedchamber, carrying all of the purchases which she would need to dress for the evening.

She dreaded attending the function. After what had transpired at the Pump Room that morning, she wanted to be anywhere but at an event full of gossips. She would receive looks of pity, of disgust, of shame. After the day she'd just experienced, she simply didn't think she could handle it.

But she couldn't disappoint her aunt. She dressed herself with Tess's help, making certain everything was as it should be. The maid styled her hair, winding the new silver ribbons through plaits and curls and giving her a more complicated coiffure than Grace was accustomed to wearing.

She almost couldn't recognize herself in the cheval mirror. The silver gown caused her eyes to sparkle in the candlelight, looking even more silvery than they typically did. Perhaps the ladies at Madam Yeats's shop had been right to insist on the silver gown after all. She certainly *felt* more beautiful than she could ever remember feeling. It was quite irregular, to think of herself as beautiful or pretty.

Just as quickly, she pushed the thoughts aside. She had no business thinking such thoughts. She was a ruined woman. No man should think those things about her, so why should she think them of herself?

The one thing which might make this evening bearable was the possibility she wouldn't see Lord Alexander. If she had any luck at all, he'd either spend the evening with Lord Rotheby or seek some other entertainment. Grace hoped he wouldn't be there. She was ill prepared to face the scandal before society, but the man who had led her to such rash deportment as well. It would be more than she could bear.

She took one last glance at herself in the mirror before she rejoined her aunt and uncle in the parlor. Aunt Dorothea was also dressed for an evening out, but Uncle Laurence had not changed his attire from earlier in the day. "Uncle, won't you join us at the Assembly Room tonight?" Oh please, let him come too. If Uncle Laurence was there, Grace could feel more at her ease. He could rein in Aunt Dorothea.

"I'm sorry, Gracie. I've promised to keep company with Lord Rotheby this evening. It seems Lord Alexander has other plans, and he didn't wish to leave the earl alone."

Her heart pounded in her chest. What other plans did Lord Alexander have for that evening? Was that the reason for his earlier visit with her uncle—simply to request his assistance with Lord Rotheby? Please let it be something as simple and entirely unremarkable as that.

She hoped beyond hope his plans did *not* include visiting the Assembly Room.

But she also desperately hoped they did.

Thirteen

As ALEX WALKED into the Assembly Room that evening, he made an effort to be seen. Quite unusual behavior for him, it was true. But tonight he would make an exception.

After the morning's incident, he must make a very public show of not only being seen, but also being seen *with her*. He wanted everyone present to understand there was a connection between them. Of course, creating such a connection became his primary task for the evening.

Sir Laurence assured Alex that he and Lady Kensington were in full support of his efforts. He also corroborated that, as suspected, Lady Grace had yet to achieve her majority at only nineteen years of age, and therefore was at the mercy of her father. He'd asked Alex to not bother with seeking the approval of her father, as the man had taken a very standoffish approach to raising his daughter. It would be best, Sir Laurence said, to take her to Gretna Greene and be done with it, and then let Lord Chatham know after the fact.

But Alex would not hear of it. If he was going to marry, he would do it the right way. Tomorrow, he was heading for London to ask the man for the right to marry his daughter. It was the only decent thing to do. She deserved far more than just decency.

So tonight, for once, he would play the part of the dandy, if only in terms of his attire—but he did it for her. Everything must be perfect. Nothing less would do. For a brief moment, he wished he had a quizzing glass with him, but quashed the thought as soon as it came. That would be a touch too much.

He'd dressed meticulously for the evening. His buff breeches and waistcoat were spotless, and set off nicely against the black of his overcoat. Thomas had shined his Hessian boots twice so they would gleam in the candlelight. His beaver hat sat atop his head at a precise angle, not perfectly straight, but also not fully askance.

Alex arrived fashionably late, to be certain Lady Kensington would have already arrived with his target in tow. The ballroom was filled with a large crowd. Dancing had yet to begin, but the orchestra was warming their instruments on the dais as fashionable people milled about. As he entered the hall, he bowed low to the Master of Ceremonies. Alex passed the man his card and waited for the formal announcement. He wanted as many people present as possible to take notice.

"Lord Alexander Hardwicke!" the Master of Ceremonies boomed out over the crush of revelers. An instant hush encompassed the hall, followed by a growing series of murmurs. His plan, it seemed, was already at work. No doubt they were talking about him.

"Thank you, sir. You are most kind." Alex pretended indifference to the hushed whispers, the covert stares, and the blatant open-mouthed gawks, taking it all in, but showing no sign of caring. Surely this meant word of his exchange with Lady Grace had spread to everyone present, and would soon fall on the ears of those unaware. "Might you inform me of the whereabouts of Lady Grace Abernathy?"

The Master of Ceremonies stared at him, open mouthed. He must also be aware. "My lord, I cannot be certain, but I believe she and her aunt are presently in the ballroom." He held a pained expression on his face, a clear indication that he had told the truth, although he found it distasteful.

Had Alex attained a rakehell's reputation since the morning? Excellent. Even better than he could have asked. He crossed through the octagon room and into the ballroom, gliding through the crowd and nodding to acquaintances along the way. Once in the ballroom, he scanned the room for Lady Grace. He needed to speak with her before someone else drew him into conversation.

Lady Kensington found him before he found her. "Lord Alexander! I hoped to see you here this evening." She pushed through the crowd, tugging a struggling Lady Grace along behind her—more dazzling and bewitching than he had ever seen her before. She looked like an angel, all aglow beneath the warm candlelight. They arrived at his side in record time; crowds posed no deterrence to Lady Kensington. "You are such a dear man. My Laurence had a pleasant visit with you this afternoon, he tells me, and hopes you will bring yourself around to us far more often. I must agree with him, as well." She looked as though she might talk to him for hours if he didn't stop her.

If looks could kill, Lady Grace's aunt wouldn't be alive very long. Even as daggers glared through the younger woman's eyes, he'd never seen anything so beautiful. "Why thank you, Lady Kensington. And good evening to you, Lady Grace."

She wore a high-waisted silver gown that shimmered in the candlelight to match her eyes. Ribbons twirled through hair dressed in a much more fashionable manner than her traditional knot. Curls spilled free and ran riot at the back of her head. A few tendrils wisped along her temples and at the nape of her neck, begging him to be touched. He anchored his arms to his side to keep from doing so.

She looked ravishing.

The orchestra had finished their preparations, and dancing was set to begin. "I do hope I'm not too late to request your hand for a dance."

She looked horrified at the prospect of dancing with him, with her jaw dropping almost to the floor. He thought she would deny him, but Lady Kensington interrupted before she could speak. "Splendid! I'm afraid she's already granted the first two dances to other gentlemen, sir. But the third dance, which," she said with a wink, "I understand to be a waltz, is free. Gracie, please pencil him in on your card."

"Aunt, I haven't been approved to waltz. I dare not defy convention in such a manner."

Blast. She may have found her excuse to avoid him, at least for that particular set.

"Oh bosh, Gracie. No one in Bath cares what Almack's dictates. You know how to waltz, don't you? Nothing else is required here, my dear. You'll waltz with Lord Alexander this evening." Lady Kensington positively beamed over her success.

A tall, lanky youth with pimply skin joined them at that moment. He looked to be hardly out of leading strings. Good. This one should pose no threat.

"Oh, Lord Warringly. You are precisely on time for your set." Lady Kensington's nose wrinkled, and Alex debated whether it was due to pleasure or distaste for the young viscount.

"Lady Grace? I do believe this is my dance." Warringly escorted her away before she could go against her aunt and deny Alex his waltz. She glanced back over her shoulder at him with a look of chagrin as she walked across the ballroom.

"You sly fox. You look positively smashing tonight, my lord," Lady Kensington said, her voice filled with amusement. "During your waltz, I'll look the other way should you decide to take her for a walk in the gardens or something of that nature. I'll not interfere."

His nerves built as he anticipated what was to come. "Thank you, ma'am. However, I don't believe it would be in your niece's best interests to be caught sneaking off alone with me at this point—not until after an announcement is made and her father has approved the match." He couldn't bear to cause her more damage than he already had. "I don't believe we'll stray out of sight."

Tonight everyone would see. That was just how it must be.

But the pleasing thought of taking Lady Grace somewhere alone nagged at him and burned his mind.

GRACE DANCED A country dance with Viscount Warringly and thought all the while about Lord Alexander. The young viscount attempted to make polite conversation with her when they were close enough to converse, but had little more to discuss than general comments on the weather. Grace didn't try overmuch to participate. The day had exhausted her, and she wanted nothing more than her bed.

Even worse than her exhaustion, she was mortified to have her aunt drag her into the public eye so soon after the morning's scandal. If her aunt and uncle insisted she stay with them and not seek employment, wouldn't it be better to keep her from society and gossipmongers? For once in her life, Grace thought perhaps her father was right. His enforced isolation might be useful for some things in life, at least.

She wondered how long it would be before word of the incident at the Pump Room reached him. If he thought her a whore before, what would he possibly think after hearing how she had *allowed* Lord Alexander Hardwicke to kiss her? He would be furious.

She needed to forget any daydreams of an eligible match, and leave to seek employment, irrespective of the Kensingtons' adamant insistence that she stay. But Grace had no desire to hurt them. She'd hate to lose the relationship she had recently forged with them. But as much as the loss would hurt, she knew there would be more to gain. She could escape Father's wrath, protect the Kensingtons from him, and keep her child, working as a nurse or a governess somewhere.

But then there was Lord Alexander. Why could the man not understand it would be easier for them both if he left her alone? After this morning, Grace had no doubt he was forming an emotional attachment to her, despite her best efforts to allay him. And try as she might to ignore him, she thought of him more often every day. He consumed her.

It had to stop. She was unsuitable for him. Grace set her mind to dissuade him tonight.

The dance ended, and Viscount Warringly led her to Aunt Dorothea, who held out a glass of lemonade for her.

"Thank you, my lady. It was a pleasure." The viscount inclined his pock-marked head toward her and then left.

"He is quite a young lad, isn't he?" Aunt Dorothea wrinkled her nose toward him again as he walked away. "I know it's not his fault, but a few more years will do that boy a great deal of good. Oh dear, I hope you didn't fancy him, Gracie. I don't think he is the one for you."

"Aunt, you and I both realize it doesn't matter who I might or might not fancy. Please stop trying to match me with some eligible gentleman, as I'm entirely ineligible." She sent her aunt a pleading look across the glass of lemonade as she sipped. "A match for me, right now, is just not possible. You have to accept the truth."

Her next partner came to claim Grace for his set. Lord Cecil Fullerton was a handsome man with broad shoulders and a good deal of height. Everything about him suited the current fashion, from the cut of his hair to that of his superfine coat. A score of young ladies eyed her jealously. He must be quite the catch in Bath.

Lord Cecil bowed deeply to Aunt Dorothea. "Lady Kensington, if you'll allow me, I'll leave you bereft of your charge for a short while." He turned his pompous smile to Grace and placed her hand on his arm. "Shall we?"

He led her to the dance floor, which soon filled with couples. She took her place across from him. When the music started, Grace attempted to fix her attention on the man before her, but soon wished she were dancing with anyone else.

"You do realize you are the envy of every young lady in the room at this moment, don't you?" He flashed her a grin, but she only saw teeth. Perfect teeth. Perfectly straight, perfectly white, perfect teeth.

"Is that so? Hmm." The man would receive no compliments from her, no matter how he fished for them.

"Quite. I must inform you, I'm the most eligible bachelor in the room. Many would go so far as to say the most handsome, as well." He brushed a hand over his waistcoat—again, a flawless hand—and drew her attention to the peacock colors adorning him.

"I see." Grace looked down the line of dancers for anyone to distract him. "Oh, look. The lady over there with the fair hair and aubergine gown is attempting to catch your attention."

He followed her gaze across the hall. "Ah yes, the Dowager Viscountess Burkes. She has been after me since before her husband passed." Lord Cecil winked at the woman and pursed his lips, feigning a kiss in her direction. "Pay her no mind, my lady. I have no desire to taste someone's leftovers. She will be no competition for you in winning my favor."

Grace shuddered as they separated to dance with a nearby pair for a few figures. She had no idea what the ladies who envied her could see in him. She only saw an utter popinjay.

They came together again. She steeled herself for another round of revulsion.

"Do you admire my cravat?" He pointed to a *perfectly* knotted neck cloth when she did not immediately respond.

"What was that? Oh, yes. It's fine." Good gracious, would he never speak of anything but himself? His pomposity knew no bounds.

"I purchased the fabric from a trader in India. He has the most luxurious silks and muslins you have ever seen." He waited while they formed a figure too far apart for her to hear. "When I brought the fabric home, I had the best seamstress in all of England sew me some new cravats. I daresay they are the envy of every gentleman in Bath. Probably all of England. None could be finer."

"Yes, it's fine, my lord." How much longer would the set last? The man was objectionable in every way imaginable. Her exhaustion didn't aid his cause either, as she was soon cranky and irritable.

When the set finally came to a close, Grace was parched and desperate to take her glass of lemonade from her aunt so she could find somewhere she could sit to rest for a few moments. However, she would find no such respite. Surely Aunt Dorothea had promised the waltz to Lord Alexander on her behalf, blast the meddlesome woman. He would be displeased if she disappeared, and the infuriating man would, in all likelihood, follow her to claim his dance.

Butany plans she may have formed were moot. Lord Alexander stood adjacent to Aunt Dorothea and rendered any escape plan impossible.

Lord Cecil turned to Grace. "I see your next partner has arrived to claim your hand. Sadly, he's not as handsome as me. I suppose you must suffer through his attentions for the duration of the waltz." His voice drifted, and surely Lord Alexander had heard every word. Lord Cecil inclined his head to the party and took his leave. She couldn't have been more thankful to see him go.

Except she now had to face a waltz with Lord Alexander.

Perhaps she could make him understand, finally, that he should place his attentions elsewhere. How she would manage it, other than stating it as plainly as possible, she didn't know. He hadn't heeded any of her prior hints, however plain she thought she had been. The time had arrived for blunt truth.

Grace took a deep breath to calm herself and faced him. Aunt Dorothea beamed in anticipation. Why was her aunt so keen to see an attachment between them? Why could she not see things as they truly were?

Lord Alexander, however, looked ready to strike the next person who dared to cough in his presence. He took a step toward her and bowed his head. "Would you like some refreshment before we waltz?" Without awaiting her response, he grasped her arm and led her toward a table laden with lemonade, gently but firmly pulling her along with him with a sense of both urgency and possession.

She did need something to quench her thirst, so she allowed him to continue, weighing her options along the way as every eye in the ballroom watched. Grace simply must make herself heard tonight.

She couldn't delay any longer. He was acting like a lovesick puppy, which she emphatically could not condone.

He handed her a glass of lemonade with his free hand, the other still firmly grasping her elbow.

Another speech was on her tongue, similar to her diatribe from that morning. But as she opened her mouth to speak, he pulled against her and hauled her through the crowd. She dug her heels into the floor and tried to remove the vise of his fingers against her arm, but she was powerless to stop her progress.

"My lord. Stop this at once."

He paid her protests no heed and stubbornly tugged her behind him through an alcove to the veranda. He looked around, and then kept going until they reached a secluded area. Apparently, he had no intention of repeating the morning's performance before of an audience. Fine. Grace intended to give him a piece of her mind, no matter how many or how few people witnessed.

He had to listen. He must understand.

She couldn't think what would happen if the man refused to listen to reason.

ALEX HAD WATCHED Lady Grace dance with her first two partners of the evening while trying to dissuade the jealousy. Surely he was only jealous due to the fact that he intended to take her as his wife. The sooner it took place, the better.

He did not have feelings for her—nothing serious, at least. He liked her. She fascinated him. Marriage to her would be at the very least a tolerable affair, with a fair amount of passion. Alex could imagine no woman he would prefer to spend his life married to, so that likely played into his feelings of envy.

Any reasonable man would be jealous if the woman he intended to marry danced with and smiled at other men. His reaction had been perfectly rational.

But when Lord Cecil, the deuced dandy, had taken her out onto the ballroom floor, Alex cringed. The infernal man was insufferable—almost as bad as Maxwell. Cecil Fullerton rankled on Alex's last nerve, and he could not hide his distaste for the man, however hard he tried. Granted, he didn't quite try.

He returned to his position beside Lady Kensington. The woman could talk the ear off anyone, but at least she had a sense of humor. He couldn't allow himself to become distracted. She spoke to him— she must have spoken to him—but he paid her no attention.

He could think of nothing but Lady Grace.

Watching her dance with Lord Cecil had been pure and utter torture. The bastard kept making vapid attempts to smile at her, obviously in search of compliments. Lady Grace played the part as well as could be expected, but by this point, he knew her expressions well—and she was quickly growing annoyed. Good! Alex was glad the fop annoyed her.

Maybe he had no reason for jealousy, after all.

But if she was annoyed…well, Lord Cecil had no right to cause her such aggravation. The abhorrent dolt. Alex had to clench his jaw shut.

Various gentlemen came to him, attempting to engage him in conversation. Alex wasn't interested. Not to be boorish, but he couldn't suffer their simpering thoughts at this point. He needed to focus his energies elsewhere, such as on the dolt who was leering at his soon-to-be-fiancée while dancing with her.

Of all the insufferable fools! Alex was fuming. Smoke must be billowing from his ears, and he was quite certain his face easily matched the redness of his hair. He could scarcely remember the last time he had been so uncontrollably, treacherously angered.

After the set finished, which felt as though it filled the span of three sets, the nit-wit Lord Cecil finally escorted Alex's future bride back to her aunt's side. He then had the audacity to say within Alex's hearing, "I see your next partner has arrived to claim your hand.

Sadly, he is not as handsome as me. I suppose you must suffer through his attentions for the duration of the waltz."

Suffer through his attentions, indeed. Alex would gladly suffer Lord Cecil through a fist to the jaw. Once the half-wit left, Alex's desperation to speak with Lady Grace alone consumed him. He needed her alone. Now.

"Lady Grace, would you like some refreshment before we waltz?" Anything to find privacy.

He didn't wait for a response. If he had, he knew she would say no, the minx. Or perhaps she would remember her aunt was holding a glass of lemonade for her and decline to go with him. Alex took her by the wrist and stalked off to a refreshment stand.

He took a glass of lemonade and passed it to her, never removing his grip on her arm. He would prefer port, himself, or perhaps scotch. Something to clear his head of all the cobwebs.

Other people leaned in, seemingly attempting to overhear any snippets of conversation between them. What would he have to do to find some privacy? Blast it, why had he thought his idea so ingenious, so brilliant to face the scandal in the open, to have their betrothal witnessed by the masses?

But that had all changed now.

He needed some seclusion with her, and he needed it now. He pulled her behind him and searched for anywhere they could be alone. The card room and the octagon room were filled with people trying to avoid the crush of the ballroom. There was nowhere acceptable indoors.

Lady Grace struggled against him, digging her heels in and trying to pull her arm free. His strength far outweighed hers, so he had no fear of her success. He would never physically hurt her, or any woman. But he needed to deal with things right now. Later would not work.

When her attempts to pull herself free failed, she called out to him, "My lord. Stop this at once." Alex ignored her protests and continued his march toward privacy.

The weather was quite pleasant that evening—a little breeze, a few clouds, but no rain. He looked around the room and found an alcove with a door leading to the veranda. Perfect. He would take the chit outside, away from the prying eyes of chaperones and gossips.

They needed to have a conversation, and they would have it tonight, by God. Right now.

There were things Lady Grace must come to understand.

Fourteen

ALEX PULLED LADY Grace through the gardens to find somewhere they could talk in private. The simple task wouldn't be so impossible if she would cease fighting him like a banshee. At least she had finally stopped ordering him to leave her alone. They would have a damned audience if she continued.

He wound through the walks of the garden, leading her by the arm. After countless twists and turns in their path, they were blessedly far enough away from prying eyes and ears to have their discussion. But where to start? He hadn't taken the time to decide how he should go about informing her of his decision. It was obvious they must marry, but Lady Grace didn't strike him as a woman desperate to be married to him. For that matter, she was loath to remain in his company.

A simple statement of the facts would be the best course of action. "My lady, we'll marry with all due haste. I'll travel to London tomorrow to speak with your father and to procure a special license."

She stared up at him lifeless glaze cast over her eyes.

Her reticence was hardly unusual, however. He pressed on. "I spoke with your uncle this afternoon, and he assures me he and your aunt are both quite pleased with the match. Our marriage will take place at the rectory in Somerton as soon as I return."

She may not be leaping for joy, but at least she was not in a rage. Delivering the details without any added fluff had clearly been the best choice, after all. Relief swept over him, and the tightness in his chest relaxed.

"I don't yet have an estate of my own, but I promise you'll want for nothing. After a brief honeymoon abroad, I'll procure property." He wished he had finished his search and could move her immediately into his home. Women liked having a home of their own—he was certain of it.

She frowned up at him with a blank look. So far, so good.

"Where would you prefer to spend most of our time? We can find a home in London if you wish to be close to your father. Or I can begin my search somewhere closer to Somerton, near your aunt and uncle. I would like to see to all of your comforts." Since he hadn't yet sorted out all of the logistics involved in Priscilla and Harry's situation, he'd just have to suit it around whatever Lady Grace preferred. She would be his wife, after all.

Her glassy eyes now stared through him. She showed no reaction that she heard a single utterance from him. Alex wanted some reaction. Anything was better than nothing. He needed to know she would be happy with him, that she was satisfied with the arrangements he'd made for her future.

"My lady, I know this is all very sudden. I know we haven't had a traditional courtship or romance. But under the circumstances—"

"Under the circumstances?" she roared at him.

Alex's eyes flew wide. Well, he'd finally provoked a response, at least. She poked a finger in his chest, and he took a few steps backward from the force of her anger.

"Under the very circumstances you've caused, do you mean? You egomaniacal, insufferable brute!"

This was not quite the reaction Alex had hoped for. He never imagined she would be anything less than thrilled to have him protect her honor.

"You didn't listen to a word I said to you yesterday, did you? Then you had the audacity to kiss me in *public*, with half of the Quality of Bath in attendance. And now—now? You have the nerve to drag me quite against my will away from my chaperone, and *inform* me we shall marry with 'all due haste.' Of all the pompous, ignorant boors, how did I become so unlucky in life to be saddled with you?" She had built such a head of steam during her tirade against him he could imagine her exhaling flames toward him. Against his better judgment, he found it quite attractive on her.

Perhaps his tactic of telling her of his arrangements instead of asking her wasn't the brightest idea, but it was too late now. "I've bungled this, haven't I? I apologize, yet again."

They stared at each other for a few moments and she continued to fume. Her eyes were the loveliest crystal shards, much like diamonds. They mesmerized him.

"My lady, might I have the honor of your hand as my wife?" She would surely warm to him now that he asked instead of informing her.

"No, you may not. I believe I made myself abundantly clear on the matter. You should leave me alone, my lord. I'm not a suitable bride for you." She wrung her hands together in obvious agitation.

He recoiled from her words. Not a suitable bride? He knew they didn't always see things the same way, but she was obviously well-born, well-bred.

"What, pray tell, makes you unsuitable?" She could never convince him to change his mind. Such an answer was an utter impossibility.

Her agitation grew as he watched. She shifted from foot to foot and he thought she might rip one of her hands free from her arm. She took her time to formulate an answer. He could almost see the thoughts fly through her mind. He fought to keep his temper in check as he waited what seemed an inordinate amount of time for her answer.

She still did not respond and his temper exploded. "Are you only an unsuitable bride for me, or are you an entirely unsuitable bride?" He only allowed a moment before he continued. "Answer me, Grace!"

Her eyes widened. She backed away from him and turned to flee before he placed a restraining hand on her shoulder. She flinched at his touch. Did she think he would strike her? Alex took a deep breath as he turned her to face him. She wouldn't meet his eyes.

"I will not hurt you, Grace. I'll never raise a hand to you in anger. You have no need to fear me, but I require an answer to my questions." He prayed she would trust him with the answer. He needed to know.

She finally raised her eyes to his, wide as saucers and on the verge of tears. "I—I cannot marry you, my lord. Please do not ask me for more. That is all the answer I can give." She trembled beneath his fingers.

"But you must marry me. I've compromised you. Your reputation—"

"My *reputation* is already in ruins, my lord, and I was compromised long before we ever met. It's the reason I'm visiting my aunt and uncle. There's nothing you can do to repair it. Please. Do not ask me for more."

She tried to escape again, but he wouldn't allow it. A silent rage, far more dangerous than his previous temper, seethed beneath the surface. Someone else had compromised her? And then left her alone to deal with the ostracism?

He yearned to face the man responsible. Alex had two younger sisters—he knew all too well the difficulties they faced in a world dominated by men. The need to set things right for her became an ache in his stomach.

Why had her father done nothing? Chatham should have insisted the bastard marry her. And if that man did not comply, he should have issued a challenge. But instead, he had sent Grace away to live with her relatives and hide from the gossip.

To say the *ton* could be less than understanding over matters such as this would be an understatement. She would never find a decent match. All of this new information reinforced his determination to marry her. She had now been compromised twice—her reputation would never survive the gossip mill.

"Grace, sweetheart, that is precisely why you must marry me. You need the protection of my name." He bordered on pleading with her before she interrupted him again.

"There is no protection you can give me. It's too late." She refused to face him, staring instead at the trees behind his shoulder.

The obstinate chit didn't know what was good for her. Alex's fury continued to grow. He was angry at the cur that compromised her and ran. He was furious with her father for not forcing the recreant to do what was right. He was irate with Grace for being so headstrong. He'd mishandled the entire situation, which irritated him with himself to no end.

She backed away from him. "I must return to the ballroom. My aunt will miss me. Please, don't try to see me again. It's better if you stay away."

That did it. A sound escaped his mouth that sounded more animal than human. He roughly clasped her hand and hauled her against him.

"If you've already been compromised, Grace, we may as well do this right. You *will* marry me." He trapped her hand behind her back and lifted her until her toes just brushed the ground. She looked up at him with frightened eyes and her lips parted in shock. Her face sat mere inches from his.

Before she could call out, Alex kissed her. His lips were hard against her silky lips, and his tongue sought possession. With a ragged moan, Grace allowed him entry.

He crushed his free hand against her backside, kneading even as he held her captive. She struggled to pull her hands free. Once he released them, they roamed over his chest, tickling in their tentative search.

He pulled his head back to lick her neck. She tasted of roses and woman. He breathed her into his senses and thought he might drown from the heady sensation. In a moment, he was hard and needy.

This had to stop now—before he went go too far—but he couldn't stop if his very life depended on it.

He needed more—her scent, her taste, her needy little sounds. He needed it all.

Grace squirmed as he slid his hands over her curves and recesses. He grasped her waist and kissed her again. Slowly, smoothly, he moved his hands up her frame.

Alex broke the kiss to look at her. Her eyes blazed liquid sapphire. She was reacting to his every touch with soft sighs and lusty moans. With the tips of his fingers, he traced the outline of her breast. She inhaled in shock, trembling against him. The nub of her breast tightened at his touch, and he throbbed in need.

Drunk with his need for her, he commanded, "Marry me, Grace," as he continued his sensual assault. He moved his mouth to her ear and nibbled on the lobe.

He stroked her to a fevered frenzy with his hands, reaching inside her gown to fondle her breasts with no barriers to his touch. Her skin was smoother than silk. It jumped beneath him as he kneaded her mounds.

Her trembling grew stronger. "I can't, my lord."

Alex pushed the top of her gown aside and freed her breasts. She was exquisite. Bouncing, porcelain bosoms with hardened, dark pink centers danced before him. He feasted on her with his eyes.

He lowered his head and took an areola into his mouth. She tasted of heaven and sweetness, a perfect mouthful. Her skin was velvet beneath his tongue.

"You can." He moved her against the trunk of a tree as his hands moved lower. He raised the skirts of her gown and shift above her knees and stroked the soft flesh of her thighs through her drawers— smooth and shapely and quivering. "Marry me. Be my wife. Let me restore your name."

She braced herself against his shoulders. He pressed his hands forward, upward, inching his way to her most private area. She did not protest when he cupped her center through the flimsy layer of fabric. Her need matched his. Boldness and appetite took over as he stroked her wetness.

A low sound rushed from her lips. "My lord. You can't. No one can re—restore my name. It's too late."

She was on the verge of climax and he hadn't even dipped a finger inside her. Good God, she was so responsive. Alex couldn't hold back any longer. He kissed her full and deep. "I need you, Grace. You must stop me now, if you don't want this." Please God, let her not stop him. How would he ever manage? Alex held his breath and waited for her response.

Her eyes clouded with need, but he refused to take her by force. She must want this also, or he would find some means of walking away from her.

She looked deep into his eyes as she answered. "Do not—do not stop. Please. I need—I have no idea what I need, but for the love of God, don't stop."

That was all the permission he needed. He pulled away from her to remove his coat and unfasten his breeches, ripping impatiently at the buttons. He laid his coat on a bed of grass and settled her atop it, then hastily undid her drawers, dragging them to her ankles and free from her body.

This would be her first experience, but he couldn't bear to hurt her more than necessary.

He was erect to the point of pain. With his arousal free, he settled between her thighs, kissing her again and again. His shaft throbbed and pressed into her belly. She shuddered beneath the intimate touch of flesh against flesh.

He suckled each of her breasts in turn to reignite the fire she had experienced earlier. "Grace, this will only hurt for a moment. I promise it won't last."

She looked straight into his eyes, a fiber of trust discernible in her gaze through a miniscule cloud fear. Please let it be fear of the unknown. He'd never made a habit of deflowering virgins, so he could only hope that was the cause.

He positioned himself at her opening and inched inside, glorying in the sensation of her tight walls surrounding him. Grace writhed beneath him and arched her hips to meet his, wrapping her legs around his body to pull him deeper. Alex couldn't restrain himself any longer. He plunged forward, burying himself in her warmth.

But found no maidenhead.

Unable, even unwilling, to stop and think, Alex set the tempo. He withdrew and thrust inside her again, eliciting surprised gasps of pleasure from her. Within moments, she matched his pace. He became almost frantic to find release, but first wanted to help Grace to hers.

She panted as he ground his hips against hers repeatedly. He hoped her sounds meant pleasure outweighed any fear or uncertainty. She couldn't know, couldn't understand, the release her body was fighting to experience. Reaching between them to stroke the swollen nub of her desire, he pressed on and increased the speed of his thrusts.

Her breath quickened and grew ragged, and her muscles tightened around him. Alex kissed her again and captured her cry of ecstasy in his mouth. With one final drive, he found completion. Intense pleasure swarmed over him as his seed filled her.

After a few moments, he realized he was pinning her to the ground, so he lifted off and moved to her side. He was still fighting to catch his breath as he tried to memorize everything about the moment. She was sheer perfection.

When Grace said she had already been compromised, he never imagined she would have been compromised quite as thoroughly as this. Simply being caught alone with a man would have been enough to accomplish her ruin. He was determined to get to the truth of the matter.

He searched her face for answers. She stared listlessly at the sky.

Getting her to speak to him, to truly open up to him, felt like an impossible task at times. Some unknown man had taken her virginity and left her to face the scandal—and any other consequences—

alone. How could any man could do such a thing and still call himself a gentleman?

But she never mentioned him being a gentleman. She had never said anything at all about him. How could he know if she had consented, as she did with Alex, or if she was ravished?

Dear God, not that. Never that.

The fear in her eyes flashed to mind—not only from tonight, but since the first time he ever saw her. Fear attached itself to Grace like a vise. But how would he discover the truth? There must be some way to convince her to trust him, to speak to him, to tell him her secrets. He need only find the way.

Her arms were crossed over her chest, hiding her beauty from him. Her shyness after their lovemaking drew him in even more. He stroked a finger down the side of her arm, wanting to comfort her, to hold her—anything to touch her again.

She rolled away and gave him her back.

He would have plenty of time to earn her trust. Grace would have to marry him now. He had been inside her. He had planted his seed in her womb. She could be carrying his child. She would be mad beyond repair to refuse him now.

GRACE LAY STILL and stared at the starless sky. Clouds drifted like blankets overhead, blocking even the moonlight. Lord Alexander shifted at her side, and his gaze felt like it was boring holes through her. She had no regrets over what she had done. She couldn't.

He'd driven away two of her demons. Fears she didn't even realize she had until they seized her in the throes of passion.

But she had been terribly afraid she would never enjoy the act of lovemaking. She never expected to have a husband with whom to experience the act, other than possibly Lord Barrow. *Perish the thought.* And if not him, Grace would never marry. It was as simple as that, in her mind.

No matter what her father thought of her, Grace would never resort to selling herself. So with no possibility of a husband, she had resigned herself to the fact that this act—the act of love—was one aspect of a woman's life she would never encounter.

However afraid she might be she would never share in the act of lovemaking, Grace had believed her other fear was more likely to hold true. She believed that if she ever took part in it, there would be no joy in it. She expected that, for her, it would always be filled with pain and fear. Her only possibility to experience the marriage bed would be with Barrow. With him, there could only ever be fear. She had never imagined such sensations to be possible as what she experienced just now with Lord Alexander.

She exulted in his touch. She could not remember a time in her life she felt as alive as she did when he coupled with her. Grace determined to never forget that moment. She would cherish it. It would be all she had of him, soon.

No matter how much he protested, she couldn't marry him. She *wouldn't* marry him. He deserved a wife above reproach, one who hadn't been tainted by a man's need for vengeance. One who was not considered a whore by her own father. His wife should bear his children, not those of another man. She should face her fears instead of running away from them.

He slid a single finger over her arm. The contact was so gentle, so tender, it threatened to shatter her. She rolled away from him and fought tears. He couldn't see her weakness. And she wouldn't allow him to interpret it as regret. He needed to know nothing would change, even after what had just passed between them.

"Grace?" Her name was scarcely more than a whisper on his lips. "Are you all right?"

His concern washed over her like a wave. Why must the man be so good, so honorable, so tender? It would be much easier to continue as she must if he were a scoundrel, a licentious rake—if he were more like Lord Barrow or her father. She wanted anything but to cause him heartache.

"I'm fine." She fought to maintain a cool demeanor. She couldn't let him see the truth.

"Who was he, Grace? Who compromised you?" He slid a hand over hers, caressing her in comforting strokes.

"I cannot say, my lord." Lord Alexander couldn't know. No one could know.

He faced her again, pain etched on his brow. "Did he...? Were you ravished?"

She controlled her reactions, careful not to let anything slip. "It is none of your concern, my lord."

His eyes flashed, and he rose to fasten his breeches. "None of my concern? How is it possible that the circumstances surrounding the compromise of my future bride are *none of my concern?*" he barked out. He paced across the garden lawn, trailing a string of curses in his wake.

"I am not your future bride, that's how. My lord, nothing has changed. I will still not have you, and you still cannot have me. We shared a moment—a lovely moment, though we likely shouldn't have done. I'm glad it can't be undone." Why had she admitted as much to him?

She pulled up her drawers and straightened her gown about her legs as she rose. "As I said before, you would do better to move on. Find yourself a suitable bride, a lady of good *ton* who has an intact reputation and does not need her reputation salvaged. Find someone other than me. I bid you good evening."

She walked away from him, back to the ballroom, back to Aunt Dorothea, and back to life as she would always know it.

Without him.

Fifteen

ALEX WATCHED GRACE walk away and fought the temptation to follow her. Ah, the cut direct. He would grant her this moment of victory. "But I shall see you at the altar, my dear."

Her reputation would suffer even more for returning to the ballroom alone, but that would soon enough be repaired. Grace would be his wife. She just needed to understand she had no alternative.

His determination that she needed his protection grew stronger than ever. Since she had been compromised before coming to Somerton, word of her disgrace might already be all over London. For that matter, word could have spread to the furthest outreaches of England.

There was no time to waste. He needed to act, and quickly.

Since he already planned to travel to London with Gil in the morning, he decided to continue with that course of action. He would visit with the Marquess of Chatham and explain the situation—short of some of the more sordid details of their encounter. But he must make it clear she had been compromised, and he intended to do the honorable thing and marry her.

Alex needed to convince the marquess that a marriage to him was the best option.

Convincing Grace could come later.

He would obtain a special license in London. Maybe Peter could do that for him. Alex had no idea how difficult it might be to convince Chatham that he was the man his daughter should marry. Sir Laurence had divulged little in their interview, but he got the impression that he did not think highly of Chatham.

Alex quit the Assembly Room without looking back. He needed to prepare for the morning's journey and to think.

THE ROAD TO London was difficult. The entire southern part of the English countryside was experiencing a torrential downpour during the three days Alex and Gil spent traveling. Several times their carriage became stuck in muddy ruts, so he had to assist the driver and footmen to free a wheel in the rain. He felt like a blasted pig that had gleefully rolled around in the sty.

On top of that, Gil's illness continued to grow worse. His coughing fits were more frequent and more severe, and Alex often saw spots of blood on the viscount's handkerchief. There could be no more denials. He was certain his friend suffered from consumption.

All the more reason he wished Gil would have stayed in Somerset. Whether in Bath or in Somerton, Gil would not be on the road to London and fighting his sickness in a cold, wet, cramped carriage.

Alex worried.

He worried that the viscount would not make it back to his beloved Roundstone Park. He worried that the Marquess of Chatham would not see things his way. He worried that he had left Grace with child. Not that he would not *want* a child with Grace. But there were already too many things making her life difficult.

If the marquess were to deny him…Alex shuddered. He must find a way to marry her. Someway, somehow, he would marry her. He would drag the chit to Gretna Green against her father's wishes if he had to, but she would be his wife. He wondered if he ought to have just taken Sir Laurence's advice to begin with, if perhaps the man had been trying to convey more to him than his words implied.

But wondering would not solve anything. He must follow through with his plan as he had it formulated.

He would not leave her with her reputation in its current state.

Travel seemed interminable. After three dreadfully long days, they arrived in London. Alex had sent a letter ahead to Peter once he decided to travel, informing his family of their impending arrival. He did not disclose his reason for the visit, just that they were coming. He wanted a room prepared for Gil.

The viscount's crested carriage rolled through the streets as Gil slept and Alex nursed his thoughts. They entered Mayfair well past dark, when most of society would be taking part in balls or routs, and other sorts of entertainments. Their presence went largely unnoticed.

Rotheby's driver pulled his carriage onto Grosvenor Square and stopped in front of Number Three, Hardwicke House. Alex never felt so relieved to be home as he did at that moment. He shook his friend awake. "Gil. We have arrived. Let us go inside."

A footman opened the door and let down the stairs as Spenser, the butler of Hardwicke House, opened the doors to the mansion Alex considered home.

Alex climbed down from his perch before he assisted Gil down the steps. He half-carried the older man inside.

"Welcome home, Lord Alexander. Shall I show you to the room I have prepared for Lord Rotheby?" Spenser executed a very brief bow, obviously understanding the urgency of seeing the viscount settled.

"Yes, Spencer, that would be splendid."

Alex followed the butler through the halls of Hardwicke House, plagued by nostalgia. He had lived in another world for the last few weeks, it seemed, as he had scarcely thought of his family and their lives in London. He rarely even thought of Priscilla and Harry.

It all rushed back to him now as he saw the paintings on the walls and the usual signs of life in their home. Scraps of his sisters' embroidery were tossed willy-nilly on tables and chairs in the morning parlor, Alex noted, and ledgers were strewn across the desk in Peter's library…the library he usually kept impeccably neat and tidy, with nary a speck of dust or a book out of place.

Spenser paused before the door to the emerald suite as they waited for a liveried footman to open the doors. Alex had requested this particular suite for the viscount in his letter, as it would not require climbing a flight of stairs and it tended to stay rather warm at night. He wanted Gil to be as comfortable as possible.

He aided the viscount into an armchair to sit. More footmen followed them into the room, unloading Rotheby's trunks from the carriage and setting them out for his use.

"My lords, I have assigned Percy to operate as his lordship's valet while you are in residence. If, of course, this will suit."

Alex glanced over to the man who waited to assist. He remembered Percy had been in the military before coming to Hardwicke House, and would likely have seen to the wounds of a number of his fellow soldiers during those days. He made a mental note to commend both Peter and Spenser on the selection. Gil would need a good deal of supervision, and perhaps medical attention, during their stay.

Gil coughed violently again and red droplets stained his handkerchief. "Percy will be fine, Spenser," he rasped out after the fit ceased. The butler nodded and took his leave as Gil turned to Alex. "I shall be quite well tonight, old man. Off with you. Go see your family." He flicked his hands and shooed him on his way.

"I will leave…but with strict orders to Percy that I am to be informed immediately should you need anything, Gil. You are a guest here. Remember that."

Alex made a pathetic attempt at a lighthearted laugh, which came out more like a wheeze, and then left the room.

Gil was right. He needed to see his family, to speak with his brother. They must learn the reason they had traveled all the way from Bath on such short notice. He knew that they would support his efforts. If needed, Peter would add his weight to the discussion with Chatham. That was simply how the Hardwicke family operated.

Alex did not want Peter's assistance so much as he wanted his support. He was a grown man, and needed to find his own way in the world. This was after all the primary reason he had gone to Somerton that spring. Taking care of these matters on his own would be at least one step in the right direction. Come to think of it, a marriage to Lady Grace Abernathy would be a step toward finding the meaning for his life as well.

But none of this was enough if he did not handle it on his own. He could not spend his life running to his brother for help every time something did not go his way.

In the hall, he found the butler giving instructions to some of the household servants. He waited until they moved on about their business.

"Spenser, are any of my family at home this evening, or are they all out?" Now that he was home, he realized how much he missed his mother and his siblings. Alex hoped at least some of them were at home.

"My lord, I believe Lady Charlotte is above stairs with her governess, and the Marquess of Grovesend and Lady Sarah are in the nursery." Alex brightened at the news. "His grace has accompanied her grace and Lady Sophia to a ball at Monahan Park this evening. They shall not return until quite late, though I am sure His Grace would be glad to see you."

"Excellent, Spenser. Please inform me when the rest of my family arrives. I should like to visit with them all this evening." He strode to the closest stairwell and took the stairs two at a time in anticipation of seeing some of the people he loved most. At some point, soon, he would need to visit Priscilla and discuss matters with her. But he needed to begin with his family.

He started in the nursery, where the door opened wide at the sound of his exuberant knocks.

"I declare, Lady Charlotte, His Grace your brother will be most highly displeased at your deportment this evening when he hears about this, and yes ma'am that was a when, not an if."

Mrs. Pratt, a middle-aged woman in a serviceable, light green cotton dress opened the door. "I daresay a single rap at the door would have been more than sufficient." Annoyance flickered across her face. The vexation fled as soon as she saw Alex instead of the expected Lady Charlotte.

"Why lord-a-mercy, Lord Alexander, I do apologize for my harsh words. You are a sight for these sore eyes, to be sure."

She reached up and patted his grinning cheek before giving in to the temptation and planting a kiss where her hand had just been. "I know you have not been gone for so terribly long, but I have certainly missed you. Come in, come in here." She swept the door wide and ushered him through it. "Children, your Uncle Alex has come home!"

As he stepped into the nursery, his niece and nephew flung themselves at him, each grasping a leg. Joseph, the young Marquess of Grovesend, attempted to climb up a leg and into his strong arms. "Uncle Alex! You have been away too long."

Young Sarah pouted and gazed up at him with wide, sad eyes. The poor, slighted little one. He could not resist her pouts, and she knew it. She often took advantage of his good nature by wheedling him until he gave in to her current demand.

He stooped closer to the children's level and pulled them both in for a hug. "I am sorry, Sarah. What shall be my punishment?"

She needed only a moment for her decision. The three-year-old heartbreaker-in-the-making with her large green eyes and strawberry blonde curls tackled him to the floor and left a peal of giggles in her aftermath. Not to be left out, Joshua took a leap and landed on top of the two. He barely missed Alex's head with his foot. Alex rolled over and pulled the children beneath him, then up above him, always careful not to crush them with his weight.

Mrs. Pratt looked on in mock horror. "Lord Alexander, you have certainly managed to rile these children up now. It is nearly their bedtime as well." She shook her head and uttered a "tsk" under her breath as she walked through the nursery and picked up after the children. "I cannot imagine where you acquired the idea such conduct is acceptable." She placed a doll into place on the bed by the window covered with lacy hangings, where Lady Sarah could easily find it when she settled in for the night.

Alex laughed out loud. "Do you claim no hand in teaching me manners then, Mrs. Pratt? Dear me, I must be an utter boor, a scamp of unequaled measure, if *you* of all people shall disown me."

He rose from his spot on the floor beneath the children, lifting them as they squirmed for freedom. "Off you go, little angel." He passed his niece to the waiting nanny, who procured the girl's nightgown. Alex tossed Joshua over his shoulder and carried him to an adjoining dressing room to assist him in dressing for bed.

"Uncle Alex! I do not want to go to bed," Joshua complained as a yawn escaped. "I am not tired. I shall not sleep a wink tonight."

Alex set him on his feet and stripped the shirt over the boy's head. The five-and-a-half year old marquess's eyes drooped, though he struggled to keep them open.

"No, I am sure you will not sleep, Josh. But you must pretend to sleep for Sarah's sake. She will follow your example." Joshua's lower lip stuck out in protest. "If you fight sleep, she will also, and then what will happen?" Alex pulled a nightshirt over the boy's head.

"Sarah will whine and cry and act like a baby all day tomorrow. But why must," Joshua paused as another loud yawn fought free, "why must I be punished for something she will do?" Fully dressed for bed, Josh returned to the nursery hand-in-hand with his uncle.

He squeezed the boy's hand. "Alas, Joshua, it happens with all older brothers of younger sisters. We must always do the things that are best for our sisters, even when they are distasteful for ourselves."

Josh continued to pout, though with less intensity.

"Your father and I, and Uncle Richard, and Uncle Neil…we all do the things that are best for Aunt Sophie and Aunt Char, do we not? Even when those things are unpleasant?"

Alex led his nephew to bed, pulled down the bed covers, and placed him inside. The little boy nodded his head, but looked unconvinced. "That is part of being a gentleman, Josh. We must always care for our sisters."

He patted the boy's head before moving to Sarah's bed to kiss her forehead. "Good night, my sweet cherub."

"Good night, Uncle Alex. You will be here in the morning? You are not leaving again?" Sarah could not hide the worry from her eyes.

"No love, I will not leave again so soon. You shall see me in the morning." He tugged firmly on her blankets to be sure they tucked securely around her and then left the nursery.

Mrs. Pratt stopped him just before he got out the door. "My lord, Lady Charlotte will want to see you. I fear she has been quite distraught this Season. It vexes her to be stuck in the schoolroom with her governess."

Alex was not surprised Mrs. Pratt would be concerned for his youngest sister. The woman had worked for the Hardwicke family since before he was born, and clucked about them all like a mother hen. As though they needed a second mother bustling about, interfering in their lives.

Char had just moved from the nursery to the schoolroom around the time Joshua joined the family, so Mrs. Pratt stayed on in her original post. Peter always said that she could keep her position as long as she saw fit. The Hardwicke siblings all loved the woman dearly.

"I was planning to stop in to see Char next, Mrs. Pratt." He gave her a peck on the cheek, eliciting a low laugh. "You know, you are a beauty. Pratt is a lucky man indeed."

Alex allowed her to bask in the glow of his flirtation and headed toward his youngest sister's bedchamber. At this time of night, Char would doubtless have left the schoolroom. He could not imagine Miss Bentley would force her charge to keep at her studies so late.

He arrived at her room and knocked out a rhythm. A feminine squeal of euphoria emanated through the doorway and he braced himself for the impending assault. Char threw open the door and flung her arms about his neck.

"Alex! Oh, goodness I have missed you. It has been purely horrid here without you." Her fair skin flushed with excitement as she babbled about nothing and everything. "Louisa Smythe had her come-out, and made quite the splash I understand. Theodora Marlborough, you know she hears all the best gossip from her eldest sister, well she told me just the other day she expects Louisa to receive no fewer than five offers this Season, and I daresay she is right."

Char drew Alex into her suite of rooms and onto a seat next to her on a well-used sofa while she continued to spurt information. "Mama insisted Peter accompany her and Sophie to all of the balls. She says he must make an effort to oversee their prospects, as you have abandoned the girls in their need and Richard is still abroad with the army. And Neil...well, you rather know he is not quite useful in any regard yet, so Mama lets him do as he will."

She stopped to draw in a breath, having somehow made it through her entire speech without seeming to breathe. "So Neil goes to his gentleman's clubs and has a grand old time, and Sophie and Peter attend all sorts of entertainments, and I have been dreadfully alone here, stuck in Hardwicke House with no one but the children and the servants for company. It has been beastly of them all, Alex, but I know if you were here, you would stay and entertain me occasionally, would you not?"

Alex imagined his sister in a few years' time as she made her entrée. The *ton* would not know what hit them.

He smiled and attempted an answer, but Char interrupted before he could speak. "Oh, how inconsiderate I have been! Do you wish for something to eat? How was your travel? Is Lord Rotheby well?

Have you had a good visit with him? What were you doing in Bath? Goodness, tell me everything." She finally paused for him to speak.

"I doubt I can answer all of your questions at once, Char, but I shall try." Alex loved Charlotte's exuberance. He found it quite endearing, though he could understand how she might be off-putting to some.

"Lord Rotheby and I have had a wonderful visit in Somerton. We spent our time going about his estate and visiting with Sir Laurence and Lady Kensington. They have become his dearest friends close by."

He paused to debate how much he ought to tell Char. She was only sixteen years of age, and the pain of their father's death was still keen for her. But she deserved the truth "Char...the viscount...I believe he is dying."

Her eyes filled with unshed tears and she gathered a tentative breath. "He is ill?" The words were a mere whisper, barely more than a sigh.

Alex placed his arm about her shoulders and drew her close to offer what comfort he could. "Yes. He has not spoken of it, but I suspect consumption." The finality he felt upon speaking the words aloud surprised him.

Her grip was a vise and her knuckles whitened. "But...but Alex. Why on earth would you allow him to travel all the way to London if he is in such a condition? Goodness, does he need anything? Should we call for a doctor?"

Alex smoothed the back of his sister's hand and gave her a gentle smile. "Have you ever tried to tell Lord Rotheby he could not do something he intended to do? Char, the man is as obstinate as a mule. He came to London to complete some business. My best guess is his business deals with his properties and their entailments, things of that nature."

"And you came back to London so he would not travel alone?" He could see the strain in her posture as she struggled to accept the news he delivered.

"That is not the entire reason for our arrival. Char...the viscount traveled to support me." A question settled heavy in the air between them. "I need to ask the Marquess of Chatham for his daughter's hand in marriage."

"You what? Marriage, Alex? Are you quite certain?" All of Char's tension melted away as she regaled him with questions. "Who is she Alex? Is she quite beautiful? She must be a diamond of the first water, to have caught your eye. Oh, Mama will be so excited! Have you told her yet? I do hope not, I wish to see her face when she hears the news. Gracious, we shall have a wedding to plan. And Peter must throw an engagement ball. Do you think Mama will allow me to attend the ball? Oh, surely she must, just this once."

"Slow down, Char," Alex said with a chuckle. "Nothing is settled yet. But yes, I am quite certain. Lady Grace will be my wife."

"Lady Grace? I shall quite enjoy having a sister named Grace." Char's eyes shone with excitement. "Have the banns been called yet?"

Char rose and walked about her chamber, then rushed back to resume her seat at his side. He laughed at her inability to stay still.

"No, Char. No banns yet. I must still speak with her father. And there is one other small problem."

"Problem? What sort of problem?" She walked away in feigned disinterest.

"The sort involving Lady Grace having denied me. But that shall all be sorted out soon."

"She did *not*. How could she deny you?"

Alex rose from the sofa and walked to the window. Charlotte's chamber sat at the front corner of the house, looking out onto Grosvenor Square. A crested carriage with liveried outriders pulled into the drive.

"They are home, Char. Shall we go down to greet them? I should like to tell the whole of my story only once. You can gloat to Sophie you know more than they, at least for the moment. It could make up somewhat for being left alone while they attend balls and such, shall it not?"

"Oh yes, quite." Char took his hand and tugged him into the hall, dragging when he fell too far behind.

ALEX SAT AMIDST the majority of his family in the upstairs drawing room of Hardwicke House. Neil, his younger brother, was still playing cards at White's that evening. And of course Richard was off in France or Portugal, or any number of other places where the British Army were fighting Old Boney. But Peter was present as the head of the family with their mother Henrietta at his side, and all three of their sisters found perches nearby to hear Alex's news.

He had already informed them all of his suspicions regarding the viscount's health and regaled them with details of his journeys. But now he would tell them of Grace.

Of course, as she had previously heard at least part of his story, Char smirked toward her elder sisters. Alex smiled over the silent exchange between the girls. No one would dare describe Char as mean-spirited, nor his other sisters for that matter. They all loved each other dearly, notwithstanding the occasional competition or familial argument. But they all loved a good competition.

Peter sipped from his glass of port. Alex thought his brother looked exhausted and silently thanked him, yet again, for the encouragement to visit Somerton.

"Alex, I cannot imagine Lord Rotheby incapable of managing his business in Bath. He had no true reason to come all the way to town." Peter took another sip from his glass and eyed his brother over the top of the glass. "It is clear he chose to accompany you. So, why? What brought you to London?"

Char remained in her seat, though she clearly desired to burst into the center of the room and shout out her news.

Alex took pity on her and cut straight to the point. "I shall call on the Marquess of Chatham to request his daughter's hand in marriage."

Cacophony broke out in the drawing room.

"Did I not tell you, Sophie, Alex has such delightful news…is it not wonderful?"

"Married? We shall host a wedding? Oh, my precious boy! Goodness, we ought to begin the arrangements at once."

"You knew *that* and you did not tell me, Char? You sneak, I shall never forgive you."

"Well, if Alex shall marry this summer, there is no reason to rush things for me, Mama. One more Season without accepting an offer will not hurt anything."

Over the din of the females, Peter caught Alex's eye. "Chatham? You wish to marry Chatham's daughter, Alex?" Concern etched his brow as he focused on Alex. The ladies noticed Peter's tone and quieted, all eyes turned to the two brothers.

Alex nodded, his mind working to grasp the meaning of Peter's apprehension. "Yes, I shall marry Lady Grace," he asserted with finality. There could be no misunderstanding amongst his family. He needed them all to be of one accord.

Peter ran a hand over his chin. Several moments passed in silence, while each brother held the other riveted with his gaze and the ladies glancing from one man to the other.

"Are you fully aware of the…the circumstances…surrounding Lady Grace's departure from London, Alex?" Peter always chose his words with great care.

If she was to be his bride, Alex wanted his family to know everything he could tell them. Well, almost everything. He would keep certain details of their encounter the night before he left Bath to himself.

"I believe I am fairly well informed. Lady Grace was compromised in London, and the man who compromised her left her to deal with the shame alone. Chatham sent her to stay with her aunt and uncle in Somerton, to keep her away from the gossip mills."

A chorus of indrawn breaths filled the air as the female members of his family learned of the contempt his intended had suffered. Peter gave no outward reaction, no sign that Alex's announcement made any sort of impact.

"I further compromised her in Bath. We had a very public…er, discussion…in the Pump Rooms and I kissed her before everyone there."

His mother looked scandalized. "Alexander Jeremiah Hardwicke, you rake! I cannot believe you would behave in such a manner. Your father and I raised you to act with far more decorum—"

Peter interrupted. "Mama, let him finish what he has to say."

She looked to have a far more detailed reprimand in store for him, but she allowed her son to continue.

Alex waited for everyone to settle down once again.

Char sat with her chin on her wrists and her elbows digging into her knees, obviously hanging on his every word and itching for the next juicy detail.

Sophie maintained her exacting, correct posture and displayed a sense of ennui—which she then destroyed with the impatience of her fingers tapping against the arm of her chair.

Peter had not changed positions at all, but continued to stroke the tip of his chin with absent-minded fervor. "Go on, Alex. Finish your story." He sent a warning look around to his sisters.

"After I kissed her, she slapped me across the cheek." Again, he was interrupted.

"I daresay, you deserved no less, Alex."

"She *slapped* you? How dreadfully unbecoming."

"Good heavens, what a scene you caused. What I would not give to have seen it with my own eyes. I cannot *wait* to tell Theodora Marlborough! She will simply die from the scandal."

Peter held up a hand, a signal for peace. "Enough!" The sisters quieted once again, though Alex knew by now it would not last for long. He determined to finish his story as soon as possible so they could revel in their excitement.

"That evening, I met Lady Grace at the Assembly Room and proposed."

"Oh Sophie, you will never guess what happened next," Char blurted out. A stern look from Peter silenced her again.

"She refused me."

Another refrain of gasps and mumbles filled the room. Alex continued with a raised voice before he could be interrupted again.

"I made it clear to Lady Grace I had every intention of providing her with the protection of my name, that she would not suffer the same shame on my account. And I traveled here to meet with her father and officially request her hand in marriage." He could see his sisters wished to interject their questions and exclamations yet again, so he pushed forward. "Lady Grace has not reached her majority yet." Understanding dawned throughout the room of what he implied. For once, no one said anything for many minutes.

Then Peter stood. "It is late. Alex has had several long days of travel. He needs his rest. Any more discussion on the matter will wait for morning." Char started to object, but Peter stayed her with his hand. He turned to Alex. "Get some rest. We will talk more in the morning."

Thankful for the reprieve, Alex nodded.

"And Alex...it is good to have you home." Peter placed a hand on Alex's shoulder and led him from the room before the girls could stop him again.

It was good to be home, Alex thought. Very good.

Sixteen

THE BREAKFAST TABLE of Hardwicke House buzzed with excitement. Lady Grace Abernathy appeared to be the conversation topic of choice, much to Alex's consternation.

He would prefer, in some ways, to go about his business and make the marriage a reality. But his family was not one to merely sit by and allow one of its members to handle such matters on his—these things soon became family affairs. He wouldn't want his life to be any different.

It was soothing, even when it meant constant interference he would sometimes prefer to do without. He sat back in his chair to answer his sisters' questions.

Char, of course, wanted specifics. "Alex, is she beautiful? Tell us how she looks."

He might as well indulge her. "She is very beautiful. Lady Grace has long black curls and eyes so light they are almost the color of ice—and she has the most perfect English rose complexion to her skin. She's very small, too. I daresay the top of her head would only reach your shoulder, Char."

She smiled at his description, but begged for more detail. "And does she dress in all the most current fashions?"

Leave it to Char to be more concerned with his bride-to-be's appearance and clothing than her personality. "You might ask me questions about Lady Grace herself, you know. She'll be part of our family soon. I am sure you'll want to know of her interests and talents, wouldn't you?"

He was needling at her to procure a reaction. Char would love Grace, despite any flaw or affliction she may have. That was simply Char's nature. But it was also in her nature to want every sort of detail a typical young lady not-quite-out in society ought to want.

She scoffed at his rebuke. "Goodness, of course I want to know those details as well. I would get there in time, you know. You should have a bit more patience with me," she scolded him, then returned to her previous luster. "So, tell me about Lady Grace's clothes." Char leaned forward, her eyes alight.

Alex shook his head at the impertinence he both loved and loathed. "Her clothing—well, I wouldn't say her gowns are the absolute height of fashion, but they are more than becoming on her. They're modest, in pretty shades for her complexion. Soft." He might have told too much with his last comment. If he knew her gowns were soft, he must have touched her. Better keep moving before Char picked up on the hint he'd dropped. "For anything more than that about her attire, you'll have to observe for yourself. I've told you enough on the matter for today. But Char, when I bring Lady Grace to London, you should offer to go on a painting excursion with her. She's an artist."

Thinking about watching Grace paint beside the Cary River in Somerton made him wish she was with him now, in London. He missed her company, though she usually was either silent or railing at him.

"Oh, how lovely! Lady Grace and I shall paint together often." Char's elation emanated throughout the breakfast room. "When will you bring her to London? I do hope it will be soon."

Mama joined them in the breakfast room, and Alex was relieved to discover she would change the subject. He had enough on his mind without trying to answer all of his youngest sister's questions.

When they finished eating, Peter rose from the head of the table. "Alex, might I have a word with you?" Unlike their mother and sisters, Peter seemed less than overjoyed by his news. The duke maintained a dour expression as they moved from the breakfast room to his library.

After the footman closed the door behind them, Peter seated himself behind his desk. "Have a seat." Once Alex complied, he continued. "Do you know what you're doing here? Have you met Chatham before? He is not the most honorable man." Peter rubbed his fingers across his chin. "There have been rumors about your intended."

Alex's ears perked up, but he refrained from reacting too soon. "I've not met Chatham before." Did he want to know the specific rumors? He wasn't certain. He stared out the open window and listened to raindrops hit the panes of glass for several moments. "What sort of rumors? Rumors about her being compromised before she left London?" He prayed that was the worst of it.

"More than just compromised."

Alex's head shot up.

Peter held his gaze. "Lord Barrow made some claims one night at White's, not long before she left Town. Rumors of her compromise at his hands had already been making their way through the gossip mill. His assertions added fuel to the flame. He claims that she initiated the act. He implied that she is fast—loose."

"Barrow?" Alex roared in pain, his only thought revenge. This was not his first encounter with the man, not by any means. "The bloody, licentious bastard, I'll have him drawn and—"

"Wait, Alex." Agony flooded Peter's face.

Alex's anger subsided by a degree, only to be replaced by fear. "There's more?" He didn't want to hear the answer.

"Barrow absconded from the country. He has been gone since the day after he made his claims at White's. No one knows where he went this time, nor do they know when to expect his return. Added to the gossip already floating about her after the broken engagement with Walsingham…well, it's not a pretty picture. Things don't look good for your Lady Grace."

Alex seethed in silence, ruminating over the information.

After several moments, Peter continued. "And there is more yet."

"More? How can there be more? By Jove, is this not enough?" He could think of nothing more than his desire to draw Barrow's cork, if not something more extreme than that. When he looked at his brother again, there was pity in his eyes.

"Chatham. He's been making waves."

"What in bloody hell does that mean?" Who cared about Chatham when Barrow needed to be dealt with?

"He's acting as though Lady Grace has been kidnapped. He claims to have the Bow Street Runners on the case, though I'm not certain that I would believe him." Peter rubbed his chin absentmindedly again. "Does she seem at all uncomfortable with where she is? Is there any reason to believe she has been taken against her will?"

Was she uncomfortable? Kidnapped? "No. No, I don't believe that could be true. But, wait…" Sir Laurence *had* suggested Alex take her to Gretna Greene.

"Wait, what?"

"Never mind. It's nothing."

Peter raised a brow, but said nothing.

Even if it were something, Alex needed to discover the truth on his own. No reason to have Peter suspecting an innocent couple of wrongdoing. Besides, Grace had arrived on the coach alone. No one brought her to Somerton. No, she hadn't been kidnapped. So what was Chatham's game? What did he hope to accomplish?

Several moments passed in silence. "Alex, do you know if it is true? Barrow has a reputation for fabricating stories to suit his purposes. He could have only wanted to ruin Lady Grace, though what purpose her ruin might serve for him, I don't know."

It took a moment for what Peter asked to sink in. "It's true. I don't know all of the circumstances, but I do know he tells the truth about the act having occurred." He would be bowled over if Grace was the only innocent he had ruined, based on what he knew of the man.

He moved his chair away from the hearth then resumed his seat. He felt over-warm with the adrenaline coursing through him. Alex trusted Peter more than nearly anyone else in his acquaintance, so he delved deeper into his suspicions. "She may have been ravaged. She won't tell me."

Peter nodded slowly. "I was afraid of that. I wouldn't put even worse crimes past Barrow. I don't trust the bastard as far as I can throw him."

Tell me about it.

Silence blanketed the room again, as the brothers determined their next step. The duke was the first to speak again. "You mustn't waste time. Go to Chatham this morning. Do whatever you must to convince him to give his consent." Peter paused for a beat. "He hasn't protected his daughter well, has he?"

Alex imagined one of his own sisters in the circumstance Grace had been thrown into. "Not well at all. I'm afraid for her. Her reputation—" He couldn't continue.

"Do you love her? Truly love her?" Peter's marriage had been loveless, and Alex knew his brother didn't want any of his siblings to suffer a similar fate.

"We'll make a good marriage of it, Peter. I'll be certain of that, if nothing else."

He didn't love Grace, did he? He was attracted to her. He found her amusing. But love? Alex didn't think it possible after such a short period of time. Love needed to be nourished, encouraged, grown. It did not happen overnight.

"You do that. Work hard at it. She's your responsibility now. You have a duty to at least try to love her." Peter stood and walked to the window before turning back to him. "I have some business I must take care of this afternoon. Lord Rotheby plans to handle his affairs today as well. I'll be taking him with me. And this evening, we've all accepted an invitation to attend a ball at Yardley Court. Mama insists you also attend."

Alex joined his brother at the window. "I'll visit Chatham House." He had no desire to attend a *ton* ball this evening. Too many cares weighed on his mind. Besides, Grace wouldn't be there. If he attended, he would have to dance and talk and make merry with the ladies, all the while thinking solely of another.

"And the ball? Don't disappoint Mama. I don't want to hurt you, but I will." A cheeky grin softened Peter's words.

He sighed. "Yes, I will attend the ball. Though I make no promises about enjoying myself." It would be much easier to suffer through the dancing and entertainment if Chatham agreed to his offer. He hoped that would be the case.

It would be easier still if Barrow appeared and he could take matters into his own hands.

AUNT DOROTHEA AND Grace worked on their embroidery together in the morning room of New Hill Cottage. They had finished their week's stay in Bath early and traveled home. The carriage was so full of boxes and packages that Uncle Laurence had decided to ride his horse instead of enjoying the conversation of the two women (which primarily consisted of the solitary conversation of his wife).

Several days had passed since Lord Rotheby had quit Bath for London with Lord Alexander, and Uncle Laurence found he had enjoyed more than enough of the ladies' company for such a short period of time.

Grace would never find a need for all of the purchases her aunt and uncle made for her. They bought her morning dresses, afternoon dresses, evening dresses, ball gowns—even riding habits! She had never ridden a horse before, and didn't think it a wise endeavor to try to learn the skill while carrying a babe. Of course, the dresses were not enough for her aunt. She had ribbons and bonnets, pelisses, parasols, and so many other items to accompany her wardrobe, she had difficulty in keeping it all straight.

They hadn't bought only one wardrobe for her, either. Aunt Dorothea thought it imperative that Grace have enough of each of these articles to suffice during each stage of her pregnancy. They wouldn't ask poor Tess to continually let out her clothing—no, that would be far too much work for the young lady's maid. After all, Tess must tend to all of Grace's needs while her lady was with child.

So Aunt Dorothea bought clothing of all sizes for Grace, in every imaginable color, and in fabrics appropriate for every season.

Grace had tried to protest, telling her aunt she was more than capable of doing her own mending and letting out—she had done both her own and her father's for a number of years, after all. No need for Tess to be put out by the workload.

Aunt Dorothea found the idea laughable.

Then Grace had argued she wouldn't need riding habits, since she didn't ride. Neither would she need ball gowns, as she intended to avoid all such future engagements—especially during her confinement. She also wouldn't need separate morning and afternoon and evening dresses, since she did not intend to be out in company. Aunt Dorothea hadn't dignified these arguments with a response. So Grace had returned to New Hill Cottage with more items than could possibly fit in her chamber.

They had been home, as Grace now thought of New Hill, for two days. She spent her days working on embroidery with her aunt, or digging up weeds in the gardens with Uncle Laurence. Some days she read novels, though she took great care to keep them hidden from Aunt Dorothea, since the older woman found them highly scandalous.

More and more often, nausea caused Grace to limit herself to her chamber. Sometimes, Tess kept her company, while other times she preferred to be alone. When around people, Grace put on a brave face. She smiled and laughed and talked, but she rarely found joy in life anymore.

But when she was alone, she sometimes cried and didn't quite know why. She had heard women often became overly emotional when they were with child, and hoped that might explain her sadness. Some deep part of her knew better.

The truth was that she missed Lord Alexander. She'd spent one night in his arms. She'd allowed herself to experience an act with him she believed she would never come to know. And now he was gone, at her insistence.

Yes, he had offered her marriage. She'd been sorely tempted to accept. But in the end, she had done for him what was right and honorable by refusing his offer.

Now she wished she could change her answer.

Grace had no right to want such a thing. He had made the offer, only because of the expectations of society. Lord Alexander had felt honor-bound to offer for her. Nothing more. And she had refused him as was her right and prerogative

No great feeling existed on his side…certainly nothing more than a simple curiosity. She couldn't allow him to bind himself irrevocably to her and her unborn child, which he did not even know would soon exist, when he so clearly felt no deep feelings for her.

Her heavy heart made her tearful again, and she set aside her embroidery with an audible sigh.

"Gracie, sweetheart, is something the matter?" Aunt Dorothea looked up from her embroidery work.

"No, Aunt. Nothing's wrong. I just don't feel quite the thing." Perhaps a lie would keep the woman from puttering about her. "I believe I'll take a nap, if that is all right."

"Of course, dear. You must get plenty of rest, I've been telling you this all along. Go on, now. Have Tess take care of you."

"I will, Aunt Dorothea." She placed her thimble, needle, and threads in a small chest, and headed upstairs.

When she arrived at her chamber though, she decided not to rest. She needed to paint—she needed to work through the emotions that had plagued her since the trip to Bath, the emotions continually stirred up by thoughts of Lord Alexander. She needed to find release.

Grace collected her easel, paints, brushes, and other supplies. She sneaked down the servants' staircase and out the side door through the kitchen, so as not to be caught by either her aunt or uncle.

It was the middle of the afternoon, and the sky was overcast again. She lugged her tools through the gardens a good distance, separating herself from the cottage. Heaven forbid if a servant should catch a glimpse of her and then notify Aunt Dorothea. She needed peace and quiet to create.

After a short hike, she settled on a location in a clearing. Open space and wind surrounded her, but little else. Setting up her easel and canvas, she selected her angle. Up ahead was a hill dotted with foxgloves and clover, with a few ancient willow trees scattered throughout. The darkened sky juxtaposed well against the scene.

Peace descended over her as soon as she set to work. She tried not to think as she painted, but wanted to let the images flow from her hands, through the brushes, and onto the canvas.

Things did not work out quite as she planned.

As she painted, the scene on her canvas took on a life of its own; it looked nothing like the sight before her eyes. Neatly organized flowers, water fountains, and sculptures sat in a garden of roses in every hue. She heard the sound of water tinkling in the fountains and the call of a bird from a nearby tree that grew just outside the area of the garden she painted.

Grace's curiosity rose as she marveled over painting something she could not see before her. Still, the garden sat clear in her mind. She saw every tiny detail, right down to the blush pink dog rose he placed in her hair.

Pink dog rose.

Memory poured over her as she continued to paint the scene from Lord Rotheby's rose gardens—the place where Lord Alexander had first kissed her. Grace flushed, thinking of his kiss, his hands, his scent—that woodsy, clean male scent so unlike any other.

Then she thought about the morning kiss in the Pump Room, when she was so angry with him—and angry with herself, if she was honest—when she had returned his passion for just a moment before striking him. Her flush deepened. The fierceness of her paint strokes intensified; her hands worked seemingly of their own accord.

Then her thoughts turned to their encounter in the gardens outside the Assembly Room. Her body tightened—a liquid pull to her center—in response to the memory of his lovemaking.

Grace no longer saw the canvas. She saw only Lord Alexander as he pressed into her from above. She could almost feel the pressure of his strong thighs against hers, the supple texture of his mouth on her own. She shuddered in her need.

A clap of thunder overhead pulled her back to the present. Blast! Grace ought to return to the house before she was drenched by the oncoming storm. She took a quick glance at the canvas. No one had touched it other than her, yet she didn't recognize it as her own creation.

The rose gardens of Roundstone Park danced before her. Where the last time she had painted, her creation had evoked darkness, danger, and a foreboding evil, this piece conjured something more sensual, more carnal.

The roses displayed their fertility. Branches and leaves beckoned the viewer closer to recline in their arms. She could almost smell the flowers' essence—heady and musky and verdant. But the fresh scent of rain in the air severed her appraisal of the painting, and she rushed to collect all of her utensils before the summer rainstorm ruined her work. With arms overflowing, she trekked to the kitchen doors of New Hill Cottage, arriving just as the clouds released their deluge.

Mrs. Finchley gawked at Grace as she rushed inside, barely escaping the downpour. "My lady, gracious heavens! What on earth have you been doing outside? You could have been caught in this storm. I daresay you would catch a chill if you had!"

The housekeeper puttered about the kitchen as she took most of the items Grace carried and set them aside. "Did my Tess know you were out from the house? That girl! She ought to look after you better."

Mrs. Finchley rang for a footman to carry Grace's load up the stairs to her bedchamber before pouring her some tea. "And that wind, my lady, why it is biting cold today. You may come down with fever yet. Drink this now, and then Tess shall take you above stairs for a rest."

It was pointless to argue with the servant. Truth be told, she was worn out after her excursion. Creating this piece had both exhilarated and exhausted her, all at once.

She sipped from her tea as Mrs. Finchley fetched a blanket from a nearby sitting room and wrapped it about her shoulders. When Tess arrived, Grace allowed herself to be led to her chamber, undressed, and placed between the sheets.

Grace slept—but she dreamed of the arms of an auburn-haired man wrapped about her.

THE RAIN STILL had not let up by that afternoon as Alex descended from one of Peter's carriages and looked up at Chatham House. He would have preferred to take his curricle, but that would force him to arrive with his clothes drenched from the storm, so he'd thought better of it.

The gardens were unkempt and in shambles. Shutters flopped about in the wind on broken hinges. Overgrown moss and vines snaked up Grecian columns, masking cracks in need of repair. The windows of the house were all shuttered, save those whose shutters hung limp from the walls. Gloom settled over the entire structure.

He climbed the ancient stairs that led to the door and thought of how life must have been for Grace as she grew up in such a place. Alex imagined his niece and nephew tromping through the gardens and shuddered. They would trip over weeds, if not worse.

This was no place for a child.

Alex rapped against the heavy entryway and waited. And waited.

And continued to wait some more.

He reached up to knock again, just as a bedraggled servant pulled the door open. The man squinted at him against the cloud-covered daylight that fought to break through. Inside the hall, darkness abounded.

"My lord. How may I be of service?" The old butler's tone suggested he had no desire to be of any service to anyone whatsoever.

Alex reached inside his coat and retrieved his calling card. As he passed it to the butler, he said "I wish to call upon the marquess, if he is in. Please inform him of my arrival." He waited for the man to do his bidding.

The servant glanced at Alex's card with a scowl before stepping back and ushering him inside out of the rain. "Wait here," he said as he hobbled off, a slight limp detectable in his gait.

As he waited in the dim light, Alex observed his surroundings. A thick layer of dust covered the tables and floor, and the rugs were in need of a good cleaning. None of the usual decorative touches he would expect of a man of the marquess's station graced the walls; no paintings or mirrors or vases of fresh spring flowers brightened the room. The furnishings were sparse and worn, and had likely been in place for generations.

Finally, the old butler returned. "His lordship will see you now. Follow me." He stepped gingerly toward what Alex assumed to be Chatham's library while Alex followed behind. No footman awaited their arrival to swing the doors wide, so the doors stood open. The butler waived him inside, without making the effort to announce him.

Chatham glared at him from his seat behind a decrepit desk. The man was likely in his forties, but he looked much older. Only a small amount of wiry, grey hair wisped over his head, his scalp shining even in the poor candlelight. He had a ruddy complexion, whether from anger, drink, or hard living, Alex couldn't determine. Stains blanketed the marquess's rumpled clothes.

Alex inclined his head in greeting.

Chatham remained seated and took another swallow from his glass. "Lord Alexander, I understand you have been dallying with my daughter. Word travels fast, you know. You would do well to stay away from her."

"You're misinformed, my lord. Dalliance is the furthest thing from my mind in relation to Lady Grace. I am afraid I shall be unable to concede to your request. I've no intention of avoiding her." Not any more, at least. Alex waited for a moment before continuing, attempting to ascertain the older man's level of drunkenness. "I assume you refer to a kiss at the Pump Room?"

He hoped the marquess's informant, whoever the bastard may be, hadn't witnessed the latter incident outside the Assembly Room—though such a revelation might, in actuality, serve to aid his cause.

"Yes. Though I wonder why you question me on that. Is there something else I've yet to hear?" Chatham gazed at him through heavily lidded eyes. "Nevertheless, stay away from Grace. As things stand, I've already discovered her whereabouts and have ordered her aunt and uncle to return her to me in London at once. Should they not comply, I'll involve the authorities. Kidnapping is no trifling matter, you know." Chatham's expression dimmed, turning sinister. "They'll all stay here, at Chatham House, where I can forestall her further exposure to gossip and scandal and where I can be certain the Kensingtons face justice."

Alex didn't waver in his resolve. "I will not stay away from her." His voice dropped. "I have come to request your permission to marry your daughter." He paused as the marquess glowered at him, measuring his words cautiously. "You're obviously aware that I've compromised her. I intend to make things right for her, so she won't suffer ostracism. Allow me to give her the protection of my name."

"Ha! You young pup, you aren't the first to *compromise* my daughter, as you so carefully termed it." Spittle flew from Chatham's mouth and his voice rose. "There can be no other reason she would have left—I mean, no other reason she would have been taken from me. I suppose her aunt and uncle felt they would protect her better than I have, yet they were poorly mistaken, weren't they? Your presence here proves it."

Alex held his temper in check. "I've done more than compromise your daughter. She may well be increasing." As much as he would prefer to avoid admitting this facet of their connection, he knew he must do whatever it took to obtain Chatham's permission. He *would* marry Grace.

"That's no concern. She'll marry Lord Barrow as soon as it can all be arranged. He's made quite a settlement on me for her. The man has a goodly portion." The bastard looked pleased with himself.

"A settlement? Barrow will pay you for her?" Disgust and fury boiled under his skin at the idea of Grace being sold. He couldn't allow that to happen. He *wouldn't*.

"She is quite a prize, don't you agree? After Barrow tasted her treats once, he even raised his offer." The fire had burned down and Chatham rubbed his hands together. "Oh dear, you didn't believe you were the first to have had Grace, did you? She can't carry your child, as she already carried his before you met her." Chatham tsked and tutted in condescension. "You are absolved of at least that one crime. He'll now pay more than the Duke of Walsingham had offered. So whatever you may want, Lord Alexander, she won't be yours."

She was already pregnant. Before they met. It all started to make sense in his mind.

Why she was *unfit* to marry him.

Why she had tried so hard to avoid him.

Why she refused his proposal.

He was crestfallen. It had nothing to do with a dislike of him, but only with her shame and fears.

His determination multiplied. "I'll double Barrow's current offer, whatever the *price* may be." His stomach revolted at the thought, but he saw no alternative.

Chatham perked up, but still scowled from across his desk.

"I have a sizeable fortune, as well. My brother has provided well for our entire family. Money is no object to me."

The marquess raised a cheroot from his desk to his mouth, chewing on the end. Minutes ticked off, and still he did not respond. Alex thought an eternity would pass him by before the marquess finally spoke. His anger toward the man grew with each passing moment of silence.

"The answer is still no. Grace will obtain a title, and I'll become aligned with the Earl of Barrow through her marriage. He has ample estates," Chatham gave a pointed look at Alex, "of which I understand you have none. Likewise, you have no title. Allow me to show you the door." Chatham stood behind his dilapidated desk and moved to escort Alex out.

Alex shook from the violence groveling at him for release. The bastard would sell Grace. To Barrow. "How soon? When will their marriage take place?" He needed time. Perhaps he could overtake the Kensingtons along the road to London and take her to Gretna Greene like her uncle had suggested.

Chatham's eyes narrowed. "That, again, is none of your concern. Do yourself a favor, Hardwicke. Forget her."

"Forget her. *Forget her?* You bloody bastard, have you no concern for your daughter at all? You would sell her to Barrow—for what? What purpose does it serve?" He kept his fists clenched at his sides so he wouldn't strike the man before he good and well earned it. He would not give the blockhead the satisfaction of striking first. "She doesn't care about a title. And she doesn't wish to marry Barrow. You cannot think he would be a better husband for her than I am. You cannot think he could make her happy—could be a good father for her child."

"Whether he will be a *good* father or not is irrelevant, since he is the father. I don't care how he treats them." Chatham reached again for the bottle and poured more into his glass until it overflowed, seemingly oblivious to the mess he created. "She will marry him and then she will be his problem. Not mine. Now leave."

Before the marquess could move around the desk, Alex spun on his heels and marched out the door, fuming his way to the carriage.

He would find a way to marry Grace. He must. No way would he allow Barrow to place one more finger on her, let alone on the child. It would be *his* child, by Jove.

Seventeen

"MY LORD, A missive has just arrived." Mason bowed low to Uncle Laurence and passed him the letter on a silver salver.

Grace glanced over from her seat huddled beneath the quilt she was working on near the hearth. The wax seal belonged to her father. She fought the desire to run to his side and rip the paper from his hands. Another urge, just as strong as the first, rose in her chest—to run away. He must have heard by now about the Pump Rooms. She ought to have left before now, gone somewhere to the north, or perhaps to Ireland. She should have left the sanctuary of her aunt and uncle's home well before now—gone somewhere he couldn't find her.

At least he wasn't there in person. She still had time. She immediately began plotting her escape, how she would leave them, where she would go. Maybe she could convince Tess to help. No— that was too big a risk. She must do this without anyone knowing.

Uncle Laurence looked at his wife for a moment before he broke the seal and read the letter's contents. His expression soured and he walked to the fire, tossing the parchment into the flames with a faint growl.

Grace had never seen her uncle in so foul a mood. "Uncle?" Her voice trembled, but she pressed on. "Uncle Laurence, what did Father write?" She couldn't decide whether her curiosity about the letter's contents outweighed her desire to pretend the letter did not exist. But she had to learn what he had said. He'd found her, after all. She needed to know his plans. Straightening her posture, she leaned forward to await her uncle's response.

"Gracie, you are to return immediately to London. His *lordship* finds your aunt and me remiss in our responsibilities to you—"

Aunt Dorothea bristled at the insult.

"And therefore we shall all go to London where your *father* can oversee our efforts to protect you from the shame you brought upon yourself."

Her aunt interrupted, all righteous indignation. "Why, that insolent man. We have been remiss in our responsibilities to Gracie? What of himself? The bloody—"

"Dorothea," Uncle Laurence chided.

She turned her glare on her husband and scowled. "The *bloody* man must be well deep in his cups, if he is under the mistaken impression he's done anything right by our Gracie, ever once in his *bloody* life. Why, I never!" She moved to Grace's side and ran a hand over her hair. "And to order us to London! Laurence, he has no authority to order us about."

"Apparently, we've been accused of kidnapping her out from beneath his nose. We're to face the authorities on these charges."

The authorities? Kidnapping? Oh dear, what a monstrous mess she'd made. Now she couldn't run away. She had to do whatever she could to clear the names of her aunt and uncle—the people who had sheltered and protected her, who had shown her love for the first time in her life. She couldn't repay them by running.

"What? How ridiculous can the man be?" Aunt Dorothea folded her arms over her chest.

Uncle Laurence paced before the hearth. "Despite the absurdity of his claims, we have no alternative. We must take Grace to London."

"But couldn't you go and clear these lies on your own? I see no reason for Gracie and me to be subjected to such an ordeal." Her aunt sat down again and ripped at the threads hanging from her embroidery project with a fierceness she rarely displayed. "Or even better, we could ask the local magistrate to come here to ascertain the truth. The London authorities should have no reason to doubt the magistrate's word."

"Whether you and I go or not, Gracie must go. Chatham is still her father, despite our wishes. He is her guardian. He has the right to do with her as he wishes, until she reaches her majority. Would you send her to London alone, then? Should she suffer through her confinement in that prison of a house? Who would care for her, if not the two of us, Dorothea?"

Ferocity radiated from Aunt Dorothea as her husband's words sunk in.

Love for her aunt and uncle surged through Grace for their loyalty and protectiveness. But she couldn't suffer the thought of them leaving their home on her account, no matter how necessary they may deem it.

But then her thoughts turned to another matter. "Uncle," she said timidly, "did my father mention the Earl of Barrow?" She feared the answer.

He reached forward to clasp her hand as he responded. "Yes, I'm afraid he did."

Several moments passed in silence.

"You're to marry as soon as the arrangements have been settled."

Good God. She would marry Lord Barrow. She would be his countess. Grace tried to settle her mind, with little success. It shouldn't surprise her. She'd known before she left London that would be her fate, should she stay.

But he ravished me.

Grace placed a hand against the slight swell caused by his atrocious deed, the swell that proved the existence of her baby. Of Barrow's baby.

What kind of father will he be?

Would he force her and her child to stay locked inside his home, much as her father had done for so many years? Would he strike the child? She couldn't tolerate the thought of any harm coming to her babe, but what could she do to stop it? As an unmarried woman, she had no rights. She would have fewer still once she married.

Her child would never know a father's love.

She needed to get outside, to clear her mind. She wrapped the quilt about her shoulders for protection against the cold outdoors. There must be a way out of this mess—she need only discover it.

"Gracie, are you quite alright?" her aunt asked, concern obvious in her tone. Grace walked to the door without answering. "Love, where are you going? Laurence, go fetch her pelisse. She'll surely catch a chill. Oh, lud."

Grace kept walking, oblivious to her aunt's distress. She needed fresh air, the wind on her cheeks, and some space to think. A footman stationed in the front hall opened the door before she walked straight through it.

Lost in thought, she wandered down the lane and away from the cottage, unaware of her surroundings and with no destination in mind. The bitter winds tore through her makeshift shawl, but she ignored the bite.

She didn't want to go back to London. Grace had settled in to her new life in Somerton and had finally found contentment. For the first time since her mother's death, she had people who cared for her, people for whom she cared. But how could she stay put? Her father was still her guardian, no matter either of their wishes on the matter. He could do with her as he wished.

Obviously, Father had concocted some sort of scheme involving this idea of her kidnapping. If only she could determine how Father would benefit from it, then she could discover a way out. Did Barrow know of their child? And how would Father be able to use that information to his advantage? Oh, blast it, why had she ever told Father about the baby to begin with? She should have simply left. This would all be so much easier if he didn't know.

She dreaded this impending marriage, but there was no escape. She could try to leave her aunt and uncle, but she doubted they would make such an escape easy for her at this point. And besides, where would she go, and how would she take care of the baby? The only real option she could conceive of—a marriage to Lord Alexander—she had tossed aside.

If only things had been different. She might have agreed to marry him and been much happier than her life now looked to be. Lord Alexander would be a good husband, she had no doubt. If she could open up to him, trust him, their life together would be more than tolerable. He might even come to love her someday.

And he would be a good father. He would never have to know that the child in her womb was not his own—babies often arrived earlier than they were expected.

But Grace had lost that opportunity. She had told him to find someone more suitable.

It had been right for her to do so. She'd done exactly as she ought, even if it wasn't the best thing for herself. How could she afford the luxury of thinking of herself, at this point? But what of her child? Would the baby not be better loved with Lord Alexander than with Lord Barrow? Alas, the opportunity was lost. She had seen nothing of Lord Alexander since she walked away from him in Bath.

She had walked away from *him*. She must always remember this. The broken heart she suffered was her own doing. There was nowhere else to place the blame.

Blast, none of this was helping anything. She forced herself to think of her future, the true future awaiting her and not the imagined future she would never experience. Lord Barrow would never make a good husband, nor likely a good father, but she had no choice. If nothing else, marrying him would mean she could keep her child, without toiling away at some job in an unknown place.

It would have to be enough.

She turned back toward the cottage and fought against the bitter wind. Tess would need to start packing again. Grace would help her. That would at least give her something to do, somewhere to focus her thoughts other than on her fears.

Fear could come later.

HIS BREATH WAS ragged as he slammed through the front door of Hardwicke House. Alex had walked home from his visit with Chatham instead of riding in the carriage. The rain had let up, and though it was unseasonably cold for May in London, the temperature didn't bother him.

He needed to walk off his anger before he returned to his family.

And what a rage he was in. Alex had difficulty remembering a time when he had come so close to losing control so completely. If he hadn't departed from Chatham House when he did, would have landed himself in prison.

The front door of Hardwicke House crashed to a close behind him, causing paintings and mirrors in the near vicinity to shudder.

Neil Hardwicke, Alex's younger brother, poked his head around the corner from the breakfast room. His sandy-blond hair with touches of the family red stuck out at ends and his blue eyes were bloodshot. "Keep it down, would you,?" He placed a hand to his temple and rubbed. "A man cannot have any quiet around here," Neil grumbled under his breath. He squinted against the light pouring through the windows and grimaced.

"I see you're up before the crack of noon." Alex gave his brother what he intended to be a playful punch on the shoulder, but instead had a good deal of force and heft behind it. "Sorry. And I see it is after noon, nonetheless."

He picked up a slice of bacon and popped it in his mouth, then took a seat across from his younger brother—whose plate was filled to spilling over. "Should we have Peter order the fatted calf killed for dinner then?" He gave a pointed look to Neil's plate in response to the look of confusion he received.

"What in bloody hell are you so chipper about?" Neil stuffed forkfuls of eggs and sausages into his mouth, effectively putting an end to communication beyond grunts, at least for a few minutes.

"Tsk, tsk. Sarcasm is not pretty on you, brother."

Before Neil could respond, Peter and Gil joined them in the breakfast room. "Good morning, Neil. So kind of you to grace us with your presence. To what do we owe this honor?" Peter then turned to Alex. "And you—will you please refrain in future from closing my front door with so much force I can hear it from the mews? Lord Rotheby and I had just returned, and I thought we must be in Vauxhall for the fireworks display."

He passed a none-too-subtle glare in the direction of Alex before continuing. "I don't wish to give my servants more work fixing doors when their time could better be spent in cleaning up after *him*," he said, nodding in the direction of Neil, who maintained his previous pace of devouring everything within reach.

Alex sighed and pulled a hand through his hair. "I'm sorry. I didn't mean to take my frustrations out on your home."

"I know it." Peter waited for a moment, allowing him time to consider his actions. "I take this to mean your interview with Chatham did not go as you had hoped?"

"Chatham? Why did you visit with Chatham?" Neil's mouth gaped open in apparent horror over the revelation, a piece of egg falling to the table.

Peter spared a mind-your-own-matters-we-are-busy-here glance in Neil's direction before urging Alex, who spared the youngest brother no glance at all, to continue.

"He refused. I don't have a title. I don't have any property. Chatham has already promised Grace to Barrow." He ground out the words, forcing them through his lips. "Barrow is paying for her. He's buying her like chattel. Chatham might as well have put her up for auction at Tattersall's, with the way he's handling this."

"Did you offer Chatham reasons to reconsider, Alex?" Gil interjected, joining in the conversation for the first time.

"You want to be *married?*" Neil dropped his fork upon the realization. "And your suit has been rejected by *Chatham?* Of all the—"

All three of the older men shot Neil a look, and he quieted again.

"I offered to double Barrow's offer. I offered to *pay* for her. Good lord, I'm sickened again just from the thought." He buried his head in his hands for a moment to collect himself. "But that wasn't the worst of it. He alleges that her aunt and uncle kidnapped her from his home. He's drawing them up on charges."

"Preposterous!" Gil's vigor returned in full force.

Peter rubbed his chin for a moment before he spoke. "That cannot be true, can it?"

He pushed away from the table and strode to the window. "I don't believe it. Not for a minute. I believe, if anything, she ran away. Frankly, I wouldn't blame her, after having met the man." Alex punched the wall, then shook the sting from his fisted hand. "He's ordered her to return, so she can marry Barrow immediately. I may have lost my chance for her, if I cannot intercept them and rush with her to Gretna Greene. But even still, she's refused me. I just don't know what to do." Her aunt and uncle would assist him in convincing her to accept. Wouldn't they? "Perhaps I could kidnap her and take her there."

Neil shook his head with force. "You can't kidnap her. Not with Chatham already accusing the Kensingtons of having done just that. There has to be another way. Besides, Barrow would be furious. Trust me, you don't want to anger him if you can avoid it. Keep thinking."

"But I have to do *something*. She's with child." Bloody hell. Why had he mentioned that? But if he couldn't tell his family, who could he tell? "I have to protect her, to save her somehow. Damn it, everything keeps getting in the way."

Several minutes passed with no one speaking. Alex stewed in his anguish, trying to find a way to change the marquess's mind. He hadn't intended to fall in love with Grace, but somehow it had happened despite his best intentions. One day he was fine, the next he was head over ears. He needed to know that he could be with her.

Finally, Gil cleared his throat. "There is something I ought to tell you which may be of assistance." The three younger men faced him,

Neil and Alex in confusion, Peter in understanding. "Hmm. How should I begin?" A coughing fit struck him, so they all waited for the earl to recompose himself.

Gil looked straight at Alex. His skin had returned to the greyish pallor after their journey from Bath to London. "I'm dying." Alex tried to interrupt but stopped upon the emergence of a staying hand from Rotheby. "You already realized that, and don't pretend otherwise. I've been suffering from consumption for more than a year now. The doctors can't do anything to slow the disease. I don't have much longer. The business I needed to handle—it had to do with my estates." Again, Alex started to butt in, and again, Gil raised his hand him. "Most of the estates are entailed and will pass to my grandson. But not all of them."

Alex questioned his friend with his eyes but stayed silent.

"That's part of the reason I asked you to visit me. Roundstone Park is not entailed. I purchased it after inheriting the earldom from my father. In my will, it was grouped with all of the rest of my holdings and would fall to Quinton. Until today.

"I changed my will this afternoon. When I die, Roundstone will be yours." Gil coughed again after his long speech, and Neil passed him a cup of tea. He took a few sips and waited for the spasm to pass. "Talk to Chatham again. Tell him you will soon inherit property. Maybe you can change his mind."

"I am not so certain it will." Neil's sober countenance gave Alex pause. "Chatham doesn't care about his daughter. Her welfare is not his primary concern. Frankly, if you offered to double Barrow's offer I'm at a loss as to why he didn't jump at your offer. Money seems to be his biggest problem, from what I've seen of him at White's. And Barrow is certainly not the type of man anyone of taste would want an association with. Surely Grace's father—well, I do hope he's not in line with Barrow. That would not bode well for him, I daresay."

"But I did propose to double the offer. I would give him more, even, if he would allow me to marry her and then leave us alone."

Peter had remained silent for most of the conversation, until now. "Then Chatham has some other motive for wanting the alliance with Barrow." Neil, Alex, and Rotheby turned to him. "I believe the rest of this conversation can wait. Mama will expect us for tea, and then we shall prepare for tonight's ball. Neil, Mama requested that I remind you she expects your joyful attendance as well." Neil stifled a groan. Peter sent a gentle smile in the direction of their ailing friend. "I believe she'll excuse Lord Rotheby, under the circumstances."

As Peter stood to leave, the others followed suit. Neil and the earl left first, with Neil making a jovial remark about feigning consumption, so Mama would leave him alone and not force him to dance all evening. Peter took hold of Alex's arm, holding him back.

"Alex, are you certain you don't love Lady Grace?" He smiled in companionship. "Your reaction to her father's denial makes me curious."

"I don't know anymore." Did he? Could he love Grace? He knew he wanted what was best for her, what she deserved. And he wanted to protect her. But was that enough for love? He just wasn't certain.

However, he had a nagging suspicion he was deluding himself.

Peter took his time before he continued. "Tomorrow, you should visit Chatham again. Try to convince him to change his mind, based on the property you will inherit from Lord Rotheby. Perhaps if he sees that you can be a more worthwhile gentleman for him to be aligned with, he will. Allow me to join you. I know you wish to handle all of this on your own, but sometimes, it's best to let our family assist us."

"Peter—"

"Don't 'Peter' me. Just allow me to accompany you. I ask no more. I won't interfere, unless you request my interference."

Alex frowned before nodding in assent. The Hardwickes stayed together. They always had, and he hoped they always would. If Peter or Neil or Richard were in the same position, he would insist on the same thing. And every single one of them would involve themselves if either of their sisters needed assistance. This didn't make him any less a man.

"After tea, I have another piece of business I must see to, but I'll be ready to join everyone for the ball." Alex needed to see Priscilla and Harry. He had to talk to her, sooner rather than later.

Peter narrowed his eyes at him. "Very well. But don't be late, or I'll be forced to take action against you. You will not upset Mama, Alex."

"I'll be ready on time. No need to worry about that."

Side-by-side, they joined the rest of the family for tea. He tried not to think of anything but the coming ball.

But in his mind, a woman with hair of midnight and a pair of ice-blue eyes danced with him. If only he could really dance with her again.

IT WASN'T YET dark when he arrived at Priscilla's house. Vivian ushered him in to the cozy downstairs parlor, where Pris was seated on a sofa beneath a quilt. Harry was nowhere to be found.

"Is he already in bed, then?" Alex moved to give her a brief kiss on the cheek. "I had hoped I'd be able to see him, if only for a moment."

"It's better this way. He would be so excited over seeing you, he wouldn't be able to sleep. I didn't know to expect you. How are you?" She slid over to make more room for him and patted the seat next to her.

"Not good." Good God, how could he hash through all of this again?

"Tell me. Let it all out." She slipped one hand behind his neck and kneaded away his tensions. Priscilla always knew just the right thing to do.

Once he started, the whole story flooded out of him. He lost track of the time as he told her of the woman he loved but couldn't have—at least not yet.

"So what will you do? If her father won't grant his permission, how will you take care of her?"

"I haven't determined that yet. This would all be so much easier if she would agree, at the very least. But taking her out of the country against her will and forcing her to marry me doesn't seem like the brightest idea. She wouldn't take that well." He raked through his hair and stared at nothing. "And even if I *do* marry her, what of you and Harry? I don't imagine she would be terribly keen on the idea of setting up a house for you nearby in the country."

"Your lady doesn't know of us, then?" Priscilla stiffened, but continued to massage the soreness from his neck. "There's no need to move us to the country. We can stay here. I believe we could even find someone else to care for us. You needn't worry."

"But I do worry. You know I care deeply for you, both of you. Harry—he looks to me as a father." Alex shook off her hand and walked to the window. "I can't leave you behind, and I can't allow you to fend for yourselves."

"You owe us nothing. Nothing." Tears filled her eyes. "You've done more for us than anyone ever ought to have done, and what's that gotten you in return? We'll be fine. Like you said, your new wife wouldn't take kindly to having us around, I'm certain. We could only cause problems for you in the country. There would be talk. You know there would be talk."

He punched the wall next to the window. "Who cares about the deuced talk?"

"Lady Grace will care, that's who. You should, as well, or you aren't the man I thought you to be." Priscilla picked her sewing up from the table next to her. She studiously worked at a stitch and ignored him.

"Devil take it," he muttered under his breath.

"I heard that." She peeked at him over her notions. "Don't forget I'm a mother. We hear everything."

"I apologize. But what would you have me do, Pris? It seems I can't win. I can neither take you with me, nor leave you behind. So now what?"

"So now you go make this happen. Find a way to marry her. And let me worry about myself and Harry for once."

"But—"

"But nothing. There's no more to discuss here." A determination like he had never before heard from her rang through in her tone.

Alex took a breath. He didn't know how he should approach this next bit—or even whether he should at all. "There is one other thing—one more piece to this puzzle." Christ, they hadn't talked about him in years. He hated to bring back the hurt and pain this would cause, but she needed to know.

"Go on."

He turned toward her to speak, but hesitated.

"I can handle it. Whatever it is, I can handle it. I'm not as fragile as you've always assumed me to be. I won't break."

If she had not broken through all she had been through, it must be the truth. He burst forth with it before he could stop himself again. She needed the truth as much as he needed to tell her. "It was Barrow." Immediately, he wished he could take those three words back.

Tears filled her eyes and ran, unimpeded, in rivulets down her cheeks. "And what will you do about it?" came so softly, he had to strain to hear her words.

"I want to rip the bastard's head off with my bare hands. I don't know what to do, Pris. But first you, and now Grace. The bastard should rot for this. He should pay." The pain in his fist from punching the wall suddenly struck him, and he rubbed his knuckles with his other hand. "I'm sorry for using such language in front of you."

Priscilla stood gingerly with the aid of the cane next to her and limped to his side. With her free hand, she touched his cheek and then placed a single, chaste kiss in the same place. "You cannot undo what he's done. And you cannot bear the weight of all of his wrongs. Let it be. He'll get his due."

"How can I let it be? Chatham will force Grace to marry the lout."

"Not if you have anything to say about it. There's always hope, Alex."

"Always?" He looked in her eyes, steadfast and unwavering, for comfort.

"Always."

Eighteen

A KNOCK SOUNDED at the door to Alex's chamber while Thomas worked to secure his neck cloth. He had donned all the proper evening finery, fussy though it may be. A top hat would finish the look. Or at least it would after Thomas finished his infernal fussing over the damned cravat.

"Come in," he called and looked up to discover his mother. "Mama. You look lovely this evening."

She wore a bold blue gown that accentuated the richness of her eyes. Her auburn hair, the color of which she had passed on to each of her children in varying degrees, had only just begun to show spots of grey about the temples. Henrietta Hardwicke, in Alex's unduly biased opinion, was the epitome of grace, elegance, and love.

She somehow brightened even more at his compliment, then moved from the doorway to a seat on a nearby chaise. "Thomas, please finish with my son's cravat and leave us. I promise you shall have more than enough time to fuss over his appearance when I'm done with him."

Alex walked to kiss his mother on the cheek as his valet bustled from the room.

She patted a spot on the chaise next to her. "Sit down, Alex. I want to speak with you." Though he couldn't imagine the purpose of her visit, he complied—he wouldn't dream of defying her to her face.

"I was very disappointed in you when you left for Somerton at the beginning of the Season, you know—"

"Mama—"

She lifted a brow to stop him from interrupting. "Hold on a moment, dear heart. I said I was disappointed in you." Taking his hand in one of her own, she looked at their interlocked fingers as she patted the back of his with her free hand. "You see, I had great plans for all of my children. Your father and I both did."

His mother looked away for a moment as a single tear fell down her cheek. She brushed at it absentmindedly. "And when Donald died, I set all our plans for the lot of you aside. My grief overwhelmed me. It became larger in my mind than anything I could want for each of you."

"Mama, we grieved Father too." Blast. He didn't know how to console his mother. For too many years, her tears were a constant companion. They had slowed a good deal recently, but it still broke his heart to see her cry.

"Goodness, of course you were all grieving. I'm making a cake of myself in trying to say this." She took a breath and continued. "But this Season—this Season, I was going to resume working toward the plans your father and I had. I've quite neglected Sophia, I daresay— she's virtually on the shelf. Charlotte is nearing her come-out. And you...well, it is well past the time you determine how you want to spend your days, you know. Time for sowing your wild oats is past. So when you left for Somerton, I felt you had defied me. Oh, Peter explained you were going to spend some time in the country and think about your life, and I know Lord Rotheby sent for you and you wanted to spend some time with him, so it had very little, if anything, to do with me."

Alex bit his tongue to refrain from telling her just how much a part of his reason for leaving she had been.

"But I wanted to find you a bride. I thought if you had a lady by your side, you would settle down and be content. But that wasn't your way." Mama slowed her speech and gazed at him with sorrow.

Then she reached a hand up to brush aside a stray lock of hair, much as she had done when he was a boy. "You always were one who needed to find your own way, weren't you? But Peter convinced me to allow you your space and time to find what you want." Her look turned serious as she faced him directly. "Have you found that? Is this Lady Grace Abernathy what will make you happy?"

She placed a single finger to his lips when he tried to answer. "Don't answer that. Not yet. Alex, I want you to have a love match, like your father and I did. I know it isn't how many amongst our class do thing, but that doesn't make marrying for wealth or title or prestige *right*. When you marry, make it count. Make it last." She gazed into his eyes with a determination that could only come from love. "Make it beautiful."

Beautiful. Leave it to Mama to boil it all down to something as perfectly simple and infinitely complex as that.

Several more tears wetted her cheeks, which she ignored. He brushed them away and rested his palm against the side of his mother's face.

"So do you? Do you love her? Please tell me you do, sweetheart, and I'll promise to love her as my very own daughter."

He desired to tell her that yes, he very much loved Grace and would make a marriage of it with her as she had done with his father. But he couldn't tell her anything less than the truth.

But what *was* the blasted truth? He exhaled louder than he intended. "I don't know if it's love. I care for her deeply…there is a certain affection in which I hold her. I want to protect her. There's even a possibility I could feel a bit of jealousy at times toward other men who might fancy her. She fascinates me—she's beautiful and quiet and passionate—an artist. But love?"

He paused and thought long and hard before continuing. "I will do everything in my power to make what I feel for Grace become love. She deserves a marriage to a man who will love her in the same way Father loved you. I intend to give her that." A few moments passed while his resolve deepened. "I'll fight to give her that."

His mother looked up at him, her eyes full of admiration. "I can see you will. Do what you need to do. You know we'll all assist you if you need it. Though I daresay you would refuse it, wouldn't you? You have become a ferociously independent man." She rose to leave him, but stopped when she reached the door. "Your father would be quite proud of you." And then she left him.

A sense of longing welled in his chest, a need to make her words come to fruition. Alex never realized before this moment how much he wanted to make his father proud, or his mother for that matter, or even Peter and the rest of his siblings, or Priscilla and Harry. He wanted desperately to be the man they all thought him to be.

But even greater than that, another need grew. The need for Grace to be proud of him.

What would *that* require? Lord only knew.

THREE OF THE four Hardwicke brothers, dressed to the nines, huddled together in the Yardley Court ballroom. They watched the crowd of marriageable-aged misses and their mamas fill the room beneath three matching chandeliers and row upon row of wall sconces filled with candles. All the candlelight cast the ballroom aglow in their shimmering glory, amongst an entire garden's worth of pots and hanging baskets bearing flowers that perfumed the entire space. An orchestra warmed their instruments in the balcony, sending a cacophony down to the cream of society.

Across the room from the Hardwicke men, Alex's mother was playing chaperone to Sophie, who looked bored but still elegant in a soft pink silk gown with her chestnut hair twisted into complicated twirls atop her head and tangled with matching pink ribbons. Mama was motioning to him. The first set would begin in a moment, and he hadn't yet fulfilled his role and selected a partner. Nor, for that matter, had either of his brothers selected a partner.

"It appears we're neglecting our duty," Alex said to his brothers. He extinguished a grin that threatened to appear at Neil's rolled eyes, hoping instead to achieve something in the line of a grimace or a scowl. For some reason, he doubted he had achieved the desired effect. "Off you go, youngster. Dance with a young miss and set her heart aflutter."

Neil wandered off, muttering beneath his breath. Peter turned to Alex with a resigned smile. "Shall we dance with the Sutter daughters? Mama hinted she'd like me to align myself with Lady Margaret, and I've yet to do anything about it."

"And just why have you been neglecting such a thing?"

Peter *did* manage a scowl, along with a perfected glare of condescension. "If you take her sister, I'll dance with her. Then Mama will be satisfied. Go on—Lady Amelia awaits."

"Is that a gentle nudge? Or a ducal order?"

Peter answered him with a sharp nudge to his rib cage.

"Oof. I see it was an order." He absentmindedly rubbed a hand against the offended area as they moved across the dance floor to where the sisters stood with their mother, the Countess of Derby.

Peter executed a deeply elegant bow to the ladies, and Alex followed suit. "Ladies. I do hope you're enjoying yourselves this evening." When he straightened, he flashed a devilish smile that seemed to bring even the countess to her knees.

The three women curtsied to him and Lady Margaret spoke. "Thank you, Your Grace. Yes, it's quite a pleasant evening. Yardley Court is rather charming, is it not?" She looked at him expectantly.

"Not nearly so charming as you, Lady Margaret. Tell me, have I come too late to request your hand for the first set?" Peter placed his arm out for her hand in a clear expectation that he had't.

She gingerly placed her hand in the crook of his arm. "Why no, Your Grace. I should be honored to dance with you." They moved off, leaving Alex with the younger Sutter sister and the countess.

He set his attentions on the mother. "Ma'am, will it be too great an inconvenience if I deprive you of both your daughters for this set?" He had not forgotten how to play the part of the gallant gentleman during his time in the country, it seemed. Chivalry was still alive and well with the Hardwicke men. Blast it.

The countess simpered, "Gracious heavens, no my lord. I see Lady Poole has arrived, and I should very much like to speak with her. We have plans for, er, for a picnic, you know." She virtually pushed Lady Amelia into his waiting arms as she left them.

Lady Amelia glanced up to him with chagrin. "I'd be delighted." They took their place in the lines next to their siblings, making polite conversation about the weather in Town of late, the latest gossip among the *ton*, and other equally ambivalent subjects with which one might converse with a young society miss without repercussions of shock or dismay throughout the set.

Alex was bored and brooding in no time. He would much prefer the silence, or even the heated disdain, of Grace.

When the set finally came to a close, the brothers escorted the Sutter sisters to their waiting mother. After leaving them safely in her care and moving out of earshot, Peter asked, "Is Lady Amelia's conversation as insipid as her elder sister's? I do hope Mama is not serious about wanting me to offer for Lady Margaret. I've no desire to marry a woman with whom it is tedious to speak. She's, but good heavens." He tilted his head to the side to emphasize his point.

"Not much better with the younger sister, I'm afraid. Perhaps you should find another appropriate young miss to court before Mama finds one for you." Alex winked at his older brother. He had no doubt that half the single ladies in the *beau monde* would gladly set their caps on the Duke of Somerton, should he give even the slightest indication of being in the market for a bride again.

"Thanks to me, you seem to have avoided a similar fate." Peter clapped a hand on Alex's shoulder.

"Look at the two of you." Derek Redgrave and another friend, Sir Jonas Buchannan, joined Peter and Alex on the side of the dance floor, wide grins all around. "With Somerton and his ne'er-do-well brother, Lord Alexander, at the ball, there will be no ladies remaining for the rest of us to dance with. All the young misses are certain to be otherwise engaged, with discussions of whom the two of you are most likely to dance with, or perchance, take for a stroll through the gardens. The rest of us might as well head over to White's and play cards, because our presence will soon be redundant," Derek said as he glanced at Sir Jonas.

Alex reached over and gave a light slap to Derek's shoulder. "I hardly think you capable of redundancy, Derek. It is good to see you as well." For the first time since his interview with Chatham, he felt a broad smile form almost without his permission.

Peter stared across the ballroom at something indeterminate. He pulled his hand up to rub against his chin in the familiar, unconscious gesture. "Pardon me, gentlemen," he said after a moment. "I see someone with whom I must speak. I'll visit with you all later, I'm certain." He left without sparing the others a glance, making his way through the throngs to a darkened corner of the room, where his mystery acquaintance waited.

Alex's gaze followed Peter until he lost sight of him in the crowd. His curiosity soon evaporated as the remaining party fell into conversation. "Your absence from Town has been conspicuous," Sir Jonas said. "Where've you been hiding yourself? And please tell me you have been up to no good."

They all laughed. "I hate to disappoint," Alex said, "but I've merely been in Somerton. Rotheby sent for me. I've kept him company. Nothing more exciting than that, I fear."

"Nothing else?" Sir Jonas asked. "Then what is this I hear of your visit to Chatham this afternoon?"

Derek raised an eyebrow. "Chatham? What on God's good earth could you have to do with Chatham?"

He wished he could have talked to Derek before this evening, but there had been no time. But still, why should he hide his current endeavor from his friends? Word would spread through town in no time if he were to marry Grace. They would know sooner rather than later. "I went to ask for his permission to marry his daughter."

"You? Get married?" Derek let out a loud guffaw. "Has hell just frozen over and I missed it somehow?"

Sir Jonas eyed Alex for a few moments, before a flicker of understanding traveled between them. "No. This is no great surprise. The Hardwickes have always been about family first—we should've expected one of them to give in soon. Hell, Somerton himself beat Alex to the punch several years ago."

Derek nodded. "True, true. So when will you leave the masses of eligible gentlemen?" he asked. "I assume Somerton will insist on a lavish affair, even if your mother hasn't. Where is she?" Derek asked as he looked about the ballroom.

Alex scanned the crowd for only a moment before he found his mother's unmistakable coiffure across the way. "Just over there," he said with an impatient wave of his hand.

"No, you numbskull, not your mother. Your betrothed. I don't believe I have made her acquaintance before."

"Grace is not here. She's in Somerton or Bath or somewhere with her aunt and uncle. Actually, she may be on her way to Town, now that I think of it." He paused a beat, again debating how much should be spoken before a gathered crowd. There could be no telling how many gossips had their ears tuned in their direction. "Chatham didn't approve. He has an arrangement with Lord Barrow." The words were bitter on his tongue.

"Surely you jest," Sir Jonas said with a somber tone. "He would prefer to be aligned with Barrow than the *Duke of Somerton*?"

Derek said nothing, but looked at Alex as though he could see inside his head.

Neil joined them before Alex could respond to his friends. "Pardon me, gentlemen. Alex, I—take a look who has just joined the ball." He gestured toward the entrance of the ballroom to a pair of older men deep in conversation.

Chatham and Barrow! The bastards.

Alex started to storm across the room to confront the two men, but Derek and Neil held him back. Derek's grip was, admittedly, the more insistent of the two. Neil would probably enjoy the scene, particularly if blood were involved.

"Wait, Alex," Sir Jonas said. "Calm yourself first. You'll accomplish nothing if you go in without thinking things through first."

He had a point. Alex focused on his breathing to slow his heart from pounding a hole through his chest.

"I take it there is more to the story," Sir Jonas said, "than you saw fit to tell us at first. What can we do to help?"

"I don't know. There may be no help." Alex tried to hide his agony, but surely did a poor job of it. His friends and brother looked on him with sympathy.

"You love her." Derek's statement was quiet, simple. True. It shot straight to the belly of the problem.

Words failed Alex, but he managed a nod of his head. Tears stung his eyes before he fought them down. He could deal with that later. He needed to be focused now. Calm. A deadly peace settled over him. Grace was what mattered. And fiend take it, somehow, he had fallen headlong in love with the chit.

"Well, what are we waiting here for?" Derek walked across the room, taking smooth, purposeful strides. The others followed him— Sir Jonas with calm gait that belied his intensity; Neil taking punchy, determined steps that showed his eagerness to join in a fracas; and Alex taking up the rear, steeling his body forward while his eyes narrowed in on Chatham and Barrow ahead, almost hunting his prey.

The two blackguards removed themselves from the main ballroom, but Alex followed them with his eyes. The foursome pursued them through a long corridor lined with candle fixtures and mirrors. Peter stepped into the hall ahead of them with two men Alex did not recognize, bringing both parties to an almost instantaneous halt. "Barrow, Chatham. Would you care to join us in the library?" Peter's tone was deceptively mild. Never a good sign.

Chatham stumbled even though he was no longer moving. Surprise flickered across his face. "Somerton, good to see you." He glanced around and his face registered recognition of the vast contingent of men who had trailed them from the ballroom. "Ah, all of you."

Barrow's eyes turned wild, flashing from man to man.

Peter held the door to the library open and gestured for everyone to enter before him. Alex sent him a question with his eyes as he passed through the doorway, but his brother only answered with a brief shake of his head.

He ached to put his fist through one of them, if not both, or at least to wrap his hands about their necks until they snapped. Instead, he did as his eldest brother expected of him. For now, at least.

Once everyone was settled, Peter began. "It seems, gentlemen, we have some business to discuss."

He moved to a table at the side of the room and poured himself a glass of port, biding his time. The silence thickened in the library.

"Might I introduce Mr. Dennison and Mr. Frost," he said after a long pause, gesturing to his two companions in turn. "Lord Barrow, you, in particular, might be interested in making their acquaintance. Though I daresay Lord Chatham will be interested, also, based on certain claims and accusations he has recently made to my brother."

Peter paused, took a sip of his port, and the tension in the room increased. "They work for Bow Street."

Barrow bolted from his seat and made for the door, with Dennison and Frost hot on his heels. Chaos erupted in his wake.

Sir Jonas shot up to assist the Bow Street Runners in returning Barrow to the room. All color drained from Chatham's face, and he slunk into the shadows of the room. Alex burst forward to attack anyone he could, desperate to plant a fist against Chatham's nose or one of Barrow's wild eyes, while Derek and Neil forcibly held him back.

Only Peter remained calm.

Nineteen

"WHAT IS THE meaning of this, Your Grace?" Chatham asked in an obvious attempt to feign innocence. His chin quivered, sending the extra chin hanging above his neck into convulsions.

In the brief moments since Peter had introduced his companions to the group, Barrow had been bodily returned to the room after a desperate attempt to flee. Alex fumed from his seat, where Derek and Neil stood at his side, a staying hand from each pressed none-too-gently into his shoulders, though he was sure Neil would allow him to break free if he felt the need to. Derek was an altogether different story.

Alex's anger at these two men threatened to explode, to overwhelm his enforced calm, to outweigh his judgment. There was Chatham's callous treatment of his daughter, his false accusation against her aunt and uncle, and his denial of Alex's pursuit. There was Barrow's treatment of Grace, which, whether he forced himself on her or not, he left her alone to deal with the shame of his actions and a pregnancy to boot. Alex couldn't even think of how the man had mistreated Priscilla. The bastard deserved no less than the hangman's noose.

But in the eyes of the law, he had done nothing wrong, at least nothing that Alex could see. Why would Barrow be more interested in the presence of the Bow Street Runners than Chatham? The marquess was the one who had made false accusations. Alex looked to Peter and waited for an explanation, biting down hard on his tongue to keep himself still. Peter may not explain things as briskly as he would like, but he always—*always*—had every aspect of a situation well thought out and handled before anyone else understood the complete scenario.

Peter turned to Chatham before responding. "Lord Chatham, I believe Mr. Frost can explain things to your satisfaction. He has some business with your friend, Lord Barrow." Peter gave a no-nonsense nod of his head in Frost's direction and took a seat before the fire.

Frost cleared his throat and eyed Barrow. Dennison held Barrow still, with the help of Sir Jonas. "My lords, it seems His Highness, the Prince Regent, has some questions for the earl."

Alex's eyes felt like they would pop free from their sockets, but he kept silent. Questions from the Prince Regent? That could only mean treason. He stared first at Barrow pulling against his captors, and then at Chatham, whose nervous eyes shifted about the room.

"Unhand me," said Barrow. "I demand to be released at once. This is preposterous." Nervous laughter escaped him, apparently against his will.

"I'm afraid, my lord, that is impossible," said Frost. "You got away from us once, but you won't escape again. You won't be leaving my sight until His Highness's questions have been satisfied."

Dennison tightened his grip on Barrow's elbow and shoved him back into place when the man pulled away, yet again, in another desperate attempt to free himself. Alex turned his attention to Chatham, whose shifty eyes had started to twitch. The marquess stood and slunk toward the door. Alex itched to manhandle him and force him to stay put, but Derek's hands against his shoulders pressed him more firmly to his seat. Sir Jonas left Barrow's side and slid into a position before the door, blocking Chatham's escape.

Sweat covered Barrow's brow and dripped from his nose onto the once-crisp linen of his cravat. "Will not escape again? Ha ha! You can't be serious." He searched the room but found no one sensitive to his plight—not even Chatham at this point, who seemed more inclined to preserve his own person. Unsurprising. The man always looked after himself first, as made imminently evident by his handling Grace's situation.

Barrow faced Somerton. "Your Grace, there must be some mistake. Whatever could—could—could these men believe—I—I've done?" His voice rose in pitch, almost with each word. Then he let out a whinny-like laugh, followed by a snort.

Peter never faltered. "Mr. Frost, why don't you detail His Highness's complaints and questions for the earl, while witnesses are present? I believe now is as good a time as any."

Alex moved to the edge of his seat. He didn't want to miss a word of this.

Frost inclined his head before turning to face the center of the room. "Your Grace. My lords. His lordship, the Earl of Barrow has been accused of treason against the crown." Just as expected. Though somewhat unexpected as well. Alex's luck was beginning to look up, indeed.

Barrow jerked violently against his captors, only to be forcibly held in his seat.

Chatham moved three steps backward without a glance and bumped into Sir Jonas, who planted his hands on the marquess's shoulders. This action both steadied the man and hindered any further attempts at escape.

Alex's pulse quickened, but he remained seated. He refused to move his gaze from Barrow. Chatham could be dealt with later. Barrow would pay now.

Frost ignored the commotion around him and continued. "His Highness, the Prince Regent, has reason to believe his informant. He's agreed to allow Lord Barrow a trial before his peers. However, Lord Barrow may not leave England again, most certainly not to travel to the continent. His Highness will not chance Lord Barrow's continued involvement in illicit activity."

Chatham interrupted. "Treason?" He overplayed his attempt at conveying shock, especially since treason had already been mentioned a few moments earlier. Chatham had no hope of convincing Alex that he wasn't fully informed of all of Barrow's dealings. These two had worked in concert. Now he need only determine how Grace's *kidnapping* played into this and how it would serve Chatham.

Frost glared at the marquess before continuing. "Yes. Treason. Dennison and I've been charged by His Highness with the task of collecting Lord Barrow for his trial."

"I refuse to go with you," Barrow said. "These charges are ridiculous—completely unfounded. Somerton, you cannot believe the man."

Peter simply raised an eyebrow, only for a moment. Just long enough to convey his disdain. He said nothing.

Neil, however, could no longer remain silent. "Barrow, you bloody dunderhead, you've done a poor job of hiding your tracks." Contempt for the man burned through his eyes like daggers. "Half the regulars at White's have been curious about your frequent 'holidays' to the Continent for some time. And more than a handful have whispered about your dealings with the French a bit too loudly in recent times for any guise of secrecy."

For a moment, Alex exchanged roles with his younger brother. He grabbed hold of an arm to forestall the hotheaded Neil from charging across the room and assaulting Barrow. If anyone was going to strike the man today, it would be him, by God.

"Your so-called 'business' with the Marquis de Fontaine put my brother in danger, you bastard. His regiment was in Leipzig!" Neil pulled so hard against Alex's arm that Derek moved in front of the youngest man. His broad frame blocked any attempt at an attack.

Peter raised a hand to silence Neil. "Let these men handle Barrow. We don't know—"

"We don't know?" Neil interrupted. "We most certainly do know the dangers Richard faces every day."

"I was saying, Neil," Peter said as a gentle admonishment, "we don't know enough of Barrow's involvement in any dealings with the French to become his judge and jury. It's best to allow these men to take him for a visit with the Regent and a trial. Allow justice to be served."

Justice, indeed. There wasn't a doubt in Alex's mind he'd be found guilty, even if he was innocent of treason. But Barrow was guilty of enough else that Alex could feel no pity for the man. Not that he would want to.

He tried to sort through everything happening around him. Barrow was a traitor, at least in Prinny's eyes. He would never go free. He would never marry Grace. That meant Alex *could* marry Grace. He would make it happen. He had to.

He was oblivious to the conversation that continued until Barrow burst free from Dennison's grasp and bowled over Chatham to get through the door. Alex came back to himself when Sir Jonas shouted, "Deuced hell," before all three men fell in a pile to the floor.

Dennison and Frost joined the fray and wrestled Barrow into submission. In the intervening melee, Derek, Neil, and Alex each let go of their holds on the others. For the first time since they had entered the library, Alex was free to do as he pleased.

Neil hauled Barrow to his feet and held him while Frost secured the suspected traitor's hands behind his back with a rope.

Alex took his chance before the man's hands were fully secured and landed a hard blow to the earl's jaw. "That," he spat out, "is for Grace."

Neil let go of his grasp on the man, and Frost backed away.

Another blow, this time to his nose. Barrow moaned and spit blood in Alex's face before he slid to the floor in pain, moving his hands to rub the injured areas. "That one is for Priscilla."

No one rushed to Barrow's aid. They all just stood aside and watched.

"You dare to strike me over two whores? And while I was bound, no less. Coward."

Before he could stop himself, Alex swung his heavy, booted foot at Barrow's stomach. The earl merely crumpled over in pain, unable to even counter with another argument.

Alex backed away and shook the sting from his hand. "That was for Harry," he said so quietly, he almost didn't realize it had come from his own lips.

"Your Grace. My lords," Frost said as he moved once again to Barrow's side, holding him as though to restrain him further, though there was no need any longer. He was in too much pain to offer much resistance. "We'll escort the prisoner to the Tower now. His Highness would like to thank you for your loyalty to the crown, Your Grace, but he asks that you keep a healthy eye on Lord Chatham until a determination can be made as to his involvement."

Through the entire ordeal, Peter hadn't moved a muscle. He nodded his head to the two Runners. "Of course, Frost. I am at His Highness's service, as always."

Frost and Dennison pushed the hunched over Barrow through the doors and away from the ball. Alex waited until the clicks of their heels against the marble floors faded into the background noise of the ballroom.

Chatham stood in a new position near the fire, quivering in fear.

"Well, I believe I've had more than enough entertainment for one evening," Peter said. "Shall we all retire to Hardwicke House and discuss what's to be done from there?"

The other men mumbled their agreement. With great distaste, Alex noted that Chatham had been included in the general invitation. Peter would honor his commitment, then, to the fullest.

Peter gave Chatham a pointed look. "I'll only be a moment. I must give my thanks to Lord Anders for the use of his library and his hospitality for the evening. Lord Chatham, you'll be staying at Hardwicke House for an extended visit."

The older man looked pained. "Am I to understand this is an order and not a request, then?"

"Understand it as you will. It's of no concern to me. But you will join us at Hardwicke House." Peter turned to Derek, then. "Sinclaire, might we have use of your carriage as well, this evening? I don't believe we have room for everyone in my carriages. We have quite the party returning this evening."

Derek nodded his assent.

"Excellent. I'll order them all prepared at once."

Peter left the library without delay.

Alex could think of only one thing. Grace could never be forced to marry Barrow now.

She was free.

GRACE PUSHED THE wave of nausea threatening to overpower her down yet again. She refused to be sick in her uncle's carriage.

But with each step of the horses, she drew one step closer to London.

One step closer to her fate. To marriage.

To Lord Barrow.

And every step also took her further from everything she loved. Well, not quite everything, to be fair. Aunt Dorothea and Uncle Laurence were with her, traveling to London. They would stay with her as long as possible.

But she had left behind New Hill Cottage, the open hills of Somerton, and a piece of her heart. She had left behind Lord Alexander.

A single tear escaped before she could squelch it, and Grace cringed as she wiped it away.

"Gracie, sweetheart," Aunt Dorothea said. "Are you quite unwell? Should we stop the carriage and rest for a bit?" The older woman reached across the empty area between them and grasped one of Grace's hands.

"No, Aunt. Please let us continue." Why must she have noticed?

A dubious look settled on Aunt Dorothea's face. "All right. But don't try to be strong, Gracie. In your condition, a woman must take care to rest. I don't wish to overtax you, and I am certain your father would understand our late arrival. Even a monster like him has feelings."

"Dorothea," Uncle Laurence warned.

"What?" she asked. "They do. Everyone has feelings." She paused for a beat, lifting a brow at him. "And the man is most certainly a monster, with the way he's treated Gracie, not to mention how he's accused *us* of *kidnapping* her."

He said nothing, but gripped his wife's fingers and squeezed in admonition.

Silence returned to the carriage. Grace stared through the windows at the countryside passing them by and wished the horses would slow their gait, or a wheel would get stuck in a rut in the road, or a highwayman would accost them and delay their arrival in Town.

But none of those things would happen. Grace's luck did not run that way.

After another long stretch of travel, the driver stopped the team to allow the Kensingtons and Grace to break for a meal. They could have stopped at a posting inn and been served, but they chose instead to picnic. Uncle Laurence claimed he preferred to sit in the bright sun for a time, but Grace believed he ordered the picnic for a different reason.

They were nearing Town—and society—and Grace was in no frame of mind to handle polite conversation with strangers, who may or may not have heard of her and her situation—or rather, any number of situations she had recently found herself in. Uncle Laurence must be sensitive to her plight.

So they picnicked on cold meats and cheeses by the side of the road under the shade of nearby trees.

"It's quite a lovely day we're having," Aunt Dorothea said. "Isn't it? I do love the sunshine, and we've had frightfully little of it in Somerton lately. Oh dear, Laurence, I believe I've stained my frock."

Aunt Dorothea rubbed at what might be a grass stain, but was possibly nothing but a damp spot on the green traveling gown. "Well, I believe we'll be in Town before suppertime. Lud, do you think

Chatham will have supper prepared for us? Oh, I am giving the man too much credit. He's accused us of a most atrocious crime, so he won't be so civilized as to feed us. I wish we'd sent word ahead to our staff to expect us. No doubt, they won't have a meal prepared when we get there. I wonder where Lord Rotheby is staying while he is in London."

Lord Rotheby? In London? Grace's heart palpitated and a flush burned her cheeks.

If the earl was in London, surely Lord Alexander hadn't allowed the older man to travel alone. However he may have behaved toward Grace, she believed him to be an honorable man. Why, he'd even tried to marry her, the foolish man, after their encounter in Bath.

That wonderful, wonderful encounter.

Which she must forget. Grace chided herself for letting her thoughts run away with her. She'd denied his pursuit and was as clear about it as she knew how to be. She had no right to hope he might be in London, and even less right to wish she might encounter him there. Not to mention wishing he would repeat his offer.

Alas, she did wish it would happen. If she could only see him again, even if for the barest of moments, perhaps she could convince herself he was not the honorable, kind, warmhearted man she imagined. Perhaps he would prove to be abominable and mean spirited, like Lord Barrow. Or neglectful, like her own father. Perhaps the pain would die, and she could stop loving him.

But perhaps she would accept him.

"Gracie. *Gracie*." Aunt Dorothea feigned impatience. "Laurence, the girl is lost in thought again. As much as she gathers wool, she should have a blanket knitted before nightfall."

"I'm sorry, Aunt," Grace said. She hated to be caught with her head in the clouds, but it happened more and more frequently. She could only blame her nerves. Or perhaps her pregnancy. Likely both. "What were you saying?"

"I asked if you had finished with your luncheon so we can continue. But please, take your time. I'm in no rush to arrive at

Chatham House and I doubt you are either. Why, look at that. You've hardly taken a bite. Eat up now. You aren't eating only for yourself, you know."

Aunt Dorothea puttered about and placed leftover food in the basket to tidy the area before they departed. Grace ate her meal without gusto, simply performing the duty at hand.

She had no desire to hurry their arrival in London. She didn't want to see Lord Alexander.

Oh, how she lied to herself. If only she could believe the lies.

Twenty

UNCLE LAURENCE'S CARRIAGE rolled to a stop before Chatham House late that afternoon. The house was as gloomy as ever, with cracked paint on the hanging shutters and the gardens overgrown with weeds and brush. Grace had no desire to step through the door.

She moved cautiously along the cobbled path with its broken stones, her aunt and uncle by her side. Uncle Laurence rapped against the dingy door. They waited for Father's old butler to answer.

How odd it was, to wait outside the house where she had grown up as though she were a guest. But Grace had come to think of New Hill Cottage as home now, and would prefer to keep things that way. Chatham House would never provide her with the warmth and love she had come to know—even to crave—in Somerton. It couldn't, after all, give what it didn't have.

But she would survive.

After several minutes passed, the butler arrived and opened the door for them. "Good evening. May I help you?" He looked down at them across a long nose, showing no recognition of Grace.

Uncle Laurence passed him his calling card. "We're here to see Lord Chatham. He's requested our presence. Please inform him of our arrival."

The butler appeared surprised and refused to take the calling card from Uncle Laurence's hand. "His lordship is away from home." The man moved back a step and took the door as though he would shut it in their faces.

Uncle Laurence stopped his motion by placing his forearm firmly against the dusty panel. "When do you expect his return?" He attempted to move inside the house.

The elderly butler blocked his entry. "I could not say." His tone implied he wouldn't say even if he could.

"Might we come inside and have a spot of tea while we wait? Our journey has been long, and the ladies would like to relax." Uncle Laurence spoke with an authority in his voice, more giving a command than a request. Grace imagined he was unaccustomed to being treated in such a manner by a mere servant, no matter who the servant's employer may be.

Her father's butler continued to stare with insolence at their small party. "You may not. I do not know when Lord Chatham will return, and I cannot allow you entry until he informs me that he wishes to see you." The aging man took a full step backward through the doorway and returned to the sanctuary of the house. "Good day to you all." He shut the door in their faces, and the lock bolted into place.

"Well, I never," Aunt Dorothea said with a huff.

Grace should be insulted by the servant's impudence, but a wave of elation washed over her instead. The fates had seen fit to grant her at least this tiny reprieve.

"Come along Dorothea, Gracie." Uncle Laurence led them back to his waiting carriage and waved off the footman. "We'll stay on Curzon Street and enquire after Chatham's whereabouts. And if we haven't found him in a reasonable time, then we'll return to Somerton."

"This is quite boorish of him, to order Gracie to return to London and then not even be at home. And that butler! To shut the door in our faces, without even offering us some refreshment. We ought not to bother with the trouble of finding the man. She's better off with us. We should just return home and take care of her, like we have been."

"Nevertheless, my dear, Chatham is Gracie's father and guardian. We don't have the protection of the authorities on our side. We must do as he asks. Especially if he has already spoken to them about his accusations against us."

"Well, how long must we wait for him? Two days ought to be more than enough time to find him, I should think. And if he hadn't turned up by then, we'll take her back home where she belongs."

Uncle Laurence sighed. "I cannot promise you we'll leave again in two days. There's much we don't know, Dorothea." Uncle Laurence rapped against the wall to signal the driver they were settled and ready to leave. The carriage moved forward with a creak and a groan.

Grace's aunt turned away from him with a loud "Hmph." She stared out the window, making a point of not looking at her husband.

THE NEXT DAY could not arrive soon enough, as far as Alex was concerned.

When they had arrived at Hardwicke House after the Yardley Court ball, Peter had insisted on allowing Chatham some privacy and time alone. He sent everyone else away, saying they could discuss everything in the morning. How he expected Alex to leave the man be for such a long period of time, when so many questions were left unanswered, he'd never determine.

Morning seemed like an eternity away.

Alex tossed and turned in his bed. He wanted to speak with Chatham again, to ask him again for permission to marry Grace. How could he rest without knowing Grace would finally, truly be his? He was almost there. But not quite.

By the time the sun began its ascent, Alex hadn't slept a wink. He tossed back the bedcovers and pounced from the bed. He didn't bother to dress before leaving his chamber and heading to the breakfast room. Peter had better be there already, if he knew what was best for him. In his hurry to start the day, he nearly flew past the footman who stood before the door to the breakfast room. The doors clanged open and he stalked inside.

To find nothing. A few servants worked to set the table, but no one else was present.

Alex was tempted to hunt down the marquess himself and get things started without Peter. But he didn't know which guest room Chatham would be in, and more likely than not, Peter would have forbidden the servants to inform him or anyone else. Damn the man and his sense of decency and propriety. He would have to hunt through Hardwicke House one room at a time to find the damned man.

Since he couldn't accost the marquess, Alex decided he may as well begin with his brother. The footman outside the door to the ducal chamber tried to block his progress, but Alex's determination won. He forced his way inside and slammed the door behind him.

"What in the name of Christ are you doing, Alex?" Peter asked. "The sun isn't even fully in the sky and you're pounding your way into my chamber. My *private* chamber, I might remind you."

Alex swept open the curtains and allowed the rising sun to blind Peter, who pulled a pillow from behind his head and placed it over his eyes.

"It is morning. We need to speak with Chatham." Why was the world moving so damnably slow today, just when he wanted life to move at its normal, entirely-too-fast pace?

"I doubt he's out of bed yet either." Peter's voice was muffled somewhat by the pillow. "Let the man get some sleep. I spoke with him briefly last night before I retired. He's not gone anywhere, I assure you. It can wait."

"It can't wait. I can't wait. Get up."

Alex pulled the blankets from the bed with one hand, and grabbed hold of Peter's ankle with the other, giving a hard yank. Peter fell from the bed and landed on his derrière with a loud thwack, the pillow still firm against his eyes.

"You arse." Peter reached out with one leg and knocked Alex to the floor.

"Ow!" Alex rubbed his elbow where it had smacked hard against the Parquet. "I suppose I deserved that."

"You did."

"Apologies. But will you please get up so we can begin the day?"

Peter glared in response. After long moments, he stood and neatly replaced the pillow and blankets on the bed. He tucked and fluffed and did any number of other tasks that were unnecessary for a man to perform himself when he had more servants at his beck and call than he ought to know what to do with. "Go and eat your breakfast. I'll be along in due time. I have more important matters to see to than your impatience."

Placing his pillows on the bed *just so* was more important than Alex's future? Than the fate of his future bride? Than seeing to it that Chatham answered to everything that needed an answer? Alex mumbled under his breath something similar to *I'll shove my breakfast down your throat*, which earned him another ducal glare, but he stood and moved toward the door.

"And Alex?" Peter asked, looking over his shoulder. "Don't wake anyone else in this manner or I'll have your hide. Everything will be handled today in an orderly manner. Chatham is now a guest in my home. You would do well to remember that."

Alex nodded in lieu of a response and returned to the breakfast room. After his lack of sleep, and then a raucous morning with Peter, he was ravenous. However hungry he may be, though, nothing could quell his desire to speak with Grace's father. He needed to know. He must hear the words.

He pushed down the urge to search the whole bloody house for the only man who could calm his nerves, then he sat at the breakfast table with a heaping plate of food. Alex could wait. He could bide his time. After all, with Barrow essentially out of the picture, Chatham must see the benefits of an alliance with the Hardwicke family.

Alex couldn't conceive how the marquess would refuse his suit now.

A MESSENGER KNOCKED at the door to their hotel room as Grace settled down to luncheon with her aunt and uncle. Uncle Laurence answered the door. "My lord, Chatham was seen last night at the ball at Yardley Court," the messenger said. "He's not returned home since."

"Is there any news of where he might be?"

"None, my lord." The messenger shifted from one foot to the other and scanned the room over again.

"Who was he seen with at the ball?"

"Lord Barrow. Possibly some others. My source was not clear on that matter."

Grace's stomach dropped. Her father was speaking with Barrow last night. Barrow was back in the country.

In London.

Here.

Her teacup rattled against the saucer in her hands, so she placed them on the table before her. Aunt Dorothea looked at her inquisitively, so she tried to resume her calm, serene demeanor.

Uncle Laurence cleared his throat. "I need more information. Find out if he left with Barrow, and force your source to tell you who else the marquess may have spoken with at the ball. It's imperative." He passed some coins into the man's hands, then closed the door. Her uncle moved back into the parlor and resumed his seat. "Well, we should know more soon."

"Laurence, I..." Aunt Dorothea said, her usual garrulous constancy missing. "Should we not return to Somerton? Lord Chatham can come there to collect Gracie, if he wishes to keep a closer eye on her. There's no reason we ought to be here now, waiting on the man to appear. If he can't face us himself with his accusations, surely he realizes he has no footing with them." She blanched, and her voice verged on desperation.

"I'm sorry dear. I know this is difficult for you. But we've traveled here, and so we'll wait." He squeezed her hand. "Give the man a chance. Perhaps he's changed."

Grace turned her head away so they wouldn't see her reaction. She brushed away the single tear that fell from her eye. No, Father hadn't changed. If he met last night with Barrow, Grace would soon be married. But not to Lord Alexander.

ALEX WAS FIT to be tied.

The entire morning had passed, and still Peter allowed the marquess to remain locked away in his chamber. Nothing could be solved without at least conversing with the man, so why hesitate?

His family sat around him in the dining room, preparing for luncheon. Derek and Sir Jonas had also joined the family, as they often did while in London, and Gil had even ventured out from the privacy of his chamber for some company. Gil sat next to Sir Jonas, and they were having a quiet discussion amongst themselves. Conversation sprinkled about the room, with delighted mirth emanating from his sisters as Sophie filled Char in on all the details from the ball the previous evening.

And Alex seethed. Heat rose from his head until it had to be visible to the rest of his family, with little trails of steam trailing upward to the ceiling.

"Lord Leith created quite the little bit of gossip last night when he danced three sets will Miss Faulkner," Sophie gushed to Char, whose eyes widened to saucers. "She swears to me that he's practically a brother to her and there's nothing there, so there's no reason for anyone to talk. But I'm not so sure…"

"She's already well on the shelf, so I don't know why anyone would gossip about her anyway," Charlotte said. "She's far longer in the tooth than you."

"Charlotte," Mama warned with narrowed eyes.

"It's true," Charlotte muttered.

Sophie raised a brow. "Miss Faulkner and Lord Leith dancing three sets in a night is no more scandalous than it would be for me and Lord Sinclaire to dance three sets in a night."

Derek hastily looked away from her, feigning interest in a gilded rococo plasterwork design on the far wall.

"Does that mean this has happened?" Alex growled. Derek may well be his closest friend, but he wouldn't stand for such behavior with his sister.

"It doesn't matter one whit if it has," Sophie replied and kicked Alex beneath the table.

He grabbed her hand and squeezed, glaring.

"Let her go," Peter said. "Don't take your anger out on your sister. For that matter, it's high time you quit your brood."

"Quit my brood," Alex ground out. "I'll quit brooding when there's good reason to quit. Not before."

Derek stifled a laugh, but then quickly sobered.

"And what do you find so funny?" Alex's belligerence threatened to explode. "Maybe you should leave."

"Alex!" Sophie said. "Lord Sinclaire is practically family. You ought not to treat him so."

"Why not? You just kicked me beneath the table. And apparently he's been dragging your reputation through the mud while I've been away. I haven't laid a hand on the insolent bastard, although if he does not remove the grin from his face in the next moment or two I'll see to it he has no reason to smile."

Mama raised her hand for peace. "Children, if you do not start behaving as the adults you seem to believe you are, I'll send you all to the nursery and let Mrs. Pratt deal with the lot of you." She turned to their guests. "I apologize. It seems my offspring have forgotten their manners."

As the footmen entered to serve luncheon, Chatham came through the opposite door. "I apologize for my tardy arrival, Your

Grace." He executed a miniscule bow first to Mama and then to Peter.

Peter stood to greet him. "There's no need for an apology. Please, join us." He indicated a chair between Derek and the dowager. Silence prevailed as Chatham joined the table. The sibling squabbles disappeared as though forgotten.

A twitch formed behind Alex's eye. He filled his plate and tried to eat, but his appetite had fled. He should wait to speak with Chatham. It would be an improper conversation to have with his entire family present. And if negotiations turned south, he didn't want Mama or his sisters to hear the foul language which might spew from his lips. They deserved his respect.

He didn't heed his own advice. "Lord Chatham," he said, "I understand why you rejected my suit toward your daughter yesterday, but would you not agree circumstances have changed in my favor?"

He could kick himself.

He needn't bother. Sophie took care of that for him. He winced in pain. She hit the exact same spot as earlier. He leveled another glare at her across the table, and her eyes issued a threat of more violence.

Chatham chewed and swallowed, then took a drink before speaking. "How so? You are aren't suddenly titled. You have no property. How are you more suitable today?"

"I referred to the situation with Lord Barrow more than to my own position. Surely a connection to the Hardwicke family, to the Duke of Somerton, would prove desirable. Besides, any further association with Barrow would only open you up to investigation as well."

"Bah. I'll find some other man for her. She's a prize, you know. Nonetheless—" He stopped himself and looked around for a moment. "I apologize, there are ladies present. I assume you know to what I refer and I don't need to speak the words out loud." He took another bite of his pheasant and didn't bother to swallow before he continued. "There's no reason for me to entertain your pursuit."

Gil tried to speak but coughed instead. Once the fit subsided, he said, "Lord Chatham, you might wish to reconsider." He paused to catch his breath. "Lord Alexander will not be without property for much longer. He'll inherit my estate in Somerton upon my death." Another bout of coughing overtook him. He held a handkerchief to his mouth, which came away bloody when the coughs ceased. "As you can see, that won't be too far in the future. One of your complaints against Lord Alexander is now baseless."

Chatham passed Alex a squinty-eyed look. "He has no title. And he won't also inherit a title in addition to your property when you pass, will he?" The marquess laughed at his crude joke, but soon sobered.

Alex's heart sunk to his toes. He had been sure Chatham would acquiesce after the situation last night. But he hadn't given the man enough credit for cruelty. He turned away in dejection and wished he could leave the room. Why had he ever brought the subject up in front of his family and friends? This was his problem, not theirs.

Peter interrupted his thoughts. "Lord Chatham, I would ask you to reconsider your decision." His voice was soft, controlled. Cold.

Alex's head jerked around. He couldn't sit idly by, yet again, and allow his eldest brother to rush in and save the day. Peter spoke over him before he could say as much.

"Under the current circumstances, wouldn't it be wise to align yourself with a family the Regent respects and trusts? Suspicion of treason is not a matter to take lightly." Peter stroked his chin with his right hand. "He hasn't brought you in for questioning yet, but that could change. Your character is already in question based on your prior associations with Barrow and your desire for a connection with him. Otherwise, the Regent would not have requested that I keep an eye on you." He leaned forward and stared straight into Chatham's eyes. "A marriage between your daughter and my brother might actually save you."

Chatham slammed his glass against the table, sloshing the liquid over the sides and onto the pristine cloth. "But he has no title!"

Alex shoved his chair away from the table. "So a title means more than your reputation? Your freedom?" He paced through the room. "More than Grace's reputation or happiness?"

"And you think you can make my daughter happy, is that it? You think you know better than I do what is best for her?"

"Yes, I do. You've ignored her for far too long."

"I have done the best I could for her." His chin quivered. "When the scandal broke out, I ordered her to stay put in her chamber, so she wouldn't have to face society in her shame. But then her aunt and uncle came along and stole her right out from under my nose, stole her from my house!"

"If the Kensingtons took her from you as you claim," Peter interjected, his voice steely, "then why did you not make such an accusation last night before the gentlemen from Bow Street? I asked them about it when I met with them yesterday afternoon. They have received no such report. It would have been a perfect opportunity to level your charge. Of course, one would think such a charge ought to have been reported long ago."

"Why, well...er, they were occupied with dealing with the traitor!"

"And you have not reported it before now because...?"

"Because I had hoped to bribe them to return her through a ransom from Barrow, if you must know. He was going to pay for her return, since she carried his child. Now I have no idea how I'll convince them to return her without bringing in the authorities. I had hoped to keep it all quiet, so they would not suffer more than necessary."

Alex burned to rip the bastard's head from his shoulders. "They never kidnapped her, and you know it. And she has been far better off in their care than she would ever be with you, or with Barrow."

"Better with the Kensingtons, has she been? Then how, pray tell, did you get your greedy paws on her? What sort of chaperones have they been for her? But what more could I expect from the whore, than she would throw herself at the first young buck who caught her eye?"

Alex flew across the room and grabbed Chatham by the throat, pulling him up from his seat. "You will not call Grace a whore in my presence." His words were controlled, even if his actions were not. "And you will apologize immediately to my mother and sisters for using such foul language in their presence."

Chatham gasped for air, and his face turned a dangerous shade of blue.

He wanted to break the man's neck. He wanted to hear the bones snap beneath his hands.

Derek placed a hand on Alex's arm and gave a firm tug. "Let him go. He can't apologize if you refuse to let him breathe. Let go."

He loosened his grip and backed away. The marquess placed his own hands where Alex's had just been and rubbed while he tried to catch his breath, falling to the floor in his efforts to do so.

Alex looked around the room at his family and friends and winced at the expressions he saw: shock, sadness, a touch of fear. And pity.

He couldn't handle the pity.

Alex took one more look at Chatham where he was crumpled on the floor, still rubbing against his neck. Then he left.

He needed air.

He needed to cool off and look at the situation with fresh eyes.

He needed to get foxed. No…

He needed Grace.

Twenty-One

As Grace and her aunt and uncle finished their tea, the messenger once again knocked at the door to Uncle Laurence's townhouse on Curzon Street. He guided the man inside, and nausea swept over Grace when she recognized him. Her trembling had to be visible. Had he found Father?

"What else have you discovered?" Uncle Laurence asked. "Have you found Chatham?"

"I've not found Lord Chatham yet, no sir. But I can tell you more of his dealings last night." The messenger looked eager to continue, but waited for a signal from Uncle Laurence. "You see, he was not only seen with the Earl of Barrow at the ball, but he also spoke with the Duke of Somerton."

Grace felt faint. The Duke of Somerton? But he was Lord Alexander's brother. Why would Father have spoken with him? And was the earl involved too?

"Some say he left with the duke, but others weren't so certain." He pulled out a paper and passed it to her uncle. "There's His Grace's address. He may be able to give you more information."

"Excellent. You've done good work today." Uncle Laurence passed the messenger a fistful of coins. "If you discover anything else, let me know immediately."

He closed the door behind the messenger and turned to Grace and Aunt Dorothea. "Well I suppose we should pay a visit to the

Duke of Somerton then. It's not yet too late for a social call, and I've not seen the man in far too long. It has been years since he resided at Somerton Court."

"But Uncle," Grace said, then faltered. What had she intended to say? She scrounged for something to say. Anything at all, really. "Wouldn't it be better if you paid the call to His Grace by yourself? Aunt Dorothea and I can stay here. Surely someone ought to wait for more news from your messenger, or possibly for Father to arrive here looking for me." They looked astounded by her scrambling. "And won't His Grace be put out by having so many visitors arrive without an invitation? Surely only one of us would be better."

Her reasoning was paltry even in her own estimation, but she wanted desperately to avoid the duke. He was bound to remind her of Lord Alexander. Something she would far prefer to avoid.

Or even worse, Lord Alexander could be there with his brother. She hadn't seen him since he left Bath, and all indications pointed to his having returned to London with Lord Rotheby. She missed him more than she ever imagined possible. But seeing him again would only give her hope when truly, she had none. Her future had been decided.

And the possibility of seeing both Lord Alexander and her father together—Grace would prefer not to even think of that.

"Now why would you think it better to call on Lord Somerton without us, Gracie?" asked her aunt. "What fustian nonsense. No, we shall all visit the duke together. I daresay he would ask after us if we weren't there. Certainly he's aware you've been staying with us. After all, he is Lord Alexander's brother you know, and we've been friendly with his family for quite some time."

Yes, Grace knew.

"And it is a perfectly acceptable hour for all of us to pay a social call. He won't be put out at all. Really, your father has done you a great disservice by keeping you so sheltered all this time. One might think you had no understanding of society whatsoever."

As usual, there could be no arguing with Aunt Dorothea. Grace resigned herself to something she would far prefer to avoid. She didn't dare feign optimism at the task, and feared her dread of the impending meeting showed on her face.

The combination of longing and trepidation grew as she secured her bonnet. She must be daft to experience so many emotions—conflicting emotions, at that—all over a simple visit, a mere social call.

They boarded Uncle Laurence's carriage. A visit to the Duke of Somerton would wait for no one, after all.

For the entire journey there, Grace could not bring herself to look at either her aunt or uncle. She dreaded walking in to the Hardwicke family home and seeing a room full of people who all looked like Lord Alexander. Had he not once told her they were all uncommonly tall, and all bore some shade of ginger in their hair? And there were so many of them.

Really, if she must meet the man's family, would it not be better to do it an individual at a time? But why must she meet them at all, since she had refused his pursuit? This was all highly bothersome.

As the carriage rounded the corner, a home far grander and more regal than her father's London home came into view. Number three, Grosvenor Square stood tall and proud. White Grecian columns stood as sentinels next around Palladian porticos and tall, arched windows. The gardens were precise rows of color situated against the backdrop of soft grey stone and brick. This home would rival even the most elaborate country homes such as she'd seen in Somerton and Bath in elegance, if not in size.

She felt thoroughly insignificant next to it—much as she was doomed to feel in the presence of its inhabitants.

His Grace must be quite an imposing figure, indeed, to own such a lavish residence in Town. Images of *ton* balls held here, like the one she had attended last Season, flashed through her mind, filled with all the glittering extravagance her imagination could muster. Such an event held here would be immaculate, perfect—everything in its place, no detail missed, nothing forgotten. It would be exquisite.

She admonished herself for daydreaming of things she would never see. A ball at Hardwicke House? With her presence? Grace pushed the thought as far aside as she could manage.

As they pulled to a stop before the structure, a tall man dashed out. Was it him? Could it be Lord Alexander? Tingles of pleasure and trepidation coursed through her body and the air around her felt alive. But before she could determine his identity, he was gone.

"Gracie, are you ready dear?" Her uncle held out a hand to her from the street, where both he and her aunt already stood.

Before she could respond, she snapped shut her jaw. She must remain composed. "Yes, of course." She allowed Uncle Laurence to hand her down from the carriage and to lead her to the entryway of the glorious house. The house she wanted anything but to draw nearer to. The house she most certainly did *not* want to enter. Her legs propelled her forward, but she felt almost as though she were floating, as though her body had taken over since her mind wouldn't quite cooperate.

Perhaps that had been one of his brothers. Or perhaps it was him, and his leaving meant she wouldn't have to face him. Facing just his family would be enough of a trial. If only she could decide whether she *wanted* the man to be him or not. This indecisiveness might be the death of her.

Before she could make up her mind, they were being escorted into the house and led through stately hallways until they arrived at a dining room. A lovely dining room. Perhaps the most beautiful dining room she had ever seen, filled with silk fabrics hanging over the windows and covering the furnishings, in rich colors that beckoned to her, and a huge table that would easily seat fifty people without batting an eye.

Of course it was also filled with people. Her head was still in a fog, and she found it difficult to concentrate or to look at these strangers and determine who they were and if any of them happened to be Lord Alexander.

Her hand was taken by another—a soft, female hand—which then guided her to a seat. So she sat. And realized that her mouth must be gaping open, yet again, even though she had firmly shut it before dismounting her uncle's carriage.

Voices rang out all around her: a loud, aggressive male voice, a sharp, forceful female voice, one very calm masculine voice. They all blended together before things shifted into focus.

"She is a whore!" Father. Father was here. With Lord Alexander's family. *He is here.* "Grace, you will come with me this instant. I swear on your mother's grave—"

No, she couldn't go with him. She tried to speak, but no sound came out.

"You are *not* taking this girl anywhere, my lord, so you may force that idea from your blithering head this instant." The female voice. Grace looked about, trying to find the speaker.

An older woman stood before her, tall and regal with the most glorious head of rich, auburn hair Grace had ever seen, tinged with only a few streaks of grey. She had a look of determination on her face that would have cowed an army as she stood before Father, towering over him, hands fisted against her hips and swords slashing through her eyes. This woman held herself with the bearing of a goddess, or perhaps the Queen.

"His Grace has informed me that you are his guest because the Prince of Wales has made the request, and so you'll not be taking one single, solitary step outside. Is that clear?" She paused only long enough to receive a curt nod from Grace's father. "And to top that, since your daughter has come into my home, she is my guest and may stay as long as she sees fit. You, sir, have no say in the matter." He stammered to interrupt, so she added: "None!"

The goddess-woman had not finished. Grace could only stare in amazement that anyone would dare to speak to her father in this way. What she wouldn't give to have the courage to do so herself.

"Furthermore, you will never use that word in my presence again. Have I made myself understood? Don't try to pretend you don't know what word I speak of, and do *not* ever use it again in reference to your daughter. Your own daughter! How could—how could—augh!" She shuddered in anger, but took only a moment from her diatribe.

Grace couldn't bear to take her eyes from the woman for long, but she took a brief glance about the room during that time, now that her vision had cleared again. Two young ladies, similar in age to herself, with varying shades of red in their hair sat about the table. Aunt Dorothea and Uncle Laurence had taken seats at the end of the table, opposite of Father and the older woman, next to Lord Rotheby. Aunt Dorothea winked when she caught Grace's eye. Two men with reddish hair and two others with dark hair completed the party. They must be Lord Alexander's family. Except, perhaps, for the dark-haired men. She searched her mind for a moment, trying to place them amongst the siblings, but to no avail.

They all stared, transfixed, upon the very same exchange she'd been observing for the last several minutes. Not upset, per se, but rather engaged.

Lord Alexander was nowhere to be seen. Good. Or was it bad?

There was no time to debate. The goddess had recomposed herself and pushed forward. "You call yourself a *father?* You arrogant, impertinent fool."

Father looked to take exception to being called a fool, but she would not be deterred, and she allowed no one to interrupt.

"And what is this bag of moonshine you've directed toward Sir Laurence and Lady Kensington? Of all the blasphemous faradiddle, that just about takes the cake. It is plain to see that these two could not hurt a fly if they tried, so I call your bluff. Poppycock! No one kidnapped anyone, and I'll hear no more of it. It seems to me, based on the way you speak to your daughter, that she would have been ridiculous and absurdly foolish to stay with you. She left you, Lord Chatham. She ran away. Is that not the truth of it, Lady Grace?"

The fullness of the formidable woman's gaze fell on Grace, along with the eyes of everyone else in the room. Even Father. She slunk down into her seat and wished she could burrow a hole to the Indies or the Americas or somewhere else—anywhere else—but there.

She had to be Lord Alexander's mother. Mustn't she? "Er, Your Grace, that is, well. Yes? Yes. I did. I left on my own." After a few words came out with no major disasters smiting her down, she gained a touch of courage, turning her gaze to rest fully on her father. "I went by coach to Aunt Dorothea and Uncle Laurence's home in Somerton and they were gracious enough to allow me to stay with them. They've done no wrong. You must drop your unfounded charges against them at once." Good God, where had that come from? She had issued her father *a command*.

Might as well continue while she still had breath. "And as Her Grace said, I won't be going anywhere with you. Ever again."

"That's right! She can stay with us," said Aunt Dorothea, apparently unable to completely bite her tongue.

Grace passed her aunt a smile before she turned to the duchess and nodded. She wished, for the briefest of moments, she could interpret the look on the older woman's face. Reverence? Acceptance?

"Well, I suppose that's settled then," the duchess said. "Shall we move on to what I find to be the greater concern here, Lord Chatham?" As she turned her gaze away from Grace and back to her father, it shifted to the cold, steely determination from before. "Which, of course, would be your treatment of your daughter. I realize that, as her father and her guardian, you are certainly entitled by law to do with the poor girl as you see fit. But really, sir, some things are simply beyond the pale. Where has all of this come from?"

Her posture demanded a response.

"You dare to question me in this manner, yet *I* am the impertinent one?" Father's chin quivered, belying his show of bravado.

"Lord Chatham," came the calm, smooth voice of the man nearest her father. This must be the duke himself. "You would be well advised to answer my mother when she asks you a question. And if you insult Her Grace again, or any of the ladies present for that matter, I shall take it upon myself to teach you a lesson in manners." He never raised his voice much higher than a whisper, forcing her to lean closer to hear his words. But his quiet demeanor disguised a grim resolve she had no desire to test.

Father's eyes narrowed, but he only followed it with, "Indeed."

"So? Go on."

He harrumphed and fidgeted and shifted his eyes about, but the dowager would not back down.

"Very well. What was your question?" Of course, Father couldn't make this confrontation easy. Grace was, at least somewhat, hoping he wouldn't answer. Hearing the truth of why he had so mistreated her might be too much to tolerate.

"Whatever could give you cause to cast such dubious names upon your one and only daughter, your flesh and blood, your child whom you should protect and love and cherish?"

His eyes settled on Grace, full of hatred and unbridled anger. She cast her own to the floor and took deep, rapid breaths, hoping to staunch a flood of tears.

"That *whore*—"

The duke was out of his chair and across the room faster than Grace could react. He pulled Father from his seat and slammed him against the wall. The crack of Father's skull reverberated in the room. He hung, suspended by the younger man's grip on the collar of his coat, his feet dangling a few inches above the floor.

"You have been warned, Chatham."

Father stared up at Lord Somerton's teeth, which had not even moved when he spoke, trembling like a small child.

"I ap—apologize. It will not happen again." Words rushed from his mouth. "Please, please put me down. I promise to mind my language."

Lord Somerton dropped him and he fell like an overused doll to the floor.

Seemingly unfazed by any of the happenings, the dowager walked over to where Father sat. She took a chair nearby. "Where does all of this anger stem from? Surely she couldn't have done anything so terrible to cause all of this."

"Her? Grace?" Father spat out the words. "Grace has likely done nothing so terribly wrong, at least if you disregard her having run from home and then whatever misguided affairs she has carried on with your *Lord Alexander*. No, it has nothing to do with her, but with what she is not."

"What am I not?" She didn't realize she'd spoken aloud until all eyes turned to her again.

"What are you not? You aren't a boy, for one thing. You cannot be my heir." Venom filled his words.

"I cannot help that, Father." Could he really hate her for that?

"Oh, but that's not all. You are also not your mother, but you look like her. You have her hair, her skin. Her eyes. You look more like her every day. I can't bear to look upon you." Was that a tear forming in his eye? Surely not.

"Lord Chatham, why does it hurt you so much to have your daughter bear the resemblance of your wife?" The dowager's voice was soft, kind. Almost motherly.

"Because after Grace was born, her mother would have nothing to do with me. The trollop carried on affairs with half the *ton*, and then she contracted an illness and died from it." Tears flowed freely down his cheeks, and his usually ruddy face was blisteringly purple. "Because I was never good enough for her mother, so she can never be good enough for me."

Something propelled Grace forward, across the room, to hand her father a handkerchief. She stood there, before him, watching him with something akin to pity. All these years, he had pushed her away and wasted his life, all because she looked like her mother and reminded him of his own pains.

He reached for her, and she backed away out of instinct. As she took her step backward, she bumped into a very tall, very male body.

"Oh! Pardon me." When she looked up, the duke reached out to steady her and then moved her off to the side, where she was suddenly surrounded by *all* of the Hardwicke siblings present. One of the sisters took her hand and patted the back of it reassuringly.

"You do realize, of course," the dowager continued, "that you've been quite wrong to mistreat your daughter because of your own grief."

He blubbered and sniffled and wiped the handkerchief across his face, making an even bigger mess of things. "I know!"

"You cannot change the past, Lord Chatham. But you can change the future."

"But how? I've made a true muck of her life, haven't I?" He looked only at the dowager, not at anyone else in the room, least of all Grace.

"She won't return with you. She's made herself abundantly clear on that matter, and I daresay she's made the proper decision there. I'll certainly support her in that endeavor."

"As shall I," said the duke.

"And I," came from one of the dark-haired men.

"I believe you know, Chatham, where I stand on the matter." Uncle Laurence remained seated with the earl and Aunt Dorothea, but he insisted upon being heard.

The other Hardwicke brother said nothing, but formed one hand into a fist and punched it against the other.

"So it seems Lady Grace has two options. She can return to Somerton under the care and supervision of her aunt and uncle—"

Father scoffed. "They have obviously not supervised her too closely now, have they?"

Lord Somerton spoke so softly Grace was uncertain she'd properly made his words out, but it sounded something like, "And your supervision has been better, then?"

The dowager continued as if she hadn't been interrupted. "Or she can marry Alex. Of course, I'm sure you can see the latter option would be the far better course of action for her reputation, since she has been quite the subject of all the latest *on dits* here, and I would imagine in Bath, and likely in a number of other places across the country. And if you truly have the intention of making her future better than her past has been, then I would suggest you consider everything that is best for *her*."

But she couldn't marry Lord Alexander. She'd refused him. He deserved better. "But—" Her voice broke off on a sob. The sister holding her hand pulled her in for a tight hug and the other girl joined them, patting her on the back, rubbing a hand over her hair.

"I believe the young ladies have heard enough of this, don't you agree?" the dowager asked the group as a whole. "Lord Sinclaire, would you be so kind as to escort them all to the drawing room? And the Kensingtons too, if you'd like. I'll order tea served, and Peter, Lord Chatham, and I will join you once this business has been settled. Neil, you go along with them."

The woman effectively shooed them all on their way, the two Hardwicke sisters practically holding Grace up as they walked. They settled in and a cup of tea was pressed into her hands where she sat near the hearth. She didn't know whether she drank. She could only think of one thing.

She would be married to Lord Alexander, if she could not find a way to stop it from happening. But surely, the dowager and the Duke of Somerton would convince Father. He would think it his best course of action. How could he not?

But how could she allow it to happen? Oh, what a dreadful, dreadful mess.

People came and went from the drawing room, conversation went on all around her, but she paid it no mind. Not until Father came in.

He looked at her, his eyes filled with sadness and guilt and maybe a touch of fear. He nodded with resolute fervor.

And she knew.

HE RODE SAMPSON through Rotten Row. Alex needed to clear his head, and nothing short of a neck-or-nothing jaunt would do.

The fashionable hour wouldn't arrive for several hours, which suited him. Company would only serve to aggravate him more, and constant interruptions to socialize and gossip would surely cause his head to explode. A few ladies and gentlemen were out and about, taking some air in the park. The Row, however, was deserted in general, and those who were there seemed content to ignore him.

Alex spurred his horse again. The wind created by their run pushed his beaver hat back from his head, but he didn't care. The hat floated away behind him. He knew not where it landed. Really, what did something so frivolous matter in the grand scheme of life?

More than ever before, he wanted to marry Grace.

Of course, all the prior reasons were still in place. He had compromised her virtue, had been intimate with her—and while she did not carry *his* child, she certainly carried *a* child. A child who would need a father. A child he would love.

But now, there was something more.

Grace could never go back to her father. He couldn't allow it. Alex tried to imagine what her childhood must have been like with a father who would call her a whore. How could the man care so little for his daughter, for a child of his own flesh?

But clearly Chatham was capable of unspeakable atrocity. Alex knew this. The man had been prepared to marry Grace off to Barrow, after all, a man who quite possibly was a traitor to the crown. A man who may have ravished Grace.

Alex shuddered.

At least he would no longer need to worry about Grace's future with Barrow. The Regent would see to it that the bastard would never step foot outside of prison walls alive again.

Cool air heavy with the scent of rain whipped his hair about his head. He heard nothing but the clop of Sampson's hooves against the hard dirt. Alex dug his spurs into the horse's side, urging him to more and more speed, the possibility of rain be damned. Wind against his face was exactly what he needed to clear his mind.

How could he change Chatham's mind? There must be a way.

Alex had a fortune, thanks to his brother. He would someday have property, whether through inheritance from Gil or through his own purchase. He could provide the marquess with a connection to the Duke of Somerton, one of the most powerful men in all of England.

What more could he want?

Without question, Chatham wasn't concerned with Grace's welfare, but more with his own status. And with a guarantee of higher respectability within the beau monde than he currently possessed, was Alex's dearth of title really such an issue?

Truth be told, Alex's problem with their earlier encounter was not Chatham's refusal. He had more confidence in his own persuasive abilities than to take the man's denial at this point as an absolute.

No, what truly bothered him was that Chatham had used such a monstrous word to describe Grace.

Whore. He filled with rage again over the thought of the term.

The worst of it was everything in Chatham's manner showed he believed what he said. The man had neither cringed nor had he shown disgust when he called her a whore. He'd looked Alex plain in the eyes and uttered the foulest thing imaginable.

When it came to the heart of the matter, Alex's actions might have contributed to Chatham's assessment. In being so plain with the marquess yesterday about his relations with Grace, even though he had auspicious intentions, he might have furthered the man's impression of his daughter. And that, Alex realized, was the true source of his anger. Not that Chatham had called Grace a whore—but that he had played a part in creating such an impression.

He was a rake. A brute. Strong enough words to describe what he'd become didn't exist.

How could he possibly deserve Grace now?

But he couldn't allow her to be with anyone else. Alex may have hurt his honor already, but he couldn't allow her virtue to suffer. He would marry her. He would find a way to convince Chatham, and he would marry Grace.

The park was beginning to fill with people, so he slowed Sampson to a canter. Devil take it, he must have been out longer than he realized.

Alex turned Sampson around and began the return journey to Grosvenor Square. He hoped beyond hope he wouldn't encounter someone he knew. He was in no mood to make polite conversation.

Two riders approached, and he cursed beneath his breath before he realized those riders were Sir Jonas and Derek.

"Have you finished with your sulk then, Alex?" Sir Jonas called out. "And where did you lose your hat? The dowager will die of shame if she discovers you've been out in public without your head properly covered."

"My hat?" He touched the top of his bare head, shocked to feel nothing but his own hair. "Devil take it, it fell off earlier and I let it fall." But his friend was right, his mother would be thoroughly scandalized if she heard of the matter.

The three men looked about to find it. Derek took off after a moment toward what Alex could only make out to be a black spot on the ground, a rock or something of the sort perhaps. That rock turned out to be his hat. Derek rode back with the beaver hat in his hands and handed it over. "Now your mother won't be forced into scandal by your behavior, as long as the gossip mill doesn't give you away."

"Thank you. I'm sure Mama would be most appreciative."

They rode together at first in silence. Alex was glad for the company because their presence prevented someone else from stopping him for conversation. But his pensive mood continued.

Despite his part in Chatham's view of Grace as a whore, and discounting his feelings toward a man who could think such a thing of her, there was yet another problem Alex must overcome.

"Will Chatham allow me to marry Grace after I attempted to kill him?"

"What was that?" asked Derek.

Alex jumped. He didn't realize he'd spoken aloud, so Derek's response was unexpected.

"I—I just—well, do you think he will? Allow me? To marry Grace, that is? I mean…I don't know what I mean." He paused to find the answers within himself. "I did strangle him, you know. That's not an easy thing to overlook."

They neared Grosvenor Square and slowed their horses, so they could have a few more moments to speak in private. Sir Jonas sent a questioning glance across to Derek, who gave an almost imperceptible shake of his head.

"What?" Alex asked. "What do I not know?" Dread settled in his stomach.

"Nothing to concern yourself with," Sir Jonas said. "Come on, they're waiting for us inside. No reason to put this off any longer."

"Put what off?"

But Sir Jonas and Derek dismounted and moved up the stairs.

A familiar carriage was parked outside the house. Try as he might, Alex couldn't place where he'd seen it before.

"Put what off?" he called out again, in a futile attempt at finding some answers before he walked into—well, he had no idea what he might be walking into. As had become something of a habit, he received no answer. Sir Jonas and Derek were already well inside the house, thoroughly ignoring him.

Alex cursed as he landed on the street and handed his reins to the groom. It was horrid enough to have his own siblings keep information from him, but to have Derek and Sir Jonas go along with it was beyond the pale.

Alone, he climbed up the stairs of Hardwicke House and entered through the front door. Who were their guests? No point in delaying the inevitable.

Spenser greeted him as he entered. "Lord Alexander, your presence has been requested by His Grace in the downstairs salon."

The butler reached for his hat and coat even as he executed a perfect bow.

"Thank you. I'll attend him immediately."

Derek and Sir Jonas had already made their presence scarce, whether by a request for their presence in the downstairs salon or by having been granted some other reprieve. He moved through the familiar halls toward the salon with a sense of fate hanging over his head.

One of Peter's liveried footmen opened the doors and ushered him inside. The room was full to bursting at the seams. His entire family was present, save Richard. Derek, Sir Jonas, and Gil were there as expected, since they were all more like family than not. Chatham stood near the window looking out into the gardens.

They all turned to face him upon his entrance. The memory of where he had seen the carriage outside before washed over him as he saw Sir Laurence and Lady Kensington seated near Gil by the fire. Alongside them sat Grace, her two icy eyes gazing at him, filled to the brim with unshed tears.

Grace was there. In London. In his home.

His body begged him to rush over to her, pull her to him, and wipe away her tears. The sight of her, even with the upset clear upon her face, rejuvenated him after spending so many days away from her. He took a breath and allowed himself to relax for the first time since he had left her in Bath.

And then he remembered himself. "Lady Grace, Sir Laurence, and Lady Kensington, it is wonderful to see you in London." He bowed to them and forced his feet to remain rooted in place.

A warm smile spread across Lady Kensington's face. "Lord Alexander, how lovely to find you here. You left Bath so suddenly and took our Lord Rotheby with you. And then when we returned to Somerton, we didn't find you there. I was greatly disappointed, I must say. But we'd hoped, when we decided to visit London, we might find you here."

"I apologize for leaving Bath so quickly, ma'am, and for taking Gil with me. I had pressing business matters to attend." What a piddling excuse.

"Oh goodness, don't trouble yourself over such a silly thing." Lady Kensington waved her handkerchief in a dismissive gesture. "We're delighted you're here. I know our Gracie has missed you dreadfully."

The color rose in Grace's cheeks and she looked away, refusing to meet his eyes. Could it be true? Had she missed him?

Her reaction rekindled his hope, but one very large impediment still stood in his way—the Marquess of Chatham.

Alex's obstacle chose that particular moment to clear his throat. "Pardon my interruption, Lord Alexander, but might it be possible to have a private word with you? There is something I wish to discuss."

He glared over at Chatham. The man had had the audacity to call Grace—the woman Alex loved, the woman he intended to marry, the woman he would give his life to honor and protect—a whore in his presence, and now he wanted to speak in private?

Lady Kensington beamed up at Alex and squeezed her husband's hand.

Without Chatham's permission, he couldn't marry Grace. He had to speak with the bastard again.

Peter spoke up. "You may use my private library if you wish. I believe that will suffice your needs, Lord Chatham."

With his glare still in place, Alex nodded and led the marquess from the salon to his brother's library. His body shook with fury. The man had to be the cause of Grace's tears; there simply was no other explanation.

He ushered Chatham inside and waited for the doors to close before taking a seat behind Peter's large oak desk. He wanted to assume an air of authority. He wanted it to be clear he was the one now in charge, not the marquess.

Alex waved a hand toward an empty wing chair facing the desk. "Please, have a seat. And tell me, what would you like to discuss?

Though I must warn you, if you haven't yet offered my mother and sisters an apology for your earlier language, I doubt I'll be very open to hearing a word you have to say."

Chatham cast his eyes away, a faint shimmer visible in the corner of one from the sun descending outside the windows. "Oh, I've offered my apologies. And I believe you'll have your mother to thank, shortly."

"My mother?"

"Yes. You see, the dowager is the one who convinced me to have a change of heart toward you."

"Mama did?" How on earth could the woman have managed such a feat when he could not? And a 'change of heart' meant what exactly? Alex rubbed a hand against his eyes, hoping to clear the fog settling over his thoughts.

"She did. Well, I should clarify. It's more Grace I have changed toward than you. I've been a neglectful father. I hope to remedy that."

"Just how do you propose to cease neglecting your daughter? And what, pray tell, does any of this have to do with me?" He moved his hand from his eyes to his temples and rubbed against the pounding blood there.

"I…well, I insist you marry my daughter."

Twenty-Two

GRACE HATED SHOWING signs of weakness, and the tears she was unable to push back would more than qualify. Sitting in the salon of Hardwicke House near her aunt and uncle, surrounded by Lord Alexander's family and friends, she berated herself for her vulnerability.

And then he walked into the room.

Lord Alexander glanced about as the door closed behind him. Grace stilled when his gaze settled upon her, and wished more than ever that she was strong enough to hide her tears.

His gaze remained on her for several moments. He pulled in a deep breath of air. His eyes changed before her, from frantic and bothered to relaxed and calm. And still, he watched her.

After another long moment, he broke his stare and included Aunt Dorothea and Uncle Laurence in his gaze. "Lady Grace, Sir Laurence and Lady Kensington, it is wonderful to see you in London." He bowed to them and her aunt spoke to him.

Grace paid no attention to her aunt's words. Without a doubt, the woman would effuse Lord Alexander with a barrage of admonitions and unsubtle hints geared toward accomplishing what Grace's father had just informed her would happen.

Hence, the reason for her tears.

She had tried so hard over this time since they first met each other to convince Lord Alexander to stay away. However much she may love him, and she had now given up all hope of convincing herself otherwise, he deserved better than her—a ravished woman, due to give birth to another man's child.

He deserved a lady with her virtue intact. A lady who felt at home in society. A lady he loved, not one he was forced to wed for honor's sake.

Honor be damned, alongside myself.

Another wave of tears threatened to spill onto her cheeks. Out of the corner of her eye, she caught the wave of Aunt Dorothea's handkerchief through the air. "We are delighted you are here, though. I know our Gracie has missed you dreadfully."

Grace blushed more fiercely than she could ever remember blushing before at her aunt's words, replacing the tears she would have otherwise shed. How could Aunt Dorothea embarrass her in such a way, and in front of his family, no less? Lord Alexander's eyes returned to hers and she looked away, unable to face him.

Then her father cleared his throat. "Pardon my interruption, Lord Alexander, but might it be possible to have a private word with you? There is something I wish to discuss." She dared not look up to see Lord Alexander's reaction. Lady Charlotte had already informed her of the events at this afternoon's tea.

After several moments, the Duke of Somerton spoke. "You may use my private library if you wish. I believe that will suffice your needs, Lord Chatham."

Nothing more was said, but Grace's father followed Lord Alexander from the room.

Minutes passed in silence, broken only by the sounds of someone sniffling. Grace didn't recognize the sniffles as her own until the women of the Hardwicke family surrounded her.

The dowager sat on the sofa next to Grace and placed her arms around her as one of her daughters, Grace was uncertain which, passed her a handkerchief.

"There, there sweetheart," the dowager said. "Lie down and rest."

The arms about her tugged gently until she lay across the sofa with her head on the older woman's lap. The sisters patted her and held her hands, and someone brought a cold compress to place against her head.

"He'll treat you well, Lady Grace," Lady Sophia said. "Our brother is a good man. Certainly better than Lord Barrow."

Lady Charlotte cut in. "But why are you so distraught, Lady Grace? Don't you want to marry Alex?"

"Leave her be, Char. Let her cry until she's finished. It's never a good idea to interrupt a good cry—you ought to know that as well as anyone."

"Girls, please be quiet," the dowager interrupted. "We're overwhelming her, I'm afraid."

Gentle hands stroked her hair and soothed her spirit. Somehow in her crying jag, the tears had become sobs that bordered on hysterics, but now returned to simple tears. And then Grace remembered where she was and who she was with. Dear Lord, she had become a maudlin watering pot! She shot up from her prone position to sit straight, and glanced around the room.

The Duke of Somerton had left, along with Lord Neil, Sir Jonas, Lord Sinclaire, Lord Rotheby, and even Grace's aunt and uncle. She was alone with the three Hardwicke women—women over whom she had just bawled like a baby.

Women who would soon be her family.

"Oh goodness, I must apologize for such unbecoming behavior. How terribly rude of me." She fumbled with her gown to straighten it and wiped her tears with the handkerchief she had been given.

"Nonsense," said Lady Sophia, the one with the reddish-blonde hair. "You'll be our sister soon, so we'll treat you as our sister. And if you can't cry with your mother and sisters, who can you cry with?"

"Oh, but I'm mortified *because* you will be my family soon. We've hardly met, and I'm behaving like a fool." Her eyes cleared, and a rather large wet patch appeared on the front of the dowager's muslin. Grace eyes widened to the point she thought they would pop out of her head. "Ma'am, I've ruined your gown!" She tried to mop up the mess with her handkerchief, but it was so full of her tears that she only made the matter worse.

Lady Somerton placed her hands over Grace's to still them. "Never mind that, my dear. Now, Grace—may I call you Grace?"

"Of course, ma'am."

"Now Grace, why don't we discuss what has you so upset? Don't you love my son?"

"Mama, what a silly question," said Lady Charlotte. "Of course she loves Alex. Didn't you see the way she looked at him?"

"Charlotte, please allow her to speak for herself." The dowager squeezed Grace's hand.

She wanted to speak the words aloud to someone, anyone. But she feared that once they were said, her heart would break even further than it already had.

But fear had controlled her for far too long.

"I do love him, Your Grace." And the tears burst forward again like a broken dam.

"Of course you do, sweetheart. So tell us, what is all this about?"

"I can't marry him."

"Why ever not? Alex wants to marry you, you love him. What's the problem?"

Grace looked up at Lord Alexander's sisters before she answered. "I can't answer that question in front of your daughters. Your Grace, they would be scandalized. You would be scandalized." She took a calming breath. "No, I cannot answer at all."

Lady Sophia sat on Grace's other side, forcing her closer to the dowager, and reached up to smooth a few escaped strands of hair behind her ear. "I can assure you that living in Town during a Season is more than enough to guarantee none of us shall be scandalized in the slightest. You can't shock the Hardwicke women."

Grace looked around at the other ladies who all nodded their heads in eager assent. "Very well. I have—" She broke off when another tear fell down her face. Lady Charlotte took one of her hands and held onto it.

She steeled herself to go on. "I have been ruined, ma'am."

The words were out. She couldn't take them back. Grace waited for shocked looks, expecting the women to pull away in disgust. But none of that happened. They continued to hold her, to stroke her, to comfort her.

The dowager spoke first. "And is Alex aware of this?"

"Yes, ma'am. He is aware."

"Then it hardly signifies. He still wants to marry you." Lady Sophia held a stern look and regarded her with knowing eyes. "But there's more, isn't there? Something you haven't told Alex, from the looks of it. What have you not told us?"

How could Lady Sophia tell? Grace wracked her mind to find something she could tell them so they would stop asking questions. But she most certainly couldn't tell them the truth.

The dowager duchess held up a hand, stopping the conversation. "That is enough for now, girls. Grace has only just met us. She'll have to learn to trust us, and we've done nothing yet to earn her trust. Why, we've berated her while she was in the midst of a crying spell." She placed her hand over one of Grace's for just a moment. "Look at me, sweetheart. Whatever it is, whatever is bothering you, it will be all right."

"I wish I could believe you, ma'am." But how could anything be all right?

"YOU INSIST I do what?" Alex asked, almost choking on the words.

"Marry Grace. And you *will* do it. You admitted to me yesterday you had done more than merely compromise her in public, so you have no alternative." Chatham looked more grim and determined than Alex had seen him in their few meetings to that point.

"I'm bewildered, my lord. You've been so adamant against me. What did my mother say to you to make this change?" Could this be happening?

"Well, I apologized for my deportment." Chatham took a moment, seeming to consider how much he should say. "She asked me about Grace, and before I knew what was happening, she had me telling all about how my wife died when Grace was a little girl."

He paused here for several moments. "I loved her mother, you know—at least at first. But she never wanted me. She strayed from our marriage many times after Grace was born, and then she contracted a disease and died."

A single tear fell down Chatham's cheek. "I was devastated, and I took to drink. I've neglected Grace far too long, and your mother helped me realize it. Grace deserves to be happy, and I intend to see to it you make her happy. I can't do it myself. But I can see from your perseverance and from your family you will do well by her. Far better than I have done."

Alex sat behind his brother's heavy desk and waited for lightening to strike. He must be dreaming. Surely this was not real. It had all been far too easy.

But nothing else happened. "I assume you would like to negotiate the terms now?" Perhaps the marquess wanted even more money than he had already offered.

"You shall marry by special license, as soon as possible. Tomorrow, if you can arrange it."

"Fine." Better than fine. Alex didn't want to wait. The longer it took for them to marry, the more likely scandal would follow.

"His Grace has offered to allow you to live at his estate in Somerton until you inherit your own property from Rotheby. You'll take Grace there, so she will be close to her aunt and uncle."

Peter had offered that? It would mean he had already discussed some of the terms with Chatham. Alex bit his lip to quell his frustration, but pushed it aside. He could deal with Peter later. "That is acceptable as well." When would the man get to the financial arrangements? They, of all things, must weigh heavily on his mind. He waited for the marquess's next provision, but it didn't come. "Lord Chatham? What do you require in terms of financial compensation? Will the sum I offered yesterday suffice?"

Chatham flushed to a deep crimson. His words were clipped, choppy. "I require no compensation."

Alex shook his head, certain he had misheard. "No compensation? Are you quite sure? I was sincere with my offer yesterday."

"No compensation. Your mother is very…convincing. She helped me to see how distasteful it would be to take money from Grace's future husband. It would be like selling her, like making her into…well, into the word I called her earlier."

"Very well. Do you have any other requirements?" Alex was prepared to give the man just about anything.

"Just a request." Chatham's eyes darted about. "Allow me—after you and Grace are married, can I come to visit occasionally? I want to try to have a relationship with her. I know I've squandered many years when I could have spent them getting to know her. I've been a horrible father to her. But I want—I need to change that. Please." He lowered his eyes to the floor.

Alex didn't give an immediate response. He gave this last request thorough consideration. "If Grace is willing, you may visit. However, the decision will rest in her hands. She has a mind of her own, and I refuse to force her to do anything she is uncomfortable with."

Chatham breathed a sigh of relief. "Thank you."

"Do not thank me. She may not wish to see you. And she may change her mind at any time."

"But you'll allow it, so I thank you. So now, what are your terms? What will you expect on my end of the bargain?"

"I have only one requirement. You will never use the word whore in regard to Grace again. Not to me, not to her, not to anyone."

"That's all? You require no dowry?"

A dowry? Surely if he expected payment for her before, the man had no means to provide a dowry.

"No dowry. Grace is enough on her own. I've no need for money, Chatham, as I'm positive you are aware."

"Then we have an arrangement."

Alex nodded. "It seems we do."

But now he must convince Grace.

Twenty-Three

GRACE CALMED HERSELF. The others who had left the salon returned, save her father and Lord Alexander. Aunt Dorothea reentered the room with an expression of glee sent in Grace's direction.

Conversation flowed around her, about the upcoming entertainments and events of the ton, along with a great deal of speculation about some of the more recent gossip. Lady Charlotte complained about how everyone else could attend, but she was stuck in the schoolroom. Grace could think of nothing to add to the discussion, not knowing these people around her, and not truly having been exposed much to London society, so she chose to remain silent.

Lady Sophia moved across the room to sit beside her. "Grace, would you like to stroll about the room with me? You seem agitated. It might help to move."

She breathed an unintended sigh of relief. "Oh, yes, that would be lovely." They walked side-by-side, ignored by the rest of the company in the salon.

"I know we don't know each other well, Grace, but I believe we'll be good friends. More than friends, actually, since you'll be my sister."

"I've never had a sister before, Lady Sophia. I do not know how one should behave with one's sisters."

"Well to start, you ought to call me Sophie and leave the 'lady' behind," she said with a kind smile and a firm pat on the back of Grace's hand.

"All right, Sophie."

"Excellent. And then you could tell me what's really bothering you. I mean really, truly disturbing you. Sisters help each other. It's part of some sort of unwritten rule book or something. Let me help you."

Much like her mother, Sophie's tone demanded attention—she would not be deterred. What was it about these Hardwickes that gave them such confidence, such eminence? It was certainly more than their station in society. Why, they weren't all that much higher in rank than herself. And they didn't comport themselves in a way that spoke to arrogance, simply one that commanded respect. If only one day, she too could walk with such an air of self-assuredness. Grace took a tentative look around the room to determine whether anyone else was listening in to their conversation.

"Your secret won't be overheard. Char has them all well entranced." Sophie slowed her gait and looked hard at Grace. "I won't betray your confidence, you have my word. This will be between you and me, no one else."

She swallowed. Grace wanted to trust Sophie, but trust had never come easy for her.

She leaned in and whispered up into Sophie's ear. "I'm with child." A fierce blush rushed to her face and she fought to maintain control over her emotions. It wouldn't do to burst into yet another bout of hysterics. If only her emotions were not so close to the surface all the time, these days. Surely it would be easier to conceal them if they didn't continuously amble their way to the forefront.

"I see." Sophie didn't appear shocked, which shocked Grace in turn. "And am I to understand the child is not my brother's, and he is unaware of your circumstances?"

She expected censure in Sophie's tone, but could detect no change. "Yes. I mean no." Blast her nerves. She shook her free hand, trying to shake some of the nervous energy away. It only served to draw the attention of Lord Neil, which then sent her heartbeat to a full gallop, because the man's face looked entirely too much like Lord Alexander for her comfort. "I mean yes, that's what you should understand, and no, your brother is not aware, nor is he the father."

"You've said you love my brother. Do you also love the baby's father, Grace?" Her voice was soft, soothing.

"Oh, no. Not at all." She shuddered at the thought.

"I should think you'd want to rush to the altar with Alex, then. I'm afraid I don't understand the problem."

Hearing such a thought from Sophie shattered her. Must the whole world conspire against her? She wished desperately she could find someone—anyone—who could understand her plight. "But I can't. He can't marry me."

"Why? Help me understand, Grace."

"Because...because he deserves better." Her voice cracked. "He deserves a lady who hasn't been ruined, who can give him his own children."

A few moments passed. "Do you think he would agree with your assessment, Grace?"

Grace blinked. "I don't know."

"And what makes you think you won't give him his own children? Or that he wouldn't accept your child as his own? Actually, if you are already with child, after what I assume was your first encounter? If that is the case, then wouldn't it be more reasonable to assume you will *without a doubt* be able to provide him with his own children?"

"Ah, well. Oh, why must you be so reasonable?" Blast Sophie for sneaking into her heart with that one, single speech, and aggravating her, all in one swoop. Everything was going against the plan.

"Because that's what I do. That's what sisters are for. We conspire together, we argue, we confide in each other, and we help each other to see reason. Get used to it. There's much more to come."

Too much more, if the course of the day didn't take a drastic turn.

Sophie winked at her. "Well, I'll tell you what I think about this whole situation. I think—"

She was cut off by the return of Lord Alexander and Grace's father.

"Grace, I need to speak with you alone, please," her father announced over the din of the room. "Your Grace, might I continue to use your library?"

The duke agreed, and Grace excused herself from Sophie to follow her father.

Once they were settled in the library, Father began. "Lord Alexander and I have just negotiated the terms for your marriage. He'll ask you to marry him later this evening, and you will accept."

The courage she'd found earlier in the day bubbled forth again. "No, Father, I won't." Where was this all coming from? It must be from being in the presence of so many others who were always so sure of themselves. The Hardwickes had been a very favorable influence on her, indeed. At least to her way of thinking.

"I beg your pardon? You will obey me, Grace. I'm still your father and your guardian, even if you won't be coming back to live with me."

"Yes, you are my father. And if you order me to marry him, I'll be forced to obey. I'll have no choice in the matter. But if he asks me, I assure you, I will refuse."

"You don't love him?" He looked bewildered, aghast.

"I do love him, which is precisely the reason I won't marry him. He deserves better than me." The pain of speaking the words out loud set her legs to shaking beneath her. Now was not the time to feel faint.

"But he compromised you. He admitted to me he's done even more than that. Why would you refuse him?"

"Because he doesn't know about the child, Father." The words came out on a sob, and she berated herself for showing such weakness in front of Father.

"The child? Why should the bloody child matter? For all he knows, it could be his own." He paused for a moment, seeming to search his mind. "Actually, he does know about the child. And he's still agreed."

"He knows? How does he know?" The room seemed to rock around her, like a ship on stormy water. She reached her hands out, grasping for something to hold onto, something to ground her, something to calm the tempest brewing in her head.

"Because I told him. He doesn't care. The child is unimportant."

Her child was *not* unimportant. And she absolutely, unequivocally would not marry any man who thought such a thing. She would leave. She would find a way. At least she would as soon as the floor stopped moving.

"Your wishes notwithstanding, I'll not marry him. You'll have to get by without however much blunt the man has promised you in exchange for me, though I cannot fathom how you have managed to extract anything from him at this point. That's all I have to say on the matter."

"Why you impertinent—"

He broke off, but Grace knew what he intended to say. She raised her chin in defiance.

"You will marry him. If you don't accept him on your own, I will command you to marry. You *will* obey." He stalked from the room.

She moved to stare out the window, bracing herself on one piece of furniture after the other in order to keep her balance. If only she had paid more attention to their surroundings while she'd traveled with her aunt and uncle. It would be much easier to escape if she knew where to go.

But she absolutely would not marry a man who thought her child unimportant. A nuisance. Another man's by-blow.

This was *her* child. She would have to find a way—some way—to give her the home she deserved.

Her. Grace was already thinking of the baby as a little girl. She took one hand from the window frame and held it against the slight swell of her belly.

I'll find a way. Everyone in your life will love you, little one. You won't grow up like I did.

ALEX REENTERED HIS brother's library where Grace was waiting for him. Chatham hadn't told him about how their conversation had gone. He'd just left and told him she was ready.

Of course, she'd refused him before. But with her father on his side, she would change her mind. She would accept. Grace would marry him.

She stood by the picture window, staring out at the fading sun, one hand resting on the windowsill. Her black-as-night hair hung in a loose knot at the nape of her neck instead of her customary strict bun. A few tendrils wisped along her brow and tucked behind her ear. He didn't want to break the beauty of the moment, the perfect picture standing before him. But she turned to face him, and her eyes pierced him through.

"Your father told me I might find you here to speak with you. Grace, I have something to ask you."

He stepped toward her but she gave him no encouragement. When he reached her, he took her free hand in his own. His hand shivered from the chill of her fingers.

"I would like you to be my wife. I want to care for you, to have a family with you. We can live in Somerton and be near your aunt and uncle, and near Lord Rotheby. I can provide for you. I can make you happy, Grace." He searched her eyes for something, anything. "Will you marry me?"

Her face showed no emotion, but she trembled beneath his touch. "No, my lord, I will not."

A blow to the stomach would have been easier to accept. He released her hand to draw his own through his hair. Pivoting on his boots, he paced the library floor. What agony this was. "There's nothing I can do to change your mind?"

"No, my lord. Nothing."

He paced some more, grasping for anything to convince her to accept him. But he found no answer. "But the scandal." Surely she couldn't face the scandal surrounding her if she refused. The scandal of birthing a child while unmarried. Of being an unwed mother. Society did not favor such women.

"Scandal does not concern me, my lord." Her voice was as cold and bereft as her eyes.

"What *does* concern you then, Grace?" His voice was rising, but he could do nothing to stop it. "What, pray tell, will put the passion back in your eyes and the heat back in your voice?" Even as he spoke, somehow her pale skin blanched further. "What will make you feel something? Anything?"

A piece of the ice chipped away from her eyes. "You think me unfeeling, my lord? Then why do you insist on continuing this charade?"

Deuce take it, could the chit not answer a simple question? Or several, as the case may be. "I most certainly do not think you unfeeling, because I have seen you feel. Nevertheless, I do believe you keep a tight cork on it all, at least where I am concerned." Most of the time. She occasionally lost her tight rein over it with him.

And here he was answering her questions instead of getting answers to his own. Bloody hell. "Answer me. What can I do to get you to feel something? Must I resort to the same tactics as the last time we saw each other?"

"I feel. I feel an awful lot more than you do, you uncaring lout." Her eyes widened in shock. Apparently she hadn't intended to use that sort of language with him. Progress.

"And why am I an uncaring lout? I believe I've made my feelings more than clear to you. I want to marry you. I want you." God, did he ever want her. Even with her cold demeanor, the air fairly crackled between them.

"Because...because...augh! Because my child doesn't matter to you!" She drew away from the window to face him full on. "Because it is *unimportant.*"

He blinked. A rather unexpected development, indeed. Apparently Chatham had informed her that he was aware of her pregnancy. "Of course the child doesn't matter. I want to marry you. Nothing will change that. How in bloody hell does that make me unfeeling?" Would he never understand her?

"Because it does! How could it not? If my child is unimportant to you, my lord, then I must also be unimportant to you. I will not have you. You may now cease your efforts, if you please."

So very proper, even in a full rage. How enchanting! There was no wonder he loved the minx. "For your information, Grace, I never said the child was unimportant. Either your father did, or possibly you assigned that word to me, yourself."

"Well, you agreed with it, didn't you?" She placed both hands haughtily on her hips, assuming The Stance—the one his mother so often took when she required submission.

"I suppose technically I did. But I was unaware of your meaning when I agreed. Your child will never be unimportant to me. Never. I will love it as my own. I only meant that the fact of your being with child would not matter in the face of my desire to marry you. It changes nothing."

"Hmph!" She still held The Stance like a professional. Grace must have learned quickly from the females in his family, in order to achieve such perfect disdain. It looked glorious on her.

"Will you marry me, Grace?" Surely now she would give in. What else could he do?

"I've told you already that I will not. Nothing has changed." The fire fell out of her eyes, and what small amount of color had filled her face now fled.

"Well. May I escort you to your aunt and uncle in the salon?" Alex pulled his hand through his hair again and came away with some in his fist. She would be the death of him. There could be no doubt.

"That would be acceptable, Lord Alexander." Her voice was thin. Grace stepped away from the windows into the library, shaking violently. Before she reached him, she collapsed into a dead faint.

ALEX CARRIED THE unconscious Grace into the salon, instigating a flurry of activity. Bodies flew about the room.

"Goodness, what have you done to her?"

"Lay her down here on the sofa, Alex. Everyone stand back."

"Is she quite all right? Peter, send for a doctor."

He laid his prone charge across the sofa as directed and stepped away from her, allowing the women to see to her. He never removed his eyes from his love.

Char rushed about, ordering servants to bring water, blankets, cloths, and so many other items he couldn't remember them all. Mama sat on the edge of the sofa, smoothing the hair away from Grace's face. Sophie, ever calm, procured some tea and a bite for Grace to eat once she recovered from her faint. Neil, Derek, and Sir Jonas wisely stood out of the way, and Peter oversaw all of the activity. Sir Laurence and Lady Kensington were curiously absent, as was Chatham, leaving Alex's family and friends to care for her.

Grace let out a soft moan, and her eyelids fluttered but didn't open.

"Alex, did she hit her head when she fell?" his mother asked. "She winced when I touched her just there."

"I—I don't know. She may have. I didn't get to her in time to catch her, Mama." He ought to have caught her. He should never have allowed her to fall, especially in her condition. The baby! "Peter, we should send for a doctor."

"No, that won't be necessary," Sophie said, her voice quiet but firm.

"But she—"

"But nothing. Grace doesn't need a doctor, Alex. Please trust me on this." Sophie lifted Grace's head and settled herself beneath it. She crooned softly, imploring her to open her eyes and drink from a cup of tea.

"Why do you ladies seem so determined not to allow me to call for a doctor? First her aunt, and now you, Sophie."

Mama interrupted his tirade. "This has happened before? She fainted before? Sophia, this isn't normal. We must send for the doctor."

"No, Mama, we can't. She wouldn't want a doctor." Sophie's voice held an edge of steel.

"How can you possibly know what she would want or not want?" Alex bellowed. "You've only known her a few hours. I'm sending for a doctor." He pivoted on his heel and marched toward the door before he saw the huddle of males. "Better yet, Neil, go fetch a doctor. And take Derek and Sir Jonas with you. Hurry."

"Stop, Alex. This is entirely normal since she is *with child.*" His sister hissed the words out as Grace's eyes opened and squinted against the light, and another soft moan slipped past her lips. "I'm sorry, Grace, I had to tell."

"With child," Mama said, her words only a whisper. Grace looked up at her in confusion. "You carry my grandchild? Oh, how delightful! But we must plan the wedding immediately. There can be no delay. I can well understand your father's hurry now, but I do wish Alex had informed me before now. Oh dear." She sniffled and wiped a tear from her eye. "I'll be a Grandmama again. You are such a dear girl. I'm so glad you will be my daughter."

Grace sat up and blinked as she looked around, her eyes settling on Sophie with a combination of hurt and a plea for help. "No. No, there's been a misunderstanding."

"A misunderstanding? You aren't with child?" His mother looked from Grace to Alex and back again.

"No, ma'am. Yes. Well, I *am* with child, but the child is not your son's. And I won't be marrying him. I'll not be your daughter, ma'am." She looked up to him with wide, sad eyes, silently pleading with him to explain. But how could he explain something he didn't understand himself?

"You've refused him again? Oh dear. But, your father…" Mama's words trailed off, and she looked up at him with an apology in her eyes.

"My father? What about my father?" Grace's voice cracked just a bit, the only indication of her fear of the man amongst the haughty air she feigned.

"Why, he left with the Kensingtons to procure a special license. He expects the nuptials to take place tomorrow. Surely he expected you to accept Alex this time, or he wouldn't have gone to such trouble. Would he?" Mama looked dubious. "He couldn't have mistaken your intentions so badly as that."

"I made myself abundantly clear to him, ma'am. I informed him that I would refuse if Lord Alexander asked me to marry him. The only way it will happen is if Father commands me to marry him, since he is still my guardian and I have no choice in the matter."

Aha! She would marry him yet. Grace *would* be his.

"I'd like to speak with Grace alone," he said to his family. "Please leave us."

They filed out of the room, leaving him alone with his love. Sophie was the last to go, and she whispered, "I'm sorry," to Grace on her way out the door.

"Your father will order you to marry me, Grace."

"Yes." She stared at the floor.

"Then why do you refuse? You could make it your choice, and not his. Why allow him to win?"

"Either way, you lose."

"What?" He couldn't temper the violence in his voice. "How could I possibly lose, when I'll be married to you?"

"You deserve better than me, my lord. You are too good for me by half. You ought not to feel honor bound to protect me, when there is nothing remaining to protect. I have no virtue. I have no dignity. I have nothing to give you." Tears slid down her cheeks, one by one, dropping to darken the soft lawn fabric of her pale pink gown.

"But I want you. Is that not enough?" He ached for her. Ached for the shame she carried. Ached to wipe the tears from her eyes and the stain from her heart. Ached to undo the damage done to her by her father and Barrow, and anyone else who had ever hurt her.

Her mouth formed the word "No" but only a squeak came from her lips.

"Why? Tell me why. Allow me to understand."

"Because it isn't your child, my lord."

"I know this. We've already discussed this."

She looked pained at his interruption.

"I apologize. I won't stop you again. Go on."

She turned her gaze to her lap. "I haven't been honest with you since I met you. I—I was ravished by Lord Barrow."

He filled with rage toward the man and wanted little more than to hunt him down where the Regent held him and rip him limb from limb. But what he did want more than that was Grace.

"I am not a suitable bride for a man such as you. You must realize that."

"And you must realize by now I've no intention of leaving you to yourself." Alex paced again, taking long strides. "Why do you allow your pride to keep you from a marriage which could erase any hint of scandal, of impropriety?"

"Pride? You think my pride is the issue here?" Anger flashed blue flames in her eyes and she stood to face him. "I have no pride left. It's been replaced by shame." She stood toe-to-toe with him, glaring up into his eyes. "I can't marry you because you deserve a wife who has a virtue to match your honor. And I *will* not marry you because you spoke only of caring for me, of providing for me, of making me happy. You spoke nothing of love."

She pushed him back a step and advanced to fill the gap. "I will not spend my life married to a man because of duty and honor, who doesn't love me as much as I love him."

"You love me?" Alex's jaw dropped.

The fire fled her eyes as realization of her admission struck her. "I didn't say that."

"You as good as did. You love me." The words were a whisper as he leaned his head in toward hers.

Alex kissed her with all the love and longing that had been building in him since the first moment he saw her eyes through the door of a coach. His lips pressed against hers before he traced the line of her lips with his tongue. She pushed against him at first. But when his tongue slid inside her mouth and tangled with hers, she melted against him and sighed into his mouth.

His hands were everywhere—in her hair, on her arms, against her derrière. He pulled her tight to him, his erection was hard and taut against the slight swell of her belly. He needed her, more of her, all of her.

She tasted of honey, all sweetness and warmth. He drank her in like liquor.

She whimpered against his mouth and wrapped her arms about his shoulders and neck, pulling her body ever closer. The heat between them roared to life.

And then Peter cleared his throat at the door. "Pardon me. I do hate to interrupt, Alex, but I believe Grace's father has returned."

He extracted himself from their embrace. She teetered and he placed an arm around her waist to secure her.

Her cheeks flushed and her lips were swollen, and she looked utterly divine. An urge to pull her from the room and above stairs to his bedchamber grew in his stomach, but he pushed it aside as once again the salon filled with people.

Chatham grinned, the first time Alex had ever seen the man smile. "I've secured a special license for you. You may marry immediately." He took one look at his daughter and his visage changed entirely. "And you *will* marry him, Grace."

Excellent.

She tugged against his grasp. He tightened his hold on her waist and pulled her closer.

"Very good, sir. We'll marry in the morning."

Grace glared up at him, pulled herself free, and marched from the salon.

And he *still* hadn't talked to her about Priscilla and Harry. For that matter, he still hadn't decided what he was going to do about them.

There was not much time left. He had to decide. Now.

Twenty-Four

AUNT DOROTHEA'S FACE was alight with joy. "Oh how wonderful. I do love weddings. Gracie, you look breathtaking in that white silk, I'm so glad we chose it for today. Lord Alexander will be stunned speechless when he sees you." She fussed about Grace, fiddling with ribbons and flowers and generally getting in Tess's way as the girl tried to secure Grace's hair in an elaborate knot.

She didn't bother to feign excitement. In an hour's time, she would marry Lord Alexander, a man who didn't love her. A man who was only marrying her for honor's sake.

A man she loved desperately.

She should be happy. She would love her husband, she could keep her child, and she would live near her aunt and uncle. She would have a family for the first time since she was a very young girl. A lot of family, for that matter, and a very interesting and entertaining family to boot.

Yet she was miserable.

It might be different if he loved her—if he wanted to marry her and was not forced to do so in order to save her honor.

But she couldn't change the situation. She would walk down the aisle and marry the man she loved more than anything in the world, and then spend the rest of her life with the knowledge that she was entirely and utterly unlovable.

Grace felt numb.

She allowed Tess and Aunt Dorothea to finish their ministrations. After they completed the task and deemed her beautiful beyond compare, and of course the loveliest bride the ton had ever seen, she boarded the waiting carriage. She sat next to Aunt Dorothea, across from her father and Uncle Laurence as they traveled to the church.

No true guests would be present. Only his family and hers, with the additions of Lord Rotheby, Sir Jonas, and the Earl of Sinclaire would witness the ceremony.

Her father took her hand to help her down from the carriage, then escorted her into the church. She tried not to shrink from his touch, but found it difficult. He couldn't fool her into thinking he was an entirely changed man overnight, simply from one confrontation with the Dowager Duchess of Somerton, even if the woman was the most imposing and convincing woman Grace had ever laid eyes upon.

Lord Alexander waited for her at the front, next to the vicar. She couldn't look at him. Instead, she stared at the walkway beneath her feet, unable to look anyone in the eyes. Father passed her hand to Lord Alexander, and the vicar started the ceremony. It all passed by her in a fog.

Lord Alexander said, "I do," and pressed her hand gently.

When prompted, she also said "I do." She had no choice. Father had commanded her to accept, so she did.

The vicar said a few more words, none of which registered in her mind. They signed the register. Lord Alexander turned her about to face their families and led her along the aisle and from the church to yet another waiting carriage. An open carriage—one that would proclaim to all of London that she was now Lady Alexander Hardwicke.

He assisted her inside and climbed up after her. The driver signaled the horses to leave, and they began the journey to Hardwicke House for a celebratory meal.

"Are you happy, Grace?"

She stared out at the passing city. "Happy, my lord?"

"Alex. Call me Alex. I want to hear my name on your lips."

She hesitated before whispering, "Alex."

He took her hand and held it in his. "I like that. I like how you say my name." A few moments passed and the tension inside her built. "I want to hear it from you more often. But you haven't answered me. I daresay that's becoming a habit. Are you happy?"

"I don't know." Grace couldn't remember the last time she had felt happy. What would it feel like? Would she even recognize it when it arrived? Somehow, she doubted it.

He stroked the back of her hand, her fingers. "I'll make you happy. Give me the opportunity. That's all I ask."

She closed her eyes and pulled in a deep breath. The air smelled of recent rain and wildflowers, and the warm, woodsy, masculine scent belonging to her husband.

"I'll try. I can promise you no more than that I will try." Was she even capable of happiness?

He pulled her hand to his lips and placed a chaste kiss on it as the carriage arrived at Hardwicke House. She shuddered at his gentle touch.

ALEX WISHED THE celebration would come to an end. He loved his family and friends, but he had other things on his mind. He wanted to show Grace how much he loved her. He couldn't live with himself if she continued to doubt him, to doubt his affection for her. His love.

They would stay in a suite at Hardwicke House for the night and journey to Somerton in the morning. He didn't want to overwhelm her on the day of their wedding by beginning with travel and spending the night at an inn along the way. He wanted to make this one night special for her—perfect even.

But the celebration continued. He sat by her side through a round of toasts, from Peter, Derek, Gil, and Sir Laurence. The whole time she wore a fake smile, one that seemed painted on her face. A small orchestra was assembled in the ballroom, and Mama declared dancing would begin immediately.

"Would you care to dance with me, Grace?" he asked as he led her to the ballroom.

With her pasted smile, she nodded and took his hand. The orchestra played a waltz. He swept her into his arms, and they glided across the floor to the music.

The world spun around them, but he saw nothing other than his wife. "I thought this day might never come, Grace."

"I hoped it wouldn't, my lord." She looked away.

A single tear slid down her cheek, and he reached up to smooth it away. It was only her pain. She loved him. He had to remember that she loved him. "Alex. I asked you to call me by my name."

She only nodded in reply.

Why couldn't she accept his love? Was he destined to a lifetime of marriage to a woman who couldn't allow him to love her? A piece of his heart broke at the prospect, and he pulled her closer in his arms, wanting to surround her with his warmth as a symbol of his love.

Alex vowed to himself that tonight he would love Grace so well that she could no longer deny it. He would do whatever it required.

But Grace would know he loved her.

THE WEDDING CELEBRATION finally came to an end, much to Grace's relief. She could think of little she wanted to celebrate less than her marriage. But the deed was done, and now Grace would have to learn her new position as a wife.

She didn't imagine life as the wife of a gentleman would be much different than life as her father's daughter had been. She would merely answer to a different master. Life would go on as it always had in the past.

After she said her goodbyes to her aunt, uncle, and Lord Rotheby, who would travel to Somerton together in a few days, her husband took her hand.

"Come with me, Grace."

So she went. The dutiful wife must obey, after all. She had no right to argue or complain.

He led her through the halls and up the stairs to a separate wing of the house. "Mama had a suite prepared for us, so we could have some privacy." He opened a large, oak door and ushered her inside.

A huge canopied bed stood against one wall, with matching tables and chairs scattered about the room. Silks draped the bed and windows in rich gold and brown.

Alex closed the door behind them. "You have a dressing room through here. I had a footman bring your trunks up earlier, so you should have everything you need." He still held one of her hands in his firm grasp. "A second sleeping chamber is on the other side of your dressing room."

Her heart pounded in her chest. Would she be allowed some reprieve then? And did she even want it?

"I had it prepared for you. But I hope you'll choose not to use it." He turned her to face him and placed his hand against her cheek. "I hope you'll stay with me tonight."

He tilted her head and placed a soft, teasing kiss upon her lips. She leaned in to him, her body disregarding her mind's commands.

But then he broke off the kiss. "I believe Tess is waiting to assist you in your dressing room."

He removed his hands from her and took a step away, granting her a chance to breathe if her lungs would cooperate. The heat in his eyes melted her core and turned her to a liquid pool of heat inside. She hurried away to her dressing room.

Tess bobbed a curtsy when she walked through the door. "My lady, your aunt prepared a trousseau for you ma'am."

"That was very kind of her, Tess." Grace stood behind the door and pressed against it while she regained her composure. Her pulse raced and her body ached in her most private areas. But he had hardly even touched her.

"We ought to get you out of your gown, ma'am. You won't want to keep your husband waiting." Tess moved to her side and removed pins from her hair. "Lady Kensington put a nightgown in your trousseau and she told me to be sure you wear it tonight. I've laid it aside."

The lady's maid worked briskly and soon had Grace's hair freed from its confines so it flowed in soft waves over her shoulders and across her back, nearly reaching to her waist. She moved to the buttons on Grace's gown next. Before she knew what was happening, she was undressed down to her shift.

Tess moved to the dressing table where a sleeping gown lay ready for Grace to don. It was a diaphanous white fabric that would expose her almost completely to her husband's gaze.

"I can't possibly wear that, Tess." Her eyes bulged and she backed a few steps away, grasping her shift to her chest.

"Why ever not, my lady? His lordship will be taking it off you, I would wager, whatever you wear." The girl's eye twinkled in delight.

"What...how do you know of such things?" Grace narrowed her eyes and the young girl.

Tess laughed. "We learn of these things and a good bit more, we house servants do. Never you mind. Off with your shift, and we'll put this pretty thing on you."

Grace gawked. "When did you become so bossy?" She had no choice but to lift her arms above her head as her servant pulled the shift from her body.

"Oh, I don't know, my lady. Maybe when I learned I'd be allowed to stay on as your lady's maid. Your husband offered me the position, you know. And since you will live in Somerton, I'll still be near my family. It's a wonderful situation, I believe. Far better than having you off with Lord Barrow, or in London. I think you and I'll do quite well with Lord Alexander, don't you agree?"

Tess settled the nightgown over Grace's head and smoothed it along her curves. "I think this will do rather well. Your aunt is a right smart lady, ma'am. Lord Alexander will want to eat you alive when he sees you like this."

Grace was already flushing in embarrassment over Tess seeing her in such a state, but the suggestion of Lord Alexander wanting to eat her alive only served to multiply her discomfort.

"Right then. Off I go, my lady. If you need me, give the bell pull a tug, but otherwise I will be far, far away." Tess exited through the door to the second bedchamber.

Grace took a few breaths to calm herself. There was no reason to fret. She'd been intimate with Alex before, and it had been a wonderful experience. Once she thought she could go through the door without running in the opposite direction, she returned to the main chamber.

Her husband stood by the hearth, kindling a fire. Candlelight danced about the room, darkened by closed curtains over the windows. He was barefoot and had removed his coat, waistcoat, and cravat. She didn't see any of his discarded items of clothing. He must have put them in his dressing room.

He walked toward her with his shirt halfway unbuttoned. Auburn hairs dotted his muscled chest. His eyes glowed in the dim candlelight. Alex stopped short of coming near enough to touch her and devoured her with his eyes. Her body burned everywhere his gaze rested, and she moved to cover herself with her arms.

"No," he said, the word a choked plea. "Let me see you." He moved closer, took her hands in his, and held her arms out to her sides.

She felt exposed, ashamed. His wedding night ought to be with a woman in possession of her virtue. And hers should be with a man who could love her.

But neither of those would be.

"You are so beautiful Grace. So perfect."

She felt anything but beautiful or perfect. But then he moved closer still, so the distance between them pulsed. He slid his hands down her bare arms and across her back, moving until they came to a stop on her behind. His hands were so large that one of them almost covered her derrière by itself. He pulled her closer, pressed her length into him. She gasped at his heat against her stomach.

Lord Alexander looked into her eyes. His were liquid pools of forest green, and the gold flecks in them were danced like flickering flames.

"I need you, Grace." His mouth came down and enveloped hers. He swept his tongue inside to stroke against hers.

A pull in her center drew her into him, and she wrapped her arms around his waist to hold him close. His scent, that glorious, masculine scent of woods and man was enhanced, musky. It washed over her in waves as they moved together and their heat combined.

He pulled the thin fabric up and touched the bare flesh of her backside with his hands, rubbing, kneading, stroking.

Her courage grew, and she lost her inhibitions. She would give in to her love for him, at least for this one night. Grace became the aggressor in their kiss, thrusting her tongue inside his mouth to taste him. Steady on her feet, she ran her hands over the hair of his chest.

Lord Alexander growled, a low sound deep in his throat. "I need to see you. All of you." He placed one arm around her waist and pulled the garment free with the other.

Grace instinctively moved her hands to cover her breasts again, but he caught them before she could.

"Please let me see you. Let me touch you, Grace." He kissed her eyelids, her cheeks, beneath her chin, along her neck. He cupped her breasts in his palms and she whimpered. Sensation ruled.

"You like that, do you? Tell me you like it." He moved his head lower and lapped his tongue over her sensitive nipple.

"Yes, I like that, Lord Alexander." She couldn't think.

"Say my name, Grace. Call me Alex." He completed the order by suckling her entire breast in his mouth.

Grace gripped his shoulders for balance. Her legs turned to jelly beneath her. "Alex. I like that, Alex." She might enjoy it a bit too much. He was welcome to stop in a few years or so.

He lowered to his knees, where his eyes were directly across from the swell of her stomach. Alex placed a gentle kiss there and held his head against where her child grew, resting for a moment and holding Grace by the hips.

His tenderness overwhelmed her. Her love for him coursed through her body so fast it scared her. She felt like she might break in two if he so much as brushed a finger over her skin.

For just that moment, she felt beautiful. Loved, even.

Grace placed her hands atop his head and ran her fingers through his shaggy hair.

He moved one hand between her legs, shocking her senses when he stroked her tender flesh. Alex slid a finger inside her and she shuddered.

When she thought she would die from the pressure building internally, he stood and picked her up. He carried her to the bed and laid her carefully across the sheets, her hair fanned out over the pillows.

He removed the last of his clothing in the flickers of the candlelight. She had never seen a nude man before, and the size of him scared her. His muscled arms, the definition of his chest, those long, powerful legs. He was glorious. She had a sudden urge to paint him, just as he stood before her, but pushed it aside. That could come later.

She needed him now.

Alex came down on the bed beside her and took her face in his hands. "I will never hurt you, Grace. Don't be afraid of me."

It wasn't fear but awe, but she had no voice to tell him. He kissed her again, deep and full, and his hands stroked her to a passionate peak again. He rose above her and braced his weight on his arms as he spread her legs with a knee. The tip of his manhood rested at her opening. She wanted more.

"Say my name, Grace. Call me by my name." His voice shook with passion and need, and an edge of fear.

"Alex." The word was a prayer on her tongue.

And he was inside her, filling her, pulsing with her. She moved her legs up to wrap about his waist and marveled that it brought him closer, deeper.

They moved as one. Her body tightened and tensed, and she would shatter to pieces if she didn't find release soon. Alex seemed to sense her need and he quickened his pace. She moaned from the most wonderful pain.

And then the world came to a stop. She crashed over the edge and held onto him for dear life. "Alex, Alex, Alex."

He spilled into her a moment later and collapsed on top of her, burying his head in her hair while he regained his breath.

"Oh, how I love you," she said on a sob. She regretted the words as soon as she said them, but he didn't react. She didn't want to love him. It would be so much easier if she didn't. Perhaps the pain would be lessened to know she was married to a man who could never love her in return if she felt no love for him.

Alex moved beside her and pulled her in close, her backside pressed firmly against his front. His breathing grew even, and he placed a large, protective hand over her abdomen where her baby grew.

Grace laid still and cried herself to sleep, careful not to alert him to her tears.

ALEX BRUSHED GRACE'S hair away from her face to watch her sleep. The tears weren't yet dry on her cheeks, so he brushed them away as well.

"Oh my sweet Grace, I love you." His words fell on the darkness of night.

She still didn't believe his love, even after their tender loving that night. What else must he do to convince her?

He pulled his wife closer and breathed in the fragrance of Grace and the scent of their lovemaking. One hand rested against the child growing in her belly. Their child. He already loved the baby as his own.

Alex drifted off to sleep, dreaming of a baby girl with midnight hair and eyes of ice.

Twenty-Five

EVERY MOVEMENT SHE made in her sleep sent blood rushing to his groin. If Grace didn't still soon, he wouldn't be able to stop himself from taking her again.

Not that that was such a horrible thought. Far from it.

But her movements increased in frequency, not to mention scale. She kicked a leg out and landed her foot against his shin. Something was very, very wrong. Even as he tried to wake her, she whimpered in her sleep. She was frightened. He leaned over her and shook her shoulder. "Grace, wake up."

Her fist swung out to strike him in the face. She would have made contact with his nose if his reflexes had been slower.

Alex used a bit more force in shaking her shoulder this time. "Grace, you're having a bad dream. Wake up for me." His voice rose in pitch.

"Ah. No, no, NO!" Her eyes flew open and she sat up in bed, struggling against him with everything in her.

"It's me, Grace. Alex. It's Alex." He held her tight to his chest, careful to keep her hands firmly locked in his fist.

She fought against him for a moment more before finally stilling in his arms. Her heartbeat slowed to a normal pace as he stroked her hair, her arms, her back.

When he pulled away from her, she still had wide eyes full of fear. "What were you dreaming about?"

She shook her head and looked away, a single tear threatening to fall.

"All right. You don't have to tell me now. It's all right." He lay down in the bed again and held her close. She closed her eyes and rested her head against his shoulder, still shaking violently.

He pulled the blankets over them and wrapped her tight. "I'll never allow you to be hurt, Grace. Never."

Alex shut his eyes. Could he keep that promise?

SHE SHIVERED AGAINST him, huddled under the counterpane in a cocoon of his warmth.

The nightmare had been far worse this time. When she awoke, she'd seen Barrow leaning over her, not Alex. It took several minutes for her to calm enough to recognize him as her husband and not as the man who had ravished her.

"I'll never allow you to be hurt, Grace. Never," Alex had said before he fell asleep again.

But how could he prevent hurting her himself? He caused her great anguish simply by not loving her, by treating her with care and tenderness, but not giving her the one thing she wanted more than anything in the world.

No, not wanted. Needed. Grace needed his love. She needed to believe he could love her, even if only half as much as she loved him.

If he couldn't love her, who could?

She turned toward him and willed herself to sleep.

And she prayed she would not dream again.

ALEX WOKE WITH the sunlight streaming in through the windows. He rolled over to give Grace a good morning kiss, but she'd already quit his bed. The spot where she had slept was cold to the touch. He grumbled under his breath.

He pulled on a robe before knocking at her dressing room door. The housekeeper had arranged for breakfast to be brought to them in bed. Grace was spoiling all his plans. How could a man be romantic if his wife wouldn't comply?

Tess answered his knock, opening the door only a crack, and informed him, "My lady is already down to the breakfast room this morning, and will be delighted to see you there, sir."

He scowled through the crack. "Be certain all her belongings are packed and ready. We leave for Somerton after breakfast. I'll send a footman up to carry everything to the carriage."

In his own dressing room, he wanted to dress as soon as possible and join his bride and family. "Can you not hurry with tying that deuced knot?" he asked Thomas. His beleaguered valet passed him a withering look but held his tongue. Alex sighed. "It seems you can't." He tried to be patient, but patience was in short supply this morning. When he was finally dressed to Thomas's satisfaction, he went downstairs.

His family filled the breakfast room to the brim. Mama and Sophie sat on either side of Grace. While Alex was glad to see his family accept his bride, he felt a twinge of jealousy that he couldn't sit next to her. "Good morning,, Mama. Good morning Grace."

Grace looked at him, her expression unreadable. "Good morning Lo—Good morning, Alex." She returned to her conversation with his mother and sister and ignored him.

He prepared a plate and sat as close to her as he could manage, across the table and down a few seats. He ignored Neil, who sat to his right, and ate his food without tasting a bite of it.

"I believe I still have some of the dressing gowns and blankets my children used when they were babies. Would you like me to have them sent to you in Somerton?" Mama asked Grace. Then she acted as though a novel idea had struck her, and not something she'd likely been planning since her discovery that Grace was with child. "Or better yet, I could travel to visit you and bring them with me. If you wouldn't mind my company, of course."

"Of course, Your Grace, you'll always be welcome. I would be glad for any assistance you can give me for the baby." Grace flushed.

Mama frowned. "Now that you have married Alex, you're my daughter. Please, let us not be so formal. If you aren't comfortable calling me Mama, then Henrietta will do just as well."

"Yes, Your Grace, I'll try to remember that. Oh, and there I go again." Her face flushed as it screwed up in concentration. "I daresay, I have so rarely had close relationships, it daunts me to use such informality."

His mother patted the top of Grace's hand. "You'll learn."

Char's face lit up. "Oh, Mama, we ought to all go to Somerton Court this winter. We can be there when the baby arrives. It would be just wonderful. May we please?"

Alex chewed his baked eggs with undue force. Would his family not grant him any time alone with his wife?

Mama turned her attention to him. "Well, Charlotte, you should ask Alex and Grace. They may want some privacy."

He bloody well did.

"That can all wait until later, Char," Peter said from the head of the table. "It seems Alex is ready to begin their journey. He couldn't even be bothered to eat his breakfast like a civilized man."

True enough. Alex tried not to scowl. "Er, yes. Well. Grace, are you ready? I believe a carriage awaits us." He shoved his chair away from the table and moved to assist her. He had planned to discuss Priscilla and Harry with her upstairs while they ate their private breakfast. Now that opportunity had been taken from him. He wished they could have discussed it before the wedding, but there'd been no time. Her aunt had whisked her away to make preparations. Devil take it. He hoped she would take the news well.

When she stood, the air carried her scent to him. He would far prefer to carry her above stairs and resume where they'd left off last night, but it would have to wait. He wanted her alone, so the carriage would have to do.

His family followed them to the door, with his sisters sniffling and simpering in their wake.

"We have only just met Grace, and you're already taking her away from us." One could always count on Char for a touch of drama. "It's just dreadful, Alex. Couldn't you stay in Town for a few more days? A week? The rest of the Season?"

"No." He bit off the word.

Sophie took Grace by the hand. "I'll write to you often." The eldest Hardwicke sister pulled Grace into a ferocious hug.

"That is enough, girls," his mother said over the din. "Allow them to leave or they won't be at an inn by dark." She slid in to replace Sophie and placed a kiss on Grace's cheek before whispering in her ear. Alex couldn't hear his mother's words, but watched as a wave of relief passed over Grace's face. "Off you go, now. No more delay. Alex, if you mistreat that girl, I'll have you horsewhipped."

"Mama, I would put nothing past you." The woman was capable of anything.

His sisters squeezed Grace into a tight hug full of giggles and squeals, eliciting a look of surprise and bewilderment on her face.

"Enough. We have to leave." Alex reached into the sea of feminine affection and plucked Grace free. Peter and Neil ducked in to give her a quick peck on the cheek each, causing her to blush profusely. Good Lord, he needed to get a handle on himself or he would ravish her right there in the middle of the street. She looked entirely too lovely when she blushed.

He guided her up the steps of the carriage and followed her inside. She sat in the center of the bench facing front, leaving him no room to sit beside her. The driver placed the steps inside and closed the door behind him. After only a moment's hesitation, Alex lifted Grace from her perch. He seated himself where she had been and pulled her down onto his lap, ignoring her indignant gasp, and then rapped against the carriage wall to signal they were ready.

He waved to his family as the carriage pulled away from Hardwicke House and took them toward Somerton. Toward home.

He held his squirming wife firmly in place and settled in for the two-day's journey. Two more carriages pulled in behind them—one housing Priscilla and Harry, the other carrying their trunks and bags and other essentials. Life was beginning to look up, indeed.

SHE THOUGHT SHE'D made herself clear by taking up the center of the seat that she wanted him to sit across from her and not beside her. Grace was mortified when Alex sat her on his lap with his entire family watching. Of course, it was a closed carriage. But there were windows. They could see everything.

She struggled against him to free herself from his grasp, but his arms were bands about her and she couldn't move. Once they were far enough away from Hardwicke House she was absolutely certain beyond any doubt they could no longer be seen or heard, Grace voiced her complaint.

"Unhand me, my lord." She tried yet again to remove herself from his hold.

He tightened his grip instead of loosening it and didn't speak until she was still. "My name is Alex." His voice was soft. Too soft.

She twisted about to face him. "Fine. Unhand me, Alex." Her voice held far more venom than she'd imagined herself capable of.

Instead of releasing her, he lifted her from his lap, slid over to one side of the bench, and sat her beside him. He kept a firm grip on her. Try as she might, she couldn't break his hold to move to the other seat of the carriage.

Grace scooted as far away from him as possible, but their bodies still touched. It was like they were fused at the hip and thigh.

Alex sighed. "Have I offended you? Have I hurt you? Why are you so upset with me this morning, Grace? I can't set something to rights if I don't know what I've done."

How could she explain to him that he was hurting her because he could never love her? That she was head over ears in love with him— far more in love than she thought healthy—and that his kindness and care, his protection, cut her to the core? Her love for him could only lead to her own heartache.

"No, you've done nothing wrong." She couldn't fault him for his lack of love for her. Even her own father had never loved her.

But his family, the Hardwickes, had accepted her without question. They had taken her in and made her one of their own. And now she was leaving them behind. Grace left a part of her heart behind with them. She could come to love them. They were rather unlike her, but that was certainly not a fault. The Hardwicke family loved each other and loved life. They were exuberant with their love.

But yet, to come from a family so full of love and life and excitement, somehow he couldn't bring himself to love her. What was it about her that made her so very unlovable?

She resented that he would take her away from them so soon. And that he did not seem to like the idea of them coming to visit. His mother had whispered in her ear that they would come to visit sooner rather than later just before they departed. It was like the dowager could already read Grace's thoughts, like they already knew her and everything about her and how she would be desperate to get to know them and spend time with them.

But now, she would be isolated once again.

Grace wondered if he would even stop her aunt and uncle from visiting, if he would keep her shut inside the house. He could, if he wanted to. It was a husband's right, after all, to do with his wife as he pleased.

She pressed a hand against her abdomen. At least she would have this child. Children loved without question—their love was unconditional. Her baby would love her, even if no one else did.

Alex couldn't take her child's love from her too. She wouldn't let him.

They traveled for a while in silence, each seething as they stared out their respective windows. He never loosened his hold on her but occasionally pulled her closer to him.

Then he turned to her. "One of the carriages behind us carries a woman and her son. She will serve as a nurse for our children."

A woman? And her child? But no husband? Unless…

"You've hired your mistress to work in our home and raise my children." A statement, not a question. "You're allowing her to bring her child—your illegitimate child—into my home. To be raised next to my children." The hurt tore through her. No wonder he would never love her. He already loved another—already had a child with another. She jabbed her elbow into his ribs as hard as she was capable.

He let out an "Oof!" and released her long enough that she escaped his grip and moved to the other side of the carriage.

"I realize I have no say in how you live your life, my lord, nor in the way you treat me. But really. There is little you could do to hurt me more, than to leave my bed to find that of your mistress."

"Grace, wait—"

"No. No, I will not wait. I'll say my piece. You have gotten it from me that I love you, and I can't deny the truth any longer. I do. I love you more than I know what to do with, and I desperately wish I didn't. But since I do, that gives you the power to destroy me." She brushed her tears away with impatience. "Living under the same roof as the woman you prefer over me will do that. Please don't ask it of me."

"Grace—"

"Don't do this. Don't try to explain it away or make me feel better or anything else. Your honor deserves more, my lord."

"That is enough!"

She flinched in her seat at his tone, and hated herself for cowering.

"She's not my mistress, and he's not my son."

"Hmph." She crossed her arms over her chest and tried to assume the same haughty air from only a couple of days before, but believed her fear showed through, nonetheless. Grace's chin quivered, however firm she tried to hold it.

"I admit, I have willingly given that impression about Town, because it was easier that way. They were safer that way. But the fact remains, I've never touched Priscilla. We've never been involved in such a way."

"If that's true, then who is she? And why are you bringing her into our home?" And why on earth could he possibly *want* to give off such an impression if it wasn't the truth.

"She's a friend. I'm her protector. I don't know what else to call our relationship. Several years ago, she was the Earl of Barrow's mistress."

Grace sucked in an abrupt breath, but bit her tongue to keep from speaking.

"He wasn't a kind man to her, but she had nowhere else to go and no one else to turn to, so she stayed with him. Barrow was violent, and she feared what he'd do to her if she tried to leave him. So she stayed. One time, Pris discovered she was pregnant. When she told him, he beat her until...until the baby was gone. Apparently, he didn't want to have to support not only her, but a child as well. When she discovered she was with child again, she tried to hide it from him for as long as she could. She could only hide it for so long. Her belly rounded, and he knew. He beat her senseless and tossed her down a flight of stairs. Then he threw her out onto the street."

"Oh my." How horrible. Thank God she wasn't married to him. How would she ever have survived it?

"Lord Sinclaire and I found her crumpled in a ball beneath a streetlight. We took her to my apartments and called a doctor to care for her. When she was well enough, she told us the whole of the story. I went after Barrow, but he'd left for the continent. When I came back, I promised Priscilla I would always care for her and her child, despite whatever else may happen in my life." He paused and looked her full in the eye. "When I make a promise, Grace, I keep it."

"Yes. I can see that you do." The poor woman. If, of course, he was telling her the truth now. He could have simply fabricated the story as a lark, as a way to convince her to change her mind. She would reserve judgment for now.

They stopped to picnic for lunch. The dowager duchess had sent a basket of breads, fruits, meats, and cheeses with them. When the driver opened the door and set down the steps, Alex alighted and then lifted Grace to the ground, holding her close longer than necessary. She took in his scent again, mixed with that of spring sun and wildflowers.

From one of the other carriages, a young boy jumped down and rushed to her husband. "Awwiks! We passed a lot of twees and wivews and stweams. And Mommy said I can go wun about some after we eat and get wid of some of my enewgy because I'm bound to make her cwazy. Can I?" He paused only long enough to look over and see her. "Who awe you?"

But Grace's attention was held rapt by the woman being helped down from the same carriage. A very tall, very strong footman lifted her down and set her gingerly on her feet, then reached inside the carriage and brought down a walking cane to place in her hands. She was really quite plain, yet something about her was very intriguing. Dull brown hair, a passable complexion, strong eyes. But not particularly beautiful. With the aid of her cane, she slowly walked toward them. While her gait was disturbed, she held herself with a proud bearing.

Had Barrow had been the cause of her affliction? Doubtless he was. Atrocious, evil man.

"Grace," Alex said as the young woman drew near, interrupting her thoughts. "Might I introduce you to Miss Priscilla Bean and her son, Harry?" He took the woman's outstretched hand and placed a very chaste kiss on her cheek.

Miss Bean started to curtsy, but Grace stayed her. "No, please. It's unnecessary. Hello, Miss Bean. It's a pleasure to make your acquaintance. Lor—Alex tells me you've agreed to be our nursemaid. I'm glad."

Miss Bean smiled, and her face came alive. "Lady Alexander, I thank you."

Harry ran in circles about them, occasionally tripping over his own feet and sending out a series of squeals. His mother grabbed onto him with one hand. "Harry, meet Alex's wife. This is Lady Alexander."

"Wady Awwiks. You are pwetty. Do you want me to catch you a fwog?"

His toothy grin melted her from the inside out. "Why, I'd love that, Harry."

"Oh no. Oh, my lady, you oughtn't to have agreed. He'll do it!" Miss Bean's eyes filled with mortification. "The next thing we know, he'll have your beautiful traveling gown covered in mud and filth and you'll have frog slime all over you."

How delightful. Grace had never been covered in mud or frog slime before. She laughed aloud, an almost giddy sound. "I'm sure that will be quite all right."

"You are." Alex looked doubtful. "I don't believe I've ever seen you anything short of perfectly put together, Grace. Are you sure you're up for this? There's nothing that can create a mess faster than a little boy. I should know. I was one."

Grace nodded to him. "Oh yes. I think it would be lovely." And she did. How very odd. "I was never allowed to play in mud or catch frogs."

A look passed between Alex and Miss Bean.

"Well, my lady, I do believe Harry can give you all the mess you desire and then some. You two should get along quite well."

"Shall we, Miss Bean?" Grace asked. "I think I'd like that. If you're all right with it, of course. But I would love to spend some time with the two of you and go hunting worms and other such things. How will I ever know if I enjoy it if I don't try it?"

Her husband's only response was, "Indeed."

Oh dear. What would he think of her? "And if it's all right with you, as well, Alex." She gave him a sheepish grin and hoped he would indulge her.

One of the outriders had laid a blanket on a soft patch of grass and arranged the basket's contents for their consumption. Alex assisted Miss Bean to sit on the blanket with a wide, boyish grin on his face. "You're welcome to do as you please, Grace. You need not seek my permission."

How terribly irregular. A husband who would not insist on approving his wife's activities? Of course, his entire family seemed to have different ideas on what is right and proper, so this shouldn't require such a vast stretch of the imagination for it to make sense.

They sat and talked while they ate, with little Harry running about them in between moments of eating as fast as he could shovel food into his mouth. Grace was pleased to discover she enjoyed the company of Priscilla, as Miss Bean insisted on being called, and they had a great deal more in common than a shared past with Lord Barrow. They both did a good deal of stitching, both embroidery and sewing, and Priscilla was a watercolorist.

As they finished their meal, Priscilla struggled to her feet with Alex jumping to assist her before she waved him off. "If it's all right, I'd like to stretch my legs before we continue."

"Of course," Alex readily agreed. "Take all the time you need. I'm in no hurry to climb back in that cramped carriage myself."

"I believe there is a creek off through the trees over there. Harry and I will go explore." She turned to her overactive son. "Would you like that?"

"Oh, yes! Yes, Momma. Hurry! I want to catch a fish." He grabbed onto his mother's free hand and pulled her along behind him as fast as her cane would allow.

Alex's gaze turned serious again as the drivers and outriders packed away the remaining foodstuffs. "Grace, your father wants to come visit you in Somerton."

Her head popped up and she returned his stare. "My father?"

"Yes. He wants to build a relationship with you." He looked her full in the eye, a curious expression in his gaze. "I told him it would be your decision, of course."

"My decision?" She couldn't hide the confusion from her voice. She'd been granted very few choices in life. What would she do with one? How would she choose?

"If you want me to refuse him, I will. I know he's not been very kind or loving to you." He paused. "But he's the only father you have. So if you want me to allow him to come and stay with us for a time, I will. You need only say the word."

"I don't know what I want." She stood and walked a few paces away from the blanket. "Wouldn't it be best for you to decide?"

He moved behind her and placed an arm casually around her waist. "No." He leaned down and sniffed her hair as he pulled her in closer.

"No? Why not? I don't understand." Grace spun in his arms and stared up into his eyes. "You're my husband. You ought to decide what's best for me. What I want doesn't matter."

His eyes darkened to almost black.

"What you want doesn't matter?" He moved away and pushed a hand through his hair, his voice strained. Alex paced for a moment before returning to the carriage. "We should move on. Get inside."

His tone told her she ought not to cross him. She scurried over to where he stood and allowed him to assist her. She took the seat facing the rear and hoped he would take her hint this time. A glance through the open door told her that Priscilla and Harry were already nearing their carriage.

Alex climbed inside behind her and sat across from her. He reached over her head and rapped against the wall, and she flinched from his movements. The carriage lurched into motion.

She waited for the lecture she was sure would come. Grace had seen the same expression countless times before from her father.

And she braced herself for the beating which always followed.

Twenty-Six

SHE SHRUNK AWAY from him when he reached over her head to alert the driver they were ready. Could Grace actually believe he would strike her? Alex was horrified. His wife thought him capable of hitting a woman. But his anger took precedence over any horror he might feel.

"Why," he began, his words slow and soft, "is what you want unimportant, Grace? Why should I make decisions and force them upon you when you have a mind of your own?"

She started to answer him, but he hadn't finished. "Why do you pull away from my touch?" His pitch escalated with each word. "Why do you flinch when I raise my hand, as though you expect me to—to beat you?"

He was near to yelling and she cowered in her seat, yet he continued. "And why, please tell me why, will you allow everyone to love you but me? Why Grace? What have I done?"

She stared at him, wide-eyed, but in anger, not fear.

"*Allow* them to love me? And just how do you propose I've allowed anyone to love me, yet somehow stopped you?" She appeared ready to pounce on him and scratch his eyes out like a cat.

"So you didn't notice my entire family fawning over you then? And you don't see how your aunt and uncle adore you?"

"That isn't love." Her chin trembled.

He slid across to her seat in a single, swift move. Alex leaned over her, towering above her, pinning her hands to her sides. "If it isn't love, then what, pray tell, is it?"

She shook beneath him but never wavered from his stare. "Kindness. Pity, perhaps. I don't know."

"That's right, you don't know. They love you, Grace. Everyone around you loves you, but I'm the only one you push away. If you're incapable of recognizing their love for what it is, then it's no wonder you cannot see mine."

"You...you don't love me." She shook her head as tears sprung to her eyes. "You cannot love me."

"Why, Grace?" he roared. "Why can't you see?"

She struggled against him, pushed him away with all her strength. Her movements set his loins aflame, and he kissed her hard on the lips, forcing his tongue inside her mouth. He slid the fabric of her traveling gown off her shoulders and freed her breasts to his touch. He stroked and kneaded first one mound, then the other.

She arched her back, pressing herself more fully into his hands. His need took control when she surrendered to him, and he forgot they were in a moving carriage.

He lifted his hips to unfasten his breeches. Alex fumbled with the buttons, his large hand bungling with the small implements, but he kept his other hand on Grace. When he finally freed his erection, he lifted his wife above him to straddle his hips and moved her skirts up about her waist, pulling frantically at the strings to her drawers.

She lowered onto him, her tightness enveloping him with exquisite torture. They moved together, hips rocking in time with the carriage rolling over the road. Grace rose and fell above him, arching into his touch, his mouth.

He nibbled her breasts. She moaned low with desire. Alex took her hips in his hands and increased the pace of their loving. She quickened around him, her eyes closed, her head rolled back. Soft little sighs sounded from her throat.

"Open your eyes, Grace. I want to watch you when you peak." He needed his own release, but forced himself to hold it at bay.

She obeyed and stared into his eyes, her frosty centers aflame with desire and need.

He thrust inside her and held her still, filling her to the brim. "I love you, Grace. I need you to believe me. I need you to accept my love."

She turned her head to the side.

"No. Look at me." With one hand, Alex pulled her head to place her eyes in line with his again and held her firmly in place. "I love you."

A single tear filled her eye and spilled over. He wiped it away with a finger and placed a chaste kiss on her lips.

"I love you, Grace."

She tried to shake her head and deny his love, but he held her head still.

"I love you." Alex moved inside her again, showing her his love with long, smooth strokes.

"I love you." He kissed her, his tongue matching the pace of their bodies.

"I love you." He moved a hand between them and stroked her taut nub.

She shuddered in his arms and tightened against him. He watched as her eyes melted from the heat. Grace cried out and collapsed against him, hiding her face against his neck.

Alex resituated them on the floor of the carriage and continued to show her his love. He pulled her legs up and around his waist and thrust deep and hard and fast, desperate for release. He held her close and murmured his love in her ear.

She reached climax again and screamed out his name as he came to completion inside her. Alex rolled them both over and pulled her atop him. Her head lay against his chest as they searched for air.

"I love you, Grace," he said as he stroked the wisps of hair that fell from her tight knot. "I've loved you since I first saw you, I believe. Your eyes have haunted my dreams since that first day, even before I heard your voice."

She raised her head to look into his eyes. Wetness covered her cheeks.

"I didn't marry you because I had to, or because honor demanded it. I didn't marry you because your father insisted. I married you because I love you. And if it takes a lifetime to convince you of my love, then that's precisely how I'll spend my life."

Her chin trembled. "You love me? Really, truly?"

The dismay in her voice knocked the air from his lungs. He searched for another way to convince her. His search was stopped by her tiny fist to his gut.

"Why did it take you so blasted long to tell me?"

She tumbled onto him and they rolled until he was above her again. She took his face between her hands and kissed him long and deep.

"I love you, Alex."

He breathed freely for the first time in a long time. "I love you too, Grace."

Epilogue

GRACE WALKED GINGERLY down the curved stairway of Somerton Court, one hand supporting her back and the other holding onto the banister.

Sophie came around the corner and rushed to her side. "What on earth are you doing, Grace? You should have pulled the bell, and any one of us could have helped you down."

"I'm pregnant, not incapacitated. You know as well as I do that I'm perfectly capable of moving around on my own."

"Still, if Alex knew…"

"Alex won't know though, will he?" Grace grinned at her sister-in-law. "You'll tell him I pulled the bell and you assisted me the entire way. Because you love me, and I'm pregnant, and I insist."

"Fine. I'll tell a bouncer for you, but only if you do something for me." Sophie had a gleam in her eyes, the same gleam Grace had come to know meant either trouble or fun, or perhaps both.

"Oh, good. What are you planning?" She almost rubbed her hands in anticipation. Almost. "I need a spot of fun, you know. I'm sick to death of being cooped up in bed."

"He only thinks he's protecting you, you know."

"I know. But that doesn't make it any easier to bear." She would prefer to be up, moving about, than stuck in bed, no matter how large her belly had grown. "But enough of that. Tell me what you have in the works."

Sophie glanced to both ends of the long entry hall of Somerton Court and pulled Grace into a nearby drawing room. She took one final glance down the hall before she closed the door.

"You must keep this a secret." Sophie fell into a sofa and tugged on Grace's hand so she would sit next to her.

"Of course."

"You have to swear to me you'll tell no one, not even Alex."

"I believe you know me better than that by now." Really, couldn't she just get on with it?

Sophie took one more look about, even though she knew they were alone and the door was closed. Good grief! "Richard's coming home. He'll be here by tomorrow at the latest." The exuberant smile on her face was contagious.

"Oh, Sophie, I'm so happy for you." She felt a small twinge in her side, but ignored it. "Does anyone else know? Your mother? Peter?"

"No, no one. Only you. He sent me a letter and begged me to keep it secret, but I was absolutely bursting with the news. I had to tell *someone*."

"Well, I'm glad you chose me." A sharper pain assaulted her, and she cringed.

"What is it?" Her sister-in-law took her hand and jumped to her feet. "Is it the baby?"

"No, I'm sure it is nothing to worry about…"

"Do not dare lie to me, Gracie."

"Really, I'm fine. Sit, talk to me. Tell me more about Richard coming home." She needed to hear Sophie's voice so she could convince herself the baby wasn't coming yet.

"Well, he hasn't sold his commission," Sophie said as she resumed her seat. "He's on a fortnight's holiday, and he couldn't have better timing, with the whole family gathered here for Christmas. And for the baby's arrival, of course."

"Of course." Grace grimaced as another pain shot through her middle.

"You are not fine, so stop trying to convince me otherwise." Sophie rose from the sofa again and rushed to the door. "I'm getting Mama. And Alex. Oh, and *everyone*." She ran out, leaving the door to the drawing room wide open. Her voice rang out, calling through the halls of Somerton Court. Within moments, the hullabaloo of her family rushing to her side broke out.

Her family. Grace liked the sound of it.

No, liked wasn't nearly the right word. Loved. She loved having her own family.

Within minutes, the room was overcrowded with the Hardwickes, her aunt and uncle, even her father. The commotion overwhelmed her.

Henrietta called out for quiet. "Enough. Grace needs calm. Can't you see how distressed she is? Here sweetheart, we'll have you somewhere more comfortable in no time." Alex pushed from behind as Peter and Neil pulled Grace to her feet.

And then a new commotion broke out when a tall, broad-shouldered man with dark, reddish-brown hair, fair skin, and the same deep green eyes Alex had, a man Grace could mistake for none other than Major Lord Richard Hardwicke, walked through the door of the drawing room and joined the party.

"I see I made it just in time."

Indeed, he had. Peter and Neil dropped their holds and she fell onto her husband in a most ungraceful heap. Her newest brother, Richard, rushed to her side to help her up again so they could haul her to a more appropriate place for birthing her child.

Grace's family was complete.

About the Author

Catherine Gayle is a bestselling author of Regency-set historical romance. She's a transplanted Texan living in North Carolina with two extremely spoiled felines. In her spare time, she watches way too much hockey and reality TV, plans fun things to do for the Nephew Monster's next visit, and performs experiments in the kitchen which are rarely toxic.

Catherine would love to hear from her readers. You can find her on the internet at www.catherinegayle.com or send her an email at catherinegayle.author@gmail.com.

Printed in Great Britain
by Amazon